D0932291

"MILE HIGH redeems the pledge every writer makes with himself: to write **The Great American novel and leave the competition dead!** The book, quite simply, administers a large dose of strychnine to American society while jigging hilariously on corruption in government and Big Business . . . a cautionary tale drawn in blood and iron filings with enough book left over to encompass a story as varied as **The Godfather, Portnoy's Complaint,** and **The Love Machine."**

—*Chicago Tribune*

"ONE OF THE VERY BEST NOVELISTS AT WORK TODAY . . . *Mile High* is entertainment, but as with all Condon's 'entertainments,' social message is an echo. What an echo."

—*San Francisco Chronicle*

"RICHARD CONDON IS ONE OF OUR SUPREME ENTERTAINERS, A VERBAL TAP-DANCER OF BE-DAZZLEMENT, FANTASY AND DARK LAUGHTER . . . Now he has abandoned vaudeville for a more ser-ious stage. The result is this savage novel about the corruption of modern America. He has written, with bril-liance and style, an indictment that forgives nothing."
—*The New York Times*

"A SUPERSONIC STORYTELLER AT THE TOP OF HIS FORM . . . Whiplash entertainment . . . full of life, larger than life."
—*Kirkus Service*

"A MAGNIFICENT MANIFESTA-TION OF AS CREATIVE AND RE-SOURCEFUL AN IMAGINATION AS IS OPERATING IN FICTION TODAY . . . Richard Condon's *The Manchurian Candidate* remains one of the unique and most startling novels of our time. Now he startles us again."
—*Kansas City Star*

"CONDON'S GREAT AND NOUR-
ISHING STRENGTH HAS AL-
WAYS BEEN HIS MANIA FOR
MANIA . . . What grips his imagina-
tion, and shakes it till splendid words
fall out, is the tic of a human bomb."
                                    —*Time*

"RICHARD CONDON HAS A
PLACE IN RECENT AMERICAN
LETTERS LIKE THE ONE OCCU-
PIED BY KURT VONNEGUT.
There is a shared maniac quality, a
reverence for the bizarre, the grand
mad gesture . . . *Mile High* is a savage
indictment of greed . . . a memorable
triumph . . . Condon overwhelms us."
                      —*Minneapolis Tribune*

MILE HIGH

by
Richard Condon

A DELL BOOK

Published by
DELL PUBLISHING CO., INC.
750 Third Avenue
New York, New York 10017

Copyright © 1969 by Richard Condon

All rights reserved. No part of this book may
be reproduced in any form or by any means without
prior written permission of the Dial Press,
excepting brief quotes used in connection with
reviews written specifically for inclusion
in a magazine or newspaper.

Dell ® TM 681510, Dell Publishing Co., Inc.

Reprinted by arrangement with
Dial Press
New York, New York

Printed in the U.S.A.

First Dell printing—October 1970

The writer acknowledges with appreciation and gratitude his indebtedness to the authors of the following books, who are historians of the events leading to and coming after the Eighteenth U.S. Constitutional Amendment:

KENNETH ALSOP *The Bootleggers and Their Era* (Doubleday, 1961)

HERBERT ASBURY *The Great Illusion* (Doubleday, 1950)

ALFRED CONNABLE and EDWARD SILBERFARB *Tigers of Tammany* (Holt, Rinehart and Winston, 1967)

VIRGINIA COWLES *1913: The Defiant Swan Song* (Weidenfeld & Nicholson, London, 1967)

K. GUNTER *Prohibition* (Walter Neale, 1931)

JOHN ALLEN KROUT *The Origins of Prohibition* (Alfred A. Knopf, 1925)

ANDREW SINCLAIR *Prohibition, the Era of Excess* (Little, Brown, 1962)

CRAIG THOMPSON and ALLEN RAYMOND *Gang Rule in New York:* The Story of a Lawless Era (The Dial Press, 1940)

CLARENCE TRUE WILSON and DEETS PICKETT *The Case for Prohibition* (Funk & Wagnalls, 1923)

Special acknowledgment is made to Norman Lewis, *The Honored Society* (Collins, London, 1964)

For Our Mexican Leader
Benito-Juarez Bennett

"The vocabulary of horror
is as limited as that of lust."

JAMES POPE HENNESSY,
Sins of the Fathers

BOOK ONE

THE MINOTAUR

CHAPTER ONE

On December 22, 1958, only two days before, they had been safe in London. On that morning one of the sixteen Phantom IV Rolls-Royces in the world had driven them to Heathrow where they boarded his father's Learstar, whose cabins were decorated to appear like the favorite rooms of the last empress of China. The Learstar had flown them to New York and Walt had made love to her twice on the way. In New York he had met her mother for the first time. The next day, in a private railroad car decorated to appear like the favorite San Francisco brothel of the Nevada silver barons, they had been taken to Hawk Bay, New York, in the central Adirondacks, where one more of only sixteen Phantom IV Rolls-Royces in the world had begun the last leg of the journey up the mountain to Bürgenstock West for the first meeting either of them had ever had with his father.

The headlamps of the enormous car paved the rain-polished road with light. A helicopter carrying a pilot and a man riding messenger with a machine rifle erect between his knees hovered above and behind the moving car, following its glow. Car and helicopter moved across a state forest of two million, two hundred thousand acres of furred hills and a hundred lakes.

The driver's uniform was black and green, the car was black and green—the West racing colors, the colors of West's signal when he put to sea; the color of money. The

driver moved the car with care through the first checkpoint
as though the armed road guards were of a different feudal
rank. He seemed to sit warily behind the wheel until he
heard the heavy slap of the guard's hand on the car's flank.

The Phantom IV glided out of the light into the dark
forest and began its climb toward Edward Courance West.

The sun seemed to sing, the birds glowed like neon in
green and silver trees and the air was stinging exhilaratingly
that morning, March 30, 1911, the day after his father's
grand funeral. Red-headed Eddie West stared at his long,
bony, Mick face in the bathroom mirror with pale, hungry,
gray eyes. He appraised himself—right profile, then left.
He pulled back his thin lips in a grimacing counterfeit of a
smile, the best he could do at any time. He watched his long,
pink hands rub snowy lather into his red stubble. He was
twenty-three years old, his father's only heir, and as of this
current week he owned a small, sound, workingman's bank,
eleven saloons, three gambling houses, eight bordellos,
downtown real estate between Fulton and Wall, four hundred and thirty thousand dollars in cash and a membership
at the bar of the State of New York, in whose practice he
would be his only client.

Everyone in his father's wide world had been at the
funeral. The White House had sent the Vice-President (Republican) and two Supreme Court justices (Democratic).
The governor had been there and the mayor and every
alderman able to stand after three nights of waking. There
had been both U. S. senators, eleven congressmen, state
senators and state assemblymen and so many judges that the
courts must have had to close. Sixty-one thousand people
had lined the way from St. Jemma's to Calvary Cemetery.
He remembered endless hedges of beards and wreaths, six
feet tall, all around the grave in ever-increasing concentric
circles of the Knights of Columbus, the Friendly Sons of
St. Patrick, the Woodmen of the World, the National Bi-
metallic League, the Young Men's Library Association, the
Holy Name Society and thirty-one other fraternal, cultural
or religious organizations. The cardinal himself had conducted the requiem high mass for the soul of the man who
had done so much to help the church acquire from the
city the site of St. Patrick's Cathedral for only eighty-

three dollars. Two bishops had prayed with contingents of the Holy Name at the wake, and there had been prayers by leaders of the Russian Orthodox Church, the Colored Methodist Episcopal Church, four rabbis and the Church of Christ, Scientist. The New York *Sun* wrote that it was the most impressive funeral since the death of General Grant. Max Emanuel Noah, great-grandson of Mordecai Noah, first Jewish Grand Sachem of Tammany Hall, had proclaimed at graveside that "the brains and heart of Tammany are buried in Calvary today."

Paddy West had been interred in a fine suit of evening clothes with a wing collar and a white silk tie, all made for him twenty-three years before by Edward J. Dillon, tailor of aristocrats. The biggest bail bondsmen of the country had stood honor guard through the three nights of the wake in the house in Oliver Street. Every big-timer of sports and the theater came into the house (and not for the first time, either) to pay his respects. The leaders of all labor were there. Paul Kelly, vice-president of the International Longshoremen's Association and owner of the Garbage Scow Trimmers' Union, a man whom Paddy West had saved from a murder sentence, came three nights in a row. Dopey Benny Fein, Monk Eastman and all the top men of the important West Side Irish gangs, Ignazio Saietta, president of the Unione Siciliane, and Little Johnny Torrio from Navy Street in Brooklyn all mourned with the rest.

They were all there because Paddy West had been the kind of a district leader who took care of his people—all of them, not only big shots—making sure they got coal in the winter, shoes and food and a place to live when they were burned out in tenement fires. He had come to the city from across the sea as an immigrant boy and he had helped it to grow into a great city with flaming fireboxes on the elevated trains and subways roaring north to 34th Street. He'd helped men of every kind and color and birth. There had been hundreds of thousands of them, all kinds—Paddy West's assembly district had them. Little Italy was his. The Lower East Side was his. Some of the West Side Irish gangs overlapped into his district. All of them—Italians, Irish and Jews—had come from countries where they'd had to fight like tigers to defend themselves from the steady wars declared on them by their own governments. The Irish were bashed and starved by the English; the Jews got it in the head from the Cossacks and the Czar; the whole citizenry of the south of Italy, and particularly Sicily, were looked on like some dumb and wild beasts by all the Italians in the north. They had to be against authority to survive. And when they got out and made it to the City of New York, where Tammany offered nothing but help and shelter in exchange for their votes, their inward-supported leaders took the guidance and the dignity. It was the most natural alliance in the world once it could get settled in. It was a democracy contained and sustained by the politicians in good working partnership with the gangs who would man the polls on Election Day with knucks and clubs and knives and guns and guide their own ethnic groups through to vote the straight ticket. It wasn't just New York. The alliance extended everywhere across the country, in all the big cities. The gangs needed the politicians for protection against the courts and the police and the law, and the politicians needed the sure vote. It was to be a long and increasingly successful marriage, perhaps never to end.

Every summer Paddy would take his people up the Hudson on day steamers to the picnic where thirty thousand glasses of beer were drunk, two to four hundred young women were laid—thus bringing about hundreds of marriages and thousands of children—dozens of noses were broken, a lifetime of memories renewed and others made. "Men and women, Eddie," he taught his boy. "That's all you need to know."

He was buried from St. Jemma's, the church he'd been married in, but very few remember that. He was taken out to Calvary in a Springfield Metallic Casket held in a new Baker Burglarproof Vault that had a Fearnaught Grave Signal to release a flag and sound a bell if the body were to move. It was fitted with a patented device of the Clover Coffin Bomb Manufacturing Company of Columbus, Ohio, containing a charge of explosive that would go off if the coffin were tampered with by resurrectionists. He was carried upon a mosque-decked, square-ended, closed, six-columned hearse drawn by six horses wearing tragic-black cockades. The hearse was followed by forty-one official carriages (there was no counting the unofficial ones jammed behind the procession for the status-sting of it) and a robed choir of six men who sang, at graveside, "Not Lost but Gone Before" and S. W. Foss's "Hullo!"

Every measure of every second of it had befitted the memory of the man whose hero had been Aaron Burr, founder and builder of the Tammany machine, the first professional American politician, a man whose accomplishments were so great that they were passed along intact to Paddy West's only son, Edward, until it seemed to the father that Burr's spirit had found a dwelling place within the boy.

It was Burr who had barred John Jay's way to the ambassadorship to England because the man was too favorable to British interests. It was Burr who had rushed into the White House demanding an embargo against England when she had gone to war against France. It was Burr who had enfranchised immigrants to create the broad and then broader base of new voters, thus breaking British colonial control of New York State. He had been the only politician to see how to use the workingman's vote in order to produce and harness political power. "The Revolution hasn't broken Britain's rotten grip," Burr said. Burr, the cold-eyed dispassionate, objective man of the world, a Princeton graduate, Washington's aide-de-camp, and the soldier who had organized the masterly retreat from Long Island. A lieutenant colonel when he was twenty-one years old, the highest-paid lawyer in the city, and he'd spent as many nights in the beds of brothels as he had in his own bed—when he was well over seventy he'd swept a girl fifty years younger off her feet and slipped her two babies.

"Burr is the man for you, Eddie," Paddy would say every week of his son's life. "Imagine him, the first campaign manager of American politics, handling the campaign for Jefferson and to his own dismay finding himself tied even with his candidate for the vote for the office of the third President of the United States, then stepping down into the vice-presidency because in the runoff he never lifted a finger for himself! Now. Think on that. Let that be the big lesson, son. Always let the other guys stand out in front and take the glory. You keep back, far out of the strong light, and win the power and the money." Paddy grinned with the joy of it, and the effect was so unexpected that the boy flinched. But the smile rarely happened again.

As Eddie whirled the boar's-hair shaving brush within

the shamrock-spattered shaving mug that had been his father's he began to expand in his mind the tremendous idea that must surely have been settled upon him by his father's spirit at some time during the three days of the wake, because it was so much of a Paddy West idea to the marrow of its being, so gloriously American, that it glowed like great masses of gold in his mind. And he could see all of it so clearly. He knew how to move it and he knew it would make him a far greater man than Aaron Burr.

In Ireland the Wests had been a Catholic Norman family, originally De l'Ouest, although Paddy had never known the shame of that. They were among the last families to resist Robert Boyle, the first Earl of Cork, in the Cromwellian rebellion. The West castle at Clogleigh was surrounded by artillery, then "all the garrison put to the sword" in 1642. Their lands confiscated, the remnants of the West family settled as tenant farmers in Kilflyn, in Kerry, where they wallowed in the present, deftly freed from the gentilities of the past, until the famine came.

When it came, Paddy's mother was dead (God rest her soul), and the family of nine, opposed to washing, slept and stank in the single room of their father's windowless mud hut, mixing their own rich smell with the smells of the pigs who shared the room and the pile of manure at the door.

The blight came on in '45. The famine began in '46. Dysentery and relapsing fever followed. Thousands roamed the countryside praying for food, eating thistles to stay alive. They began to leak out of their country. First to Liverpool, Glasgow and South Wales, then to Australia, last but most powerfully to the United States, jammed starving and diseased into unseaworthy ships.

A million died at home before Paddy West got away, including three brothers and four sisters. The British at last had begun to issue corn, but the Irish didn't know what it was and most of them couldn't or wouldn't eat it. Paddy filled his pants and a sack with it and made himself eat it after he saw how they cooked it, but on the road from Killarney to Cork he preferred to eat weeds. But he had luck. He came on two drunken English soldiers and in the right place for it, so he clomped them both on the heads with a flat rock and found six shillings in their pockets, all unaware that he had started on his life's work. He ate the corn, cooked or raw, and watched for lonely soldier drunks at night until he earned enough for his Cunard passage— about twenty American dollars' worth. Then he bought steerage space aboard a three-hundred-tonner, although it was known that in the year before, thirty-eight thousand of the fleeing Irish had died at sea or soon thereafter. But he didn't die at all. He found himself on the other side of the Castle Garden immigration shed in New York with eight shillings in his pocket. He walked along South Street, dizzy, looking at the thickets of ships' masts standing against the sky along the quay as far as the eye could see, their jib booms thrusting across the width of the street, almost touching the buildings.

He had thought he had forgotten what the smell of food could be like, what it could do to the belly and all concentration of will. He had survived forty-two days of ocean crossing on only the food he had brought aboard the ship because that would be the only food there was. Now, as he walked and goggled, he could smell oysters and hot clam chowder. It shook him. All his usual indifference to food was replaced by such longing that his hands shook, but one of his great strengths of character was his suspicion. He would not risk getting a short rate for his eight shillings when he turned them into American money. He'd wait until he could be sure he was getting an official rate from a bank or a mercantile counting room. He'd heard plenty about waterfront, big-city crooks aboard the *Marriam Murphy* for forty-two days. He stared the fine food smells down and set out to find a bank, wandering dazedly past pubs and ship's chandlers, boardinghouses and sailors' slop shops, street stands, horses, whores and sailmaker lofts. Someone was playing a piano somewhere.

Paddy West was seventeen years old, tall and strong. Gold had been discovered in California five months before, and the news was emptying the port of seamen as soon as the ships touched the piers. The men only wanted to ship out to California, around the Horn or across the Isthmus, so crimping had become an industrial necessity and overnight there sprang up sophisticated systems for shanghaiing sailors. Crimps were the civil equivalent of the naval press gangs which had roamed England in search of naval man-power during the Napoleonic Wars.

Paddy West knew all about crimps. He had crossed next to a man and woman who had lived in Liverpool and had lost three sons to the bastards. On that crossing Paddy had promised himself, writ in vomit, never to go to sea again or set his feet on anything that floated. The man and the woman had been talking about the South End and Lime Street in Liverpool, but he was here now and he could see what was happening, and he knew if he answered any greeting from a warm and friendly stranger he'd find himself on the floor of a foc'sle bound for China.

He moved warily and got his first job as a fish-market porter on the very day he landed. He became a citizen of the United States on the second day. They paid him twenty-five cents to take the oath along with sixteen other men, all of them crouched and huddled sideways to be able to lay but one fingertip on the Bible to swear allegiance. There just weren't enough Bibles to go around. The witnesses who that day swore they had known every one of the applicants for eight years or longer, all those years spent in the City of New York, had good, steady work out of it, but the Tam-many judges in the State Supreme Court were often hoarse swearing them all in. All the new citizens had to promise to vote the straight Tammany ticket of course. It was a thrill to be a new American, and he was never to forget that. Still and all, he spoke to none of his fellow indoctrinates. Paddy West wouldn't talk to anyone except his employer because any man on the street might be a crimp.

The two flourishing crimping organizations were those of Fernando Wood, a U.S. congressman, and Ma "the Casker" Steinet. She was called the Casker because if something slipped and a shanghaied man died on her hands she'd stuff him into a cask and send him off to sea that way, collecting her fee nevertheless. Fernando Wood owned a tobacco shop in Pearl Street, then he acquired seven sailing vessels while trading with a pack of cards, and so entered the shipping trade. When his crews began to desert in order to make their way west to California he immediately began his eventually extensive crimping business as a sideline. Meanwhile, forging ahead in city politics, he rose to be chairman of the Tammany Young Men's Committee, then won the Democratic Congressional nomination in 1840. In Congress, Wood crusaded for Navy drydocks and for full pay for overseas consuls. And despite complete indifference on all sides, he encouraged a nut professor to string wires from the Wood Congressional committee rooms to corresponding rooms on the other side of Capitol Hill, and thus Professor Morse's amazing telegraph was demonstrated publicly for the first time.

Congressman Wood was skillful with guns, knives, clubs, fists and pokers—widely admired. In 1848, when 212,000 immigrants arrived in New York, including 117,000 Irishmen, Wood, who was always dreaming and planning for Tammany Hall, organized the Instant Citizenship Committee that had so flattered Paddy. While Wood went well on his way to becoming mayor he was also establishing himself as one of the two top crimps. He did indeed become mayor in 1854, and moved instantly to attack municipal problems by banning the driving of cattle through downtown streets, by putting the police into uniforms against their will, and before settling down with his and Tammany's ideas of the real business of being mayor, established the seven hundred and seventy-six acre Central Park in Manhattan at a projected cost of three million dollars.

Fearing Wood's crimps—because he truly admired Fernando Wood—Paddy moved out of his waterfront boardinghouse and walked north almost three miles every night to a farmhouse where he could lock himself in. He avoided the Irish shantytown along the old Bloomingdale Road just farther north because the crimps were drawn to it like flies to a jam pot. At the fish market, if any jolly smiler spoke to him and invited him off for a drink Paddy would ignore the man. Because of the crimps, he refused to drink for the rest of his life, from the day he set foot in America. If the same jolly stranger spoke to him twice Paddy would stop what he was doing and stare the man down. If it happened a third time he would hit the man with a short piece of lead pipe he kept in his trousers, because crimps are brutal men, then sell the man to Ma Steinet, getting five dollars. After three of Wood's men went down under Paddy's pipe and disappeared he thought they had crossed him off as a seafaring prospect, but his employer told him that he had been called uptown and told to fire Paddy or lose his license. That was that. Mr. Wood was very offended. When the *Hilda M. Hess,* the Antarctic whaler that was lying out in the upper bay, was loaded and ready to leave port, Mr. Wood had said that Paddy would be on it.

"What'll I do?" Paddy asked.

"Get inland. Go to Pennsylvania."

"I can't."

"Why not?"

"I'm goin' inta politics here."

"Over Mr. Wood's cold body, you are."

"I'm young. I'll wait. I ain't goin' ta wait until I go vomitin' around the world in a whaling ship."

Paddy never returned to the farmhouse. He knew Wood's crimps would be waiting for him along that dark road. He went straight to Ma Steinet, an evil-smelling old woman but Wood's competitor.

"Wood's crimps are after me."

"You're not the first."

"He got me outta me job."

"Go find a priest. Why tell me?"

"I want a job. But not on no ship."

She stared at him unpleasantly.

"I use me eyes," Paddy said, earnest and unsmiling. "I'm a good crimp. Put me on as a runner." The runners were rowed out to meet the incoming ships, as far out in the harbor as they could get to, to board them with grapnels, then go into the foc'sles with booze and even go aloft with the crew to help them stow the muslin. They'd tell the sailors anything to get them to jump the ship when it docked, then to move them, drunk and helpless, into the boss crimp's boardinghouse.

"You'd fall outta the rowboat," Ma said, but she admired the way he never smiled but just jutted his fat lips outward and stared through her with hard eyes to some distant objective. She could feel the coldness of him, strong enough to put out a fire. "All right. You can be the drayman," she told him. Drayman was low man in the crimping trade. When the runners got the seamen ashore the draymen moved their gear to the boardinghouse, then after Ma had signed them on an outgoing ticket, the drayman carted the doped, drunk and sometimes dead bodies back to the wharves, now stripped of their money and their gear.

Paddy took the job. He got a dose of pox his second night in one of Ma's boardinghouses and never touched a street whore again for the rest of his life. Ma paid him room and board and three dollars a week and Fernando Wood forgot about him. Good luck continued. Young Bill Tweed, leader of the Cherry Hill gang, had founded the Americus Vespucci Volunteer Fire Company. Because of Paddy's strength he won himself the right to wear one of Bill Tweed's red shirts and became a star member of the Americus Engine Company Number Six, known all over the city as the Big Six, champions for outracing and outmaneuvering any volunteer fire company in Manhattan; fighting it out with fists at the water hydrant if the race was close. It was thrilling to see them race against the Eight Company down Broadway, the great red-shirted men teamed like horses to drag the engine—its box—brightly emblazoned with the head of a snarling Bengal tiger—with Big Bill Tweed jogging beside them and blowing his silver trumpet, while fire buffs and children tumbled and ran all around them. Their fame spread far beyond the city. When Millard Fillmore became President they were presented to him at the White House. The Number Six company did a lot for Paddy West.

Paddy didn't drink or whore and now he gave up smoking because it cut his wind. He was the industry's model crimp. He could bring in more sailors with a stern stare than another crimp could with a bottle of booze. If any woman in any of the three saloons the Casker owned ever spoke to him, Paddy would knock her down. Soon all the top whores on the waterfront came to show him doglike devotion. He organized the best of them in his own little band and took over the organization of their sales and promotion. But he spoke to them only through his helper, Jiggs Tobin, a Roscommon man who was saving to buy his own horse and hack.

Working for Ma, running the girls and cashing bets on the Big Six weren't the only sources of income for young Paddy. He taught himself to be an accomplished pickpocket, no mean feat for a farm boy with hands like a cow's udders. Ma Steinet would watch him watching the runners roll the drunk sailors and then get drunk themselves. She'd admire the way Paddy would walk among them, lifting the money out of their pockets. In that way he was an honest thief. He never stole from strangers or the sober. She was pleased with his steady ambition and the no-nonsense, teetotal way about him. She jumped him over the ranks of runners into the first vacancy as boardinghouse master when he was only twenty-two years old—six feet, two inches tall, one hundred and ninety pounds, without a smile or a frown, but never stupid-looking for any of that.

Until a crew was ordered by a shipping company, the Casker's boarders were housed warmly and fed well for two dollars a week from each man. She ran saloons in each doss and specialized in seafaring men. Whatever it was she offered, it was so right for sailors that even though men knew they had been shanghaied before from one of Casker Steinet's places, most of them returned again and again.

The boardinghouse Paddy ran was close to the river and had a trapdoor for lowering the drugged men into small boats to be run out to the big ships that waited impatiently for their crews in the harbor. For supplying crews Ma got the advance notes issued by the shipping companies against two or three months' pay for each man she dropped aboard. The runners got five dollars a head per man, the boardinghouse master got 10 percent of Ma's estimated gross, which was about 2 percent of true earnings, but Ma never objected to Paddy running the whores or picking the runners' pockets.

Any boy's ambition modifies as he grows older. The year Paddy landed was the year of the appointment of the first American representative to the Vatican, and he dreamed of parading past the Swiss Guards in silk knickerbockers. However, by 1856, after fighting in the forces of Mayor Fernando Wood, Paddy had worked himself along in the party councils at least far enough so that he made seventeen hundred dollars out of securing, but not serving, writs of condemnation of the new Elevated Railway Company, and six hundred and fifteen dollars as the professional friend of the workers in the shoe industry. He was among the first one hundred members of the Order of the Knights of St. Crispin, formed to protect the seniority rights of shoemakers against cheap competition from beginners. Paddy opened his first saloon in the sixties (which, in 1878, became the first saloon in the nation to install electric light). When

George Leslie robbed the Manhattan Savings Bank of $3,000,000 in broad daylight, although two of Leslie's men went to jail for it, Paddy West saw to it that Leslie was not brought to trial, because of "lack of evidence." Paddy was becoming one of the men to see in New York government.

But when Ma Steinet died in 1860 Paddy was just getting started. He was twenty-eight years old. He was managing all three of the Steinet boardinghouses, all fourteen runners, three draymen, five boatmen, seven slop shops that sold the seamen the gear that the boardinghouse master stole from them before they were drugged and shipped out. He was shipping master, i.e., employment agent-crimp, for twenty-six shipping companies. Ma went feeble three years before the end. She was bedridden. She told Paddy she loved him like a son, then spat on the floor beside the bed and smiled at him as coyly as a young lover. She knew to a dime how much her business brought in. She told him that if he would keep his stealing down to not more than 20 percent, she would leave him the whole business and the "goodwill." He was stealing 55 percent. He asked her if she'd put the intention in writing. She declined. She maintained sensitively that signing a paper such as that could only help her to die more quickly, and again she was pleased with him because he didn't bother to express horror at such a thought.

"If you don't trust me, who can you trust?"

"Me brass knucks," Ma said wanly.

"Would you trust a judge?"

"Are you daft?"

"Supposin' I can figure out a way that will keep you safe?"

"How?"

"Supposin' the biggest bank in the city was in charge of the paper, and this bank had to be satisfied you died a natural death—?"

"A bank is only men, Paddy."

"But there has to be a way!" His voice went harsh. It frightened her. Her breathing became disordered again, because one of her troubles was that she took in more air than she gave out—the cardinal rule with everything else in her life. "I got a sister in Perth Amboy," she wheezed. "She has two sons. One is a doctor and I wish—I wish—"

"Whaddaye wish, Ma?"

"Never mind. Maybe I wish I had two sons in Perth Amboy."

That amused Paddy but not to the point of smiling. He laughed. It was a quick single sound as though a hand had been caught in a slammed cash drawer. "If you had two sons," he said, "they'da been shanghaied twice by now."

She cackled gratefully over the compliment, then worked on trying to breathe again. "If I signed it, it would have to say that I leave three thousand dollars to each boy and four thousand to my sister plus my jewelry." She nearly winced at the look in his eyes.

"What jewelry?" he asked.

"Where you can't find it."

"All right. You accept the two boys."

"I accept the two boys *with* the biggest bank. And I write the paper. No lawyers. And the paper has to say that you have to work for me until I die no matter how long it takes and that I have to die natural or you get nothing."

Paddy stood up. His menacing bedside manner was gone. "I'll get the pen and paper. You decide which bank. Then I'll be off to Perth Amboy. And I want to say this. I appreciate it. I won't take you for no twenty percent. Five percent, no more, and that's settled."

She managed a two-tone sigh. "Just don't steal more than twenty percent, Paddy, and I got a good deal."

After Ma died Paddy set his course for politics as though he were pulling Engine Number Six. He leased the three boardinghouses to Charley Gleason. He sold the slop shops to Larry Meagher, and over the twenty-two years with Ma and his bands of fancy girls and his various overrides he had saved forty-one thousand dollars and he now owned leases and buildings and land. When he burned the boardinghouses that stood between Fulton and Wall Streets after the leases expired, he collected another three thousand in insurance. He built tenements on the land with a good bank loan that the Party arranged for him at fair rates.

Paddy's first leader at Tammany Hall was Fernando Wood. Then he prospered under his old fire captain, Bill Tweed, then moved along to Honest John Kelly, Squire Croker and Mr. Murphy. They had all been great men, each in a different way, none as great as the greatest, Aaron Burr. He served them all with pride and pleasure, staying well back, out of sight as much as possible. He opened the first of his string of saloons in Franklin Street, just across Center Street from the Tombs prison and the Criminal Courts Building, which Bill Tweed had built for the city at a cost exceeding the original estimate of two hundred and fifty thousand dollars by twelve million, two hundred and fifty thousand. Bill Tweed knew, and proved it to Paddy West with a finger pointing to the careers of Commodore Vanderbilt, Mr. Astor and Jay Gould, that this was the American way, and a man was nothing without his money.

Paddy knew that money was respectability, politics was power, and power was money. His visible movements held no more expression than his face as he went on his way to acquire all these. He taught the art of silence and invisibility to his son years later. "Let them others have all the fame and take all the risks," he counseled daily. He would have little Eddie write lists of sentences like that fifty times every evening. He offered the boy a bonus of two dollars a month when Eddie was nine years old if he could remain silent and unsmiling and speak only to answer questions, and the boy collected from his delighted father month after month. Paddy was the hardest kind of hard Irish and he wanted his boy to carry that on. Eddie was raised as another kind of foreigner by his mother, a startlingly, even shockingly different kind of foreigner. But his father's way was stronger, and the boy grew up to be a Kerry man surviving in the midst of famine; a hard, alien thinker who was pleased to have all others indulge their emotions.

Paddy settled the bands of girls into the first of his three brothels, then expanded. The houses were placed in the gay districts, each in a building with one of his saloons. After he got the saloons going, Big Tim Sullivan gave him "the license" to open his first gambling setup. It prospered from the start. However, the hub of hubs, the diadem center of all of his life's work, was the Franklin Street saloon, which became one of the most famous saloons in the city from the day it opened in 1871. By 1880 it was *the* gathering place for all the big politicians and gangsters; prizefighters, judges and jockeys; prosecutors and defense lawyers; pimps, con men, bail bondsmen and leading actors. Paddy presided over all of it, approachable but unsmiling, thick-lipped and thick-limbed, the guardian of Tammany's prestige and power at the doorway to the Tombs.

It was his cardinal rule that every alternative had to be investigated before he turned anyone down, and the *only* reason for refusing, in every instance, was disloyalty. Every morning at nine he dressed in a black suit with a black vest and a black tie on a white shirt with a high celluloid collar and climbed into the original old hack owned by Jiggs Tobin (whose loyalty was of the highest) and was driven from his house in Oliver Street to the corner three blocks north of the Franklin Street saloon, where, rain and shine, he would step down daintily from the cab and walk with slow majesty along the street, distributing largesse as he went—twenty dollars' worth of nickels, dimes and quarters.

He entered his saloon, walked up one flight of stairs to the small, nearly bare, office with its picture of Aaron Burr, the current Tammany leader and the incumbent cardinal. He ran everything from there even though, as district leader, his political headquarters was on Madison Street. One day a week he ate lunch in Mulberry Street, always the same: that raw ham, spaghetti with the meat and tomato gravy, no wine, one coffee. One other day each week he ate lunch in Rivington Street, always the same: some of that cold fish, boiled beef, some boiled carrots, a little more boiled beef and one coffee. He wanted the voters and the gangs to see him, to see that he wasn't one of those who favored the Irish. During peak business hours he presided over the barroom, always available. Throughout the winter he attended the important fires in his district and saw that the burned-out were housed by his block captains and clothed and fed. He handled the drunks and the dispossess cases personally in the courts and attended weddings, funerals and bar mitzvahs.

He was a flannel-mouthed, burly fairy godfather to all who were loyal. He got the boys out of jail. He saved them from hanging—until January 1, 1889, when he began to save them from the electric chair. He never refused a touch. He never forgot to collect interest on the touch. He was for the city. He helped get the subway built after having gotten the contractors' applications turned down. He did as much for builders, lawyers, cops, judges, businessmen and bankers as he ever did for the criminal element. He was a community leader in the greatest democracy, all of it exquisitely organized precisely along the lines of the church itself by Honest John Kelly, one of the best of them. The individual's vote was captured by the tenement captain, who reported it to the block captain. All the block captains were members of the election district committee and accountable to an election district captain. In the church chain this was much like an altar boy helping the parish priest, who reported to the bishop (the election district captain), who reported to Paddy West, district leader, the equivalent of a cardinal. He reported to the executive committee of Tammany Hall, the city's Curia, together with thirty-three other district leaders, and directly to the Leader of Tammany himself, their pope. All of them along the chain handed out bail money, Christmas turkeys, coal, jobs, justice, and clothes in return for votes and loyalty.

The birthday of Columbus had been a Tammany holiday celebrated long before Tammany encouraged that it be taken over by Italo-Americans. Paddy always made it his policy to celebrate this day exclusively with Italian voters. On October 12, 1887, as Patron and Grand Marshal of the annual Columbus Day ball, when he was fifty-five years old, Paddy West, a bachelor, first rested his eyes on Maria Corrente.

He was seated with friends, runners and lobbygows along the wall of the ballroom when she danced past him, fluidly correct in the arms of her father, Giuseppe Corrente, a leading importer of olive oil and cheeses. The room had been splashed with bunting in the colors of the Italian and American flags. Planks on sawhorses, covered with pastel crepe paper, bore up under pyramids of ham and cheese sandwiches, piles of glistening sugar cakes. Among these stacks waiters worked to fill pitchers and glasses with new red wine. The music was loud and happy. The children ran at top speed in and out among the dancers.

She was beautiful, strikingly Italianate, with a fulfilling loveliness of full body and an ivory-cast, haughty face. Her hair and eyes were very black. She was aware of dignity. He longed to see her smile, to see a burst of white teeth beneath those soft-seeming lips. But she did not smile. She

seemed altogether remarkable to him, perhaps because of
some quirk of digestion or twist of light or canting of sound
and time. He felt himself breathing differently. He tried to
understand it. He was fifty-five years old and these rushing
feelings were neither pleasant nor welcome. It must be the
light that made him see her this way. But everyone else
looked as they always had, the beauties and the deformed.
It is always the approaches of light that show beauty to the
mind and the memory, then seal it there irrevocably, to be
recalled whenever the present is too much to bear.

He rummaged through his mind and tossed out what had
passed for emotions out of the neatly kept portmanteau of
his feelings, all folded neatly, but he could find nothing to
match what he was feeling now as he conjured the sounds of
her voice and the smells of her body. She was unique to him
because no one or anything had every gripped and twisted
him into such a strange and frightening shape before, like
some dopey swain with iron balls and a bleat built-in to
voice and glance—a thing that brought laughter to the
world. By dancing past him she had removed him unfairly
from his husk as a powerful chief, a man who walked anywhere with plopping heavy feet if he chose to do so, but
toward whom all others stepped lightly and with deference.
She had risen from beneath the surface of time—which he
had always controlled, beyond (perhaps) growing a bit
older each year, but never seriously so—summoning his
wistful lust and confounding his plans. She had frozen him
in time: he was wearing the head of a much older man like a
mask covering the face of a boy her age. She was too young,
she was too beautiful, or whatever it was she was that was
doing all this to him. He could not discern who and what
might be mocking him.

Paddy West had set world's records for caution in his
time. With him it had never been a matter of moving when
the road ahead had been cleared. It was his fixed policy to
refuse to move until the road ahead had been paved, brilliantly lighted, and a golden city settled at the other end of it.
Then, with an armed police escort before him and behind
him, he would be on his way. But this girl was beyond these
rules. He spoke in a choked voice to Vincent Stoppaglieri,
a Brooklyn contractor, seated at his right. "Who's that girl?"
He kept his voice bored. It was a polite inquiry, as though

he had decided he must show some interest in the events of the evening.

"Whicha one?"

But she was gone. "Oh. Ah. She's gone now. She was dancin' wit' Joe Corrente."

"Ah. The daughter. Please."

"Why?"

"She'sa go onna terlet, she'sa think she makes candy."

"I don't get your drift, Vinnie."

"She'sa too good for thisa kinda place. She'sa gung to be big balleto dance."

"What's that?"

"Balleto is how they dance inna opera."

"They *dance* in the opera? All this time I thought the opera was singin'."

"Mosta they sing. Some-a time they dance. Whenna they dance, they dance balleto. It'sa nice."

The daughter came haughtily past again. It wasn't a big ballroom. Each time she passed the large mirrors at each end of the room she seemed to renew herself by drinking in deeply of her image as it floated past, and Paddy put it down to filial excellence that a girl should so savor a dance with her unbeautiful father. Young men attempted to cut in, but she froze them more rigidly than if she had asked them to wait just one moment until she could get the head of Medusa out of her purse. Her father sweated and looked miserable. Neither he nor the girl smiled or spoke to each other. Helpless, Paddy watched her leave just before half-past ten, and beyond the one casual inquiry to Vincent Stoppaglieri he didn't ask about her again and let the evening go on as though he had (properly) forgotten her.

He led the grand march with Mrs. Carlo Fratelli, wearing the old, reliable blank expression on his fifteen-inch-long face. After that he made the speech he always made, a paean to all Italians in America, the greatest Americans of them all. Then he went home to his house in Oliver Street and sat up until dawn to think things through in his methodical way. He reached the conclusion after some hours that the only thing in his favor was that the girl was Sicilian and might therefore carry enormous family feelings and do whatever her father asked her to do. Jesus, the girl looked like she was twenty-two years old, for Christ's sake.

He did not have time for mooning. Dick Croker was the new Leader, and it was the year the Hall had to recapture the mayor's office and deliver the patronage. It wouldn't be easy. Henry George had the labor backing. Teddy Roosevelt at twenty-eight had all the strength to make a lot of noise. Whoever Squire Croker chose to run against those two would need total support in every district. All that work plus Monk Eastman's gang tearing up the district night after night, which kept Paddy in judge's chambers and filled his head. However, he had *some* time. And he had his own competent information service. Over the next few weeks he was able to put together a dimensional picture of the girl. Her father had sent her to the old country, then to Paris to study dancing. In the fall she'd start as a dancer with the Metropolitan Opera Company. What she did was a mystery to him until he found out it was only "toe-dancin'," then he knew all about it. For whatever ideas a young girl gets, she used the name Mary Courance instead of Maria Corrente. Her father was opposed to her becoming a professional dancer and offended that she had decided to change her name, even though one canceled out the other. That part of it, the father's opposition and the girl's rebellion, gave Paddy cause as to the Sicilian upbringing being in his favor, but he reasoned that this was America and God knew everything was different in America.

He moved automatically through his work, never once able to concentrate on it. She was in his mind all the time. The need for her intensified even after prayer. He clung to his patience and waited for a sign, but he would not make an overt move because risk to Paddy was what bubonic plague is to a public health officer—something to be stamped out forever.

Then the sign came. It was in the form of an urgent message from Don Carmelo "the Wolf" Lumia, president of the Unione Siciliane, asking him to meet with his *consigliere,* Don Salvatore Purpi, in a Broome Street restaurant. There was no doubt about the unusual urgency of the summons, all the more extraordinary because Don Carmelo was very much the "man of respect," never exigent or ruffled. Paddy went to the meeting with the hope that Lumia or the Unione faced total disaster or at least big enough trouble to obligate them to him far beyond any payment with money.

He was shown to a table at the back of the restaurant, which smelled gloriously of cheeses, salamis, garlic, and cooking sauces, looking as out of place among the other diners as a hod carrier singing tenor at La Scala. Purpi and two of Don Carmelo's *caporegimi* stood up as he approached the table. Paddy was the personification of political power, and nothing took precedence over that among *mafiosi*. Don Salvatore was a dear little old man with murderer's eyes, not as cold as Paddy's but perhaps cold enough to chill a magnum of champagne with a glance. He had never worked a day in his long life, and all the rich experience he had acquired along the way had made him counselor to the boss.

Paddy insisted on shaking hands ponderously, calling each man by name, asking for their children. He accepted a cup of coffee. Don Salvatore asked, equally politely, how the election would go.

"Croker will run Congressman Hewitt, Sal," Paddy said. "We'll be all right. He's rich enough to hurl charges of nihilism and socialist peril at Henry George, and that kid Roosevelt don't mean nothin'." He sipped the coffee. "What's this trouble in Don Carmelo's letter, Sal?"

"It's no good, Paddy. Two cops is dead and a kid. She's Italian, so we can handle it, but the cops are Polacks and Judge Gant won't lift a finger because he says the Polacks vote like they was one man."

Paddy whistled.

"They have three of our soldiers, and the lawyers can't even find out where they have them, so we can't do nothing."

"How did they get picked up?"

Don Salvatore shrugged. "They was like standin' there when the cops got it."

Paddy considered the information. "Well, Sal," he said, "there's always more button men, ain't there?"

"These are Don Carmelo's sister's kids. Two of them. We got to get them loose."

Paddy's heart sang. He thought of the girl and his nether parts became ascendant, his lust like the taste of good wine. "Well!" he said cheerfully. "This is the toughest one yet, ain't it? Where's a telephone?"

Don Salvatore led him out of the restaurant with the two troop commanders bringing up the rear. The procession went down the street to a horse room that had been paying

Paddy tribute for many years but that he had never set foot
in before. He made a call to Rollo Gant, asked a few questions and listened with care. He hung up, did not speak but
led the way back along the street to the restaurant. When
they were seated at the table again he said, almost tasting
Maria Corrente's mouth, almost feeling her legs wrapped
around him, "No wonder Judge Gant won't move. Yiz may
all be cooked."

"Whassamatta?"

"Sweet Jesus, Sal, it's only less than a month ago when
the Fratellanza killed Chief Hennessey in New Oreleens."

"What the hell?"

"I know. I know. He butted in. But he was chiefa police
and every cop in this country was hot about it, and now,
Sweet Saint Joseph, Sal, yiz have killed two more cops and
shoot a little kid to make it all the worse." He mopped his
brow with a silk handkerchief to indicate that he was
enormously agitated. "I'll tell you this. You can't blame
Rollo Gant for going to sleep on this one."

Don Salvatore was grim. He did not look endearing any
more. "Tell me somet'ing, Paddy. You not gunna do
nuttin'?"

Paddy drummed on the tabletop with his fingertips. "If
I do something, Sal, it's not because we need yiz in the election. Make sure Carmelo understands that. This is between
you and me only."

"You mean if you fix it, that's between us and you?"

"Right."

"I unnerstan'."

"I better talk to Carmelo and whoever else he wants to
have there."

"When?"

"The quicker."

"We get back to you, Paddy."

Don Salvatore got up. They shook hands, then Paddy
shook hands with the others. The three men left the restaurant and Paddy sat on at the table feeling spiritual now about
the girl. The carnality had passed. He lit a cigar two nuns
had given him the Saturday before, and since he didn't
smoke, he let it burn like incense in the thick, white soup
plate in the center of the table. He took to dreaming of sons,
then of a beautiful old age when that would come, as it

probably must. The spiritual feeling about the girl didn't last. The other came back to him with rush of blood and he had to adjust his clothing surreptitiously. He decided at that moment that he would undress her instead of letting her undress herself. If she went off to undress in some room away from the bed it could be forever before she came out again, and he knew he couldn't stand up to the waiting. He changed the subject in his mind abruptly; otherwise he felt he'd be out raping milk-wagon horses. He thought about buying her a fur coat. The restaurant proprietor approached, rubbing his hands almost to shreds and asking if Paddy would like some prosciutto or maybe one or two little artichokes?

"Very good of you, I'm sure," Paddy said. "Perhaps you'd send out for a small bottle of just plain grape juice?" The proprietor was off like a racing dog. Paddy watched the blue cigar smoke rise and curl, swaying in the air before him like a beautiful ballerina bending herself toward him. He enjoyed the grape juice and formulated his campaign. He left a dollar on the table and the proprietor snatched it up and followed him, pleading with him to take it back, throwing it from hand to hand like a hot chestnut. Paddy stopped his forward course long enough to acknowledge that the man was registering that he couldn't take Paddy's money. "Give it to the Little Sisters of the Poor," Paddy said. There was more than one way to pay for a cigar.

The meeting with Don Carmelo was held at 10:15 that night in a railroad flat on East 116th Street. Muro Scarlata had come up from downtown. Concetto Canapa was there from Brooklyn. Salvatore Purpi ran the meeting for Don Carmelo. Everyone but Paddy smoked black rope and they all wore hats from the wardrobe of *Tosca*.

"This here is the best part of the indictment handed down by the New Oreleens grand jury," Paddy was saying as he took a piece of foolscap out of his pocket. "Last month that was, remember." He began to read the paper. " 'The extended range of our researches has developed the existence of a secret organization styled "Mafia." The evidence comes from several sources fully competent in themselves to attest its truth, while the fact is supported by the long record of blood-curdling crimes, it bein' almost impossible to discover the perpetrators or to secure witnesses.'"

"What we need to hear that for, Paddy?" Don Carmelo asked. Muro Scarlata spat, ringing the brass cuspidor. Paddy continued to read as though he had not been interrupted. "'The larger number of the society is composed of Sicilians who have left their native land, in most instances under assumed names to avoid—'"

"What is this got to do wit' us?" Scarlata asked. "You t'ink we got all night here?"

Paddy looked at him with all his impressive coldness and kept staring. When he was ready to talk he said, "I don't want any horse shit from any little dago. I run the show, you ginny bastard, an' if anny of you get away with skin it'll be my doin', so shut your mout'."

No one protested.

"All right," he continued. "This is what it's got to do wit' you. Last month the people of the city of New Oreleens rioted after the Fratellanza killed the Chief. They took eleven of your people out of the city jail and lynched them, and when a ship wit' eighteen hundred Sicilians came into the port it was turned away. Then they started wit' legal proceedings to deport all Sicilians, and now you've killed two cops and a kid and maybe you'll have the same thing on your hands. You can be lynched on lamp posts and the rest can be sent back to the old country—that's what the hell it's got to do wit' you."

"Listen, Paddy," Don Carmelo said gently, "What you gunna do?"

Paddy stood up. "You better find me three guys who look something like the guys they pinched and tell them they'll have to take the fall. I'll be back here tumorra night at six." He insisted on shaking hands with each one before he left, including Muro Scarlata, and asked after their wives and kids.

When they met the next evening he told them he thought it all could be worked out. There would be two blocks of money needed for the payoff. He said, after all, Judge Gant had to be handled because it was his assembly district, but the cops wanted their payoff to be indirect because it was two of their own people who were killed. "I got them to agree to accept a reward and some department medals and citations. It'll be a nine-way split, and what we want now

will be the best thing for the neighborhoods and the newspapers. You people will have to stay way in the background,
but I want yiz to call on the Sicilian business people and
make them form a Sicilian-American citizens' committee to
tell the Polacks how bad they feel that this here thing happened. Make it look like every little kid and every grocery
store all chipped in wit' the reward money—and it's got to
come to thirty grand. That's three thousand for each of nine
cops and three for Rollo Gant. The city'll pay for the medals.
Now, we want a real respectable business fella to head the
committee. Someone like Joe Corrente, he's in olive oil."

"You want him, you got him," Don Salvatore said.

"I think you ought to allow five hundred bucks each for
the families of the two dead cops," Paddy said. "And get
eight or ten little kids in their first communion dresses to
lay flowers on the grave of the kid who was shot, God rest
her soul, and have the three fall guys ready to give theirselves
up to my cops Tuesday morning. We'll do it in Prospect
Park because there has to be a little gun play, but we want
it safer this time. I think I should tell you, Carmelo, that
the cops is gonna kill one of the three guys, then the other
two will stand trial."

"Perfectly all right," Don Carmelo assured him.

"And I'll tell you this. Now that I got it all organized
it sounds easy as pie, but it took one helluva lot of doin' all
the same."

"What about my three button men?"

"Oh, them. They're sprung by now. They let them out
at five-thirty. Insufficient evidence."

Paddy went to Atlantic City for the sea air and stayed
there until "brilliant police work" apprehended the killers
of the two policemen after a running gun battle in Prospect Park that resulted in the killing of one of the men,
Gaspare Minasola, forty-nine. His companions confessed
to the killing of the two officers and the child and would be
brought to trial without delay. The trial was delayed, as it
turned out, for twenty-two months, but the men were ulti-
mately sentenced to two and a half years in state prison
with time off for good behavior.

Paddy was alone in his Oliver Street house one evening
about a month later, listening to "County Kerry Airs" sung

by Dame Elizabeth Blue on the Gramophone when Don Salvatore Purpi came to call. Out of deference to his visitor's nationality as well as his sanity Paddy turned the music machine off. He found a bottle of red wine given him by the Carmelite nuns of New Jersey and they sat down to talk.

It developed that, first of all, Don Salvatore had come representing all Sicilians in New York to thank Paddy for what he had done for them and to get an idea of just what it was going to cost for his indispensable services. Paddy shrugged it off. He didn't want anything, he said. That seemed to startle, even frighten Purpi, who began to talk rapidly about how he was an old man who had seen much of life and that he knew it was not right for anyone to be allowed to serve yet refuse money, because the world could not get on that way. If a man worked, if a man delivered just as he had said he would, then it would be unworthy of everyone concerned if that man did not receive his just due —and besides, every transaction should be separate.

Paddy took his time. "You know me, Sal. I'll take a little envelope if it'll make you and the boys feel better. It'll only go to the nuns annyhow. But—there is somethin' else. Somethin' close to me heart—"

"Name it. You have only to say it, Paddy, because we know you are a fair man."

"Well, you'll find this as hard to believe as annything you've ever heard, but I'm a shy man when it comes to women. For one thing—I mean, it's the God's truth, ain't it?—I'm not a young man. I mean, I'm first to say that. But just the same, Sal, there's this girl I want to marry, and, well, she's younger an' all. If you know what I mean."

"Lemme repeat. We must be sure. You say you wanna get married?"

Paddy nodded earnestly.

"I see. Good luck. God bless you. And keepa you."

"It's not an ordinary situation, you see. I never met the girl. Although I seen her, of course. But she's never seen me and doesn't know I'm on God's earth, if you want the truth of it."

"I see," Don Salvatore said sagely, completely baffled.

"But she's an old-country girl, a Sicilian girl, and I thought—I mean, after all, the girls do what their fathers want, don't they?"

"It depends."

"But if Carmelo and you was to go to the father—"

"Aaaaah!"

"I give it a lotta thought. I mean, it could be a good thing all around for a man to have his daughter marry me, if you know what I mean, an' I think you do."

"It will be an honor, Paddy. What is the father's name?"

"You know—the Correntes. Joe Corrente. The olive-oil fella. His daughter Maria is the one."

The *capo mafioso,* Carmelo Lumia, and his *consigliere,* Salvatore Purpi, called at the Corrente offices. The air sang with wonderful smells: *crescenz* and *parmigiano, quartirolo* and *teleggio.* As they were shown into Corrente's room he became very pale. He knew well who they were.

They were two men of respect. They showed no suggestion of either violence or power. They entered the room humbly, with deference, two elderly men who were unpretentiously dressed and very respectful. They showed their awareness of his place in the world, of his dignity and of the marks of his success. Their manner conveyed that what they wished most was to be of any large or small service to him. It filled him with dread. He leaped to his feet upon short, trembling legs and said in the dialect of northwestern Sicily, "Good day. Good day. You honor me by coming. Please seat yourselves and tell me how I may make you in any way more comfortable." The two men sat down and faced Corrente across his desk. Don Carmelo's voice was mellifluent and admiring. "We are here to express the gratitude and admiration for the way you organized the Italian community of Brooklyn at the time of the recent sadnesses."

"Thank you. I was happy to work on that. Judge Gant came to me and he said it would be a good thing because of what happened last month in New Orleans when the Matrangas and the Provenzanos had the disagreement. Over the docks." He knew he must sound as though he were babbling, but he didn't mind because these two men undoubtedly thought all people talked like that.

"Then you know Judge Gant. Do you know Patrick J. West?"

"I have met him. At the ball each year. I certainly know who he is. A very important man."

"Judge Gant is a boss, of course," Don Carmelo reminded gently. "But Patrick J. West is a very big boss."

"I know that," Corrente said. "I am sure of that."

"And he is a friend," Purpi said with emphasis. "He is a friend of the friends."

Corrente began to sweat lightly. He was a short round man with a pencil-line mustache, something terribly *démodé*, over a soft, uncertain, pink mouth. He had to clear his throat to answer, lest he squeak. "But surely it isn't possible that there is anything *I* can do for Patrick J. West?"

"Yes, there is," Don Carmelo said.

"There is?"

"I bring honor to you, signore. Patrick J. West wishes to marry your daughter."

"My daughter?"

"Yes."

"Which daughter? I have nine daughters."

"The daughter who is called Maria."

"*Maria?*" Corrente looked at them as though they had either gotten the girl's name wrong or made a terrible mistake. He seemed stunned, incredulous. Slowly he felt his strength returning to himself now that he understood, as a businessman, the nature of their visit.

"The daughter who dances the balleto," Don Salvatore said.

Corrente wanted to laugh. Happily. With composure and pleasure. He felt positively arrogant with the new power. There was, after all, a sweetness in truth and justice in life. He wanted to laugh until he sobbed and hiccupped. Since his wife had died thirteen years before, his daughter Maria had been the scourge of his life, as she would be of any man's. He could not believe his good fortune. He would be rid of the home-grown harridan in a manner that no one, not even a priest, could find fault with, and by doing so the Fratellanza would have fallen into his debt. And his new, elderly son-in-law was such a power in this city that he wanted to sing when he thought of all the hotels that would be forced to buy his cheeses. He almost felt affection for Maria for making all this possible. Aieee! And now—to *business*!

"My little girl—you would say one of the most beautiful girls you have ever seen. I have shoveled money into her education. She has studied in Rome and Paris."

"You lose a daughter, yes," Don Salvatore said. "But do you not also gain?"

"How? How, signori?" he pleaded to be told. "What compensates for the loss of such a daughter? A daughter who was to have begun a brilliant career in November on the stage of the Metropolitan Opera?"

"Have you been paying a small tax to the little brothers on the docks when you land your imports?"

"Always."

"Splendid, then," Don Carmelo said. "As a wedding present to the father of the bride we are going to give you one year free of those little taxes."

"But you make me appear ungrateful! What am I sacrificing after all, only—"

"Fifteen months," Don Carmelo said with finality.

"I thank you. But never mind my little business. What of the young man she loves and whom—if she marries—" He bit his tongue for telling such a lie. Maria had never acknowledged the existence of any man. If it were possible to accuse a girl of rape, then her mirror would accuse her.

"Two days after the wedding," Don Carmelo said, "you will be named a Commendatore of the Order of Saint Maurice and Saint Lazarus by the grateful Kingdom of Italy."

"Also every Italian-language newspaper in this country will run that news on its front page."

"It would honor Patrick J. West if I could be knighted before the wedding," Mr. Corrente suggested.

"Good. That will be done."

That night Giuseppe Corrente did not knock timidly on his daughter Maria's door, the only private chamber in a house filled with women. He kicked it open. She glared at him. He kicked it shut behind him.

"Are you drunk or something?" she shrilled. "What are you doing in my private, personal room? Have you lost your senses?"

"Maria, have you heard of the Wolf? Carmelo, the Wolf, Lumia?"

"What has that got to do with me?"

"He came to see me today."

"I don't care who came to see you today. Get out! Everything will be covered with a male stink in here."

"A man the Fratellanza needs very much, a man they regard very, very highly, a man for whom they would be happy to torture and kill—this man wants you."

"*Wants* me?" Her long, beautiful hand squeezed her full firm breast.

"Your body."

She screamed involuntarily.

"But he wants to marry you. His name, his place, his fortune—all yours. He wants to marry you *in a church.*"

She fainted.

He didn't touch her as she lay on the floor. He sat on the edge of her bed and mopped his underarms with any cloths, such as handkerchiefs, curtains, the pillow slip, hoping his male stink was at its apogee. She stirred at his feet. She picked herself up, tottered to the full-length mirror and touched herself longingly in eight or ten places, perhaps wondering if she could store them in safety and visit them alone. She wheeled on her father. "Why should I be sacrificed to save you?"

"Oh, no, no. You have it wrong. They didn't come to threaten *me.* If Don Carmelo sends men with knives or throwing acid, they will go directly to *you.*"

"Papa! Papa, darling! What did you tell them?"

"I told them you would respond as a Sicilian woman."

Patrick J. West took Maria Corrente as his bride on December 1, 1887. It was a sudden wedding. Mr. Corrente urged that there be a minimum of delay. It was a quiet wedding, performed at St. Jemma's by Bishop James Fagin Ryan, assisted by Father Passanante, the bride's own confessor. All newspapers reported the event decorously on the society pages. No mention was made of the age of the bride or the groom. Among the wonderful array of wedding presents they received were seven hundred bath towels and sixty-seven color paintings of the Sacred Heart of Jesus. Although a honeymoon at Niagara Falls had been announced, the couple proceeded directly from the reception for a few friends at the Patrick J. West Democratic Club to their house in Oliver Street. The bride had fainted several times during the wedding ceremony and at the reception, and in her malaise had tossed the seven-tiered wedding cake at her sisters instead of the bridal bouquet. Only her family and the Mafia knew that the bride met her husband for the

first time at the head of the aisle in the church when Mr.
Corrente gave her away. The bride spoke only in Sicilian.
Her father, always at her side, interpreted for her by saying,
"My daughter tells you that she is a Sicilian woman, Your
Grace, and that she speaks in the dialect of her country because this is the most meaningful day of her life." She
seemed reluctant to cut the wedding cake at the side of her
groom for the benefit of the photographer from *Il Progresso*
until Don Carmelo Lumia spoke to her briefly, perhaps explaining what the picture would mean to her father. She became very pale but she agreed with alacrity, although she
fainted during the pretty rite.

When the bride and groom reached home alone she still
had not spoken to him, and other than marrying him, had
not acknowledged him from the moment they had met. His
anger was mounting like the white smoke of the papal election signal, and in a very short time her disdain caused him
to lose his head—or, to be fair, it was the combination of her
disdain and his lust—and he clubbed her with his hard,
baggy fists, then took her sexually wholly by force. She
fought and clawed under him and screamed all through the
act. It was his masculine opinion that after this clear show
of domination she would come to her senses, because although he was not entirely an experienced man with delicately reared women, he had commanded many a battalion
of whores, and he had a firm, if unilateral, belief in what
women responded to.

When she became conscious again he went to her side and
attempted to soothe her by rubbing her wrists with Irish
whiskey, but she fought him off as though he had come to
rape her once more, snatching the bottle and striking him
with it and slashing his right cheek severely with her nails.
The same degrading combination of lust and anger got him
so aroused that he raped her again, throwing her to the floor,
whisking back her once-immaculate wedding gown to her
chin, her new drawers in shreds from the first great encoun-
ter, and flinging himself through the air upon her body as
though he were a small boy and she were a sled. She rolled
to one side, screaming piercingly. He landed with heavy
force on the floor and almost knocked himself unconscious,
but the inequity of it all kept him alert, and his great hairy
hand clamped upon her ankle and drew her slowly under

him, pinning her with his elbows, his knees, then his hips
with their gross passenger.

When it was over this time he lay on top of her like a
landed manta ray, gasping and frightened that he was having a coronary for, at last, his age had protested horribly.
She grappled him off herself and rolled away. He mewed
piteously that if he had to take it from her every time he
wanted a little piece throughout their married life, he might
well find himself at death's door. Jesus! What a wedding
night after so many long months of such glorious dreams.
The injustice righted him. "What the hell is wrong here?" he
raged. "You're my wife. Here we are. This is alla sacred
jooty for botha us." She hawked and spat at him, then tried
to kick him swiftly in the groin, and they had the last exchange of their life in the English language. "Every time you
want to put that big hairy thing in me," she said in a shrill,
strident voice, "you'd better get Carmelo the Wolf and some
button men to hold me down."

"Why—you shameless little cooze!" he shouted at her
from the floor.

"And remember this, you old mess. My father, that wet
little shit, told me I had to marry you because I was a
Sicilian woman. All right, you rancid, goat-bellied ruin, I
will become a Sicilian woman from now until you are dead."

She never spoke to him in English again. When he spoke
to her she answered obscenely in the Alcamo dialect that is
not, in any way, as dulcet from a woman as, say, Parisian
French. If he wanted her body he had to fight her desperately
for it. She exercised with forty-pound iron dumbbells and
grew stronger and stronger while he felt himself grow
weaker until, after a short while, the whole damned struggle wasn't worth it. She let herself go. She seemed to live on
pasta and grow fatter by the hour. She wore the same shape-
less black dress at all times and her dank black hair looked
as though it had been arranged with an egg beater. She
would not leave the house except to buy food. She cooked
and served him only Sicilian dishes—*riso chi cacuocciuli* or
farsumagru or *pomaruoro o gratte,* all a terrible mess to
Paddy, a meat-and-potatoes man. He came home to eat less
and less often. Neither her father nor her sisters visited
Maria, and in a relatively short time it was as though no one
remembered that she was in that house or that she had ever

married or that she existed at all. Except her son, Eddie.

One of the first two rapes "took," as the old wives would say. She swelled up and in exactly ten lunar months from her wedding day she gave birth to their son and demanded so shrilly and hysterically of Father Passanante that the infant be christened Courance that the priest prevailed upon Paddy to include it as the child's middle name. He became Edward Courance West, an odd enough name for a Sicilian-Irish baby.

Until her son was fourteen years old—which was as long as the boy had her—she spoke to him only in Sicilian. She treated him distantly, with her special, stupid haughtiness, and the boy thought of her as a queen, regal in beauty and in bearing. The more he adored her the more she took care of herself, and her little raisin-eyes found their way out of their pillows of fat. She began to clean and scent herself. She cast off the black rag of a dress for other dresses, engaging and colorful, and after a while even took to going to the ladies' barber in the neighborhood to get her hair dressed stylishly. Then, when the boy was fourteen and his heart totally hers and filled with love and joy of her, she ran off with a woman who sold silk stockings from door to door. She left behind a letter, in English, for her husband so that he would be sure to know what she had done. A door had opened for her. No one had been able to understand what had been wrong with her for all these years, but the touch of the lady sales agent's hand and the look in her eye at that moment had put everything right in one flash.

Paddy and his son responded bitterly to her desertion. Eddie held it against all women for all of his life. He never stopped seeking revenge upon every one of them for what his mother had done to his father and what she had done —the greater betrayal within the lesser one—to him.

Eddie West saw his mother as a coldly beautiful snarler who spoke in a mysterious code that separated her from the rest of the world. The Dance itself and her aborted world triumphs as a dancer were in imagination totally achieved by her because they had been denied her. She paddled on her back in a limpid pool of wistful fantasies, always looking back to where she had almost begun. She transmitted her own frustration to her son and gave it form for him. Frustration at never being able to get through to her, at having to hear her speak a language that he thought no one else could speak, describing with disdain and emasculating indifference a world he could neither enter nor imagine. He would beat upon walls because he could not beat upon her. In his boy's mind, then within his deserted adolescent consciousness, he thought of all women as repositories of some enormous secret that could not be dislodged unless it were shaken out or beaten out or stamped and kicked and strangled out. The discovery of this secret, this enigma, would explain the mystery of women and prove the key to open the mile-high doors that separated one vital part of him from the other deadened part with which he was forced to live.

When she left him it was not that something wonderful and irreplaceable had vanished, leaving him unloved and alone. While she was with him he felt more unloved than after she'd gone. His father loved him and proved that every day, then proved it again and again. But when his mother went away without revealing the enigma's explanation and thus releasing the lock within the mile-high doors, his frustration multiplied itself, then squared itself, broadening, lengthening and deepening until the enigmas (more of them and all of them) were sunk at the center of a gigantic cube that was his "peculiarness," standing alone on the barren plain of his existence at the geometric center of his frigid brain.

When she was gone he convinced himself that it was not just his mother who was alien and hateful and the creator of frustration and pain, but all women, because the only opposite of his mother was his father, his father and the people his father brought to see him—heavyweight champions of the world, famous actresses, high-riding jockeys, Presidents of the United States, all activists, people who revealed, never concealed, amiable, outgoing, attentive and interesting. As the years went on he thought he had forgotten everything he had felt so keenly in that first month of nights after she had gone away, but the pain of the frustration had settled deeply into the cold mists inside his head, so deeply that he was not aware it was still there. Except that he hunted women, preferring the compliant, extroverted, instantly surrendering, totally available. And when, as it happened several times in his life, these total availables suddenly revealed an antic selfishness that thwarted him, the gigantic old frustration was dragged out of his head. He had then to shake, strike, stamp and strangle to try to rid himself of the old locked-in secret. Although he thought later that he had at last seen a glimpse of the explanation with his own wife, the echo of his mother's meaning-within-no-meaning was still heard.

His father's public essence was strong and whole, but the boy could not match its splendid shape with the grotesque private form his father assumed inside the house, and thus was never able to see his father whole. Outside, the father was a giant figure, all-powerful, feared/loved. People came to him to try to realize their fortunes through him; the singers sang sweetly and the magicians their wonders did perform. But inside the house this majesty shrank into gabbling garrulousness that pleaded as it followed the icy, foul-tongued mother up and down stairs, in and out of rooms, apologizing for something that the son could not understand. "Maria! Wait! Listen to me! I have two tickets for a center box at the opera wit' all that beautiful dancin'."

She would halt and turn on the stairs, look far down at her husband and say in Sicilian, "Why don't you cover those tickets with dog shit and eat them for breakfast?" Only the boy understood what she had said. One dark winter afternoon (she would not use electric light because it was "not Sicilian"), while she was making pasta and talking to the boy, they heard the father move behind the kitchen door in the stair hall, secretively, trying to learn something desperately important to him. His mother began to talk more and more torrentially in Sicilian, flinging the dough, slamming it into the marble tabletop. After a while the father's steps moved away and after a while his mother's voice became calm and distant again.

That night the father came into the boy's dark room and sat on the edge of the bed and asked what the mother had been shouting so passionately that afternoon. Eddie told him she had been describing the grace of the great Sicilian dancer Evalina Perseguitare, the first dancer to remove heels from her slippers to assist her *batterie*, one of the most brilliant inventions of the ballet. She was also the woman who was credited with having perfected the *entrechat six* and who, in order for her feet to be seen as her Achilles tendon sent her into flight, shortened her skirts to mid-leg; but it took one hundred years more for them to go still higher, to the knee. The ballet is life in the air, Mama said. The ground is there only as a point of departure. Humans stay imbedded in the ground, Mama said; Gods and dancers defy the fly-paper and soar, free of all restraint.

"Does she always talk like that?"

"Sure. She wants me to know all about it."

"Why?"

"I'm going to be a dancer."

"*Eddie*!"

The boy thought his father was electrified with elation. "It's a wonderful life," he said dreamily. "The world is at your feet. You travel and you see all the beautiful things of Rome, London and Berlin. I start my lessons in two weeks, then after a while Mama and I are going to Paris."

Paddy was sick with horror. He groped his way out of the house. When he returned the next morning he gave Eddie ten cents to buy himself some of that special cake at Boehm's, six blocks away, then he went into his wife's room, talked to her briefly about her plans to turn the boy into a ballet dancer, then beat her unconscious and left her bleeding, stuffed far under the bed like a chamber pot. He stopped talking to her forever on that day. That afternoon he took Eddie with him on his rounds, and from then on, in the weekends and during winter, summer and autumn holidays he took him to baseball games, horse races and boxing matches without much letup and began his basic education in the uses of power and money. Eddie forgot about dancing. His father told him to put it out of his head, that it was work for women and that men had a damned sight more of better things to do in their lives than balance on their toes and jump in the air in tights.

The people around the courts—the cops, the gamblers, the businessmen and the madams—got used to seeing Eddie at his father's side. Every leader of Tammany Hall from 1900 forward knew the boy as though he were a favorite nephew; so did the gang leaders. Paddy West got a big kick out of having Eddie talk Sicilian with the Italian mobs and some of the most famous killers of their time. Ignazio Saieta made Eddie an honorary member of the Unione Siciliane, which Eddie made stick when he got older and decided he needed it. The Irish gangs took for granted he was Irish. So did the Jews. The Italian gangs knew he was a Sicilian and that nobody and nothing could change that. His father, whose ponderous wisdom no one ever doubted, was careful to keep the balance correctly weighted. He taught Eddie the value of concealing from the Jews and the Irish (and everyone but Sicilians) that he could speak the Sicilian language. "They're a canny, clannish people, Eddie," he said, "and they'll like it best if you show the Sicilian to them alone. When in doubt, think like Aaron Burr, Ed. Ice in the veins is money in the bank, and always take the long view."

On the day Eddie became fourteen his father chose Lorette des Anges, the leading soubrette of the day, eight times the cover girl on the *Police Gazette,* to "break Eddie in." He took the boy to her beautiful flat in Murray Hill on a clear, sunny Sunday morning and had a glass of champagne with them before he left Eddie there. Eddie was pleasured so much he thought his hair would leap off his head in one piece. All in all, in a choice between his mother and father, there was never any real contest for Eddie's soul —not apparently, anyhow.

The day after the first time he was ever laid Paddy told him he was going to be a lawyer and that he would be going away to school in New England to prepare for college and be ready to handle the kind of boys he would meet there. Eddie was a bright boy. Paddy could line up the best sponsors. Eddie qualified for the junior form at the Gelbart Academy, where the boys were taught odd speech, something not too unlike the speech at Cambridge University in England—although no one ever identified it for Paddy West or the boy would not have been allowed to stay. Eddie entered Yale at sixteen, Harvard Law School at eighteen. He was admitted to the New York bar when he was twenty, a prodigy, on July 4, 1908.

Each summer, from the time he was fourteen, his father rented a large cottage at Canoe Place, Long Island, and conducted his business from there while Eddie entertained friends from school, all of them talking high in their noses, swallowing vowels and vocally punching at odd syllables. The speech stayed with Eddie for all of his life. He was an aristocrat, so, it followed, he spoke like an aristocrat.

Paddy worked out a clear policy for the selection of his

son's roommates. Eddie was always younger than the other boys, although usually taller and always more worldly. Therefore part of his standard equipment when he went off to Gelbart was autographed pictures—James Jeffries, Lorette des Anges (in spangled tights and inscribed "Stay warm for Lorette, baby doll") and a signed cabinet photograph of William McKinley (Republican), twenty-ninth President of the United States ("For Edward C. West, a grand young American, The White House, January 27, 1904").

To develop his roommate system Paddy procured a list of the forty-one members of Eddie's class at Gelbart and had his bank run down the credit ratings of their families. Together he and Eddie selected the six top ratings, and on arrival at school, Eddie set out to cultivate those six whether they had shale acne, congenital idiocy, or were immediately nicknamed "Shitty" by the other boys. "It's the long view that sees you through, Eddie," his father taught. "Don't forget, Burr married an old whore for comfort in his old days. You got to go to the money, Ed—money don't go to you." Working his points with Tammany sureness, Eddie always managed to be assigned to a room with the best-connected boy in his class (next to Eddie), but an important part of the system was to move on to a new roommate every year so that the greatest amount of future ground could be mapped. This required a strategy that would not hurt, offend or alienate the current roommate. "I've talked it over wit' t'ree of the biggest men in Wall Street, Eddie," Paddy said. "All independent of the other. Everyone of them said the same. The only good anybody gets outta schools is meetin' the right people. The rest is all a lotta Latin an' chowder."

Twice a year, at Christmas and at spring holidays, Eddie would take his current roommate and the next year's roommate with him to New York. Paddy would put the boys up in a big suite at the Astor. These sessions always clinched next year's roommate and held the current one as a friend forever. In the years to come Eddie was able to move at the inner core of the great newspaper and magazine publishers, the bankers, lawyers and industrialists, all because of Paddy's (and Aaron Burr's) superior planning. When Eddie got the two young men to the Astor Paddy really laid it on with a trowel. He moved his "afternoon office" uptown to the boys' living room, and in and out of the doors of the hotel suite would walk such figures as George M. Cohan, Philadelphia Jack O'Brien, Al Smith, Isadora Duncan, Georgie Mountin, the jockey who won the Preakness, and Winston S. Churchill, who was in New York on a lecture tour. On the last night of the heavenly visit, after a quick tour of all the principal museums and lunch at Jack's, when they were all dressed for dinner and he was opening a magnum of champagne (which he did not drink), Eddie would announce the surprise. There would be a discreet knock on the door and into the room would come three beautiful women (one of them always the glamorous, famous Lorette des Anges, who was always assigned to the current room-mate) and really wonderful fun would begin. The room-mates never got over that part of the program. For some of them it was the only thing they remembered about their youth. All of it gave Eddie a sound appreciation of power.

It wasn't only an education in material things. "Use their religions, Eddie," his father taught. "Sometimes that's a good handle on a man. But remember Burr. The old, long, ice-cold view of everything. Religion is only the politics of the centuries." That was the only lesson from Paddy he never learned. His mother had been a savage, primeval Catholic. His wife was to be a rote devout. These two women had such formidable influence on his emotions that he was herniated by religion, which was for him an emotion never to be examined, only felt.

As soon as he was admitted to the bar his father explained that he was now qualified to run the family's little bank. It was a miniature bank run in a street-level store on West 14th Street, having four big safes in the cellar that could have been opened with the stick of a taffy apple but were safe safes because they were Paddy's safes and the criminal element needed Paddy. The bank had been established in '81 with a capital of ninety thousand dollars for the work-ingmen in the neighborhood. The saloon chain, the whore-houses, the gambling joints were throwing off good money. Because he never failed to deliver less than 98 percent of the vote, and on one occasion had delivered 107 percent, he was always so well regarded by the leader that Tammany saw to it that certain city funds, and later on, state and federal funds, were deposited in the West National Bank;

and the gamblers and West Side gangs always used it as their bank.

"Banks are the great power stations," Paddy taught. "It's as clear as day. The more money they put in your bank the more power you got, but the beauty part is the more power we get the more money they put in." Both of them were dead certain about Eddie's place in politics. "Yes and forever," Paddy taught. "Look what Aaron Burr did with politics for a power base. He damned near owned Mexico. Now, mind you, to get it started I had to do it out in front where they could all see me workin'. But not you. There's warmth in the shadows you never dreamed of, Ed. There's much beauty behind a mask. Run the people who you put there to run politics and let them run everything but the bank. The bank is the only place the world sees you out in front. Give them the glory and a ham sandwich. You take the rest."

Edward Courance West at twenty-one became the youngest bank president in the history of the state. The bank was three blocks west of Tammany Hall, which had moved uptown from Franklin and Nassau in '68. To install his son, Paddy had torn down the building the street-level store was in and built a four-story edifice, with a vault for the sweet little bank whose capital was now eight million, two hundred and ninety-one thousand dollars and eleven cents (as of the 1909 year-end audit).

When Paddy died suddenly after a lifetime without a sick day, Eddie was twenty-three years old: March 24, 1911. Leaving the Franklin Street saloon with Willie Tobin, Paddy passed a horse that had just been frightened by a noisy automobile and had reared high, startling Paddy, who had grabbed the reins to pull the horse down to his level so he could slam it a good punch in the mouth. He knocked the horse to its knees, then picked it up again to send it spinning over on its side in the shafts. Then Paddy made a rattling sound in his throat, grabbed at his chest with his huge right hand and fell down on the pavement. Willie ran into the saloon to get a bottle of whiskey and to call Doc Solomon, the coroner, who was at the bar talking to a police captain. By the time they got back to Paddy he was dead.

He was seventy-nine years old and might have lived to be ninety had he remembered Aaron Burr and not lost his temper just for the sake of slugging a horse. Just as Burr might have been President had he not lost his temper and shot Alexander Hamilton. Eddie made careful note of both errors and withdrew a few steps backward into greater coldness. But error to one side, Paddy West had died as active, powerful, teetotal and unsmiling as always. His life had been a chapter in the ever-unfolding American dream, inspiring and evocative. A principal thoroughfare of the City of New York was named for him, West Street—as had been Sullivan County, Foley Square and Plattsburg, New York, for other great men who had striven to widen the base of democracy.

The day after Paddy West's magnificent funeral, as he scraped red rubble off his cheeks, Edward Courance West, aged twenty-three, encountered the merest ghost of the idea that was to make him one of the great kings of the world but that was to finish the expansion and terminate the glory of the American dream by several centuries. Everything that followed the execution of his idea in American history was to be looted and sacked by him, drained and left hollow, and he was to be only most obscurely (by not more than three people) identified with it. From the moment the perfume of that idea lingered over him Eddie West thought about very little else. He began forthwith to organize all the affairs and details of his inheritance so that they might be administered at once by his appointees.

CHAPTER TWO

The first step was to talk things over with the Leader, himself a saloon keeper who had been a horsecar driver on the 14th Street crosstown line, a job obtainable only through political wirepulling because it was a cash business and unreported fares were considered to be a fringe benefit. The Leader had worked hard and had spent very little and by the time he was twenty-four he had enough to lease his own saloon—soup and beer for a nickel with all the free crackers, cheese and bologna you could eat. Beyond members of his family (of which he considered little Eddie one) he was not a communicative man. Politics had been his only interest for all his life, and from the day of the opening of his first saloon and the establishment of his famous Fanwood Club he worked day and night, summer and winter, to deliver the vote when it was needed, so that in proper time he was made docks commissioner and was able to put four or five hundred thousand dollars aside and expand his chain of saloons. He was a political genius. He was what Paddy West believed Aaron Burr was and which Aaron Burr had not been.

He lunched every day on the second floor of Delmonico's at Union Square, right by the Hall, at a table that rested on four tiger's paws, the room being known to the press as "The Scarlet Room of Mystery," its door guarded by lads from the gas house district. Eddie got there early to be sure of a seat next to the leader, who was so glad to see him that he nodded at him. They ate caviar, tortue verte au sherry, filets de sole à la Nantua, suprême de volaille aux truffes fraîches, haricots verts à la crème, pommes de terre à la parisienne, parfait de fois gras à la gelée de porto, asperges vertes, bombe Montmorency and friandises. The Leader and Eddie shared a bottle of seltzer. The others at the table drank beer. The Leader did not countenance talking during meals —he rarely did what might be called chatting at any time— and would glare at anyone who talked while dining, or have him removed from the room. When the cigars came out the Leader rose and walked gingerly to the small table at the far corner of the room that had only two chairs. Eddie followed him. They sat down. The waiter served coffee, then went away. The Leader puffed on his cigar, then raised his eyebrows, signifying that Eddie could speak.

"About the leadership of the First," Eddie said. The Leader pursed his lips. "I want John Kullers," Eddie told him.

"John *Kull*ers?"

"Yes."

"You won't run yourself?"

"No."

"You'd run it like Paddy ran it, Eddie. That's what we have to have."

"John Kullers will run it that way because I'll be telling him how."

"Have you thought about the Eyetalians?"

"What about them?"

"Paul Kelly was in to see me this morning. He wants Jimmy Lehner for leader in the First."

"In *my* district?"

The Leader shrugged as though he were shifting a grand piano across his shoulders. "That's politics for you."

"Well?"

"You better talk it over with him." The Leader stood up. The meeting was over. "Straighten it all out, Eddie. We don't want trouble."

Eddie went to the Franklin Street saloon and sent out a runner to locate Paul Kelly, who, since winning his murder trial with Paddy West's help, had applied to the courts to have his name changed back to Vacarelli. He had retired from the gang business and had gone into the labor-union business and had changed his residence from the Lower East Side to East 116th Street. By the process of elimination it was determined that Vacarelli must be in a poolroom in East Harlem, his uptown headquarters.

He greeted Eddie warmly in the pool hall. They spoke Sicilian. Eddie said he wanted to have a little meeting someplace, so Vacarelli stopped playing pool and they went outside to sit in a wagon.

"What's up, paesano?"

"I just left the Leader."

"Yeah? I saw him this morning."

"I know. He said you wanted to take over my district."

Vacarelli shrugged. "Why not? It's near my business." He ran the waterfront.

"Because you don't know politics, Paolo. It's a family profession and very complicated." Eddie was calm and reasonable. "What is it you think you can get out of the leadership that I can't get for you? Did Paddy ever let you down? I'm Paddy now." Eddie was taking the sincere, straight way because he had a lot to do that day and all this blather was such a minor part of it. Vacarelli didn't have a chance of taking over the First, and all of them knew it; this was just to reestablish his position and maybe win a few points if he could.

"You gonna be district leader, kid?"

"I'm running John Kullers."

"He's all right, but he's yours."

"Ours, Paolo. John and I will take care of everything for you."

"That's good."

"You'll tell the Leader it's all straightened out?"

"I'll tell him today." They shook hands and Eddie went downtown.

The biggest men in the city were in the Franklin Street saloon, retasting the vigor of Paddy's funeral. Some, who had five days of alcohol in their systems, were misty-eyed or openly weeping. One leading actor was asking all who would listen if they had caught him when the news of Paddy's death had come to him. Eddie shook a lot of hands and accepted a lot of commiseration with his long face and his cold eyes and his blatted Gelbart Academy accent. When he found the chance he told the head bartender to send Willie Tobin upstairs as soon as he could be found. Willie was Jiggs Tobin's son, a bail bondsman Paddy had used as a runner to the judges, the police and the prosecutors across the street. Paddy had made Willie take the bar examinations three times until he had passed. He was two years older than Eddie, a born lobbygow and second gravedigger.

Willie came into the shabby office cautiously, as he did everything else, closing the door behind him. He was a small-boned, dapper man with a vaguely epicene air. Eddie didn't tell him to sit down so he didn't. "How long were you with Paddy, Willie?" Eddie asked.

"Since I'm thirteen. Half my life almost. God rest his soul."

"This was Paddy's office, but this afternoon your name goes up on that door." The offer seemed to make Willie nervous. "'William Tobin, Attorney-at-Law,' it'll say. It's your office now."

"Why is that, Eddie?" Willie's teeth were working on his lower lip.

"New brooms sweep efficiently, and I'm the sweeper here, Willie. John Kullers is the new leader. John will run the district and all the saloons. Rhonda will handle the cathouses and I'll make an arrangement for the gambling rooms. But you'll run all the contracts. No more than that. It's work you know well. I wouldn't ask for the impossible."

"But how'll I know which contracts to take? Paddy always decided that."

"You'll know because I'll tell you. There's the phone. And you'll always know where I am. And I'm bumping you to thirty a week." Eddie got up and put on his hat. He looked slowly around the shabby office. "I'll never be back here," he said and started out. Willie called him.

"I think it oughta be fifty, Eddie."

"Thirty. When I see how you settle in I'll put you on a percentage basis and you'll make some real money." He left, closing the door loudly. The telephone rang. Willie picked it up.

"Hello?"

"Who's this?"

"Bill Tobin. Did you expect Paddy?"

"Lemme talk to Eddie."

"No."

"No? You know who this is?"

"Tell me what you want and I'll get back to you." There

was an uncertain pause at the other end. "Or hang up," Tobin said.

"You don't wanna know who this is?"

"So far what for?"

"This is Mike Segal."

"Hello, Mike."

"Hello, Willie."

"There's been a change, Mike."

"What?"

"Everybody calls me Bill."

"Why not?"

"What can we do for you, Mike?"

"I got a contract. Benny needs a gun permit. Unlimited."

"I'll get back to you tomorrow."

"Jesus, it's got to be late this afternoon."

"I need Eddie's okay and Eddie's on a horsecar somewhere. I'll get back to you by five o'clock."

"Call me at Benny's. We need the permit by tonight. In case."

Willie Tobin had failed the bar examination twice on his father's orders. The Tobins were crafty Irish who looked at the world out of the corners of their eyes and used a smile like an entrenching tool. Jiggs Tobin had decided long ago that Paddy West was the Tobin family career. It wasn't that the idea was all that different from the old days. The Tobins had always served a chief in the most comfortable position that he had to offer. They knew the value of a smile and all the kind of talk that could foam out of those kinds of smiles. Paddy West was a bigger chief in the City of New York than any goatskin-clad Druid cringer of a Tobin had ever found to keep a roof over his head. Jiggs knew how to work Paddy. He'd gotten two city jobs out of it, jobs that required no more of him than showing up once a week at the Sanitation Office to pick up his pay check. And he'd gotten his own horse, hansom and hack license, the dream of his life, without it costing one cent because he knew how to think ahead of Paddy while always seeming to be thinking far behind. That was why he made Willie fail those examinations. It paid to look dumb when you were working for a pea-brained elephant like Paddy West, and there was no better way to prove how dumb you were and no better way to write in-

surance on Paddy's gratitude than making him not just a
benefactor for sending the lad through law school and keeping him on a job loaded with money and power but for turning him into a *superior* benefactor. Paddy couldn't have
passed the bar examination if he'd taken it fifty-eight times,
but under the Tobin family system it was proved he was
fifty-eight times smarter than this Tobin clot who muddled
along and couldn't get to be a lawyer until the third time.
Jiggs and Willie and Bridey Tobin, God rest her soul, had
many a laugh over that. In fact Paddy West gave them more
fine entertainment and good rib-aching fun than anything
shown in any theeayter.

Willie wasn't smarmy. If he had discovered the Tobin system he could never have lived long enough to protect it. On
the surface he was a tenth-generation fink, to the world and
the Wests. He was the kind of dim-witted—well, damned
near dim-witted—twit who always absolutely miraculously
not only got the job done but got it done quick and in the
best way.

Jiggs Tobin said the secret of rising as a courtier was to
demonstrate every day of your life that you were abjectly
dependent on the boss's orders, that you couldn't move
across a room unless the smartest captain God ever sent to
earth charted your course and did all your thinking for you.
You had to insist on getting orders, then you had to be vocally grateful for receiving them, marveling all the way that
the human mind could coordinate and project such intricate
boxes within boxes, each containing a new and more splendid pearl. Then, of course, Jiggs said, you go out and get
the job done your own way and do it fast and at the least
cost. If the Man ever—which wasn't likely—complimented
you on a job well done in a tone of astonishment that you
could find your ass with either hand, then—instantly!—flash
the dumb-ox expression across the face and look him square
in the puss with dismay and stammer out like you couldn't
comprehend why the hell he should be praising you when
all you was doing was trying to carry out orders which,
thank God, were so detailed that how could you make a
mistake?

Jiggs was a master tobin, but Willie was far better at the
family profession than his father, which made the father

ecstatically proud because he had been just that much better an ass-kissing stumblewit than *his* father.

Willie was a new kind of tobin. They had always been lumpy men, with shoulders for pushing through a crowd ahead of the Boss, with eyes like awls to everyone but the Boss, with stained teeth and heads of hair like sea grass, tangled and long. They had been farters and belchers and friends of the rubber mat under a spittoon.

Willie was effete compared to the tobins who had lived before him. He was light-boned and graceful. He was a dude who put his savings squarely on his back and who had set himself to the task of wheedling jeweled stickpins out of Paddy, because people gave Paddy every sort of thing they kept in the backs of their bureau drawers when they didn't have money to give, because, after all, that was what loyalty meant in Paddy's eyes, not just the straight-ticket vote. Willie wore his beige hair in three, beautifully kept waves that ascended like lights from the elegant widow's peak that he had become so grateful to find on his forehead. Willie wore a ring on each hand that he had coaxed patiently out of Paddy, claiming that rings and stickpins bespoke affluence when he dealt with the cops in the Tombs and the judges and the DAs in the courts across the street. He was a nimble tobin in every way, but he was hauntingly epicene and therefore a new tobin. He specialized in merchandising the soft answer and the sweet request, and it worked, because when he had to he could put the old feudal steel into his voice and back them all down, because, as the newest of a long, long line of tobins he knew well his place and his power of place within the fief.

"It isn't an assignment that will be long or demanding," Eddie said to William Glass, dean of the Law School at Columbia University. "Just library research. Nights and weekends."

"Law students need their nights and weekends, Mr. West. That's when they learn to be lawyers."

"Law students can use money too. And I'll pay well." Eddie's tall, white, stiff collar seemed to support his long neck and bony head, giving him a swamp-bird's dignity.

"We have our graduates, the young lawyers who don't immediately set the world on fire." Dean Glass lifted a card file from a desk drawer and began to riffle through it. "Here is a brilliant young man. Arnold Goff. Straight As, and we haven't had many of those in our history. Editor of the law journal too."

"I'll take him."

"He's a lawyer, Mr. West. Explain your problem and he'll tell you whether he'll accept your offer."

Goff's office was in the St. Paul Building at 220 Broadway, below Chambers Street. Goff was a medium-sized man with soft skin, as pale as cigarette paper, with pale, shiny hair, wearing a black suit and a mauve necktie. He had the hardest eyes Eddie had ever seen, and that made Eddie marvel; harder than Paddy's and colder; harder than those of the men who had sat in Paddy's office above the saloon. Goff shook Eddie's hand, motioned him to a seat, but did not speak. He had mastered the compulsory law course wherein lawyers are taught to let others do all the talking in order to create an aura of mysterious wisdom and to avoid revealing the extent of this wisdom.

It was a pleasant small office with two windows that looked up Broadway, and off to the right, one could see City Hall. The walls displayed diplomas and impressive certificates, but those hung above reading level were dental-school diplomas that Goff's fiancée had bought at auction. There were also many pictures of large numbers of men in white aprons who were eating beefsteaks in happy congress, all the pictures framed in pencil-thin black wood and also purchased in quantity by Goff's fiancée from the estate of a defunct restaurateur.

Goff didn't say as much as "What can I do for you?" He sat in repose, with his fingertips touching under his chin, waiting for the petitioner to explain his presence.

It was child's play for Eddie. His father had challenged and rewarded him for not speaking long before his school days. That and his money gave him an edge. They sat in silence for one minute. Then three minutes. After about four minutes Goff said imperturbably, "What can I do for you?"

"I am an attorney. Dean Glass said you were a gifted briefs man."

"Thank you." Goff did something indefinable with his pale left hand, exposing his open palm, making a loosely clenched fist, then opening it to release nothing, thus turning his two words into a sardonic statement.

"That is what I know about you as a lawyer. What will I find when I investigate the rest?"

"Do you think that will be necessary?"

Eddie nodded pleasantly.

"If it is necessary to investigate an attorney at law beyond questioning the dean of his law school, then the retainer must be extraordinary. If that is so, why aren't you in Wall Street talking to one of the big firms? I would add that it might be more in line if I were to investigate you."

"That seems indiscreet for an attorney at law to say."

"I'm not in a popularity contest."

"You can investigate me. I am Edward Courance West. Paddy West's son."

Goff sat up very straight and his hard eyes began to be transformed into eyes that were looking at the golden medina. He stood up, walked around his desk and shook Eddie's hand again. "I am very glad to know you, Mr. West. Now let me tell you about myself." He moved slowly back to his chair behind the desk talking persuasively as he went.

"I am Arnold Goff, twenty-five years old. My father is head of Goff Lite-Wayts, a leading dress house on 39th Street that has a triple-A rating. I am an only son and my parents are proud of me. I am unmarried but engaged to a young woman, Bella Radin, age twenty-three. Her family runs nickelodeons, and we will marry as soon as my circumstances permit. My father would happily finance the marriage, and for that matter so would hers, but we have declined these offers. I have had no clients other than my father's firm, which I refuse to charge. I could pick up cases around the criminal courts if I wanted to live like that, if I had become a lawyer to do that. So, on the surface, I have no income. But I have. I gamble for a living and I am good at it. Not lucky. I am in the strictest sense of the word a professional gambler. Lightning calculator. If the truth were faced, I am even better with figures than I am at the law. But full-time gambling is out of the question while my parents are alive. They educated me to be a lawyer." Goff's telephone rang. "It's either my father, my mother, or Bella, my fiancée," he said ruefully. "Want to bet, Mr. West? I'll give you a good price." The phone rang again.

"What price?"

"Bet ten against those three names and win a hundred."

"What price if I name the caller, against those three?" The phone rang.

"Name the caller and you get twenty-five to one."

Eddie took out his wallet. "Can you cover a hundred dollars?" He slid a one-hundred-dollar bill across the glass-topped desk.

"You're covered. Who's calling?"

"A man named Willie Tobin," Eddie said. Goff picked up the phone and spoke into it with a casual drawl. "Hello? Who is calling, please?" He handed the instrument across the desk. "It's for you, Mr. West," he said almost gaily. "Mr. Bill Tobin."

"Mike Segal called with a contract for an unlimited," Willie told Eddie. "It's for Benny. Okay?"

"Okay," Eddie said. "Give it to Judge Ornstein. He's Supreme Court in Suffolk County but he's sitting in Brooklyn today as an extra to help clear up the calendar. Tell him I said hello to his wife." Eddie hung up and pushed the phone back toward Goff. "This is the retainer, Mr. Goff," Eddie said. "I want you to compile a precise legal history of the prohibition movement in this country. You are authorized for up to four assistants at fifteen dollars a week for sixteen weeks each. I want it as close to county by county as you can get it."

Goff had become very pale. His lips looked blue. His eyes looked harder because they were desperate. He had saved eighteen hundred dollars toward his marriage and the money was banked jointly with Bella Radin, who was patient and understanding and believed in him as a gambler as in everything else, but there had to be limits, as with everything else. He would have to borrow an additional seven hundred dollars from his father to cover this bet. How could he explain such a bet? It wouldn't be easy. He had to pay off within twenty-four hours, because this expressionless man with his long neck and cold, bony face just happened to be one of the men in the city who could make or break a lawyer.

"I suggest a fee of three thousand dollars, payable in advance," West was saying. "That fee should convey how important this brief is to me and how painstakingly it must be made." Before the bet Eddie had decided to offer a fee of a thousand dollars, but the bet took up the slack. The net cost for the brief would now be only five hundred dollars and he would have put a lock on Goff. "I'll pay for clerical expenses weekly as they're incurred, but the brief must be completed in one hundred and twenty days. Can you do it?"

Goff answered slowly, knowing he had to say he could do it because there was no other way to get the money to pay back West. "I think so. But I'll need six assistants."

"I'll pay for four. If you want six, you pay for the extra two."

"What if I can finish in ninety days?"

"Twenty percent bonus."

"Sixty days?"

"It can't be done in sixty days."

"Just supposing."

"I'd pay a fifty percent bonus," Eddie answered.

Goff figured it like a baseball bookie figuring bet hedges from behind first base. A bonus of fifteen hundred dollars would pay a hundred assistants for one week at West's rates, but he had no intention of paying anybody fifteen a week. With enough assistants—mainly with Bella and her relatives, the smartest family in the United States of America—it could be done in two months. He could win the bonus, and almost make a profit after paying off the bet, for a case that any Wall Street firm would have charged West fifteen thousand for, if they would have accepted it at all. But, and a great big but, he'd have West on his side and they wouldn't. That was the big bookmaker edge.

"I want social explanations insofar as they exist," West was saying. "Why has the temperance movement struggled so long and why have they failed so miserably decade after decade? I want geographic and economic reasons. Earnings. Plant costs. Book values. Inventories. Brewery and distillery locations. Trade associations will have all that. A brief, in short, whose limits are confined only to the talents of the man who writes it. When can I see an outline?"

"Sunday?" This was Friday.

"Sunday?" Eddie said. "Better make it Wednesday."

"Not if it counts against the bonus time limit."

"We won't start counting until Thursday morning"—and Goff had gained five and a half days; by the time West okayed the outline they'd be well off and running.

Eddie spoke slowly. "I hope we will do business again, Mr. Goff. But there is a very special rule for that. The fact that I am your client must be regarded as privileged information. You may not tell *anyone* that I am your client."

"My fiancée is my effective partner."

"Let this be understood. If I hear it around that I am organizing information about the prohibition movement, you will be sorry."

"I'll tell my fiancée, Mr. West. I'll take my chances with that."

West shrugged, put on his hat and got up. He took out his wallet and gave Goff a card. "Reach me through this man," he said. Then he put two one-thousand-dollar bills and two five-hundred-dollar bills on the shiny desk top. "I always pay cash." They shook hands. West walked to the door. Goff said, "Mr. West, we forgot the bet."

"Oh. Yes. The bet."

Goff scooped up the two thousand-dollar bills and one five-hundred-dollar bill and extended them to Eddie. "I always pay cash," he said, grinning broadly even though he was very pale and his hand trembled slightly.

CHAPTER THREE

Pick, Heller & O'Connell was the most widely influential and distinguished law firm in the United States. Their clients were the principal owners of the republic. Pick, Heller & O'Connell did on a gargantuan scale what Paddy West had done municipally all his life. Lawyers were the managers of America in the exquisitely powerful sense of managing all the managers of business, industry, religion and government. They made all the dangerous decisions. They handled the negotiations in which no manager or proprietor could safely appear. They were the high-yield gold thread in the tapestry of American wealth and power. The thread crossed all boundaries, entered all strong rooms, and infected/guided all of the consciences of a most unified colossus. The lawyers were not only the intelligence of a monolithic establishment, they were its fusion. They interlocked with other lawyers, communicating in a special dialect. Their fabric was strengthened each year by the top 10 percent of the graduating classes of the law schools of five universities.

Pick, Heller & O'Connell employed two hundred and sixteen lawyers in their main offices in Wall Street. They practiced marine law in offices at Bowling Green, where they maintained a staff of twenty-seven lawyers.

Eddie West had direct entry to the counsels of the firm because his roommate in his second year at Harvard had been C. L. Pick, Jr. Furthermore, Francis A. O'Connell was chairman of the Metropolitan Citizens' Committee for Good Government and had known Paddy West well. But Eddie didn't think those credentials would be good enough for what he wanted. He would be greeted by Mr. Pick or Mr. O'Connell, then turned over to a junior partner, and that simply would not do. He had pondered the problem. He had a first-class mind. He decided it would be better to cause each of the senior partners—C. L. Pick, F. Marx Heller, Francis A. O'Connell—to become individually and immeasurably indebted to him. The nature of indebtedness was that it had to acknowledge superior power. If it should occur to all of them at some later date that they had been framed, they would also be aware that if he had been able to frame them once he could frame them again, so they would do what he would ask. A part of his plan would offer shock and surprise. Its biggest part would depend on the fact that their advanced years and almost hermetically entrenched position at the top would have made them rusty at self-defense in the over-simplified arena of New York politics. As he saw it, no matter what they did in their panic, no matter how much muscle and cunning they brought to bear, he would be able to close all the doors.

The plan began with the arrival of eight city firemen, under a lieutenant, all wearing fire helmets and rubber coats, who swarmed through Pick, Heller & O'Connell's fourteenth-floor office checking wiring, pounding on walls and vents, then clearing all personnel off the floor, interrupting many serious client conferences. Word was passed immediately to F. A. O'Connell, who did not bother to leave his office to shout at the firemen but telephoned the fire commissioner. He lost his temper, which two doctors had warned him never to do again, when the only satisfaction the commissioner would give him was to ask that he have the senior fire officer present telephone him at once.

O'Connell was a blond, red-complexioned man who dressed as exquisitely as any standard duke. He went out to find and halt the firemen and discovered that *two* entire floors had by then been cleared and condemned. He found the fire lieutenant outside C. L. Pick's office on the sixteenth floor. Inside that office the extremely fragile, elderly C. L. Pick, doyen of all American corporation lawyers, was conferring with the head of the country's largest steel company who also happened to be the head of the largest investment bank. "Sorry, buster," the lieutenant said to O'Connell, "this wiring is a sin and a shame. It all has to come out. Lives are endangered here. Go to it, boys." He signaled three firemen with axes and they began to chop at C. L. Pick's wall that was lined with irreplaceable paneling that had been removed at enormous cost from the walls of the town hall in Littlecot, Lindfield, Sussex, England, and was four hundred and nine years old. They could hear Mr. Pick's tiny screams from within as the axes broke through. Despite O'Connell's attempt to fling himself on the axemen, the two outraged elderly men inside the room came into full view. The banker, a man with a nose like a boxing glove, cried out in tones that might have shattered windows, "What the hell are you doing?" and C. L. Pick shrilled, "Arrest those men!"

O'Connell charged the fire lieutenant with a chair and forced him to stop the axemen and to agree to telephone the commissioner. During all this the third senior partner, F. Marx Heller, slept on soundly on the leather settee in his office on the seventeenth floor.

On the following morning Heller was visited by investigators from the United States Customs Service who asked him to accompany them to Ellis Island for questioning on charges of smuggling. Heller was very stout and white-haired with used, stained tea bags under his eyes, whose perpetual expression was that of a man who is struggling not to bite people. Also he was more suspicious than a failing prince. He did not answer.

"Did you cross from Le Havre on the liner *Connubia* late in the summer of 1907?"

"Yes."

"Did you occupy staterooms A-402 and 403 on that crossing?"

"I don't remember."

"The records say you did."

"What about it?"

"I have a warrant for your arrest."

"Who issued the warrant?"

"Judge Heneghan. Special Sessions."

Heller spun his chair away from them and looked out the windows at the confluence of rivers. "Come back in forty minutes," he said. "I have to talk to my partners."

"We'll be waiting right outside," the shorter man said.

"I wouldn't try any tricks if I were you," the other man

advised him. They left. Heller told his secretary to find Mr. O'Connell and get him there on the double.

O'Connell burst into the room. "I haven't got the time, Marxie, whatever it is. The Leader was in Albany until noon today and I've got to get up to the Hall to see him or we'll never be able to hold up our heads again." He started out again.

"*Halt!*" Heller roared. The younger man stopped and turned. "Lock the door," Heller said, "and pull up a chair very close, on this side." O'Connell moved himself into place. "We are being framed," Heller said in a soft whisper.

"No! How? Why? Who?"

"The Fire Department condemned three floors?"

O'Connell nodded with agitation.

"Two customs men are waiting outside. They have a bench warrant to take me to Ellis Island for questioning on smuggling charges."

"No!"

"Yes. Now hear this. One: We are being framed, and that is so heinously unthinkable that I will skip over it for the moment. Two: I am going with these men to Ellis Island ——"

O'Connell began to object. Heller gripped his shoulder. "Listen to me! If we protest this thing and begin to defend ourselves legally, we'll be falling right into the trap being set by whoever it is out there who is out to get us."

"Get *us*?"

"If we fight right now everything will go straight into the papers, and what client could have confidence in us if we couldn't handle a silly thing like a fire violation or the clap-trap nonsense of a smuggling charge? Nozzir. I'm going with these men and listen to them for twenty-four hours. Tell my wife to go over and stay with my daughter tonight. In the meantime, you and C.L. go for the Leader's throat and tell him that if he doesn't clean this mess up now we'll run a reform ticket next November and fill up a war chest that will back Tammany right out of politics."

A middle-aged secretary broke into the room. "Mr. Heller! They've arrested Mr. Pick!"

"*Whaaaaat?*"

"Miss Sage says she heard the police charge him with

complicity in the murder of Tessie Quintell, the Golden Girl of the Tenderloin."

Heller stared at O'Connell glassily. "Get over there, Frank."

"To the *Tombs?*" Criminal law was a mystery to O'Connell.

"Send young Charley Pick to the Tombs. You get uptown and strangle the Leader."

O'Connell was shown into the Leader's office. The Leader was wearing a dark woolen shawl around his shoulders as he sat in a tall rocking chair behind the vast desk. He wore a high-crowned straw sailor hat of the kind affected by retail butchers. "Sit down an' take a load offa your feet, Frank. What'll you have?"

"Anything. Straight."

"Southern Comfort for Mr. O'Connell, Artie," the Leader said to the man who had ushered O'Connell in. "It's the best thing for you, Frank. Mostly fruit. I used to work with Louis Herron, the bartender who invented it in '75. It's a patented drink, of course, you know, but the missus makes this for me at home. Anyone can make it, you know. Add fresh peaches and peach brandy to bonded bourbon and let it stand in an oak barrel for eight months."

"Listen to me, you—"

"It's a fine drink if you like peaches, peach brandy and bourbon. Say, I found out about them tambourines."

"What tambourines?"

"You remember at that Holy Name breakfast when I asked you where I could get some tambourines wholesale? That was you, wasn't it?"

"No! Now listen, goddammit—"

"Anyway, I had the word wrong. It was tabourets. Man was thinking of startin' a shish kebab joint but he switched. How's the missus?"

"C. L. Pick is an old and delicate man. They have him downtown in that—"

"It looks like my boy Peter will be made a monsignor and be sent off to the North American College in Rome. He'll have to learn Eyetalian, you know, but that's nothin' to them fellas. Marty, the other boy—"

O'Connell belted the Southern Comfort, stood up, leaned

far over the desk and stared at the Leader three inches away from his astonishingly blue eyes. "New York City police have arrested C. L. Pick and have thrown him into the Tombs on a charge of complicity in the murder of some tart. New York City firemen came into our offices yesterday and ripped it up with axes. Marxie Heller has been taken to Ellis Island on charges of smuggling. What the hell are you going to do about that and who the hell is responsible for this shameful mess?"

When Mr. O'Connell left Tammany Hall he was shaken and frightened. The Leader had not only been greatly shocked, but every bit of it had been news to him.

CHAPTER FOUR

Eddie West, handling routine work at his desk in the bank, waited for the call that had to come. It arrived at 11:35 A.M. Mr. C. L. Pick, Jr., was calling.

"Ed?"

"Yes, Charley?"

"Is your secretary on the line?"

"Are you on, Miss Mechanic?"

"Yes, sir."

"Get off, please." They heard the click. "Go ahead, Charley."

"Ed, never mind how or why, but they have my father in the Tombs on a murder charge."

"Charley!"

"Can you do anything?"

"You're goddam right I can do something. Go to the saloon just across Center Street, in Franklin Street. I'll get there as quickly as I can."

"Thank you, Ed."

"Charley, please! I'm so glad you thought to call me." He hung up, grinning. He sauntered to the hatrack, popped on his high-crowned derby and left the office.

By the time the Leader had sent for John Kullers of the First Assembly District and O'Connell had watched Kullers pull the same true-blue blank stare that convinced O'Connell that he had nothing to do with the setup, and by the time Kullers had taken him to the Franklin Street saloon to find Willie Tobin to get him to call Eddie (while the Leader be-

gan his tirade at the Fire Department, carefully avoiding
doing anything about the Tombs until he could find out
more about what was going on but promising everything),
Eddie had met C.L., Jr., had heard the whole outrageous
story and not only had C. L. Pick, Sr. out of the Tombs but
had removed every shred of paper relative to his arrest and
detention and turned them over to Charley.

He packed the tiny, dazed old man into a taxi with his
son. The cab drew away from the curb just as O'Connell
came sprinting across the street from the saloon. He called
after Eddie. Eddie turned. "Pardon me, sir," O'Connell said,
"but was that C. L. Pick you just put into that cab?" Eddie
stared at him coldly until O'Connell apologized and properly
identified himself as C.L.'s partner. Eddie confirmed the
passenger's identity, adding that he had roomed at law school
with Charley Pick and that he had been happy to help out.
O'Connell was greatly impressed. The Leader had been helpless. The district leader who very nearly lived in the Tombs
was helpless. But this young lawyer had done everything
required. "Who are you?" O'Connell asked.

"I am Edward Courance West, president of the West
National Bank."

"But how—?"

Eddie shrugged charmingly. "My father was Paddy
West," he explained, "and I'm happy to see that they still
remember him in there. And now—Mr. Heller. We'll have
to do something about him. Want to come along?" O'Connell
fell into step beside him. "And after that the goddam Fire
Department," he said.

Eddie stopped. "The *Fire* Department?" O'Connell explained in an angry torrent. Eddie grew indignant. "Someone must be framing you, Mr. O'Connell."

"Yes. That's what it is. And if I have to spend every
dime I ever made I'm going to find out who it is."

Eddie gripped O'Connell's shoulder with sincerity. "First
we'll see that your partner is off Ellis Island and comfortable,
then I'll just have one good, hard look into this whole thing.
When I get finished you can be sure of one thing, Mr.
O'Connell—we will have gotten to the bottom of this."

"He's one of the finest young men I've ever had dealings
with," F. A. O'Connell told his partners in Marxie Heller's

office, because the walls in C. L. Pick's office were being restored, "and I think we're obligated to try to do something substantial for him and get it all settled between us before he gets here."

"Can't offer a bank president money," Heller said.

"Yes, we can, Marxie," C. L. said in his trembling flute of a voice. "We control funds and we can see that a fair portion of them are deposited in the young man's bank.

"Yes. That's the way," O'Connell said. "We won't ask him, we'll just start depositing."

"Marxie, you can persuade Mr. Morgan to speak to the Treasury people about reallocating some of their funds in the city."

"If he comes in with proof of who did this to us," Heller growled, "by God, I'll open an account with him myself."

Mr. West's arrival was announced. They offered him a drink, but he didn't drink. They offered him a cigar, but he didn't smoke. Then Heller couldn't stand it any more and he asked if Eddie had found out who had been trying to frame them.

"You have enemies, gentlemen."

"I should hope so," Heller replied.

"There is a certain man—politically and otherwise very powerful—whose name is Paul Kelly, born Paolo Vacarelli. He is boss of the waterfront among other things."

"The gang leader?"

"Well, he calls himself a labor leader now."

"We have never had anything to do with him," C. L. Pick said flatly.

"Of course not," Eddie reassured him. "But Kelly handled the arrangements. A certain person hired Kelly to have you harassed, thinking you would make an uproar and all of it could get into the newspapers. Hoping, I would say, that it might ruin you."

"Who is it?" All partners leaned forward.

"At this moment the name is unknown to me. If you wish, I'll have another talk with Kelly. However, Kelly's client is said to be a well-known figure in the shipping business. I thought perhaps you might be able to deduce who he might be." The law firm had been in publicly fought litigation for nine years with the Evans-Dwye Steamship Lines and had won, so far, eleven of the seventeen law suits filed.

The litigation and its bitterness had seldom been out of the financial pages. Heller banged his fist down with force on the arm of his chair. "It's Evans!" he yelled. "Let's break his goddam back!"

CHAPTER FIVE

Arnold Goff's finished brief was delivered directly to Mr.
West by Goff's fiancée, Miss Bella Radin, to his apartment
in the Buckingham Hotel on Fifth Avenue at Fiftieth Street
in one day less than the maximum bonus period—completed
in fifty-nine days. It was five weeks after West had rescued
Pick, Heller & O'Connell and, in a way, identified their op-
pressor. ("Because I value your son's friendship, Mr. Pick,"
and "I am an attorney before I am a banker, Mr. Heller, and
I ask you to banish from your mind any possibility of rewarding me for what is nothing more than professional
courtesy," and "If there is the slightest repercussion from
Paul Kelly or *whoever* his client may be I will depend on
you to ring me at once, Mr. O'Connell.")

The Goff brief was magnificently comprehensive. It com-
prised eleven volumes of about five hundred pages each,
neatly typed in double spacing and bound sensibly, volume
by volume, in buckram. A sixty-three-page précis accom-
panied it as well as a bibliography. Eddie was pleased. It
was a Friday afternoon. Before she left he asked Miss Radin
to please tell Mr. Goff to come to see him at the hotel on
Sunday at noon.

Eddie untied his tie slowly as he stared down greedily
at the massive brief, standing in the center of the high-
ceilinged, enormous room that had been combined from two
apartments to recreate the feeling of the interior of an English country house of the first third of the nineteenth century (just about the time his father was escaping the Irish

famine by teaching himself to chew and swallow English corn). He had installed a nine-foot-high white marble fireplace. The facing sofas were deep-dimpled black leather, each with hundreds of shiny black buttons. He worked at a heavy, wide library table that stood on a thick Chinese rug with royal blue markings on a field of gold. The room had two large, square standing safes, each covered with a Spanish shawl, each wired to explode five seconds after forced entry, each holding nests of locked strongboxes, because the West operation took in and paid out large amounts of cash at all hours of the day and night.

He took a bath, put on silk pajamas, a dressing gown, woolen socks and slippers, poured himself a glass of ginger ale, then settled down at the table to begin examining the brief. He read until three-fifteen the following morning, then slept until nine o'clock, when he showered, shaved, dressed and had a light breakfast. He read again until ten that night, slept until five the next morning, then read until eleven forty-five. Goff arrived promptly at noon, wearing the same mauve necktie he always seemed to wear.

"Don't you have any other ties?" Eddie asked as greeting.

"I only wear mauve ties. I have twenty-two mauve ties."

"Why?"

"My fiancée likes mauve. Besides, it goes with black suits and white shirts and I collect those too."

Eddie asked him to sit down and offered him a drink.

"I don't drink," Goff said.

"I don't either."

"Let the chumps have it."

"I liked your brief."

"Good."

"What do I owe you?"

Goff handed Eddie an envelope. Eddie removed the bill and studied it.

Bonus	$1500
Assts. (4)	
16 wks at $15	960
Typists (5)	
12 weeks at $12	720
	$3180

"What's this sixteen weeks for assistants?" Eddie asked. "You did it in eight weeks."

"You authorized four for a hundred and twenty days."

"And that's a lot of money for typing."

"Is it? Can you buy a typist for only twelve dollars a week?"

"You haven't charged me for supplies and typewriter rentals."

"My treat, Mr. West."

"All right. This is a fair statement. I'll pay it." He took out his wallet and tossed it across the room. Goff caught it. "Keep the wallet as a memento," Eddie said. "My treat." Goff took the money out of the wallet and counted it. His face flushed deeply. "This is exactly three thousand one hundred and eighty dollars," he said slowly.

"So long as it's correct."

"Now I guess you expect me to ask you how it happened that there was exactly three thousand one hundred and eighty dollars in the wallet."

Eddie shrugged.

"You put a plant on me." Goff was deeply offended and it showed. "Were you trying to tell me something?"

"I thought you might like to work for me," Eddie said. "And I like to have suspicious people working for me. Plants don't happen to suspicious people, not to careful people. For instance, as I told you the day I retained you, I don't think you should have told your girl who your client was."

"What's the job?"

"I want a man to handle money. We do informal short-term financing. There are other payments and collections."

"Is it legit?"

"No."

Goff drummed on the arm of the chair with his white fingers. "Then it isn't something I could do as a lawyer, is it?"

"Entirely up to you."

Goff stared at him with those hard, hard eyes.

"You said you wanted to be a professional gambler. I own three gambling houses. I need one manager for all of them. I'd want you to see that you got yourself publicized as a gambler. I'd like it if everyone thought of you as Arnold Goff, the sportsman."

"Why?"

"Gamblers are always handling large amounts of cash—passing it from hand to hand."

"What's the pay? I assume I could keep what I win."

"You may keep it if you bet your own money, and you're not likely to get any of mine for that. I'll pay you two percent of all the money you handle, going out and coming in. Until you learn the trade you can have five hundred a month on a drawing account."

"I'll need to talk it over with Bella, Mr. West."

"Marry her, sure. But why tell her my business?"

"Because we want to be a family. Because sometimes life is nice. Maybe most of the time. I wouldn't be giving her my respect if I only shared the good things with her."

"She was my plant."

"What?"

"I said your fiancée was my plant with you. I paid her a hundred dollars. She told me how much the bill would be when she brought the brief Friday afternoon. She told me how you refused to charge me for the rent of the loft because it was your father's and you got it for nothing. Now, that was chump stuff. That was silly and sentimental."

Goff looked stricken. He didn't speak. His right hand pressed hard on his diaphragm. He looked as though he were going to be sick.

"A plant is a plant," Eddie said. "Anybody can set a plant, because money is grease and I've got the grease." He stared down at Goff with ice-water contempt. "Never tell anyone anything. Never trust anyone. When you told her who the client was she was in business for herself."

Goff's face was sunken. He gripped his whole lower face with his widely opened right hand and clung to it tightly as though his head were himself, all of himself, and he needed to grip hard to hold everything together.

When he spoke, minutes later, he said, "When do I start?"

"Wednesday night. Be here at eight. We'll have dinner, then I'll take you on the rounds. Would you like some tea?"

"No, thank you, Mr. West."

CHAPTER SIX

After Goff left, West went out for some air. He strolled up Fifth along the Park, then down the other side of the avenue, apparently window shopping but actually preoccupied with the problem of concealing his youth at the moment of the key confrontations, searching for some technical way he could get around this serious disadvantage. But the answer would not come. When he got back to his flat he assembled pads and pencils and editing crayons in schizoid order, then at 2:23 P.M. he began the editing for publication.

> When rum became the currency of the slave trade in the last half of the 18th century, Americans drank more than at any time in history and this thirst grew as rum became one of the important factors in the colonial economy . . .

Eddie grinned with pride in himself for conceiving exactly how it could all be accomplished as he read that the first prohibition law had been passed in the colony of Georgia in 1735 and that all those for whom the law ostensibly had been passed immediately neglected their work and devoted themselves to plotting how they could insure a free and ample supply of ardent spirits. The first moonshine stills ever operated had started to work. Rum runners from the Bahamas began an extensive trade. Blind tigers sprang up in every Georgia settlement until there were as many drinking places per capita in the colony as there were in London, and bootleggers worked in all districts selling rum from peddler's packs.

> . . . the movement to prohibit alcohol must be seen, in the largest sense, as a struggle between rural and urban America. The first colonists brought with them the doctrine that rural life was good, that city life was wicked. The farmer was the backbone of the nation. The new Constitution was written to protect rural rights, i.e., disproportionate representation in the U. S. Senate of the rural countryside as against the cities. State capitals were founded in isolated rural villages such as Albany and Harrisburg. State taxation gave the power to the rural people, whose taxes were not sufficient payment for it. Birth in a log cabin was essential to the suitability of presidential candidates.

By eleven o'clock that night Eddie was marveling and making carefully separate sidenotes on such things as the most famous medical man of his time, Dr. Benjamin Rush, Surgeon General of the Continental Army and signer of the Declaration of Independence, and his pamphlet of 1785, "An Inquiry into the Effect of Spirituous Liquors on the Human Body and Mind," laying out fundamental lines on which all prohibition efforts to follow would be argued.

> . . . for the transition period between drunkenness and temperance Dr. Rush recommended the use of laudanum or opium mixed with wine.

> In 1788, Fisher Ames, the man who had defeated Samuel Adams for Congress, campaigned on this statement: "If any man supposes that a mere law can turn the tastes of people from ardent spirits to malt liquor, he has a most romantic notion of legislative power."

> However, the College of Physicians in Philadelphia was influenced by the Rush Report to send recommendations to Congress in December 1790, when the legislature was considering new revenue laws against West Indies rum and the Rush Report caused the formation of the first temperance associations in America.

The first temperance society in the world was organized in March 1808 by Dr. Billy J. Clark, "a young and intrepid physician" of Moreau, Saratoga County, New York. Within the next decade temperance societies were formed in Connecticut, Massachusetts, New York, Rhode Island, Vermont, New Hampshire, Maine and Pennsylvania. Only candidates who guaranteed to support a prohibition law, state-wide, were endorsed for the legislature, and it was demonstrated that the people would vote for him regardless of party lines. The individual response of these citizen-voters, however, was so overwhelmingly in favor of hard liquor and against all laws that sought to prohibit their manufacture and sale that every manner of bootlegging and moonshining was resorted to until the temperance movement lost all it had gained.

Eddie was awed by the stultifying *emotion* that managed to wreck perfectly sound plans decade after decade. He had solid admiration for the firm grip of the temperance movement on the schoolbooks used in all public schools that taught from the earliest grades that alcohol was evil, but he deplored that none of them seemed to see the path by which they could follow up and consolidate such gains. The profit motive was missing, he decided. No American movement could hope for success unless great numbers of people could be helped to share in the clearly available profits from their work. ". . . 122,000,000 copies of *McGuffey's Reader* were in the schools and they formed the minds of rural Protestant America," and "In 1873 the Women's Christian Temperance Union persuaded the Congress and state legislatures to pass laws requiring temperance teaching in all public schools. By 1902, every state and territory except Arizona had such a law, but a foremost critic wrote: 'There can be no indoctrination without misrepresentation.' A sample instruction in all schools: 'A cat or dog may be killed by causing it to drink a small quantity of alcohol . . . it often happens that the children of those who drink have weak minds or become crazy as they grow older.' "

Clearly alcohol *in the cities* was the terrible threat to the nation from the point of view of the temperance societies.

The census figures showed that wicked city dwellers and the foreign-born were nearly half the population of the United States. This made the drys desperate and entreated urgency. The old rural America was being attacked.

... Frances E. Willard, 34, Dean of Women at Northwestern University, was elected president of the Women's Christian Temperance Union in 1879 when the Union was organized in twenty-three states. Within a decade she had established branches in every state, city, town, village and hamlet, and the total prohibition movement took over the control of the most vigorous part of the prohibition industry. These gallant helpers praised the mothers and the schools that indoctrinated the young for thirty years. They pointed out the great evils ascribed to the Pope, atheists and the devil, to jazz and to bootleggers, expressed the dread of the great social change and the struggle as to whether citizens shall be free to drink alcohol as a test of strength between social orders. Through this great trumpet it was established, hopefully forever, that the determined rock of prohibition was the granite base on which the evangelical church militant is founded, and with it are involved an entire way of life and an ancient tradition. The overcoming of prohibition will mean the emergence of the cities as the dominant force in America—as dominant politically as they are already dominant economically.

When he finished editing, West called Willie Tobin to have him begin to choose a printer-binder whose price would be right in consideration of the city printing business Eddie would be willing to swing his way. He asked Willie to have such a printer at the hotel at nine-thirty the next morning. He awoke his secretary by messenger to her father's house at one-fifteen in the morning. His note asked her to assemble five typists for emergency work on day and night shifts and asked her to come to the hotel the next morning at nine forty-five with two strong office boys and a wagon to transport eleven volumes of typescript to the assembled typists at the bank.

At a quarter to four in the morning he changed his mind.

He called Arnold Goff at the 38th Street gambling house and asked him to please secure the use of his father's loft for emergency typing, then he sent another messenger to awaken Miss Mechanic's family so that she could receive the revised instructions.

After he had discussed the project with Miss Mechanic and the people from the printer-binders and they had all left with the typescripts to take them to the loft, Eddie donned police-issue storm rubbers, a warm scarf and a greatcoat and went out in the rain to march with the Tammany contingent in the procession of fifty thousand people mourning the deaths of one hundred and forty-three women who had been trapped in the Triangle shirtwaist fire.

After the parade he and John Kullers went to Delmonico's for a business meeting. They ate downstairs. The Leader was still touchy about not having been warned about the Pick, Heller & O'Connell plan. Kullers was a bulky, pink man who wore silver-rimmed glasses and examined everything he touched—plates, napkin hems, handshakes and cigarettes. After holding a short beer up to strong light for minute analysis he sipped it.

"What do you expect to find when you stare at beer that way, John?" Eddie asked.

"You never know. Eleven years ago some smart guy slipped a goldfish into a beer on me. And I caught poison ivy from a baseball bat. Always look is best, Eddie."

"You know a man named Arnold Goff, John? A lawyer?"

"I don't think so. But bring him in here, let me look him over top to bottom, and I'll tell you exactly."

"I'll send him to you tomorrow. He's going to run the gambling and some of the payoffs for me."

"Is that so? How'll I know him? We don't want me talking that kind of business to the wrong guy, do we, Eddie?"

"He'll be wearing a mauve necktie, John. A middle-sized, pale man."

"Got you." The waiter set a steak down in front of Kullers, who pierced it at one end with his fork (which he had previously scrutinized) and lifted it slowly off the plate, watching it closely.

"What do you think you might find there, John?"

"It could be anything, Eddie. A man in Twin Lakes,

Pennsylvania, put itching powder on a steak and gave it to his brother-in-law as a joke. The man choked to death before his eyes. What can I do for Goff, Eddie?"

"Get to know him. Put the word out that I sold out the houses to him. After he operates for four or five months I think we could recommend to the other leaders that he handle all their contact work for police payoffs and like that. It could mean cleaner politics on election day. What do you think, John?"

"I like it. And I think the boys'll go fer't." He lifted a huge baked potato out of its dish and slipped a jeweller's loop over his right eye to go over the surface of the potato skin carefully. "Your father, God rest his soul, coulda told you what the blight did to the potatoes in Ireland. The blight come from right in this country, you know."

"Let me know what you think after you look Goff over," West said.

It was Wednesday night and Eddie and Goff had dined at Mouquin's. "I'm selling you the three gambling houses," Eddie explained, "then you'll assign them back to me. Think you can run them?"

Goff gave him a wintry smile.

"Two percent of the net to you. My man keeps the books. As soon as I sell out to you we won't know each other, except as depositor and banker. This is the last time we'll be together in public. You are about to become a famous gambler. I'm just a banker, nothing more or less. If you want to talk on the phone, call Willie Tobin. If you have straight political problems with cops or with muscle, call John Kullers. This is the operating policy: Any client is entitled to win up to twenty-five hundred dollars. That's fair both ways. But if a client pushes to win more than twenty-five hundred, then you send a mechanic in to take it back from him. Don't take it all. Drop him down to a thousand ahead, then pull the mechanic and let him try to start to run it up again."

"You must have three marvelous operations."

"Yes. My father thought so. He established the bank with a lot of that money. You'll think so, too, when you count your two percent of the handle. But I have other plans in work, and in a few years, when you count your two percent from all that, you'll know that the three gambling houses were only your front, my friend."

He left Goff at the 45th Street house at two-fifty the next morning and went to a brownstone on West 37th Street. He strode past the parlor and went to the back of the building on the main floor, entered what appeared to be a cloak-room, then let himself into a small, cosy room where a colored waiter in rich gold and purple brought him a bottle of Vichy water. Five minutes later Rhonda Healey came in, an extremely handsome, thirtyish woman who wore a long sequined gown and long sequined gloves and hair piled on top of her head in a haute-bouffante style that had expired about nine years before. She greeted Eddie warily and sat down at the small table. She had been Paddy's last sweet-heart because he had been certain she had never been a whore. "I know whores for over sixty years," he told Eddie, "and Rhonda was either big-time show business someplace or she's from a rich family and just likes to be around this business. Aaron Burr was in and outta fifty notch joints and never fooled once."

"I missed you at the funeral," Eddie told her.

"I was there."

"They told me."

"He was a great man."

"He was."

"What can I do for you, Eddie?"

"Before Paddy passed on we had talked about plans for reorganization when the right time came and—"

"Am I being fired?" She started to stand up. He waved her back into the chair.

"Why should you be fired?" he asked after she had perched on the edge of her chair for a while.

"That's what I meant—I was shocked to think—"

"But why should you think it?"

She couldn't look at him. Paddy had proved she wasn't a whore but he hadn't proved she wasn't a thief.

"The way you did that—it was as though you wanted to run away," he said regretfully. "Now I'll have to run an audit on you and your bar and your towel count and your financial life." They stared at each other. She shrugged. She said, "I've been dragging two hundred a week. You couldn't have found it. I sell them my own wine."

"If I couldn't have found it why did you tell me?"

"Because before you'd let a woman beat you out of anything you'd tear this whole business apart."

"You're smart."

"Okay, Eddie. I'll be gone in the morning."

"No. I'm glad we had this talk. You were too good to be true, and to be honest, it had me worried. I mean, Paddy trusted you, and that was preposterous for Paddy. Let it go. What I came in to tell you is that I want to sell all eight cat-houses to you, then have you sign them back to a few companies of mine. After that you'll be in charge of the whole operation."

"You mean Paddy owned *eight* of these joints?"

"This is the best one. Your end of the operation will be two percent of the net, and when the word gets out you are the owner maybe some people will try to move in. If that happens call Willie Tobin at the Franklin Street saloon or at the New York A.C. He'll take care of everything. As always, I'm just another customer. Okay?"

"Sure, Eddie. Gee, thanks."

"You'll have eight times the field to look over for me, Rhonda."

"I understand, Eddie."

"When anything new, strictly along my lines, my particular taste, comes in, just call me at the hotel and leave a message. Just say, 'Miss Healey called.' Okay?"

"Sure, Eddie. Certainly."

Edward Courance West saw everything with dimensional, indefectible clarity. He was able to compute all odds at a single glance. He observed with almost superhuman keenness, weighed what he saw instantly, then acted upon it. All factors were balanced to the milligram and were made to march toward the great objectives, no matter how distant. The alarming flaw in his psychological equipment—although in the American history he would write with his life nothing would appear to be flawed—was that the terrain he viewed and judged and acted upon could have been that of another planet. It had no connection with what was really there, with what needed to be coped with in other people's reality. His bank, which was to grow into a repository for several billions of dollars, he regarded as a sort of useful front, a status symbol to anchor and justify all his other activities within the societies of the planet he was visiting. He dusted a large amount of capital with a wistful greed for power; sifted both ingredients, stirring well, into a great lump of inevitable circumstances; yeasty and promising; then waited for the dough to rise. In commerce this is vision; in politics and war-making, statesmanship. In that more invidious branch of self-serving, patriotism, it would be called unselfish courage; in religion, holiness.

To Edward Courance West the prohibition of alcohol was merely the greatest business opportunity since the Industrial Revolution. He did not see it as an infringement of rights. He felt that the mighty mass of Americans would rather vote as they were told as a welcome alternative to thinking. He did not judge that the consequences of prohibition, which he most surely foresaw—because the extent of those consequences was the measure of his business opportunity—were anyone's business but his own. When he got his plans moving he was amazed that so few others immediately grasped what he was trying to do—only C. L. Pick and Arnold Goff. It neither surprised him nor dismayed him that as he took his plan forward into realization it was only the criminal element/politicians and the people who actually owned the nation he was about to ruin (the financial establishment) who understood where his banner of The New Businessman would lead them all. All he saw, very simply, was a chance to make two or three billion dollars and to evade taxes on all but a minuscule fraction of it. That simple fact justified every minute move upon the landscape of that other planet that he had examined so carefully through his strange telescope. Chaos has always been the legacy of mystics.

CHAPTER SEVEN

It took eleven weeks to type, correct, print and bind thirty-two copies of the book *The Business of Prohibition,* by Edward Courance West, President, West National Bank, New York. Each copy had a printed fly leaf that said: "This Is Copy No. —— of a Limited Edition of Thirty Copies: Eastern Edition" (or "Midwestern Edition"). Each edition was numbered up to five only, so that the value of the volume and the reader was increased, the distribution of the over-all printing going to six national regions of the country. It was a fat book, printed in eminently readable but not large type. One-third of it assessed the historic side of the prohibition movement. One-third exposed the corporate side of the alcoholic-beverage industries. Everything built to the final section, which showed the value of plants and factories and agricultural investments that produced ardent spirits, beer and wines; values of stocks on hand by case and barrel; locations of warehouses and their inventories; values of buildings, plants and retail sites; over-all gross income, net income, taxes paid. This section listed retail outlet groups by number and kind: bars, package stores, food stores, sales by railroads, hotels, restaurants and steamship companies. It established the average cost per drink per region, profit per drink, drink sale totals, bottle sale totals, bulk sale totals. It reflected on the greatly reduced values of all investments in every area of the alcoholic-beverage industries and their suppliers of raw materials and offered financial projections of the reduced worth of all economic units within sections represented by the agricultural, transportation, distilling, brewing, restaurant, hotel, bar and other related industries should prohibition become a law. It compared tables showing how investors might divest themselves of holdings in all related industries and what prices they could command under the controlled circumstances and at what prices it was estimated they could reinvest in the same industries and divisions of industries (a fraction of the original values).

In almost all ways it was a mystifying book. It was as though a fascinating message had been torn in half, then only one half of it exhibited. In a sense, at least to the casual eye, it did not seem to be trying to establish any point. The only flat recommendation it made toward prohibition (if it really did favor one side of the question) demonstrated why it was likely that once the movement renounced its historic drive to secure local options and state-wide prohibition and aimed its strategy at winning a national law, the prohibition movement could win forever by gaining a constitutional amendment in its favor. *How* this single, seemingly elemental strategy was to be carried out was not examined.

Eddie sent the thirty books to Pick, Heller & O'Connell with a list of thirty designated recipients who in his educated opinion as a politician, gambling-house proprietor, banker, and bordello keeper represented the eighteen greediest, the seven most hypocritical and the five wealthiest families in the country. The silent approval that would accompany the offering of the books by such an exalted law firm, the keepers of the keys, was the most vital and essential part of the plan. Four months had passed since he had rescued them from disaster. Paul Kelly had willingly agreed to sit in their offices and admit that he had been paid to undertake their disgrace, but refused to state who had employed him. They were more than grateful to Edward West, they were restive to be shown the way in which they could discharge their obligation.

The three partners were waiting for him in C. L. Pick's slightly renovated office. Mr. Pick was staring dreamily at the new door that now led into the room at the unlikely place where the fire axes had destroyed the priceless Littlecot paneling. The panel destruction, the incomparably formidable client's reaction, and his own visit to the Tombs had marked the beginning of his decline, and he was to retire from the practice of law not five months later. The unexpectedly placed door drew his attention away from clients and what they needed urgently to say to him. A glazed look would come over his eyes and his vaunted ability to concentrate and achieve had simply faded away.

Marxie Heller was smoking a very large cigar but not enjoying it. He hated cigars but believed they cut his appetite. A helpless food addict, he was constantly fighting his enormous weight; he could resist almost everything except eating.

F. A. O'Connell wore a fitted green suit with high-slash back vents and deeply marked lapel stitching. The handkerchief pocket had been placed extremely high to lengthen his line, and he wore a natural linen vest with narrow lapels to lift up that attenuated line. He had already crossed into that part of the afternoon when he brooded about being able to catch the most comfortable train to Long Island. When he had begun the practice of law he rode home on the 8:14 P.M. He now aimed at the 3:10.

The partners had assigned the reading of West's book to a junior lawyer and each now had in hand a copy of the lawyer's report, which said, in part:

> Certain sections of the book constitute a history of the prohibition movement in the United States. Other portions go into vast detail concerning the corporate motivation of the alcoholic-beverage industries and contain extraordinary, almost irrelevant, information relating to almost all phases of those industries. It is difficult to say why. At one moment the author seems hardly interested in whether the prohibition movement succeeds, then in the next he appears to be a fanatic dry. He seems to resent the financial success of the A.B. industries, but not for moral or religious or industrial reasons. His strategic and tactical recommendations to speed the enactment of the prohibition law are lucid and closely reasoned. The author is an attorney and the youngest bank president in New York State (West National Bank, a family-owned institution of this city whose December 1910 statement shows audited assets of $22,000,000; i.e., a small, commercial bank).

"What does the book mean?" Heller asked Eddie.

"Why did I send it to you?"

"Yes."

"The book needs its limited distribution under the best sponsorship, which is your firm."

"But—what does the book mean?"

"Why did I write it?"

C. L. Pick stared at the new door, looking slightly drugged. They waited for Eddie's answer, which was not instantly forthcoming because his father had taught him to take his time for maximum results before saying anything, much less answering something. C. L. Pick spoke for him in the interval in a dreamy voice. "Beauty is in the eye of the beholder," he said. "Where Mr. West stands will depend on the reader."

Eddie attempted to wag his head and deliver a rueful, boyish grin at the same time, something he was not at all good at.

"It is the last part of the book that is vital," Mr. Pick said.

Eddie took some folded onion-skin paper from his pocket. It opened into three sheets. "You have my list of thirty," he said smoothly. "It is possible that you represent most of those on the list and know all of them. All I am asking is that you send each one a copy of the book with this letter." He handed one onion-skin sheet to each of the partners. O'Connell and Heller read what it said. Mr. Pick was content to let it rest on the desk in front of him.

"Dear ————," the letter said, "It could be extraordinarily vital in a meaning of futures for you to read this book. If you wish to discuss it after you have studied it, that should be arranged as rapidly as possible. Very truly yours,————."

"That's all?" Heller asked.

"That's all," Eddie said.

"But what the hell does it mean?"

"What is the *objective?*" O'Connell asked crossly, irritable that they were getting dangerously close to the time when he should be leaving to catch that train. Mr. Pick tottered to his feet, always facing the new door but walking somewhat in crab fashion toward the door he had always used. "It could be a very good thing, Mr. West," he said, not looking at Eddie or at anything but the door. "You may be sure we will be happy to distribute your book and to await the outcome with the keenest interest." He sidled out of the room.

Eddie followed him at once. O'Connell started for the new door to catch the train.

"Wait a minute here!" Heller called out. "I'm not clear on this. What the hell is the boy trying to do?"

Mr. Pick's sere, distant laugh was ghastly.

CHAPTER EIGHT

The water-smooth, indifferent Italianate girl sat in a green rayon wrapper with a poorly embroidered dragon on its back in an ornate bedroom in the 41st Street house that had a big brass bed and a little pile of hand towels between the bed and the bathroom door. Utterly bored, she was staring at the window curtains, her hands reposeful in her lap. She was very dark, with large eyes, and she had large, high tits on an ectomorphic frame—long feet and hands with fingers as thin as pencils, long legs and a short waist. Her head was held fragilely high over her soft, soapy shoulders by a long, narrow neck. She was neither pretty nor not pretty, just effective-looking, her appearance emphasized with heavy make-up. She was youth racing through transition.

Mrs. Healey had set her up for the trick she would be turning. She didn't mind. What the hell, it paid triple and her old lady got the same thing every Saturday night for exactly nothing. And it would keep her on light action for a couple of days, just fooling around with the off-duty girls and making spit-babies.

His eyes were like muddy winter water when he came into the room. He was holding himself together as if the last twenty yards had been too much to wait through. His nails were digging his thighs. The door opened, and he went in and stood at the middle of the yellow coffin shape of light as it fell into the darkened room from the hall. He closed the door. He smelled to her like the cages at the zoo. They never smelled like people when they were like this.

All the meetings were to be held in C. L. Pick's office. The first meeting was with the executive vice-president of the largest investment bank in the Midwest. The bank officer, Mr. Padgett, immediately demanded the point of the meeting.

"All right. What's it all about?"

"Money," Eddie said after one of his better lengthy pauses.

"How?" Padgett was no pauser. His value to his bank was his instinct to go for the throat.

"It's all in the last third of the book. We would own most of that."

"But can it *work?*"

"Oh, it can work," C.L. said dreamily, staring at the new door. "Of course one would need to see a prohibition law on the statute books."

"What about that?" Padgett asked Eddie.

"If I didn't have a plan for handling that we wouldn't be here. The details are all in my safe at the bank. It will take not less than three days to go through all of it."

"I can make the time."

"Before you make the time perhaps you should know the requirement."

"How much?"

"I'll need seventy-five million dollars and the possibility of a twenty percent overcall."

Padgett turned, aghast, to stare at Mr. Pick.

"Mr. West is not offering anyone all of the investment. He requires a national spread of investors. The company will be a limited partnership in its form, Mr. Padgett. Two hundred shares will be issued, one hundred shares will be sold. The buyers will own fifty percent of the company, which will be a Swiss company with not reportable income, all shares being issued to bearer. Mr. West will be the only general partner and sole operator of the company. He will assume general liability and will hold the other one hundred shares."

"What's the requirement?"

"Not less than one half of one share, which would require three hundred and seventy-five thousand dollars, or any number of shares up to a maximum of twenty shares, which would cost fifteen million dollars."

"Let's be realistic here," Padgett said emphatically. "Mr. West is a pretty young fellow to expect to take down fifty percent of that kind of company."

"We are not haggling, Mr. Padgett," Eddie murmured. "Take it or leave it." He had suddenly realized when they lighted up like this that it was all as good as he had thought it was and that this was the answer to his being so young.

"It isn't Mr. West's age, Mr. Padgett," Mr. Pick explained. "It is his unique point of view, which is the result of his experience. You are not a New Yorker or you would know the extent of the connections of Mr. West's late father, Patrick J. West, one of the great political leaders of our city, friend of as extraordinary a cross section of American life as one could imagine, ranging from the Presidents of the United States to—well, for example, to the leaders of criminal society in our national life. I would say, after considerable thought, that it might be quite impossible to find another banker of Mr. West's over-all practicality for this situation. Mr. West is also a lawyer. For another thing, the passage of the prohibiting law itself may be nine years away, and in nine years, of course, Mr. West will be that much older."

"The book guaranteed five years. Prohibition by 1916."

"The book guaranteed nothing. There may be a war. Wars delay some things."

"But what *money* are you putting up to demand fifty percent?" Padgett cried in anguish, turning back to Eddie.

"I'll be using three hundred thousand dollars to get me the best entry into the present prohibition movement so that I can help from the inside. That will cost you nothing. I'll be using part of that fund to plant the right people with the distillers' and brewers' associations to make sure they make mistakes. And I'll be giving my time, which is quite a bit more money than three hundred and seventy-five thousand dollars for a half share each year and considerably more money than three million, seven hundred and fifty thousand dollars and for ten half shares over the next ten years. I own my bank, Mr. Padgett. I'll be working for prohibition and against its enemies. I'll be buying shipyards in the Bahamas, acquiring Army, Navy and U. S. bonded warehouse stocks of liquor before anyone else can get them, setting up the capital flow to finance the wholesale regional organizations and the organizations within those organizations to distribute and sell the liquor stocks, later to manufacture liquor stocks, later to buy breweries through us and make and deliver beer to this country. I've got to head the group that chooses the next President of the United States in the elections that will follow the enactment of a national prohibition law because the tone of prohibition enforcement has to set properly throughout the drinking nation or we'll have twice the job on our hands. That's one of the reasons why I have to have a national spread of influential investors. Further, I'm going to have to educate about thirty or forty men whom the community might possibly call disreputable, who will educate the three to five thousand extremely disreputable men who will employ a half million roughnecks who will move the liquor, sell it and serve it regardless of legal punishments. If bribery becomes necessary, and it will, Mr. Padgett, it will have to be done on a———"

"Conjectural bribery is a condition of Mr. West's extrapolation," C. L. said softly.

"It's all planned," Eddie said. "As far as I see it, it's all done. All it needs now is capital, and that's why we're here. Seven hundred and fifty thousand dollars a share. Two years after prohibition gets under way each share will be worth about seven-million-five. In five years about seventy-five. In twelve years, about five hundred million."

"Who else has seen the book?" Padgett wiped his mouth with the linen handkerchief from his breast pocket.

"You'll never know, Mr. Padgett. And the others'll never know that your people have seen it."

Padgett was slowing down. "Well—uh—how can that amount of money be handled without a finance committee?"

"I'm the finance committee." Eddie looked at him coldly, feeling stronger for having forgotten how to smile such a long time ago.

"In any event," Mr. Pick said, "all funds will be expended by double signature—Mr. West's and either mine or one of the senior partners of this firm. All accounting will be done from Switzerland. Each limited partner will be given a statement of account quarterly."

Twenty-two investment units—investment trusts, institutions, individuals or holding companies—bought one hundred shares of Horizons A.G., a corporation formed in the town of Grabs, Canton of St. Gallen, Switzerland. The

Swiss lawyers had offered the city of Chur as the corporation base, but E. C. West had studied the map and advised counsel that he would prefer Grabs if it were much the same corporately. It may have been the only joke West ever attempted.

The largest holding among the limited partners was twenty shares, bought by a colossally wealthy eastern family trust. The smallest holding was one half share offered by the general partner from his 50 percent to Pick, Heller & O'Connell. Records of the owners of the bearer shares, for purposes of profits distribution, were locked in vaults of the Grabs branch of the Forster-Appenzeller Bank.

E. C. West grew a rich, brown mustache as heavy as any worn by the Imperial German General Staff, then on maneuvers in Silesia. Even Willie Tobin, whom he had known since childhood, was instructed to address him and to refer to him as E.C. and E. C. West, respectively. In 1912, just three and a half months after the formation of Horizons A.G., the Swiss banking system developed and secured its government's endorsement of number accounts, which were protected by federal law from disclosure by any Swiss bank of any depositor's identity, and the Horizons A.G. accounts were therewith transferred from name to a number.

E. C. West had made an excellent start. He owned 50 percent of a company that had seventy-five million dollars in cash on deposit and had earned it with an investment of three thousand, six hundred and eighty dollars to Arnold Goff for the presentation brief, two hundred and twenty dollars for a fire lieutenant, one hundred dollars to two customs agents, the promise of a promotion to the police officers who had detained Mr. Pick, plus cab fares, incidental expenses and casual entertainment.

As an afterthought he changed the formative name of The Crusade for Tomorrow Foundation to The American Crusade Incorporated, a nonprofit Delaware corporation, on whose engraved letterhead appeared the names of the flower of American community leadership—not only the six contributing members who had made the crusade possible but many of the twenty-two investors whose presence anywhere would be incandescent.

E. C. West was elected as its executive secretary and

empowered to seek a voice in the councils of the Anti-Saloon League, the Women's Christian Temperance Union and the Prohibition party. E. C. West became the crusading peer of Wayne B. Wheeler, Bishop James Cannon, Jr., the Reverend Purley A. Baker, William E. Johnson, Ernest H. Cherrington, the Reverend George Young and William Jennings Bryan. With Wayne B. Wheeler entirely sold, as E. C. West's first great goal, they worked out the telling shift into the strategy of national (as opposed to state or local) referendum.

The question of time limit on ratification was worked out with Senator Warren G. Harding (Rep., Ohio), with whom West became the closest of friends. The two men had a great deal in common to begin with, to be sure, and when their busy schedules permitted they slipped off to New York, over a series of eight or ten weekends, where West was able to show the senator the sort of wonderful, wide-open time he had perhaps heard about but still couldn't quite believe existed in such opulence. On the fourth, fifth and seventh weekends Mr. West invited Senator Harding's political counselor, Mr. Harry Daugherty, to join them. If such a degree of palship were possible, Daugherty and West became even thicker than West and the senator. It was marvelous. If the boys wanted to gamble, they won. They never lost once on what must have been a dozen trips up to New York and they played at three different gambling houses, all deep-carpet houses with the best champagne and many beautiful women. The senator expressed a passing, if wistful, admiration for the queen of the *Police Gazette,* Miss Lorette des Anges. On his third visit to New York with E. C. West the senator was delighted to discover her as his dining partner at Reisenweber's. He made such a tremendous hit with her—for he was an extremely handsome and amiable man—that, in his words, she just seemed to "crumble all up" at the end of the evening and practically pleaded to get into bed with him.

Daugherty avowed to Mr. West that he "really knew New York like no other man." Some of the bordellos he got them into were about the most luxuriously sensual the two men had ever seen. And the women!—they said they just couldn't believe there were women like that. Mr. Daugherty half jested that there hadn't been one jeer or catcall when he

had taken his first girl up the grand staircase. The senator
asked E.C. how he could just seem to take over all these
places and E.C. answered imperturbably, "I own them"—
a really good laugh.

Senator Harding's views on ratification were that with-
out a limitation he feared that several senators who were
shaky on the enactment might turn wet. Behind closed doors
E. C. West told Mr. Wheeler that this was a trick of Senator
Harding's, who believed the amendment could be defeated
in this way. But West and Wheeler knew the strength of the
dry movement in the Senate and the House. They asked
Senator Harding how much of a time limit he had in mind.
Harding said he thought five years would be sound.
Wheeler and West then offered him a six-year limit, and
Harding immediately proposed this on the floor of the
Senate and it was adopted. Later, while the Eighteenth
Amendment was pending in the House, West was strolling
along a corridor in the Senate Office Building with Bishop
Cannon, chairman of the Anti-Saloon League's legislative
committee. They encountered Harding, who grinned broadly
and told them that the time limitation they had agreed on
meant the end of any chance for prohibition, because the
amendment could not possibly be ratified by the states
within six years. West and the good bishop grinned even
more broadly. "Senator," Bishop Cannon told Harding
calmly, "the amendment will be ratified within two years.
We know that three-fourths of the states are ready to ratify."

The amendment was ratified by a majority of the states
of the United States of America in twelve months and
twenty-nine days.

E. C. West had begun his work with the Anti-Saloon
League as assistant to Ernest Cherrington, chief of the
League's educational and publications division, late in 1911.
Soon, under his fanatic urging, the League was publishing
more than forty tons of a powerful assortment of publications each month, an amount that reached more than 250,-
000,000 book pages and ranged from weekly, bimonthly and
monthly periodicals to pamphlets, tracts and folders, even
including one national daily. By accepting West's counsel
as a full-time consultant the Methodist Book Concern and
the WCTU, in their combined output equaled the amount
of League publication.

In 1914 Mr. Wheeler announced that the expenses of the drys had reached a peak point of two and a half million dollars a year, 90 percent of which came from "the little people of the country." He recalled for the press that "in only one case did the national organization receive as much as fifty thousand dollars from a single source, The American Crusade Incorporated, and only five persons contributed ten thousand dollars or more. Furthermore, we have spent less than one hundred thousand dollars directly in electing drys to the Congress." It was like killing a dragon with sandpaper.

In 1912, E. C. West was named liaison officer among the League, the WCTU, the Methodist Conference and the Prohibition party. He was now at the executive council level, and he began to bring some of the most influential men and women in the United States to meet Mr. Wheeler, Bishop Cannon and William Johnson, who complimented these leaders effusively on their achievements toward a dry America. The great names E. C. West revolved through the doors of the prohibition movement were limited partners of Horizons A.G., friends and associates of those partners, clients of Pick, Heller & O'Connell or founders or friends and associates of the founders of The American Crusade Incorporated. They were powerful publishers, great bankers, leading industrialists, famous lawyers. And the flow was so constant that it began to seem that E. C. West was vitally connected with almost everyone of consequence in the nation. He was such an alert, forceful and gifted young man.

Every one of Mr. West's visitors impressed upon League executives that in his opinion it was excruciatingly important to abandon the local option and state-wide prohibition strategy in favor of a national referendum. Late in 1912 the League moved to endorse that constant recommendation. Only William Jennings Bryan demurred, but he had never been right in his life. The three principal prohibition agencies announced for the first time their total solidarity and accepted as their common goal the total abolition of the liquor trade. The original and basic plan to dry up the United States by steps and stages, first in villages, then in towns and counties, then throughout whole states, until the nation had been overcome was abandoned forever. The new policy required an amendment to the Constitution, therefore every professional politician in the United States on every level of government was to be enlisted—not necessarily through outright "purchase" of his cooperation, although if that became necessary it would be done.

E. C. West's central strategy was to bring every imaginable pressure on candidates and officeholders; to maintain an espionage system that would reveal the enemy's plans; to unload on the voters a barrage of truths, half truths and imaginative postulates that would synthesize the educational work of the previous thirty years; and to refuse to falter even if it became necessary to bring direct pressure on individuals in politics through business, banking and even family connections. All permutations and combinations of effect were directed toward the end of causing the Senate and the House of Representatives to act in the national interest by delivering the legal preconditions that would then place the issue squarely before the people of the United States—who could, after all, be persuaded to do absolutely anything, E. C. West assured his partners.

"If ever any subject was thoroughly discussed before the American people it was the prohibition issue. If ever the American people had a full and fair chance to make up their minds and declare their decisions at the polls in the election of candidates for legislative office, it was in connection with prohibition," E. C. West told *The New York Times* in 1923. "No other amendment ever before brought before the people of this country has received such uniform support from both political parties, from every section of the country, and has been ratified by such an overwhelming majority of the states."

With the decision taken to push for a national amendment in 1913, E. C. West was moved upward to places on both the finance and legislative committees of the League, retaining his portfolio as interagency liaison with the other major agencies.

It was Clarence Padgett who actually "discovered" Warren G. Harding. A great many of the interests of the bank that employed Padgett were in Ohio, and naturally he was very close to the George Cox machine in Cincinnati, where it operated from a saloon headquarters. Cox put Harding into the State Senate in 1901, and he stayed there, except for a run for governor in 1910, until he was elected to the U.S. Senate in 1914. Harding wasn't any deep thinker, but he didn't have to be. He was as amiable as a whore at a bankers' convention. The only time in his life he ever voted against the party line was over a local-option bill that the party wanted passed. His "manager," Harry Daugherty, made him vote dry because the Anti-Saloon League wanted that option badly, and the party would be a lot quicker to forgive him than the League. And the League remembered. When Harding ran for the U. S. Senate, Wayne B. Wheeler himself publicly forgave Harding for owning brewery stock, saying that the stock was the only payment Harding could get for the advertisements the brewers placed in Harding's newspaper. He was a country courthouse senator in 1914 and President of the United States six years later—his progress having been achieved with the private support of the League, which, publicly, on E. C. West's emphatic advice, had refused to support either presidential candidate.

Padgett "found" Harding in the gubernatorial campaign in 1910 and he talked him over with George B. Cox. "Warren ain't much," Cox said, "but he does what you tell him to do." E. C. West liked the sound of that. He went to Ohio to meet Harding and consequently also met Mr. Harry Daugherty. "He's a big, sweet dummy," West told his partners. "And I have to agree with Daugherty—he looks like a President. And heaven knows, he's the easy-going opposite of Woodrow Wilson."

In the Spring of 1919 Horizons A.G. was in full agreement on the make-up of the 1920 ticket, and gradually West impressed the importance of this opportunity on the leaders of the League by his tested method of bringing in distinguished visitors to underscore his confidence in the candidate. In turn the League, unaware that West's business and industrial forces were on the same tack, began the line-up of the cadres of the senators of the old guard who would handle the nomination under the orthodox convention proceedings.

The League, indeed the entire movement, was thrilled at the victory of their "hand-picked" new President at the very outset of the force of the Eighteenth Amendment as the law of the land. Then the sound of clinking bottles was heard through every open White House window.

"We're beside ourselves with admiration out here," Padgett told West on the telephone from Chicago. "You did it! You actually went and did it!" West did more than that. He introduced Elias H. Mortimer as the official White House bootlegger.

CHAPTER TEN

In the years between the formation of Horizons A.G. in 1911 and the day constitutional prohibition went into effect everywhere in the United States at 12:01 A.M., January 17, 1920, E. C. West had greatly consolidated his position. He had married and had had one son, Daniel Patrick. His efforts for the prohibition movement (his day-to-day work on its behalf among national leaders), his closeness to the President and the administration, the nature of his partners in the Swiss company, the increased strength of his position with Pick, Heller & O'Connell, his wife's father's influence and the influence of her family had greatly enhanced the yearly statements of the West National Bank. It was now a bank of the first echelon with total resources of $455,493,-531, as of its annual statement issued on December 31, 1919, with deposits on that date totaling $301,768,091. West's national influence was seen not only through his stunning successes for the prohibition movement. He had won the admiration of the national business community for the decisive assistance he had brought to the desperate labor unrest, particularly in the steel industry in 1915-16, when he had organized an army of effective strikebreakers from New York and elsewhere, mainly through Dopey Benny Fein and Paul Kelly. This experience had given him insight into the labor opportunity that he was to bring to fruition in the garment industry in New York in 1925, installing his friends Louis Buchalter and Jacob Shapiro, then, earning while learning, moving upward while he promoted still other labor leaders to effective control of the labor movement.

Before C. L. Pick's death in 1916 (when his place in the firm was taken by West's old roommate, C. L. Pick, Jr.) the old man had asked E.C. to visit him at Locust Valley. He was quite weak by then but wholly amiable. "Was it you or Evans Dwye who framed us in 1911, Eddie?"

"Why, C.L. I——"

"Have no fears, my boy. It's just one of those tiny things left unexplained that have interest only to me. It was you, wasn't it?"

"Yes, sir."

"My word!"

"There was a good reason, C.L. I had to do it because——"

"I know. I know," the old man said, staying him with a fragile hand. "We could never have taken your bizarre plan seriously—nor could we possibly have sponsored it—if we had not been so grotesquely indebted to you. It was good thinking, Eddie. You were born a master criminal, perhaps the greatest I have ever met in a lifetime of practicing corporate law."

E.C. thanked him because he knew the old man meant it as a sincere compliment.

"Do you still own those six lots of your father's between Fulton and Wall?"

"Yes, sir."

"You must build a new bank there. A skyscraper filled with money." He sighed. "Ah, how I envy your coldness of spirit, Eddie, your inability to understand that mortals feel pain." He delivered his sere and ghastly laugh. "You paranoiacs are the true romantics."

CHAPTER ELEVEN

If one is vaguely ashamed of being the son of a woman who wore a black shawl and who spoke only Sicilian, who spoke to one's father only in obscenities knowing that no one but her son could understand her, then one does not marry beneath oneself, simply because of the conviction that there is no one beneath one. If one spent eight telescoped years acquiring ten years of education at the Gelbart Academy, Yale and Harvard, in terms of envied personality, envied by all one's peers, and if one then became the youngest bank president and in relatively short order formed a company having assets of seventy-five million dollars, then went on to help direct one of the greatest social movements any nation has ever known, then one does not seek the hand of some mere commoner. Neither did Edward Courance West.

Irene Wagstaff was a red-blonde with very fair skin and pale green eyes, therefore she did not in any way resemble E. C. West's mother. Irene Wagstaff's bosom did not bulge exceedingly nor was it flat. She had skin for a botanist to wonder over and a look of such youth and freshness that all thought of giving and taking pain went out of West's mind, although not forever.

Her father was Walter Wagstaff, a railroad president— more than sufficient station for the times. He was a director of a large steel company, of the leading cooperative of the coming citrus industry, of an industrial chemicals complex and of an automobile-manufacturing firm near Detroit, Michigan, that seemed capable of doubling its value every year. He was also a consecrated prohibitionist, because liquor dragged down the efficiency of the workingman, and he and his daughter were devout Catholics.

Irene was twenty years old, one of two children. Her religious conviction was prodigious, if unilateral: Mass every morning, Communion twice a week, and a confessor more regularly used than other girls' hairdressers. She was a throwback Catholic. She was fulfilled by the show-business side of the faith as opposed to the theological, by the costumes and processions and glorious singing that had been designed for ages and times long gone when there had been nothing to do for diversion except make love, go to war, work to exhaustion or respond to the slogan that church services were better than ever. Irene was an endearing but never immoderately bright girl. She was in no way stupid; she never tried to pass her Catholicism along. When she met Edward, for example, she didn't ask him whether he was a Catholic or, when they were courting, whether he would attend Mass with her or take Communion with her. She just went to church and got enormous pleasure out of it, as one gets from a classical play one has seen and enjoyed many times, a play with a simple plot or perhaps a plotless, mindless ballet. Irene was intact. She was one of those oddities who are either born whole or who somehow, as impossible as it seems, grow up whole. She made people happy merely by sitting and walking and being. She made E. C. West marvel.

Their meeting was correct in every way. West was a leader of the prohibition movement. His crusading activities were regularly reported in the national press. Because of that, because he was a banker and because he had requested it through the League's lecture bureau, he was invited to address a meeting of the American Bankers' Association on topics of prohibition. The members were circularized with a warning not to miss the meeting. As a bank director, Walter Wagstaff attended the luncheon, gorged on his own dry convictions. He was stunned with admiration for the speaker. When the meeting was over, Mr. Wagstaff sought West out to introduce himself. In the course of their very brief talk Mr. Wagstaff said that he didn't suppose Mr. West got to New York very often, and E.C. explained that he lived in New York, that he spent only the first three days of each week in Washington. "In that case," Mr. Wagstaff said, "why don't you come to dinner next week?"

Casual students of the West legend might have said that he fell in love with Irene the moment he entered her father's mansion on Fifth Avenue, measured the vast entrance hall with his expert eye, took in warmth from the huge Delacroix that hung on a stair landing facing the door and entered the pleasant library of rare first editions.

He and Mr. Wagstaff shared a half bottle of Poland water. The two Wagstaff daughters entered the room together. One was more lovely than the other, depending on the lighting each one found to settle in, and the lighting that fell on Irene was superb.

Within the week E. C. West had convinced himself that it was time he married. He was impressed by Walter Wagstaff. Marriage would lend another dimension to his position both as a banker and as a crusader and it would permit him to undertake more formal entertainment, which was becoming really quite necessary. It would aid in dissembling the impression he gave of being too young. And he had fallen in love with Irene. They became engaged three months after they met. Irene was quite pleased too.

Irene saw her fiancé (and everything else within her view) in the same manner that she saw the church: as he and others represented him to be; as the church and others said the church would be forever. She wanted serenity above all else, and she would not countenance deceit and gossip and scandal about others. A great storm of the period was caused by the findings of the Pujo Committee of Congress, which her father and Edward and her sister Clarice discussed over and over again at dinner until she had had to register her own belief that the committee must be mistaken, that what it charged could simply not be true. The committee's report had stated that a dozen men, headed by J. P. Morgan, James Stillman, George Baker and the Rockefeller family, controlled the money markets of the United States. It asserted that they controlled: "a hundred and eighteen directorships in thirty-four banks and trust companies having total resources of two billion, six hundred million, seventy-nine thousand dollars; thirty directorships in ten insurance companies having total assets of two billion, two hundred and ninety-three million dollars; a hunderd and five directorships

in thirty-two transportation systems having total capitalization of eleven billion, seven hundred and eighty-four million
dollars; sixty-three directorships in twenty-four producing
and trading corporations having a total capitalization of
three billion, three hundred and thirty-nine million dollars;
twenty-five directorships in twelve public-utility corporations having a total capitalization of two billion, one hundred and fifty million dollars." Altogether the twelve men
represented three hundred and forty-one directorships in
one hundred and twelve corporations having aggregate resources that were four times the size of the British national
debt.

Irene deplored. Mr. Wagstaff justified. E. C. West envied
but did not despair, because among the twelve men were
some of his partners in Horizons A.G.

Not being in the remotest way paranoiac, Irene's reac-
tions to Edward were not at all like his to her. He acquired
the fixed idea that he was being persecuted by "them" because "they" separated him from her for three days each
week. He experienced heady delusions of grandeur when Mr.
Wagstaff put his private railroad car at his disposal for his
journeys to and from Washington—a private car that had
gold dinner service, wine bins, jewel safes, a sunken marble
bathtub, nine complete and different sets of slip covers for
the furniture, electric partitions to enclose or widen rooms,
a staff of four uniformed by Wetzel, a parlor organ and a
garage for a car at one end with its own ramp and sleeping
space for a chauffeur and a mechanic. And her religious
devotion induced him to falsify and pretend to the Wag-
staffs that he had been a ravenously devout Catholic all his
life, even though he paid for that in vicious responses of
memory that made him see his mother shuffling under that
black shawl on her way to seven o'clock Mass every morning
of all the years.

Irene loved him. At first she liked what she saw and
what she was told about him. Then she liked it all better and
better. He was handsome in an imperial way and a stunning
dresser. Her sister, Clarice, crooned over his name and proclaimed that he was "the absolute dark-horse catch of the
year," so Irene began to improve on what she saw and made
him trim his mustache to something less formidable.
Slowly, through her father's eyes, she began to see also a re-

markable achiever, a young bank president whose board of
directors held a collection of some of the most important
men in the United States. For such an unneurotic, unfrag-
mented woman respect was the only solid frame of love a
woman could feel for a man. And her father had said, "He is
young to achieve such an eminence among such doctrinaire
people, that's one thing. But the main thing, the important
thing, is that a man of his age is able to see the vision of a
nation no longer reeling under the yoke of alcohol. Youth
knows idealism, yes. Youth is the time for idealism. But to
be so determined to move that idealism into tomorrow, to
give one-half of his time with no hope for direct profit at his
stage of life, at an age when other young men feel that every
second must be used to further only themselves—by God,
Irene, that is admirable."

Two days before the wedding the groom went uptown to
see Paolo Vacarelli. They sat in the wagon in front of the
poolroom to have their meeting.

"Hey, Eduardo," Vacarelli said. "What's all this blue-
nose stuff you're doing?"

"I'm going to tell you soon, but not now. Only one thing:
it's good."

"Good for what?"

"Good for business."

"What can I do for you?"

"I'm getting married. We're going to Europe for the
honeymoon."

"I read about it."

"We land at Naples, then we go to Palermo."

"That's the way you going, hey?"

"I want a yellow handkerchief from you to Don Vito."

"Yeah?"

"It's a little soon for what I have in mind, but my people
think there's a war coming, so I've got to talk to Don Vito
soon, while I can. Can you do it?"

"You mean will I do it?"

"Yes."

"But you don't want to talk about it? You just want me
to send you in blind."

"It's going to be a very good thing, Paolo. Before I get
back, Don Vito is going to tell you that too. Okay?"

"Okay, Eduardo. You got it."

"Send it to the bank tomorrow."
"You got it."

They were married by the cardinal at St. Patrick's at a nuptial High Mass with a *fantastic* organist and choir (Irene thought), and it was a most important social event for Catholic New York. Irene was thrilled to hear the cardinal call Edward "Eddie" and to speak so fondly of his father. In all the time she had been going to St. Patrick's they had never met the cardinal, who was now—as Clarice put it— "an old friend of the family."

Bishop Cannon and Wayne B. Wheeler came to the church. They approved of his projected sixty-day "holiday" because he would receive the press at all European capitals to provide an "intimate explanation" of the prohibition movement. Mr. Wheeler said jokingly, "I'd go easy on those European wines if I were you."

On their wedding day, June 17, 1913, they sailed for Naples aboard the *Conde di Orselino* for a grand tour honeymoon.

Don Vito Cascio Ferro, *capo di capi* of the Sicilian Mafia, a charming, cultivated gentleman of immense dignity with a long, white beard, was wearing linen knickerbockers and a gray, piped Norfolk jacket when he entertained E. C. West at luncheon in his palazzo facing the Bay of Palermo from the higher base of Monte Pellegrino.

In 1909, as a "personal response" to the effrontery of the police commissioner of New York, Theodore Bingham, who had sent police lieutenant Joseph Petrosino to investigate the Mafia, he had personally shot Petrosino to death at the center of the Piazza Marina in full view of more than one hundred witnesses, then had returned to his carriage to be taken back to the dinner party from which he had excused himself, a party attended by the high aristocracy of the city. Of the twenty murders of which he was acquitted in his lifetime Don Vito admitted to only the Petrosino affair, for which he was never charged. "It was a challenge," he would say. "My action was a disinterested one, taken in response to a challenge that I could not afford to ignore."

E. C. West put the yellow silk handkerchief marked in one corner with a large *V* for Vacarelli into a heavy manila envelope. He sealed the envelope with a wide band of wax, marked the wax in three places with his signet ring, allowed it to harden, then took it to the hall porter of the hotel to ask that it be delivered by hand. The porter summoned a page, then noticed the addressee's name on the envelope. He stared at West. He waved the boy away. He put on a flat cap with a shiny black visor and left the hotel to deliver the envelope himself. He returned with an invitation to lunch for the following day written in Don Vito's hand on heavy parchment, rolled and tied with a striped green, red and black ribbon.

West's carriage rolled past medieval monuments and chirragesque buildings, across the city through the hot sunshine, up the slope higher and higher until he could see out across the pavonine harbor and feel the ancient sleepiness of the crumbling city that had been founded by the Phoenicians, occupied by the Romans in 254 B.C., conquered by the Byzantines in 525 A.D., taken by the Saracen Arabs in 830, overrun by the Normans, sacked by the Spanish, absorbed by Italy in 1860 and was presently owned by the Mafia.

He was greeted on the threshold of the rich Sicilian-baroque palazzo by his host, who spoke to him in Sicilian. He was taken to lunch in a tree-shaded, fountain-cooled, flower-scented patio. They spoke of the world, of American politics, and of the ballet (about which West was most authoritative) while they ate pasta al sarde, melanzane alla siciliana, spada a Ghiotta and a rush of exuberant Sicilian sweets more baroque than the city's architecture. West felt his mother's presence overwhelmingly through the food more strongly than music could bring back any other memories of her. They sipped coffee. West refused a cigar.

"It was good to hear from Don Paolo," Don Vito said. "He has done well in America."

"He has won the respect of all people," West answered. "Why did he send you?"

"He has introduced me to you so that I may tell you about a new business I am developing."

"Please," the elegant old gentleman urged, "you must tell me about that."

He did not speak again for fifty minutes. He listened intently. When West had finished he said, "What you say is very interesting. If I may say so, you speak a very good Sicilian."

"Thank you."

"I like big thoughts. But yours are a hero's thoughts, and I found that I was asking myself if they were not too big."

"America is big."

"You mean Sicily is small. You are right. I agree. Sicily is small and I am old. But I am experienced. I have had long tenure. The Honored Society is over three hundred years old and it forgets nothing, so I am that much more experienced by serving it. What there is to know about the business we do I have learned well."

"Are you telling me that what I have described to you cannot be accomplished?"

"Only you can prove that. I want to see that it can be accomplished. I am only telling you that none of us could ever have had such a magnificent conception of business as you have shown me today."

"Thank you." West allowed almost fifty seconds to pass before he spoke again. "Prohibition, Don Vito, is most peculiarly American. It could not be carried out anywhere else, and I say that with pride. Americans are split in half into nature and content. Not the nation, but the people. The nation is totally and mystically unified, but each American is split into two halves—on one side his origins, on the other side the enormous opportunities that confront him.

"We are people who fled civilizations. Think of that. We are the offspring who could not succeed under the established, civilized circumstances, whatever they were—and all the backgrounds varied. We struggled through hardships to get to the new land, then we found a fantastically rich world. Having left the old countries penniless and hungry, our fathers had to convince themselves that they would build a better place. They taught that to their children. It created tremendous idealism. It created tremendous gullibility. The prohibition movement is, after all, only lip service to idealism. We want the ideal of prohibition while knowing at the same instant that when we get it we will continue to live as we have always lived: the wine drinkers will go on drinking wine, the people from the beer countries will have to have their beer, the rest will want liquor. But they must serve the ideal. They must seem to be striving for yet a better world, carrying on their father's dreams.

"But it is such a rich country! It can grow anything, feed and fuel the world, realize any whim for any man. And because we are split in half as I have explained, one half does not know what the other half is doing. Poverty may bring faith, but riches bring things. We must have faith, so Americans have achieved a faith in things. Therefore, what the American people are faced with is a craving for reassurance that they have kept the true faith, the universal faith, the faith of loss and deprivation—which is prohibition. Simultaneously the other half is a quivering maw of national sensuality—sensation, tactilities, gluttony, satiety—the essence of total self—all making us dependent upon our riches, faith's opposite. That is why what we have been discussing is good business, Don Vito. Truly, it is not a question of the size of the opportunity but only a question of having been born, then trained to understand the market."

"Formidable!"

"Thank you."

"We will help you."

"Thank you. Before I ask your help I must tell you what I am prepared to pay for it."

"Before I can tell you if what you offer to pay is enough, I must know how much help you want."

"I want from you one trustworthy man who is bound to you as well as he will be bound to me. That man must have your powers to call on the obedience and the trust of five hundred, perhaps a thousand, other men of respect. I want to know only the one man, because it is important to the survival of the plan that only one man know me."

Don Vito was silent. He poured more cognac in his glass. "I understand," he said.

"For the one man, then—to support the work of that one man—for helping him to find the unquestioned loyalty of the five hundred other men—that is the help I have come to ask for."

"What does this one man do? What do the five hundred do?"

"There are three major divisions in the work we will have. Finance for the work of the one man plus five hundred men plus five thousand more they will find. Next, procurement of stocks to be sold by the one man and the five hundred men and the thousands—tens of thousands of others—whom they will find. I have my finance officer. I have my procurement officer. The one man will be in charge of distribution, sales and—very important—enforcement. The five hundred men who are loyal only to him will do all that for him."

"How much will you pay?"

"Two percent of my net."

"To him or to me?"

"Two percent to you. Two percent to him."

Don Vito leaned forward extending his open hand. "We have made a deal, my friend."

Irene was waiting for him in bed when he got back to the hotel, naked and pink, smiling, they both thought, rather lewdly. "Did you have a good meeting, dear?" she asked huskily.

"Excellent," he said, stripping off his clothes.

CHAPTER TWELVE

They went to Rome the next morning, then to Vienna, St. Petersburg, Berlin, London, Paris and to Zurich for meetings with the Horizons A.G. bankers. It was one of these bankers who told them about the Bürgenstock. A letter from the cardinal had preceded them to the Vatican, and they lunched with the Pope: a salad, cold chicken, a glass of Frascati and black coffee. Chatting, Irene said she had seen photographs of Queen Elena and thought she was quite the most beautiful woman she had ever seen, and suddenly it was arranged that they should meet Queen Elena (and the king) at a court ball.

The king wore the uniform of a general and the Collar of Annunziata. Irene wrote to Clarice that night to say that she was seriously thinking of asking Edward to buy Clarice an Italian title for Christmas.

In Vienna everyone was abuzz about the war everyone was sure was about to start. Edward and Irene drank their morning coffee at Konstantinehügel and bowled along the Hauptallee in their carriage, and the bankers led them gingerly through Viennese society, called "the haughtiest in Europe." She wrote to Clarice to say that no one was received at court unless he had sixteen quarterings or unless he were an Army officer, and all unmarried girls smoked Havana cigars. They were there in the last days of June. Although they had missed the Derby by three weeks, the gambling season was at its height, but Edward was a priss and wouldn't gamble. In a letter to Clarice Irene pretended to have visited Sigmund Freud "in the hope that he would be able to recommend something to do about your case." At the end of the six-page letter she attached a postscript saying, "I was only fooling about Freud, actually there is no hope for you."

The Wests did not enjoy St. Petersburg after a thirty-seven-hour train journey. They were annoyed by the customs officers, baffled by the language and were utterly bored with the constant gossip everywhere about the coming war. Irene thought the Russians would do very well in a war. Almost every man they saw on the street was in some sort of a uniform, the policemen being the most splendid of all in black, with orange or bright green lapels and dashing astrakhan caps. Building janitors wore gorgeous scarlet blouses and caps with brass plates. They spent an entire morning at Fabergé's wonderful shop. Edward bought her a beautiful gold cigarette case and she bought him a jewel-encrusted scent flask. He pretended to believe it was meant for brandy and said she had bought it only to shock Bishop Cannon.

Berlin was miraculously gay and not in the slightest apprehensive about everyone's keenly anticipated war. They stayed at the Adlon, which was only five years old. The Kaiser called it "my hotel." Everything in it was so solid and massive: dark-yellow, clouded marble pillars ornamented with precious metals, and twenty page boys lined up like toy soldiers, always ready for the Kaiser to pass in review, which he did, regularly, once a week. Lorenz Adlon told them that there were a quarter of a million bottles of wine in the cellar, and Edward used the reference half-humorously in the mass interview he granted to the German press on his special subject, America and prohibition. He was quoted as saying, "What we are doing in America is, in a sense, very good for the Adlon Hotel, because in a very few years' time Americans will have to journey to the Hotel Adlon's quarter of a million bottles if they want to drink the alcohol that can poison their minds and bodies." He also commented, in passing, on the new German army tax of 1½ percent on all property, saying, "Americans simply would not tolerate such taxation."

To enrage Clarice, Irene took special lessons in dancing the minuet and the gavotte from the official court dancing teacher. The Kaiser did not approve of modern dances, and although the Wests were not invited to a court ball because, as it turned out, the Kaiser did not approve of prohibitionists either, a banker friend was happy to arrange for the *Tanz Probe* and the minuet instructions. Clarice wrote Irene (the letter reached her in London) that this was "the silliest thing you've ever done and a wanton waste of money. Who in the world will you ever find to dance the minuet with?"

Berlin most certainly was not all fun. Because of what he had said in the press about the "intolerable German Army tax" Edward was challenged to a duel by an Army officer who felt deeply that the Army's honor had been impugned and that only blood could remove the stain. Edward chose pistols, asked Herr Gabel, a German banker, to be his second and was very cool about going through with the whole sinister business. He most certainly could have been killed if Frau Gabel had not told Irene. The two women rushed to the field, in the Tiergarten, with four policemen. The Kaiser himself had taken a stand against dueling just two months before. The party rocketed through the dawn behind steaming horses and got there just as the two men had begun to pace away from each other, Edward (he said later) thinking cold-mindedly of Aaron Burr. Irene began to yell, then ran across the field, the police behind her, and threw herself not at Edward but at the bald, scarred Army officer ("He must have been in *fifty* duels!" she wrote to Clarice), who stood at attention and permitted himself to be arrested providing no policeman dared to lay a hand upon him. The Wests were escorted back to the hotel to pack, then were taken to the railroad station by the police and told to leave the country at once. They boarded a train for London. The whole escapade excited Irene so much that she jerked down the window shades of their railway compartment, threw off her clothes and had Edward mounting her before the train was out of the station.

London was *marvelous!* It simply couldn't have been better, Irene wrote Clarice, even though Berlin had to be recognized as the high point. She told Edward later that she gave the Berlin adventure credit for the conception of Daniel, who arrived at precisely the right moment of the human gestation cycle figuring from the time that German train had chugged slowly out of the station.

Cabarets ruled London. Irene was able to keep Edward on a dance floor for every night of the three weeks they were there, then hardly ever again in his life. They met the Asquiths who were friends of Walter Wagstaff's, and they met Emily Pankhurst who was a friend of Mr. Wayne B. Wheeler's. They stayed at the Savoy Hotel. Irene had never seen such enormous bathtubs. At her request the hotel sent the bathtub manufacturer's representative to see her and she ordered six of the great white boats and, keeping two for themselves, had the others sent to her father, the cardinal and the Leader to arrive at Christmas.

There was a heat wave. Mr. Walter Hines Page, the American ambassador to the Court of St. James, may not have been rich (for he was only a book publisher), but he refused to allow his family to live in what the American government had provided as housing for its envoy—a hovel in Carlos Place. Irene told the ambassador that she was totally and absolutely on his side, but when she wrote to Clarice about it, Clarice wrote back asking what Mr. Page and the American government planned to do about the living conditions of the American Indian.

While in Paris, Edward decided to visit some people living outside the city who sold cognac, and Irene wanted to do her best to decide among Poiret, Worth, Cheruit, Lanvin and Pacquin (all well within Paris), so they were separated for three days. Not that it was the very first time. Edward had had to rush off to Scotland to see some men who sold whiskey and they had been separated for two days. Irene wrote to Clarice, "I have bought three sets of pale, flesh-colored tights that I must wear under transparent Persian trousers and a brightly colored silk tunic that is cut *very* low in front. My oriental slippers curve up almost two inches, and for my turban Edward has somehow managed to imprison a live mouse with deep pink eyes in glass as a living ornament. The difficulty is that we cannot see how we are to feed him now that he is locked in there." Clarice did not write to her sister again. When the Wests returned to New York she refused to call on Irene. When Irene went to find her she hid, and they had to give a ball to lure the offended girl into the open where Irene could explain that it had all been a hoax.

Edward had a new Cadillac Torpedo sent from New York

to surprise her and they drove it to Zurich. The business in Zurich was over too soon for Irene, who thought it the most civilized city she had ever been in. Then the weather became unusually hot, and Herr Boos, the managing director of the Forster-Appenzeller Bank, suggested that they should enjoy a respite at the Bürgenstock before the time came to embark for New York. They drove from Zurich to Zug to Lucerne. They left the car in Lucerne and boarded the lake steamer for Kehrsiten and because they were approaching the absolute peak of their lives, all unknowingly of course, everything seemed to expand to heroic proportions of euphoria. They stood in the bow of the lake steamer with their arms around each other's waists.

All the strange newness of being married and the peril within the small and large adjustments that had been made from the moment they met seemed to vanish as they were pulled up the mountainside by the cable railway. Even Edward accepted the extraordinary sense of serenity. He had been under pressure from the day they had left New York, worrying about the boobs who would be fumbling with the prohibition movement at home, coping with seasickness, dreading failure at the meeting with Don Vito, preserving circumspection in the careful, not entirely tentative meetings with distillers and vintners, and writing daily, even thrice daily, throughout the travels, to Willie Tobin, Arnold Goff and Pick, Heller & O'Connell. He had not ever become impatient with Irene or short-tempered. Throughout the tour he remained almost a caricature of a man in love.

They were settled in a large suite in the Grand Hotel after Irene had patted the group of stuffed animals in the reception hall and they and the porters had choked and sneezed on the clouds of dust that the pats had brought up. The rooms were above a wide terrace at the edge of a cliff above the cerulean lake that seemed so far below them that, twenty years later when he stood beside Al Smith at the top of the Empire State Building and Irene had been dead for almost four years, he had said, to no one at all, "Only halfway up to the Bürgenstock."

They had walked up the back pathways to the top of the Tritten Alp and they had soared to its summit on the Hammetschwand lift, which was enclosed by a glass shaft and was the highest and fastest lift in Europe. He had read to her from Haydn's *Dictionary of Dates* (concerning the history of the world to the summer of 1885) under gaslight as they sat on wicker furniture painted blue and white in the great main hall of the hotel. They had dined with all other guests at long, common tables, with a bearded, authoritative, portly guest, who would be either a doctor, a lawyer or a clergyman, presiding at the head of each table, and the maître d'hôtel would watch over it all with eagle eyes and snap his fingers peremptorily for the waiters to rush in with the changes for each of the six courses.

After they left the Bürgenstock they held to the illusion that they had been the only people on the mountain: the food and wine had appeared, but one did not remember how; the three hotels on the long estate were filled to the last room with guests, but one did not remember them as having been there. Only they were there, facing each other and striving by constant copulation to repopulate the planet. There was the final illusion that eternity would be too short a time but that, since youth is well known to last forever, they would double eternity when they had the moment to get around to it.

Just as E. C. West had made one "joke" in his lifetime, and that not a memorable one, he also allowed himself this single romantic period. It began on his wedding day, picked up momentum as they moved across Europe, then found the square root of itself upon the Bürgenstock. The day they left for Paris he turned off some tiny petcock within his soul and allowed the gigantic tenderness and euphoria to begin to diminish very slowly, as sand falls to the inert chamber of an hourglass. It was gone soon enough.

CHAPTER THIRTEEN

Early in 1914 E. C. West launched the League's concentrated antivice campaign that urged that attention be paid to the heinous connection between alcohol and commercialized vice. Ruthlessly he exposed the fact that harlots were encouraged to solicit customers in the back rooms of saloons and received commissions on alcoholic drinks they were able to sell. When these prostitutes were arrested, the saloon keepers paid their fines. In Chicago alone, West thundered to the press, nine hundred and twenty-eight tarts were counted in the back rooms of two hundred and thirty-six saloons in a single night, and the back rooms of four hundred and forty-five saloons had contributed directly to the delinquency of fourteen thousand girls in Chicago every twenty-four hours. Something had to be done. In response the National Retail Liquor Dealers' Association hastened to endorse the Anti-Profanity League of America and urged all saloon keepers to display the League's cards behind their bars.

In 1913 Congress was at last compelled to make a move toward correcting the interstate shipment of liquor under the protection of the federal government. The Anti-Saloon League rammed through the first great national victory of the dry movement with the passage of the Webb-Kenyon Law, which provided heavy penalties for the shipment of liquor into a dry state. When the national board of trustees met early in 1913 to discuss the forthcoming twenty-year jubilee convention of the League, they voted that the time had come to strike out for national prohibition. Everything was concentrated on the Congressional election of 1914. All Protestant denominations were behind the drive, working through state leagues that directed the campaign locally. "We loosed an avalanche of letters, telegrams and petitions upon Congress. We started with about twenty thousand speakers, mostly volunteers, all over the United States. We went into every Congressional district," West told the Chicago *Tribune* after the victory, "and we triumphed even beyond our hopes."

But it would be at least two years before the League would control two-thirds of the votes in either house. Sure, patient strategy kept them from pressing for an amendment to the constitution in 1915 or 1916. "Had we attempted otherwise," E. C. West wrote in the *American* magazine in the mid-twenties, "we might have delayed passage for several years. The strategy of the day dictated holding off, insofar as rushing Congress was concerned, but we repeated the results of 1914 in 1916, and we won again. And we knew that the prohibition amendment would be submitted to the states by the Congress just elected."

President Wilson called the 65th Congress into special session to declare a state of war with Germany. The President had a war program for Congress. He insisted that this take precedence over any dry legislation. However, the League did get the Food Control Bill passed as a war measure, and in its final form it prohibited the manufacture of distilled liquors from any foodstuffs. It went into effect September 8, 1917, and it was generally conceded that alcohol, at least as hard liquor, was finished forever in America.

At last the victory of victories was realized: a resolution submitting the Eighteenth Amendment to the states was adopted on December 18, 1917. On January 16, 1919, the Secretary of State announced that the states had ratified the amendment and that its purpose as a law of the nation could go into effect one year from that date.

E. C. West and Don Vito Cascio dined at the Hotel Sofitel at the Gare Maritime in Cherbourg in May 1917. West had arrived for their meetings that morning aboard the *Aquitania* and had spent the day talking with the farmers from the Calvados cooperatives. The two men enjoyed a simple meal of baked clams in a sauce of breadcrumbs, butter, lemon, shallots and white wine. They didn't talk business because Don Vito was travel-weary. After dinner they strolled back to the ship. West had booked two staterooms, one on each side of a large sitting room with a private deck. As they breakfasted the next morning the ship was being moored at Southampton. They spent the day and the evening working in the big stateroom. At eleven that night, when the ship was at sea, they took three turns around the deck and retired.

It was a comfortable eight-day crossing. They worked ten hours each day and continued to talk about their plans at meals. When the ship reached New York West disembarked, and he never saw Don Vito again. The old man remained aboard to be visited during the eighteen hours in port by his special delegate in America.

The agenda during the crossing began with their examination of the draft of the Volstead Act to enforce prohibition, over which E. C. West had labored for four years in the most exhaustive planning of its loopholes. In a special sense the Volstead Act was to be their license to operate. They analyzed the characters and abilities of the leaders for the twenty-three marketing areas. These men had been proposed by Don Vito's special delegate for his recommendations. "His Sicilian people are very sound. Torrio is excellent, for example. Masseria is fine. I don't know the American choices except by hearsay and his recommendation, and he knows his business."

"Yes, he does," West said. "I gave him his head. I recommended no one. With my father I've been around the New York people all my life, but he chose better men than I would have picked."

"Well—we've been at this business longer than you."

They went over the Horizons A.G. warehouse stocks in the Bahamas; Cuba, the Florida Keys, Nova Scotia, St. Pierre and Miquelon, Lunenberg, Mexico, Vancouver Island and Canada. West told the delighted old man that after the passage of the Food Control Bill, which had finished distilling forever in the United States, Horizons A.G. had purchased thirty-seven distilleries together with their inventories and had arranged to have half the contents of 600,000 barrels of government-bonded bourbon and rye whiskies siphoned out and replaced with neutral spirits and water in warehouses around the country.

They went over the operating manuals with care, and Don Vito approved of West's thoroughness of method. "We have never needed such precise planning, because there hasn't been anything new in our business for hundreds of years. But men accustomed to basics such as extortion or strong-arm work or running some gambling and a few whores will have no concept of how to move around in this new big business. Sometimes you're going to think you brought in a lot of chimpanzees to run your bank, but their individual styles of working have to be taken into account. One man is a blusterer and he takes chances. Another man uses a gun or a knife to solve all the problems. Let them have their styles, but let them learn the fundamentals of the new, big business, which is what you have given them here in this operating manual, Zu Eduardo. They must have it drummed into their heads what you want them to deliver and how much it is going to cost them and precisely how much protection they can count on."

West explained the long-term effects for Horizons A.G. that the Goff-supervised short-term commercial banking would achieve. He told how Tobin would function as a procurement and collections officer. He related the work of both men to the work of Don Vito's special delegate, who would be in the field on an operational level supervising recruitment at first and tightening every bolt by teaching the operating manual and, where necessary, seeing that it was enforced. "He and Goff have the personal element to cope with. Tobin has it to a lesser degree. They'll all be dealing with undisciplined, uneducated and often illiterate immigrants whom we will be turning to rich men overnight—so fast, in fact, that they'll think they did it all themselves."

"That's the big problem," Don Vito agreed. "A bunch of hoodlums who think they did it all themselves. Guys who can only think with their knuckles or guns will think they planned their way into a million bucks, and if they don't, the newspapers will convince them they did."

"Mostly it takes money—in terms of ships, trucks, garages, guns, warehouses, breweries, distilleries and gasoline. These men haven't learned to count that high."

"The main thing—and I will say this again and again to

Benito when we have our meetings—is that they have to understand that none of them have to think except the way they've always been thinking or else this whole thing will be too big for them," Don Vito said emphatically. "I had to kill a dentist once. He was a good dentist and had been a friend of the friends all his life. But he had trained so hard and he took so much pride in being a dentist that he began to forget the ethos of our business. He began to complain that if it was found out that he was a friend of the friends, it could hurt his position. Not his practice, you understand. Even if he had been a very bad dentist they would all have had to flock to him because he was one of us. But for his *position* as a dentist. Among other dentists in the different international dental conventions he had to go to—that was his use to us, as an opium courier. We had made him a famous dentist among the dentists of the world, but he didn't understand what he was doing and he wanted to get out, so I killed him. The lesson is: Never send a man on a boy's errand. Use brutes where they must be used and be glad they cannot think. Keep searching for the people who see life as we do and give them a chance to think."

West explained the basis of the operation. "They will all need capital to go into what you call the new, big business. Your man will instruct them as to whom they can borrow from for quick, safe, sure action. We lend them the money on short term—turning the money around in thirty days for twenty percent interest. We lend them the money to buy the merchandise. Your man gives each local leader a list of eight or ten suppliers who all work under Tobin. They all buy from us at sixty dollars a case, liquor that cost us, on an average, about four dollars a case because we buy it by hundreds of thousands of cases. All right. They will need ships, boats and crews, weapons, payoff money and fuel to get their stocks into the United States, because, in the first phase at least, we'll sell it legally outside the country. Again we lend them the money, for that and for the trucks to move it and for weapons to protect it and for men to guard it, distribute and sell it. All short-term commercial banking. Thirty days at twenty percent. Now—the business will move through four phases. The first phase will be to use the available American stocks we've been stockpiling. Every idiot and his brother will think they've doped it all out. They'll plan to steal from the warehouses or hijack it or get it with forged government withdrawal permits, and, frankly, with the administration we are about to have in Washington, they'll be selling the real permits like bakers selling bread. But we've been stockpiling in the states and in Europe and in Canada since 1913. Not that we won't get more than our share of those withdrawal permits. For example," West continued with not a little self-appreciation, "I bought thirty-four wholesale drug companies, because they will control both medical permits and the permits to withdraw denatured alcohol. The denatured alcohol is for antifreeze and hair tonics and things like that. But the way I saw that the law was drawn, once that alcohol changes hands—once, that is, it goes from one wholesale drug house to another—the second firm cannot be prosecuted or made to account for what it has done with the alcohol. There is no problem in extracting the foreign agents; then the alcohol is ready for use in liquor again. That's a part of Phase Two—when the so-called available stocks seem to be running out.

"We've stockpiled sugar—my God, do we own sugar!— and stills. Your man will set up the stills with families in the big city slums, so many of them that even if the enforcement agents were going to stay honest they couldn't find more than ten percent to stamp out. And we'll give them industrial alcohol and druggists' denatured alcohol just to whet their palates for more drinkable stuff. Then we'll move into Phase Three and run stocks in from Canada, the Bahamas, Cuba, Nova Scotia, the Keys and Vancouver Island. Naturally, there will be small operators buying in Europe and Canada, but our commitments will have to be served first because we placed the orders—the *continuing* orders— first, and the home-country distilleries will have their own native market demands to meet in terms of supply."

"What's Phase Four, in the name of heaven?"

"Our own distilleries operating inside the United States. We'll be running our own breweries from the very beginning, of course, because the Volstead Act, as I wrote it, permits the manufacture of quote cereal beverages with an alcohol content of not more than one-half of one percent unquote. When it reaches the consumer it will be four-to-six-percent beer, I assure you. By the time we're ready to distill our own hard liquor the local politicians and the police and

as a matter of principle, neither company questioned or refused applications for life insurance submitted by Arnold
Goff on the lives of others—all the policies having Mr.
Goff (or one of Mr. Goff's forty-three companies) as bene-
ficiary. Nor was there any undue investigation or delay in
paying claims in the event of the sudden death of any of
these policyholders. By and large it was an extremely profitable branch of insurance practice because the policies carried
high premiums for extremely short terms, and the premiums,
naturally, were paid through Goff by the borrower.

If an operator had an Atlantic rum fleet, he had capital
requirements requiring a revolving fund—maintained at a
level of a million and a half to two million dollars—for
liquor purchase (from Willie's branch), all ships, high-
speed boats and shoreside trucking equipment, plus insurance, payroll, fuel, warehousing, garaging and protection.
He had to hire large amounts of capital, and he had to hire it
from Goff to spend it on Willie.

Not that he didn't get full service for it. For example,
through Edward's friends in the White House Willie was
able to acquire two hundred unused Liberty motors that had
been built for torpedo boats in World War I at 12 percent
of their original cost. They had bought boat yards in the
Bahamas. The motors were fitted into new hulls and the
finished boats were sold for 165 percent of their original
cost. After sale the boats were berthed in New York along
the Brooklyn waterfront and at a marine garage on the East
River with direct access to Hell Gate, and also Bayshore,
Long Island, and at Westhampton. Each boat came equipped
with a Horizons amulet, a dory hung over the stern for protection against the Coast Guard, who were paid to harass
free-lance operators. With the amulet, the Coast Guard
escorted the boats into port safely. This offshore arm of the
government was an alert, enthusiastic organization that was
ever willing to help. During the peak holiday rush periods,
for example, Coast Guard Cutter 203 loaded on 700 cases
at sea along Rum Row, then unloaded them at the Canal
Street dock for seven dollars a case, which they shared
partially with the New York policemen who helped off-load
the cargo.

Of course it was neither profitable nor possible to buy
everyone's cooperation. There was occasional trouble.

Willie's branch concentrated all its lawyers in the Knicker-bocker Building at 42nd Street and Broadway, where they established a pattern of rapid legal assistance that was a model in every way.

The large breweries were operated under lease from Horizons by the gangs in the principal national market areas. This was an enormously profitable business; in 1928 whole-sale beer sales in Chicago alone amounted to $196,680,000. But the operating expenses of the gangs were high: police, federal agencies, armed guards, insurance and brewery rental were some peripheral factors, in addition to which they were required to pay one-sixth of their gross to Horizons.

Further capital was borrowed through Goff for the oper-ation and maintenance of all other income-producing activi-ties demanded by the operating manual that Horizons enforced: narcotics, brothels, gambling, nightclubs, race tracks, roadhouses, slot machines, policy rackets, laundries, restaurants, dance halls, speakeasies, booking agencies, sugar brokerage, labor organizations, alky-cooking, taxis and strike-breaking and extortion rackets.

The national capital requirement of all mobs in all na-tional market areas came to a substantial four hundred and twenty-six million dollars annually, which might have been a perilous risk for Horizons A.G., through Goff, the mo-nopoly banking agency. However, all loans were secured with life insurance policies in Arnold Goff's favor. If the borrower died naturally, the policy would honor the amount of the debt. If, as sometimes happened, there were unintelli-gent borrowers who did not want to pay the debt, they knew they would be putting a break-even price on their heads. Which is to say that although Arnold Goff became one of the mythical figures of modern American crime, and although he was gifted and clever with numbers, he was only a technician, who worked for 2 percent. By 1917 he was already about the most exciting figure to be pointed out at a race track or at a Broadway opening. By 1921 he was the sort of hoodlum-sportsman about whom people enjoyed believing anything. He had fixed the 1919 World Series, not less than two world championship prize fights and a baker's dozen of big stake races.

Yet he didn't seem at all sinister if you didn't happen

to look into his eyes. He had talcum-pale skin, noodle-soft, and shining hair. He was a full-time ladies' man with a stable of mistresses and still time for the big whorehouses. He had a chin dimple, and there are chin-dimple buffs just as there are women who hang around musicians. He continued to be a fence for stolen jewelry even after the enormous action started, but more often than not, after the sets were broken up they were most likely to rub off on some pretty girl. Fencing wasn't the only part of his business that he held out on E. C. West. He financed a chain of bucket shops, the rawest kind of Wall Street stock swindle; but like everything else he did or tried to do, sooner or later it came to West's attention.

At the time he attempted his first double-dealing with E. C. West, Goff held life insurance policies in his favor totaling eleven million four hundred and twelve thousand dollars, which meant that his 2 percent share of the short-term loan action represented by the policies would be two hundred and twenty-eight thousand, two hundred and forty dollars. If that was an average thirty-day, short-term aggregate loan, then Goff's income from banking alone (and it was the big banking that made all his other income possible) could be figured roughly at two million seven hundred and thirty-eight thousand eight hundred and eighty dollars a year—tax free.

The short-term commercial banking was done through forty-three Goff companies that had been incorporated in eleven states but that operated regionally in the nation under such banal names as Goffair Mortgage or Arnlegal Furniture or Allgoff Enterprises. The collections were made by these companies and remitted on the same updated thirty-day loan basis to the West National Bank in New York. William Tobin, executive vice-president of Horizons A.G., a Swiss company, held power of attorney on each of the forty-two Goff company accounts. Using these at the end of each fiscal quarter, he withdrew 98 percent of all Goff company funds and caused the West National to remit these funds to the Horizons A.G. numbered account at the Forster-Appenzeller Bank in Grabs.

That it was a sound system was proved by the fact that it was never investigated, even after Goff was shot to death on April 19, 1928. Goff's own life was insured in two policies of seven million five hundred thousand dollars, each in the favor of Horizons A.G. of Grabs, Switzerland.

Regardless of what caused his death, Arnold Goff's problem was never entirely one of greed. His major problem was that he hated E. C. West. As those things so often seem to happen, he hated him for the most irrational of reasons.

On the first day of each calendar quarter Goff was required to meet with the head of the West National Bank. He was the representative of forty-two companies that deposited with the bank, therefore anyone would have seen that these were normal business meetings. He would be driven to the bank building between Fulton and Wall, forty-seven stories high with a lobby displaying enormous murals by Roja-Hunt depicting man at his nets bringing in the fruits of the sea, and the lobby floor seeming to shine with gold. E. C. West's office, on the thirty-third floor, was reached through a series of rooms like Chinese boxes, each room with a different decor and each manned by a bulky civilian who bulged above a different exquisite desk.

Arnold Goff did not hate West because West had made him a multimillionaire. He hated him because at the end of every one of their meetings since 1911, originally held in the old building on West 14th Street, West would always dismiss him with that contemptuous false smile that might have been peeled off the front page of the *World* and say, "Now, don't tell Bella Radin what we talked about today."

On January 2, 1924, everything seemed to be just the same. Goff was passed through the exquisite guard boxes into the last room, where West was sitting soldier-straight as always, confidently handsome and physically healthy and, to Goff, as attractive as a fish cake with a mustache. They greeted each other. Goff sat down. The meeting invariably opened with West handing him the bank's statement showing that his forty-two accounts had remitted 98 percent of their bank balances to a Swiss bank. Goff had always been convinced that West was just an ice-water banker with a little more than the usual banker's larceny in him. He thought West had happened to inherit those three gambling houses and had never really been a part of them. He considered West a smart square who had figured out this clever banker's dodge of short-term credit for businesses that weren't legit, but he never ever conceived that West had anything to do with mobs and booze and vice, because West had not intended him to think that way.

That morning his revulsion for West rolled over him like waves of icy water. He blurted out what he refused to contain any longer. He didn't wait for the bank statements to be extended.

"Listen, Mr. West. Do you know what it cost me to be allowed to sit here and do business with you? A law practice!"

"It wasn't much of a law practice, Goff."

"And did I ever tell you—or maybe you read it in the papers and it slipped your mind—that my father killed himself in 1919 and left me a cowardly note that said he was ashamed of me?"

"He might have been ashamed of you. I'm ashamed of you myself. But he killed himself because he was in the terminal stages of cancer."

"Are you trying to tell me that you didn't make a fortune betting the way I told you to bet on the 1919 series?"

"Betting?" West looked at Goff as if he were drunk. And he was almost drunk. It had been a three-day New Year's Eve celebration. "I don't bet."

"All right. So let it go. Okay. Never mind. What's the difference? What I'm talking about is this. For a hundred dollars you sold Bella away from me."

"Bella?"

"Bella! Bella Radin!

"You look as though you're going to vomit, Goff." West opened a desk drawer and took out a silver flask. He slid the flask across the desk. "Hair of the dog." Goff opened the top of the flask gratefully and took a long swallow. He leaned back in the chair and closed his eyes.

"Now—shall we go over these statements?"

Goff shot an accusing finger at him. "You took her away from me!"

"I bought information from the woman. That was thirteen years ago. She accepted one hundred dollars that she said she was going to deposit in your joint account. But you wanted to lose that woman. She took the money for you, but you were glad for the excuse to drop her."

"All right. Never mind. What's the difference?"

"If you think she can be had for money, go buy her back."

Goff's eyes filled with drunken tears. His instability shocked West. "It's too late. She got married. She has kids."

"Goff, what do you want? Please tell me what you want?"

Goff's trembling finger leveled at his enemy again. "Just don't mention her. When I walk out of here, don't say what you always say. For the first time in thirteen years just don't say it—okay?"

"Is that all?"

"That's all."

"Now may I get on with business?"

"Go ahead."

"Have you read about the daylight robberies of the bank messengers carrying negotiable Liberty Bonds that have been going on over the past eighteen months?"

"Yes. I saw that." Goff sat up quite straight.

"Why did you organize those robberies?"

Goff stared. His face darkened visibly because he could not have grown paler. "What are you talking about?"

"You're a thief."

"Now, just a minute here!"

"You are a cheap package-snatcher—or should I say a mastermind of package snatchers?—and you disposed of the bonds through those tinhorn bucket shops you organized."

"Who said that? That's a goddam lie. Who said that?"

"Goff, I want the money to be handed over to Willie Tobin before this bank closes on Friday."

"*You* want the money? That wasn't your bank that was hit. They never hit your messengers."

"Call it a fine."

"A fine. The bonds were worth five million dollars! God knows how many people could have been involved. God knows where all that money could be now."

"I hired you to work as a moneylender, not as a thief. You endangered my business when you had those packages snatched. Bring the money to Tobin by Friday afternoon or you'll be out of business."

That sentence, which West thought could close him out, composed Goff, and his eyes showed their old, hard hatred. "You know banking, Mr. West, and you figured out a very good thing for me. But you don't know the people I work with, and you don't know how to put me out of business."

West studied him the way a great chef de cuisine might

look at the daily garbage. "Friday afternoon, Goff," he said.

"Up your ass," Goff answered and walked to the office door. As he touched the doorknob West called out to him and he turned. "You forgot your bank statements," West said, holding them out. Goff returned and accepted the envelope. He walked to the door again and West called out again. He turned.

"Now, don't tell Bella Radin what we talked about today," West said with mock severity.

When Goff reached the pavement on William Street he was nearly ill with rage. He forgot that he had driven to the bank in his car or that his driver was standing at the building entrance. He strode past the man, who came after him, touching his arm. Out of reflexive frustration Goff turned and struck the man heavily in the face, making him stagger sideways. Shocked at what he had done, he felt his anger cool. As curious crowds began to gather he helped the driver to right himself and, mumbling apologies, hurried the man toward the car. The driver was as astounded by the blow as by the fact that for the first time Goff had acknowledged him at all. They got into the car and Goff peeled a fifty-dollar bill off a large roll of money and leaned forward to drop it in the driver's lap.

There were fourteen telephone messages at the hotel, but he ignored them. He ran a very cold bath and lay in it for ten minutes because that was what relaxed him most. He got into pajamas and a robe and called room service to send a waiter into his kitchen to make him a cup of Ovaltine. In about twenty minutes he felt calm and sleepy. It was five minutes to six. What was he in such an uproar about? He stretched out on the bed and began to sort everything into its place, but not all of the pieces would fit. How in God's name had West known he had engineered the bond heist? How had he found out he had floated the bonds away through the bucket shops—and how did he know Goff owned bucket shops? What was wrong here?

The only thing that could give Goff satisfaction gave him enormous satisfaction. West had had a fair run in the money-lending business. Ninety-eight percent of that kind of a turnover for thirteen years should be enough for the greediest banker in the world. West was finished now. It was all Goff's business now—100 percent Goff's. He felt so good about it that he began to marvel at the brass of the ice-water bastard demanding to be paid five million dollars from somebody else's bonds and calling it a "fine." He was willing to steal the money from Goff, then call it a fine for stealing. Well, the cold-ass grabber had made his own square bed and he could have it. West saying he was going to put him out of business was a very funny line. Goff fell asleep.

He awoke to the sound of his doorbell ringing and to a pounding on the door. He rolled out of bed and put on a light. The noise stopped. He started across the living room toward the door when the ringing started again. "Shut up!" he shouted. "And you better have a goddam good reason." He opened the door.

Three men stood there. Incredibly, one was Joe "the Boss" Masseria. He tried to register that before he saw that the other two were Frankie Yale and Frankie Marlowe. Joe the Boss hadn't shown himself out of his neighborhood for years because he had decided that it was dangerous to call attention to himself. He did the thinking. He had lieutenants to do the work. He ran all the rackets in New York: booze, narcotics, the Italian lottery, vice, extortion—name it, they belonged to Joe the Boss. Charley Lucky ran Manhattan for him. Ciro Terranova ran uptown and the Bronx. Frankie Yale ran Brooklyn for him. Joe ran all the big hoods, all the rackets, and he was head of the Unione, and in all the years he had done business with Goff they had met only once.

What the hell was this? He stared at Frankie Yale, his pal, his contact, the man he did business with and with whom he had had many a wonderful time. Goff was in the nightclub business with Frankie Marlowe and they owned a couple of fighters and a couple of horses together. Goff knew so much about these three men that the way they stood there looking at him was frightening. Frankie Yale was the richest man in Brooklyn, it occurred to him fleetingly. Yale had once sent a pair of diamond cufflinks to a newspaperman because the man had written that he was "the Beau Brummel of the underworld." Joe the Boss was maybe three and a half times bigger than Capone—not Capone's scrapbook, Capone. Frankie Yale was *the* specialist for fancy hits. He handled only very big hits. He had killed

Jim Colisimo and Dion O'Banion as a favor. And Marlowe was Yale's chief gunman.

"What is it, boys?" Goff said shakily. "What's the matter?" His voice broke. Masseria pushed him on the chest and sent him backward into the room. Marlowe locked the door.

"Frankie, listen——" he said to Yale.

"Shuddup."

He had *made* Yale! He had made all of them. Without the money he had lent them they would be nothing—stevedores sweating on the docks or pimps or strong-arms. This was too much. Something had gone wrong. "I never keep cash here," he said. "I swear there isn't six grand in the whole place."

"Arnold?"

"Yes, Joe?"

"I got a contract to hit you."

"Hit me?" He looked frantically from one face to the other. His mouth became unsteady and he had to grit his teeth to stop trembling. "Why? Whose contract? This is impossible. I do everything right. I help everybody. I helped you. Who wants me hit?"

They stared at him and he slid downward into a chair.

"Who?" Masseria asked resentfully. "You wanna know who? You think I turn out to handle goddam hits, you son of a bitch? You think I come alla way up here and Frankie comes alla way from Brooklyn because *we* wanna hit a fucking shylock?"

Goff was trembling uncontrollably. "They can't pay you what I can pay. There isn't anybody in this entire business, coast to coast, who can pay you more than I can pay. Lemme walk outta here with a suitcase and get on some ship. I'll go so far nobody'll ever see me again. I'll be like dead. You'll collect twice—from them and from me. Okay?"

Masseria nodded to Yale. Yale grasped the front of Goff's robe and pajamas and pulled him to his feet. "Why don't you do what you're told, you prick."

"Do what, Frankie?" Goff was weeping. "I'll do anything. Tell me what."

"Tomorrow when the banks open you get outta here and you take a payoff from certain bonds you got and you bring it downtown to a certain guy, you know who."

Goff gaped. He couldn't seem to make himself understand. "You mean—*West?*"

"Shaddopp!" Masseria roared. "I don' wanna know who! You unnastan'? *You* know who. That's enough. You hear?" Yale hit Goff in the gut with all his professional force and dropped him retching on the floor. Masseria walked up beside him and kicked him viciously in the head with his heavy shoe. He rolled Goff over with his foot so that Goff was staring up at him. "You get me mixed up wit' people like this again," he said with heavy anger, "and you'll wish to God somebody would take a contract to come in and only kill you.

In 1912, because of his extensive political connections, William Tobin, a well-known New York attorney, was named to the action committee of the National Brewers' Consortium and to the defense committee of the Personal Liberty League of the Distillers' Appeal. For the entire alcoholic-beverage industry he was able to swing into action such hopeless projects as the employment of dozens of costly experts to analyze dry strategy—which was available in the daily newspapers for two cents—and the beverage industry's boycott of firms that he pointed out as opposing traffic in beer and spirits (because they had tried to discourage on-the-job drinking by employees), such as the Pennsylvania Railroad, Procter & Gamble, and the United States Steel Corporation, which were then blacklisted. The Heinz Company was cited as an enemy because its founder was president of the Pennsylvania Sunday School Association, which had endorsed prohibition.

The Tobin Committee was able to raise rages among companies and consumers alike. Tobin succeeded in setting the brewers against the distillers and the vintners against the brewers, so that each secretly expected to drive the others out of the market; the brewers, particularly, had hopes of arranging to manufacture the only national alcoholic beverage. He also advised groups to bribe the wrong politicians, who would then vote dry or run shouting to the newspapers. Each dummy "front" organization Tobin formed for his industries to fight the prohibitionists was somehow exposed and destroyed. Wherever possible he guided the alcohol manufacturers to do everything wrong, every possible public and private mistake. All in all, Tobin made popular mistakes for his people, wholly aided by the fact that Americans had been educated for a generation through the WCTU's educational committees. Americans deeply wanted the brewers and distillers to be guilty.

His job well done, Tobin left political contact work in 1914 to accept a post as executive vice-president of Horizons A.G., a Swiss corporation dealing in imports. The new appointment made Tobin very happy. He was miserable when he was separated from Eddie, filled with dread and woe, since all the while he served the wet cause Eddie forbade him to attempt to come within a mile of him. They could not be seen together. Tobin could understand that that was necessary functionally, but it made him miserable, and were it not for the fact that he had to telephone Eddie every night to get his instructions and find out what it was he would be required to do next, he simply did not think he would have been able to stand it.

But that was over now, thank God. Eddie had given him a wonderful six-window office directly over Eddie's own office in the new West National Building. A direct telephone connection had been sunk into the building wall within a copper cable where no one could tamper with it. Willie Tobin had never known any other life than working for the Wests. Paddy had chosen him when he was thirteen because he had been so silent. Paddy had put him through law school and had broken him into politics; then Eddie, marvelous Eddie, had polished him.

Willie was a small-boned man, elegant in his movements and his almost epicene taste in clothes, with large, limpid brown eyes that stared passively, even adoringly. He had a wonderful flair for scarves, which he wore instead of ties— not in public, of course, but at the office, since he saw no one but the staff personally; everything was done on the telephone. He still had the knack of silence, because he knew Eddie admired that, but with the staff he could rattle on like a blue jay. He had an entirely male staff. He thought that was much the best thing, considering the types who might possibly decide to visit the office—a bunch of hairy gorillas. Willie just seemed to vanish at the end of the working day. He never invited even the closest staff people to dinner or to his place even though some of them had very, very big eyes over that prospect. He'd taken some of them to lunch. He'd taken a few of them to important performances of the ballet or to really good art shows, but never just one of them, in fact never less than three of them. He certainly had no women friends. He was absolutely crazy about Irene West—that was clearly there for everyone to see except Irene and Edward West. But when the staff people talked it over at *their* places almost every night of every week of the year they decided that Willie adored Irene because she was so close to Eddie that some of that wonderful stuff must rub off on her.

Willie's life, public and private, was like a human extension of a complicated telephone system. Edward West always knew where to find him simply because he tried not to stray from the telephone unless Eddie had okayed it first. He placed and took eighty and ninety telephone calls from New York, most states and Europe in the course of his twenty-four hour self-imposed duty. He concentrated the essence of these calls into précis form and took them himself to Eddie's office every morning, heavily sealed, names identified in code. He was, or became, absolutely indispensable to Eddie. But he made no grandiose efforts to advertise his brave activities. He did prodigies of work without showing effort. He murmured rather than spoke. He had the analytical ability to think his way through the consecutive parts and movements of a watch, but only the extremely observant (which did not include Edward West) knew he was as intelligent as he was because he really did work hard at diverting attention from himself. "You are not there to bellow opera arias," he told himself.

He was passionately interested and extremely learned about the dance because, incomprehensibly, the dance was the topic Eddie most enjoyed talking about—in fact it was the only topic that was certain to soften him, to relax his mind and the stern muscles of his face. Sometimes, when this happened, Willie would miss seeing those wonderfully strong, stern lines. But in a way he knew he was making Eddie happy.

Willie had started with the Wests at two dollars a week. When Paddy died he was making twenty-two as Paddy's confidential man, then Eddie had raised him to thirty. By 1924 he had nine million dollars banked in Switzerland, earned by his commission of one percent of the handle on liquor procurement and one percent on national collections. He didn't find very much to spend it on. Besides clothes, elaborate birthday and Christmas presents for Eddie (and Irene) were about the only expensive items. He had a wonderful wardrobe of just about every kind of wonderful clothes in closets and chests and stored trunks and some day when he really got the chance he was going to rent a sixteen-room apartment on Fifth Avenue, live in four rooms and line the walls of all the rest with closets for his wonderful clothes. He kept canaries. And after a few years of banking so much money he began to collect one each of every automobile ever made. He got his back up for the first time with Eddie and really did have to stamp his foot when he was told they were going to move to Bürgenstock West for good. He simply refused to budge until Eddie had agreed that he could take his car collection with him.

Sunday was usually his quiet day. He just relaxed in the apartment with the canaries, doing needlework on ladies' evening handbags, a recreation he had learned from that ruffian of an old lawyer, F. Marx Heller. He was able to complete three bags a month of his own designs, and he sold them to an uptown outlet for thirty dollars each. He lived at the New York Athletic Club on 59th at Sixth in a comfortable seven-story brownstone building. Every morning and night he took an ice-water plunge in the eight-foot-square tank the club kept for drunks—which had a fifty-pound cake of ice floating in it at all times—then had a wonderful deep, *deep* Swedish massage from Fred or Barney. He never fraternized at all in the club and only tipped on Christmas Day and June 25 lest they get some idea that he was somehow trying to make himself popular.

He really preferred the bachelor life, he told Irene, because his hours were so irregular and there was so much traveling (which was true at least in the early years). Eddie could call him at all hours of the night to pass on instructions to the special representative or to sober up some big-time trial lawyer in the ice-water plunge or to take sixty or seventy thousand dollars downtown to Arnold Goff or to find the right sort of cooperative doctor to help out at Rhonda Healey's request. He really liked Rhonda. She put up with so goddam much.

When he had just about settled himself in the new Horizons offices, with the most divine view of the two rivers anyone had ever seen, Eddie (and Irene) got back from that endless honeymoon, and he was sent off to Europe in Eddie's wake.

He had two steady travel beats after that, and the way it seemed to work out, Eddie always sent him to the Bahamas, Cuba, the Keys and Mexico in the summertime and to Canada only in the winter, for God's sake. And he had a lot of travel inside the country. Eddie broke the ground, but he had to finish the arrangements to take down half of the six hundred thousand barrels of government whiskey in 1915. Then he and the special representative had to get it moved, then to see that it was stored safely. There were about twenty gallons to the half barrel, or about four million cases of uncut whiskey. They had to begin to buy garages practically in wholesale lots all over the country, and Eddie made Willie qualify for a realty board license so that he could split commissions with local realty agents on the sales. They'd be needing garages soon enough anyway, and, all told, the three hundred thousand barrels of whiskey cost only two dollars and eighty cents a case, including all pay-offs and transport. Naturally this didn't prorate the cost of the garages, but it included the grain alcohol and water mix that they had used to fill the barrels to the top again. It was a terribly difficult job of organization, but Eddie *and* the special representative had said Willie had a *genius* for logistics. The genius part that met the eye was that five years later they were selling the whiskey that cost them two-eighty a case for sixty-four dollars a case. And it was so good that after the buyer got it he cut it again.

Eddie wanted him to go to Europe before the war started in order to finish all the details Eddie had begun in France, Scotland and England while he and Irene were on tour.

Willie closed for three million five hundred thousand cases of Scotch at a unit cost of eight dollars a case, including shipping costs, for delivery to their warehouses (which he had bought or built) in the Bahamas and in the Keys not later than July 15, 1919, under a delivery schedule that was to begin—wartime shipping slowing things down as it could —on April 15th, 1915. He bought seven hundred and fifty thousand cases of red and white wine and a hundred thousand cases of vermouth in France because Eddie had reasoned that although they could get it cheaper in Italy and Germany by holding the wine off the market until the market stabilized, the rich Americans would have sour palates from lousy red wine and they'd be ready to pay eighty dollars a case for French wine that had cost six dollars a case in the big bulk lots. By that time they wouldn't know one wine from the other—beyond red and white, of course— so Eddie had him buy the hard, hard reds of the Côte-Rôtie, which was wine that demanded plenty of aging, and they took delivery on that at once. Wanting to be fair with the American people, Eddie did not accept delivery on any white wine (an assorted bag) that was more than two years old. The label printers would see to all the details of marques and vintages. He bought one million two hundred thousand cases of champagne at eleven dollars a case because Americans had been brainwashed into believing that they could drink only champagne to celebrate or commemorate important occasions—otherwise they would suffer bad luck; and they got ninety-five a case for it.

He finished up the heavyweight cognac arrangements in the southwest, then went back to Paris determined to see an "exhibition" before he left because everyone said that was the thing to do. Little did he know that, having become the greatest individual customer for French wines in all history, the vintners would have been happy to stage an "exhibition" for him themselves, throwing in all wives and daughters.

He did see one in the Rue Chabanais and not only disapproved of it but (privately) thought it a silly waste of time. Publicly he did his best to pretend to be most enthusiastic, whereupon the banker they used in Paris immediately felt it necessary to fix him up with this cow-cunted young whore who couldn't speak a word of English, and they had sat in a drafty room for a half hour until he felt it was safe enough to come out. He had had to give her fifty dollars (with a finger to his lips), and she had rushed him and kissed him and he had almost vomited because God knew where *that* mouth had been!

He sailed out of England for Canada, where he reserved

stocks of neutral-grain spirits for delivery, at order, beginning in February 1922; he had also stockpiled a matching quantity of neutral-grain spirits in the States. He bought eight hundred thousand cases of Canadian whiskey, then went to Cuba, where he reserved two hundred thousand cases of light and two hundred thousand cases of barreled rums in a general Caribbean mix. When the major reserving/buying was completed he began the work of warehousing his stores in the more expensive storage facilities inside the States and in the feeder stations ringing the country. When all arrangements were completed, in December 1918, they had a total of sixteen million four hundred thousand cases on reserve order or ready to be shipped.

Eddie had acted shrewdly. He knew that the mad scramble to make a killing would start just before the ratification of the amendment. But he also knew that there could not possibly be enough liquor in Britain, France and Canada for the nationals of those countries in addition to thirsty Americans and that the case-unit prices would soar tremendously. And he was 100 percent right.

Eddie had known about the brewery loophole that would appear in the Volstead Act because he himself had put all the loopholes there. Many discouraged brewers didn't have the interest left to hold onto their plants for a long pull, and none of them had any interest in making "cereal beverages." They were willing to sell their breweries to Horizons A.G. or they were willing to lease their breweries for the duration of prohibition. If a well-placed brewery could not be bought or leased, it was Willie's job to have its directors brought to trial in a federal court and to have the breweries closed under injunction. That usually brought the owners around.

The limited partners of Horizons A.G., who were influential in the various regions, were very helpful in brewery acquisitions. When prohibition came and the manufacture of "cereal beverages" with an alcoholic content of not more than one-half of one percent was legalized, the breweries (Horizons leased a hundred and forty-two of these to local mobs in the national marketing areas) ran full blast making "near beer," which they delivered to the speakeasies together with a container of the alcohol that had been removed from it at the brewery. The bartender could then return the alcohol to the beer barrel with a compression pump or pour it into the glass by hand—as the customer preferred. Then the Chicago chemists came up with wort, which was green beer with no alcohol at all, so there could not possibly be any legal objection. When these barrels were delivered the speakeasies needed only to drop yeast into them and let the beer ferment on the premises, so that the hangovers were so much less horrible. Beer was an enormous profitmaker (and yielded one-sixth of its gross sales to Horizons A.G.). It cost six dollars a barrel to make and sold to speakeasies for fifty-five dollars a barrel. Beer outsold liquor over the bars at the ratio of twenty-three to one.

Chicago was a very big beer territory. It handled sixty thousand barrels of beer a week. New York wasn't as big for beer per capita, but its yield was four times that of Chicago from everything else; and New York was handling one hundred and thirty-seven thousand barrels a week. Nationally, when the share of Horizons A.G. was one-sixth of eight billion dollars—quite apart from the wholesale liquor business, the brewery rentals and the short-term credit banking —New York was the biggest gross unit producer of all national market areas with nine hundred million a year. But of course Chicago had the biggest star attraction of any market area, Al Capone.

When Eddie finished his estimates in 1930, averaging the income for the decade just spent at a gross of thirteen billion dollars a year, it was established that the rackets and their dependent industries had become the biggest American industry then and in the nation's history.

Willie supervised 193 employees in the West National building and 74 in the field, plus 11 buying representatives and expediters who worked outside the country. The field people were used to verify inventories and to check duplicates of deposit slips against lading bills and gross-income figures filed under the special representative's control. It was not a complex structure. The mobs borrowed capital from Goff, who was Horizons A.G. but did not know it, to buy/ lease from Willie Tobin, a Horizons employee, then shared one-sixth of their gross operating profits with Benito Rei, who was Horizons A.G. and also the special representative of Don Vito Cascio Ferro, *capo di capi*, chosen to assist

E. C. West in a most important phase of the over-all operation.

At eight-thirty on a March morning in 1915, while E. C. West was going through the morning mail at the League office in Washington, Congressman Rei was announced. Rei had just begun his second term in the House. He and West had had several pleasant meetings, usually at lunch, in the regular course of West's friendly coverage of the members of Congress as a member of the League's legislative committee.

Rei was an Illinois Republican, a well-balanced, well-educated man who held a degree from the Wharton School of Business of the University of Pennsylvania. He was a regular on everything except Italo-American legislation, but in no way a party hack. His most effective strength was his ability to influence other members on voting difficult bills.

"Are you wet or dry this morning?" West asked affably as the congressman sat down. Rei was neither wet nor dry. He would vote on the prohibition issues as the party required.

"It feels a little bit more wet out this morning," Rei said. He refused a cigar.

"What can we do for you?"

"I bring a message."

"How very kind of you."

Rei smiled, took a long white envelope from his inner pocket and slid it across the desk. It wasn't sealed. West pulled at the flap and a yellow handkerchief of heavy silk fell out showing a large *VCF* embroidered in black in one corner. Startled, West looked quickly at Rei. Rei smiled blandly. "I have been to the old country on a holiday," he said. "Don Vito sends to you fond greetings, Zu Eduardo."

Zu, in the Sicilian speech, was the closest to a title any man would accept to indicate that he was a "friend of the friends." The tremendous excitement of the moment covered West's forehead with a light sweat. The thought of his mother filled his heart like a soaring flight of primrose flamingoes. If only she could know! If only she could be there to see that the leader of the brotherhood, the *true* leader, had acknowledged that he was merely a soldier of the son of Maria Corrente.

Rei and he met the following morning on the enclosed deck of the 10 A.M. ferry leaving South Ferry in Manhattan for St. George, Staten Island. They went over the operating manual together.

The working manual Rei was to administer would be applied to seventy-two major and twenty-six minor gangs working in the twenty-three national market areas, whose leaders, lieutenants and business managers were to be recruited wholly by him—Sicilian as well as non-Sicilian, Jewish, Irish, Polish and Negro. Each gang would be accountable to Rei operationally through its leader and financially through its business manager. Rei would undertake all the essential protection approaches there were on a high emergency level. The labor force for each gang was to be recruited by the leader and the lieutenants from among the available force of bank robbers, car thieves, gunmen, gamblers, pimps, strong boys, hold-up men and muscleheads. The gang leader would work within the broad lines of the unwritten operating manual, interpreting it wherever he chose except in areas of payoffs, collections, procurements, and short-term capital borrowing. Each gang, depending on whether it was major or minor, agreed to develop, to exploit within their abilities, income opportunities derived from: alcohol, narcotics, brothels, gambling, nightclubs, race tracks, roadhouses, slot machines, laundries, restaurants, dance halls, hotels, speakeasies, breweries, labor organizations, band booking, sugar brokerage, strike-breaking, taxis, political poll-watching, shylocking and extortion. When required by Rei, each gang leader would follow his orders or supply whatever assistance might be necessary as well as agree to submit to Rei's arbitration, or to the arbitration of his delegate when Rei should consider arbitration necessary.

Rei was a native American, three years older than West. He was a trained business administrator and a factor in state and city politics and more than cognizant of the byways of national politics. His brother, Ira King, was an important banker in California.

Rei did not run for a third term. In 1916 he became president and chief executive officer of the National Immigrant Investment Bank, a small bank of long standing that Horizons A.G. capital acquired and recapitalized at six million dollars and that Horizons owned. With the aid of Rei's own connections and the assistance of Horizons' limited partners, as well as through the cooperation of Pick, Heller & O'Connell, it became a repository for substantial federal, state and municipal funds. It began to handle more and more industrial transactions. It became the correspondent bank of the Western Alliance Trust (Ira King's bank) and the West National Bank in California and New York respectively. Horizons partners and other national leaders served as the bank's directors.

Each of the gangs in each of the national market areas was required to form companies through which income for Horizons A.G. would flow, and in return for the opportunities and protection afforded them were required to pay to Horizons A.G. one-sixth of the gross earnings from all activities, indirectly. Willie Tobin held powers of attorney on these accounts through his seventy-four field representatives, and he would withdraw Horizons' one-sixth share from each of the twenty-one hundred and nineteen companies on the last day of each month and remit these collections through the West National Bank to the Horizons account in Zurich. Quadruplicate slips went to Rei, the regional representatives, the gang's business manager and to Tobin. Punctuality in collections and a right count were enforced by Rei.

The first killing Rei ordered (as the Horizons A.G. administrator) eliminated (Big) Jim Colisimo, a vice industrialist and gang chieftain of Chicago's South Side, on May 11, 1920, one hundred and fourteen days after prohibition had become the national law. Rei's administrative problem had been aggravated by the fact that prohibition did not invent the gangster. Colisimo's operations had been earning about a half million dollars a year for many years, but he was a stodgy, old-fashioned vice operator, and the scope of his understanding of the new opportunities and his interest in exploiting them was limited. His death, a stile that separated the old-style hit-or-miss criminal from the superbly mechanized and fluidly organized big-business-organization criminal, was a historic moment in the developing American meaning.

It began there—the watershed of modern American crime —and it resolved moral factors for every American born thereafter, instituting approaches to social, governmental, financial and international problems that were henceforth to be based upon an entire people's contempt for law and authority. As it developed it learned. For example, on April 28, 1929, at E. C. West's insistence, Benito Rei ordered an organizational convention to be held at the President Hotel at Atlantic City, New Jersey. Each leader present was a Horizon A.G. franchise holder with a clearly defined territory in which he exploited business opportunities that had first been coordinated in the West operations manual and in which he held monopolistic power.

At the convention Rei insisted upon and enforced a cartelization and streamlined the enforcement procedure from a wasteful, overlapping, scatter-shot and haphazard punitive system to a centralized, organized single-unit national murder-squad system that was more efficient and, more important, more controllable in the blatant yellow-press, public-relations sense. West was tired of useless and wasteful/impulsive killing, therefore it was rechanneled and made industrially pragmatic. The essential cartelization was necessary to spread the industrial energy to all parts of the company's branches, equally in and throughout the twenty-three national market areas. It was West's conception of the carefully phased development of an industry that had demonstrated a greater growth rate than any other in American history. And all projects confirmed that, if carefully planned and prudently cultivated, it would continue to lead the rest of the nation for many decades afterward and, given proper managerial impetus, for the long, long-range forseeable future.

When he had had his first meeting with Benito Rei aboard the Staten Island ferryboat on that March morning in 1915, that was the true dawn of the new America. He had said with his even voice and straight-forward look: "Let all of them make names and money for themselves." For the industry he created, for the first industry of the greatest democracy in the world, the words were prophecy and became the nation's lodestone.

Even the humbler hoodlums did well. The estate of the late Vincent Drucci was in excess of four hundred thousand dollars. Jack Zuta, business manager for one of the smaller mobs, the Aiellos, left behind balance sheets, promissory notes, cancelled checks, ledgers and transaction records showing that, out of the gang's weekly average income of four hundred and twenty-nine thousand dollars, the amount of one hundred and eight thousand, four hundred and sixty-nine dollars was paid out weekly to "M.K.," Oberta's code for Rei—"Mafia King." The Aiellos were a poor-relation, church-mouse sort of gang.

Hymie Weiss, the earnest Polish-American who caught up the mantle of Dion O'Banion when it fell, was only twenty-eight when he was shot to death, but he left an estate of one million three hundred thousand dollars. Jimmy La Penna was so unimportant that he made no effort to try to conceal his bank accounts from the government, thus making it simple to discover that in one calendar year he had deposited eight hundred and four thousand, one hundred and seventy-six dollars and ninety-seven cents in his personal bank account. In the following year, when organization reshuffling had reduced him to an even smaller status, he banked a total of three hundred thirty thousand sixty-six dollars and thirty-nine cents.

A former whorehouse waiter named Greasy Thumb Guzik, whom Rei had chosen to become business manager of the Capone organization in Illinois, told the police during the James Ragen murder investigation, "I got more cash than Rockefeller and there's twenty of us with more than I have. No one's going to push us around."

West had wanted them to make names for themselves, as indeed they did. The names they made on one occasion became part of a parlor guessing game at a party given by the Wests for the visiting Prince of Wales. Irene invented the game because she thought it would amuse the royal guest. Everyone took a turn at recalling the names of gangsters as recorded in the adoring, gee-whiz daily press, always the daily fan magazines of big-business crime and an important factor in its rise to American industrial leadership. The guests thought of such names as Cheeks Ginsberg, Charley Bullets, Schemer Drucci, Bugsey Siegal, Yankee Schwartz, Dingbat Oberta, Klondike O'Donnell, Bummy Goldstein, Joe Bananas, Uncle Goldberg, Jimmy Blue-Eyes, Shimmy Patton, Blinky Palermo, Potatoes Kaufman, Dandy Phil Kastel, Piggy Lynch, Fur Sammons, King Angersola,

Spunky Weiss, Gameboy (and his brother, Honeyboy) Miller, Tootsie Cohen, Joe Adonis and Dimples Wolinsky. Only the highest Russian political leaders and ranking American military figures cherished more infantile pet names, but, as E. C. West explained to the prince, "I imagine they all wear their childish names the way savages wear paint or tattoos—to frighten away enemies and evil spirits."

Prohibition fused the amateurism and catch-as-catch-can national tendencies of the early days of the republic with a more modern, highly organized lust for violence and the quick buck. It fused the need to massacre twelve hundred thousand American Indians and ten million American buffalo, the lynching bees, the draft riots, bread riots, gold riots and race riots, the constant wars, the largest rats in the biggest slums, boxing and football, the loudest music, the most strident and exploitative press with the entire wonderful promise of tomorrow and tomorrow, always dragging the great nation downward into greater violence and more and more unnecessary death, into newer and more positive celebrations of nonlife, all so that the savage, simple-minded people might be educated into greater frenzies of understanding that power and money are the only desirable objectives for this life.

CHAPTER FOURTEEN

Daniel West was born on May 15, 1914, on the same day as his father's favorite mistress's favorite dachshund, missing by six days the first Mother's Day-by-law in the nation's history, which had been thunderingly sponsored by Senator Heflin of Alabama.

Daniel was born at West Wagstaff, his parents' new country house at Sands Point, Long Island. The house and all its grounds had been blessed by the cardinal the day before Irene and Edward occupied it. This was not any ritual gesture. Irene planned that she and Edward were to be buried in West Wagstaff's rose garden when they died and she wanted to be able to think of it from the beginning as consecrated ground.

To commemorate Daniel's birth, Grandfather Wagstaff established an investment account in trust for the boy and suggested that it wouldn't be a bad idea at all if Edward were to match his one hundred thousand dollars. Edward, who had just tied up eight hundred and thirty-two thousand dollars in the completion of West Wagstaff for Irene and Daniel, said he certainly wouldn't try to vie with Walter Wagstaff when it came to giving presents, but he would be entirely willing to take personal charge of the investment of the trust's fund. "If you ask me," Grandfather Wagstaff said, "that's even better." Edward, despite his relative youth, already had major interests in nineteen companies and was a director of eleven. He was as good as his word. He invested the infant's money in Canadian neutral-grain spirits and increased its value twenty-two times in 1922, then reinvested it.

The mother and child did very well. Humorously enough, the baby was a dark, sharp-featured Sicilian-looking infant, which baffled everyone. Edward dashed in to see his wife at the first signal from the doctor. He was bursting with pride. He had had a good night's sleep. Irene had been considerate as always and had been delivered of her child after Edward had been refreshed by his nine hours of sleep, after he had had a good, hot breakfast, and after he had had the chance to talk to the bank and to Willie Tobin. He kissed her lovingly and caressed the red-blonde hair away from her forehead. She smiled at him happily, looking no more worn than if she had just returned from a strong ocean swim. "How is he?" she asked faintly.

"The doctor says fine. But they haven't shown him yet."

"Do you think we should have him baptized now? This morning? Just to be sure?"

"Well, they said he's a very healthy baby."

"We can always do it again at the church and have a nice party afterward. Suppose someone dropped him? He'd never go to heaven. He'd never see God."

"I'll ask the cardinal, darling. It certainly seems like a good idea to me."

Two nurses, quite ugly but wearing enchanting uniform caps, came in with the baby—one to fight the father off if that became necessary. But the father hung well back. The nurses gargled over the bundle of blankets as they handed it to the mother and drew back. "He's beautiful—oooooh, he's so beautiful, madame," the fat nurse said.

"You may look now, sir," the escort nurse told Edward. He sidled across to a point three feet away from the side of the bed to beam down at the sleepy red face. Suddenly his eyes filled with tears. "Why, he looks like my mother," he said, the words tangling themselves in the lacy intricacy of the emotion.

"Oh, Edward, darling!" Irene said. "You are so sweet. You really look as though you might weep."

The nurses withdrew.

"It's so unexpected," Edward said.

"Perhaps he'll be a dancer. Would you like that? Wouldn't that be wonderful?"

The tears brimmed over in his eyes. "Yes," he answered. "Yes, it would."

E. C. West was twenty-six years old in 1914, but he offered exterior sternness and had achieved such significant positions in fields as varied as oil production, insurance, aluminum, transportation and banking that no measure of him could be taken in terms of his age. He was welcomed at the White House. Not less than once a month, because of his relentless crusading for the Anti-Saloon League, he was to be found on the front pages of American big-city newspapers—but never as just another blue-nose; whenever he was photographed he used that dazzling, overwhelming smile that was seen by no one except newspaper readers.

When the Wests had returned from Europe in September the year before, they hadn't been able to begin to entertain because they had had no house. Before they'd sailed for Naples they had approved the final plans for West Wagstaff. Irene spent most of her time working with architects and decorators and landscape gardeners, and in a short time she became quite visibly pregnant, which made her all the less interested in entertaining, no matter how keen Edward was to start.

Edward dropped right back into his old, demanding schedule, dividing his time between Washington and New York, between the League and the bank, and needing to double his efforts at the bank because he had only half the time to accomplish what had to be done. But he did not relinquish his commitment to the League, and he was tremendously admired for this. He was far too tactful (and far too busy) to arrange such a thing himself, or risk upsetting Irene and her family in some public adventure, so he had Rhonda Healey find him a mistress and set her up in a flat in Washington close by the League offices—an assignment that was carried out well and in short order.

The 1914–15 year was a wonderful year. War came just as he had predicted on his return from Europe when he had so advised the President publicly. The League was now pushing full ahead for the Eighteenth Amendment to the constitution. The twenty-two partners of Horizons A.G. were more than pleased with all developments and were so impressed with Edward that they had begun to ask him to serve on boards and to invest where they were investing. All this interest had been somewhat accelerated by the Wagstaff connection, of course. Walter Wagstaff was the *old* establishment, industrially and socially, and most certainly a power in the land. Having him as a father-in-law seemed to add to Edward's maturity.

The Wests wintered in Palm Beach, renting the Gelbart house belonging to the old headmaster of Eddie's beloved old school, until Irene could decide whether she wanted to build or buy in Palm Beach. Then they bought a house on East 55th Street in New York and gradually settled into a migration schedule that found them on 55th Street from late October until early January, blissfully at Sands Point from April until October and at Palm Beach in between. Old Professor Gelbart at last agreed to sell his house to Edward because he was an alumnus and because he had three hundred thousand dollars.

Next to Edward and Daniel, the house at West Wagstaff was Irene's greatest pride. It was so perfect from every perspective of space and decoration, or gentling therapy against the world, that Walter Wagstaff was convinced that "someone used a wand on this place." It was a close reproduction of Willmott House in Wells, England, for the building of which Lady Evelyn Willmott had left to the architect, Robert Adam, an "open credit with my bankers" before going off to Italy with Lord Hunt of Ludlow and scandalizing England. Adam had created "a small, sweet house" within and without. The first floor had a living room, drawing room, library, den, terrace, dining room, bar, kitchen and service rooms. The second floor had a paneled Georgian drawing room, seven bedrooms with carved wooden fireplaces, six master baths, sitting rooms and dressing rooms. The third floor had seven servant's rooms and baths.

It was an exquisite, femininely beautiful house whose classic Doric columns on the front side had lengthened capitals; its frieze and pediments were softened and lightened by delicate wooden swags across the upper portico. All of the proportions throughout the house were treated and flattered and made more wondrously deceptive by the artful entrance of light from unexpected places: the south side of the house was one-third glass and the window on the stair landing had been placed to use light as a cosmetic on the main hall. All the proportions were Adam harmonies.

The ceilings were delicate stucco forms connected to painted medallions of white touched with gilt against backgrounds of pastel green, lilac or blue. The curtains and furniture and carpets followed the sweet designs of the rooms, which followed the embracing design of the graceful house. The rooms were octagonal, circular, square or rectangular, but they seemed to have been conceived as a single unit that made ineffable use of all available space. Some rooms had apsidal ends or arcaded columns, which Adam had used if he considered a room too narrow or too long.

Irene burbled with joy as she pulled Edward along behind her from room to room—so proud was she of what had been accomplished—telling him that the house would stand forever, would be a monument to Daniel's children and Daniel's children's children.

There were many touches of fantasy. They had an enormous canopied bath with walls of yellow Siena marble and a tub carved from a block of the same stone, having four gold goose heads as faucets. In an adjoining alcove, off the bath, stood a modern barber chair where Edward was shaved and trimmed every morning by his valet and where Irene's hair was "done" by her extraordinary French maid.

As he grew older, Edward grew more and more devoutedly Irish and even restored things to give his old father retroactive comforts he had not had. The dining room was finished in warm opalescent satinwood and the furnishings were arranged to face two principal paintings by Jack Keats, "Kerry Market" and "Home of the Heart," which were set into two large wall panels. Edward had never bothered to mention it even to Irene, but when he had had his grandfather's house, or rather his dwelling within the piggery at Kilflyn, Kerry, entirely restored, the architect-builders had battled him vehemently but had of course at last had to give in to his insistence that two bathrooms be included in the perfect little restoration.

The chandelier in the dining room when lit looked like a blanketful of diamonds that had been tossed, then frozen in mid-air. Adjacent to the dining room was the two-hundred-year-old barroom that had been bought, packed, and transported from an old tavern to Kilflyn and that Edward somehow managed to imply had come from his father's house there. Its dimensions, which were thirty-two feet by forty feet, were something more than double the size of the sleeping room of the piggery in which the entire large West family had lived before the famine.

Outside, on sixteen acres, were gardens on several levels going down toward the Sound, one secret garden totally enclosed in sculptured walls with stairs leading to hidden grottoes. Twelve Italian cypresses, each weighing five tons, had been barged into West Wagstaff from the sea and had been replanted along the silver-stoned driveway that wound through billiard-table lawns and parterred gardens to the great door, which opened to show the superb flying staircase, cantilevered as it wound upward past Boucher wall tapestries woven in the royal factory at Beauvais at the time of Louis XV.

Edward had asked for a house in which they could entertain. He had got that and much more. Beginning with the summer of 1914 they began to entertain at the rate of hotel keepers. Edward saw it as solid, good business policy. Irene enjoyed it. People sweated out the arrival of West invitations, because Edward had studied how to balance guests with the same Burrian objectivity that Paddy had brought to his science of choosing college roommates. The Wests entertained in their houses, aboard a chartered yacht, at beach picnics in summer and winter, at dinners, musicales, masked balls, teas, lunches, at the race track and, twice a year, in a string of field boxes that were provided by Mr. John McGraw at the Polo Grounds.

The Wests did not entertain at restaurants or cabarets, first, because Edward was so prominently identified with the prohibition cause that they did not think it correct to play host in the midst of public drinking, and second, because that sort of entertaining might possibly be necessary or proper in some foreign city but surely not in the city of one's homes. However, after prohibition people just didn't seem to want to stay at home any more. Cabarets, with their formal floor shows, gave way to nightclubs, where the customers entertained each other just by being there.

Edward had not continued as an officer of the League after victory had been won. Everyone knew that he had devoted seven of the most crucial years to the movement in the most electrically effective manner in spite of a demand-

ing business life and purely out of the strength of his convictions. Nonetheless the Wests continued to entertain at
home in the old way, and people were delighted to accept
because the bag was always such big game—the Vice-President or Enrico Caruso or Legs Diamond or Mary Miles Min-
ter or a Russian grand duke. But soon guests began to get
restless earlier in the evening and would wonder aloud to the
hostess what might be happening out in the night.

In 1919 Edward became interested in a subject that was
to absorb him over the years until it became the single,
major fixation of his life. It began with his acquaintanceship
with A. Mitchell Palmer, who was Wilson's Attorney-Gen-
eral and had approached Edward to sound him out concerning possible League support of Palmer's possible candidacy
for the presidency in the 1920 elections. Palmer had been
extremely active in warning the nation about subversive
aliens and threatening to disclose Socialist/Communist plots
of which he had proof. Edward, although secretly committed
to Harding's candidacy, had been terribly upset, even dis-
proportionately upset, by the intensive propaganda cam-
paigns the Soviets were carrying out following the dread
Bolshevik Revolution in Russia, and when an identical
Workers' party was established in the United States he saw
it almost as a personal threat to everything he had not yet
accomplished. He was chatteringly grateful to Palmer for
his country-wide mass arrests of all dangerous political and
labor agitators.

He was himself then deeply involved with helping the
American labor movement to open up and express itself
through the use by the business world of armies of strikebreakers. It had been an extremely profitable venture and it
had kept his organization in touch with the leaders who provided the strong-arm divisions. But it had also occurred to
him—it occurred first to Willie Tobin, as a matter of fact—
that if a Workers' party were to foment a revolution in the
United States, among their first targets would be Edward
Courance West. The rag-tag section of labor representing
Communists and Wobblies had been fiercely against the
whole successful strike-breaking movement because it had
thwarted their own Bolshevik plans. He pressed on, nearly
frantically, in Congress for criminal syndicalist laws to be
invoked against radicals. In 1919 he declared a war against

Communists and all they stood for, and that militancy was to be enforced for the rest of his life.

By 1924 Willie Tobin had completed his massive transference of helpless love to Irene, the safest object of a feeling he could not otherwise have coped with. Serving her in any way, just being there as a good spaniel would be there, became a way of life for him, and when the three of them could be together sharing the intimacies of the day's occupation, it was all sheer heaven *sur glace*. While Edward had to be in Washington, or traveling, or working late, Willie served as the family friend to escort Irene to dinner parties or the opera. Irene was very fond of him. She knew Edward and Bill had been boys together and she understood that Bill was the American representative of some Swiss company Edward was interested in. Once or twice she had tried to match Bill with Clarice, but then Clarice had gotten married; then she had tried Bill and someone else and the someone else had gotten married, and so on. Soon she forgot she had been made vaguely restless over the fact that Bill was single.

One night in the winter of 1924, after a dinner party the Wests had given in 55th Street for a film tycoon named Winikus, they all found themselves seated at a huge table at the Silver Slipper, a Broadway nightclub whose partners included Arnold Goff and Frankie Marlowe. Irene had tried to raise objections about going there because she knew it made Edward uncomfortable, but there was no getting out of it. Mrs. Winikus was fascinated by gangsters. The main problem was how to seat sixteen people in the most popular nightclub in the city at midnight on a Saturday. And they were the hosts. People made telephone calls to all sorts of other people in some very odd places but to no avail. Edward, seeing that Irene was becoming distressed at her guests' disappointment, said to Willie, "You knew some of those people, didn't you, Bill?" Tobin said he did. He went to the telephone and called Arnold Goff at Lindy's.

"Arnold, I'm sorry to bother you."

"Any time, Bill."

"I find myself in one of those things."

"Anything."

"I'm with Ed West and his wife and about fourteen other people and they all want to sit ringside at the Silver Slipper."

"I'll handle it personally. Don't even bother to call me back. When will you be there?"

"Forty-five minutes?"

"Plenty of time. Fine."

They were seated at ringside center and Tobin was regarded with awe by Irene and Mrs. Winikus—Irene because she had had no idea that Willie could be so effective and Mrs. Winikus because she wondered if possibly Willie could be one of those "underworld higher-ups" people always seemed to be talking about in her husband's pictures, who, of course, she knew did not really exist. Irene was at one end of the table, Mrs. Winikus was at her left, facing the dance floor. Bill was on her right. "Do you know any gangsters?" Mrs. Winikus asked him in a careful, low voice.

"I suppose everyone knows a gangster or two," Willie said.

"Well, I don't. Not outside the film business, that is. In fact, you're the only one I know who does."

Irene was very pleased that her guest of honor was so entertained so she said, "Which ones are the gangsters, Bill?"

"If I remember my *American Weekly*," Mrs. Winikus said, "that lumpy man in the corner is a terrible killer."

"Which one?" Irene's eyes peered through the heavy tobacco smoke. It was very difficult to see or to breathe. The music was very loud and the waiters kept bumping into everything. "I can't see a thing, dammit. What's his name? I may remember him from the newspapers."

"I *think* it's Frenchy Marton."

"Oh, dammit! He's notorious!" She kept looking, focusing on closer tables. "Bill, who is the man with the terribly hard black eyes and the chalk-white face? Over there, at the table with the two men who seem to be smoking the same cigar?"

Willie turned in his chair to look where she was indicating. "Uh—oh. That's Arnold Goff."

"No!" Mrs. Winikus said incredulously.

"The sportsman?" Irene asked.

"Sportsman!" Mrs. Winikus snorted the word.

"The—uh—gambler," Willie said.

"He has fixed everything there is to bet on, and he certainly looks like he takes dope," Mrs. Winikus said.

"Oh, I suppose these people take dope on crackers,"

Irene said. *"I* read somewhere that they call Mr. Goff 'Mr. Underworld.' Isn't this thrilling, Jane? We are embedded in gangsters. Do you know him, Bill?"

"Well, yes. That is, I've met him." Reflexively, he looked down the table to where Edward was lighting someone's cigarette. Tobin felt extremely important, which was extremely rare for him. Important in Irene's eyes. He thought, if this is what happens when she hears I know Arnold Goff, whatever would she do if I introduced her to Pal Al, the people's darling, Capone?

Irene's interest, somewhat reluctant, was the polite response she felt it proper to show, just as, in a drawing room, where the hostess has said casually that she and Chandler have just acquired Rembrandt's "The Night Watch," would she like to see it? Irene would have had to show great interest, not because she was all that wild about Rembrandt but because it would mean so much to her hostess. Here was old Bill positively alight with all this new-found attention, and here was one of her guests of honor enjoying every second of everything she thought was happening around them, so Irene decided she would have to pretend that Arnold Goff was Rembrandt's "The Night Watch."

"Do you know him well enough to invite him to join us, Bill?"

"Why, yes, as a matter of fact. Goff was the chap I called to get this table."

"Then do ask him to come over, and please get him to bring his dreadfully sinister friends."

"Oh, my God," Mrs. Winikus said, "I can't *stand* it!"

Bill got up and made his slender, elegant way through the mire of yacking, yelling yahoos just as one of the men at Goff's table slipped off into the smoke.

"Everything okay?" Goff asked Tobin.

"Couldn't be better."

"Meet Herm 'Hot Horse' Levin, a great handicapper and a prime manufacturer of twenty-nine-ninety-fives, in case you have a friend you'd like to outfit in a few classy dresses at wholesale."

"Any time," Levin said.

"This is Mr. William Tobin," Goff told him.

"I came over to invite you fellows to join our little party," Bill said.

"Has anybody consulted Mr. West on that?"

"I am here as courier from Mrs. West."

"Oh. Well, who can say no to that? Right, Herm?"

"Anything you say, Arn."

The three men struggled back to the West party and Tobin made the introductions at Irene's end of the table. The others were unreachable back in the thick murk.

That night, as they were preparing for bed, Edward said, "Why was that cheap gambler sitting at my table tonight? How did he get there?"

"*Cheap* gambler? Mrs. Winikus said he had arranged for the only crooked World Series ever played. And he seemed a very nice man."

"I asked you: How did he get there?"

"I asked Bill to bring him over."

"How did you know Tobin knew him?"

"He told me. Jane had pointed out this notorious gang-leader, Frenchy Marton, who was actually too far away for anyone to see, then I saw Mr. Goff and for something to say because Jane was so fascinated, I asked Bill who that was, then one thing led to another, then Bill, who just does things because he's so *sweet,* said it was Mr. Goff whom he had called to get the table, so I asked him to ask Mr. Goff and Mr. Levin to join our table. We thought Mr. Levin was some heinous gangster, but he turned out to be a dress manufacturer, which I thought was *very* amusing."

"Irene, never do that again."

"But what was wrong?"

"This is what was wrong. Those places are nothing but low marketplaces and——"

"But they're marketplaces for everyone. All the men at our table tonight were doing business *except* Bill. The most sinister thing that happened was that Mr. Levin gave me his card and made a mysterious mark at the corner of it that means, he told me, that I will get the real wholesale price if I buy dresses at his place."

"Irene, Arnold Goff is about as low a specimen of human life as anyone can find anywhere. He is a suborner, probably a murderer, a cheat, a fence and a narcotics peddler and a few dozen other rotten things. He lives in a state of multiple mortal sin and if I were asked to name the lowest living American I would unhesitatingly name Arnold Goff. Now do you see what was wrong?"

"Yes, dear."

"But it was not your fault, Irene, it was Tobin's fault."

"No."

"I'll see him tomorrow morning."

"Edward, I said no. Bill is a gentleman who saw that Jane and I were hopelessly, childishly diverted by all the goings-on at the Silver Slipper nightclub, and he did what he did because I asked him and because he is gallant."

"Well, he won't do it again."

"Edward, when I make a mistake I have a right to the blame. I will not share the blame. You simply have to promise me you won't mention this to Bill."

"All right, goddammit."

"Edward! I don't think that taking the name of the Lord in vain makes you very much better than your estimate of Mr. Goff."

"Aaaarrrgggghhhh!" He kicked a wastebasket across the room.

CHAPTER FIFTEEN

The year 1928 opened well. Transfers to the Horizons A.G. account in Zurich had averaged out at a steady $25,917,154.-19 weekly for 1927, to be reinvested as foreign capital in the booming stock markets in Europe and the States. The liquor industry had stabilized well. The organizational shape-up of fewer and fewer small gangs in the national market areas and more and more large outfits had continued nicely and desirably. They were well into Phase Four, the national return to American distilleries. The country was prosperous, and this had meant a sharp increase in the public consumption of entertainment, gambling, narcotics and vice. The demands for the excitement of it all had helped shylocking and had expanded extortion activities and labor organization. Sickeningly, the Bolsheviks had seemed to gain a strong foothold in Soviet Russia, but Edward's European informants said this could not last, while that goddam Willie Tobin kept bringing in what he called "proof" that communism was not only permanently established in Russia but that the Russian government was determined to send it on the march to overthrow the United States. Tobin was like some babbling schoolgirl about it. He kept insisting that his "information" showed that Edward Courance West was not only a prime target but a *lever* and that they had many secret agents trying to get "information" that would "expose" Edward Courance West. He refused to believe it, but it made him sick, nonetheless. It could not be true, but if it were true, he would fight them as they had never been fought in their rotten lives.

If organized labor was a tremendously profitable business, it was also the key mass in American life where the Bolsheviki would attempt to strike, and he kept his finger on labor's pulse and had specialists, such as Louis Buchalter and Jacob Shapiro, and hundreds of their lieutenants throughout the labor movement report to Bill Tobin the slightest evidence of Communist infiltration, which, God damn them, was where Tobin was compiling the most revolutionary information on Soviet plans any agency, official or otherwise, had ever seen. The government had nothing like it. The President was a child in Communist affairs. Let them get their own information. He would sit and sift and judge what his people were constantly ferreting out and when the time came to act he would act. The certain point was that there did not seem to be any immediate danger. As America continued to grow, as the market continued to rise, as the people grew wealthier and more secure, the Communist conspiracy did not have a chance.

The year 1927 had been a record-breaker for everyone and it seemed that there was no stopping it. He had acquired a substantial interest in sixty-seven companies and sat on the boards of fifty-four of these. However, it had not been a good year entirely. Don Vito Cascio Ferro had died in Palermo's Ucciardone prison. He had been arrested in 1927 by Mussolini's police prefect, Cesare Mori, on a trumped-up charge of smuggling. He had ignored the court during his trial, much as if he had been sitting in his own flower-lined patio overlooking the bay. When his lawyer had appeared to be pleading for leniency, Don Vito gratingly had admonished him for speaking "in conflict with my principles and my authority." He was permitted to address the court before it sentenced him. He spoke briefly and disdainfully to the judges. "As you have been unable to obtain proof of any of my numerous crimes, you have been reduced to condemning me for the only one I have never committed. May God have mercy on you." Don Calogero Vizzini succeeded Don Vito. He was cordial and most helpful to Congressman Rei when the banker arrived in Palermo in the late spring to pay his last respects at the grave.

The anxiety over the Soviet threat (which could not be

coped with tangibly enough) and the pressures of work, travel, decisions and public appearances (four honorary degrees in 1927) were all taxing, and Edward had to release the tension somehow. In March 1928, Rhonda Healey called Tobin at his new sixteen-room apartment at 64th and Fifth Avenue, where a clever architect had managed to use twelve hundred and eighteen square feet for closet space, to say that Eddie had beaten up one of her girls so badly that the girl was in critical condition at the Midtown Hospital and that she was afraid, when she regained consciousness, her brothers were going to force her to tell where it had happened and who had done it to her and that the worst kind of trouble could develop. Tobin hurried to the hospital.

The girl had a fractured skull, a broken jaw, multiple fractures of the right arm and seven badly splintered ribs that had edged her over into pneumonia. She was on the hospital's critical list. It was a simple matter to hold off the police investigation, but her family were waiting—in the hospital—in a near hysterical state. Did Mr. Tobin wish to talk to them? He thanked the doctors, but he said that meeting would have to wait for the moment. He paid a nurse a relatively large sum to sedate the three brothers without their knowledge, and for their own good (and for the good of the hospital) because in their enraged grief they were approaching violence; this was managed with coffee and with milk. He left instructions as "lawyer for the patient" that no expense was to be spared for medical care. He telephoned Congressman Rei from the telephone facing the waiting room and the three leather-jacketed brothers. They were very large men who sat, red-eyed and despairing, bursting irrationally into questions at each other in loud voices. They were workingmen. He hoped they were teamsters or stevedores.

"Hello, Ben? Tobin. Fine. Yourself? Good. Ben, we have a little emergency here and, to tell the truth, I don't know exactly what kind of muscle is needed, but suffice to say, for the moment anyhow, one can't buy one's way out of this particular contretemps. I'm at the Midtown Hospital in New York. Yes. That would be marvelous. Suppose you ask him to ask for me at Manny Wolfe's at the corner of Forty-ninth and Third? Fine. I'll be at the bar. Thank you,

Ben. And you can be sure this is very much a business call involving our peerless leader."

There was no change in the girl's condition when he left fifteen minutes later. The brothers were much calmer, however. In thirty-five minutes he saw the bartender nod in his direction and two men who introduced themselves as Al and Reggie Sciortino joined him. Willie explained the problem in vague terms, because that was not what they were there to discuss. "Suffice to say accidents are accidents, but the three brothers will not accept that it could be an accident. And the point is if they started backtracking to the girl's employer and making a lot of noisy trouble there, if they began to beat up on one of the girl's coworkers and got some kind of an idea of who had caused the accident, that would all be pointless. They are very large, very strong, very violent, agitated men and they have to be discouraged."

"If we get them outta the hospital, there ain't nothing to it. Was the broad a hooker?"

"Yes."

"You the mout'piece for the operation?"

"Did anyone tell you to ask me any questions? Do I have to make the same phone call all over again?"

The other man touched his forearm. "He's only human. Forget it."

"I'm genuinely sorry," the first man said.

"I have no idea how these things are done," Willie sniffed. "The girl's name is Carmela Palermitano, and her brothers are in the fifth-floor waiting room."

"Okay, fine. We'll handle it," the older brother affirmed. "You want them hit?"

"The point is this: They have to be completely discouraged from persisting in following up the idea of who caused this accident. If you can talk to them and discourage them, that would be fine. If you have to beat them to discourage them—well, they have to take their chances with the rest of us." Willie was losing patience.

"But if they won't listen?"

"As I said, quite distinctly, Mr. Sciortino, they have to be discouraged. What you have to do to discourage them is your job."

Carmela was able to see him, with Rhonda Healey, in

five days. The brothers were no longer at the hospital. Rhonda introduced Willie as her lawyer. Carmela said she had a bad headache but otherwise everything was okay.

"Every job has its on-the-job problems, Miss Palermitano," Willie said.

"Yeah," Carmela answered.

"But, on the other hand, every cloud has a silver lining."

"Yeah?"

"I want you to take this little check—it's for fifteen hundred dollars—and I want you to sign this little paper—one of those formalities—"

"It's okay, Rhond?" Carmela asked.

"Baby, how can you lose? He's also paying all expenses."

Carmela signed the paper. Then she looked at the check. "Gee, thanks, mister."

"Enjoy your rest here," Willie told her with kind interest. "Order whatever you want, and if you feel like having your hair done every day, just pick up that phone and order it."

Carmela smiled gratefully. "First I got to get this plaster cast offa my head," she said.

Danny West was fourteen years old and in his freshman year at Gelbart, to which his mother had agreed to send him with much trepidation because it was a "mixed" school, i.e., Protestants were allowed to attend. Irene was driven to see him once every week and obeyed his instructions meekly not to enter the school grounds more often than once a month. They met at the back of an ice cream parlor in town.

That March, after she had returned from her regular weekly visit, Irene found a letter waiting at the 55th Street house. It was typewritten. It said: "Dear Mrs. West: It is time you knew you were married to a pervert who beats and tortures prostitutes for his pleasure. He has nearly killed a prostitute named Carmela Palermitano. She is now in serious condition at the Midtown Hospital in New York, quite near your house, suffering from multiple fractures. Very truly yours, A Friend."

That night she and Edward dined alone and she told him about the letter, saying it was insane and frightening.

"Let me see it," Edward said.

He read the letter. He folded it and put it in his wallet. "This is outrageous," he said. "This little letter is going to the postal authorities tomorrow."

"Can they trace it?"

"That remains to be seen. I am *very* upset about this. Irene, in the future I think it best that you do not touch any mail that comes for you. We may be able to keep the sender's fingerprints intact that way. That is to say, your fingers might smudge his prints."

"But, darling, the mailman will have handled it and heaven knows how many people at the post office."

"That is true. Well, I can only say that this is a rotten, desperate thing to do to a man and his wife—as fruitless a gesture as it is."

The next day West had Willie transfer the Palermitano girl from the Midtown to a good, small hospital in Brooklyn so that she would be nearer her family. He leaned hard on the postal authorities to no avail. He retained the typewriter expert, Martin Tytell, but aside from Tytell's opinion that the message had "probably" been written on an old-fashioned Oliver machine having a circular keyboard and showing weak stems on the *t*, the *f* and the *j*, there was no clue to the identity of the sender.

"This could be a Communist trick, you know," Willie said.

"How?" Edward shot the question.

Willie shrugged. "They have to break you. If they can get at you through Irene—if they could smash your marriage—"

Edward said, "I won't accept that theory yet, but I most certainly will not rule it out."

In April the second terrible disaster of the year fell upon the Wests when Walter Wagstaff and Clarice were lost at sea in a storm off Palm Beach. Their deserted sloop went aground below Daytona. No trace of them was found. Edward chartered a Ford Trimotor and he and Irene flew to the scene, where Edward took personal charge. Both the Navy Air Arm and the Coast Guard did everything they could. At last they gave up hope, and Irene asked Bishop Nolan to sail with them out into the deep water all along the coast, where he consecrated the ocean and asked for the Lord's mercy on their souls.

Irene was distraught. She couldn't bring herself to leave her father's house so soon. She was shockingly grieved and shocked to see that death could possibly come so unexpectedly to a woman as religious as she. She kept thinking, too, that if Danny hadn't been at school for his first time away from home, she and Edward would have gone to Palm Beach with Clarice and Daddy and would have been aboard that sloop with them and Danny would have been an orphan boy.

After a week of hopeless searching, Edward simply had to get back to his duties at the bank, but Irene pleaded to remain at Palm Beach. He went to New York without her. She returned without announcement three weeks later, tired and weak, and found a typewritten letter waiting for her on the silver tray in the hall at West Wagstaff. It was a registered letter, so it had been separated from the mountain of messages of commiseration.

"Dear Mrs. West:

It was too bad you did not follow up the information concerning your husband's brutal abuse of the prostitute Carmela Palermitano. I have enclosed in this envelope a key to the apartment of Miss Alouette Tazin (the only such name in the telephone directory), who lives on Park Avenue in a flat that is paid for by your husband, who visits her on Monday, Wednesday and Friday afternoons between five and seven o'clock. See for yourself. Use this key. However, you may choose not to believe me again. Therefore, why not visit the prostitute Carmela Palermitano at the Sante Croce Nursing Home at 1192 Smitter Street, Brooklyn. Ask her who mutilated her. With all my best, I am, Sincerely yours, A Friend."

Irene telephoned Edward at the bank. He was not there. It was a Wednesday afternoon. She fought sin. She fought fear and faithlessness. She locked herself in her sitting room and knelt to pray. She prayed that this overwhelming temptation to evil would depart from her. She prayed for forgiveness for betraying Edward, though loving him as much as she did, by believing what a poison-pen letter, already once denied, told her. She could not win over herself. She telephoned the Sante Croce Nursing Home in Brooklyn. She asked if Miss Carmela Palermitano was a patient there. She was. She telephoned the Midtown Hospital. She asked for the records division and inquired if they had recently treated a patient named Carmela Palermitano. They had.

Irene had herself driven to the nursing home. It was twenty minutes to six when she got there. Miss Palermitano was wearing a stiff white casque. Her right arm lay straight along her side, fat and ridged with white plaster from her wrist to her elbow. Her face was pale and there were black rings under her eyes. She didn't speak when Irene came into the room, as she pulled up a chair beside the bed and sat so that her eyes were at the level of Carmela's eyes.

"I've come from Edward West," she said.

"How is he?"

"He—is—fine."

"I'm gladda see you. Evvey time somebody comes from Eddie West I make a little more money. I have nothing but troubles since he put me in here, believe me. I got a brother who was knocked off. My mother . . . my mother went to bed, she won't get out. As far as I'm concerned, the whole thing started with Eddie West."

Irene closed her eyes, and it took all her strength to open them again. "Do you hate him?"

"Why should I hate him? That's what he does—he can't help it. He's like a queer or something. He paid me. I knew what he liked. What the hell?" They sat silently, then Carmela began to put two and two together. "You his wife, honey?"

Irene nodded.

"Then you got a real problem, lady," the sad-eyed patient said.

Irene sent the car away. She walked. Later it began to rain so she went into a movie house. When they stopped showing, it was a quarter to twelve. She walked. The street clock above a jeweler's said twenty-five to two. She got in a cab and asked the driver to take her to a hotel. "What kinda hotel?" he asked.

She sat for a moment to try to think of a hotel. "The Ritz. On Madison," she said.

"In Manhattan?" the driver asked incredulously.

The clock in the hotel lobby said twenty after two. She paid for the room for two days in advance. When she awoke the sun was shining. Her wrist watch said one-twenty. She remembered what Edward liked to do to women. She dressed and walked to St. Patrick's and gathered peace in the dimness. Then she went back to the hotel. The hotel clock said five minutes to seven. She went to bed. She awoke at four-twenty the next morning, got dressed and went walking. She ate lunch at 96th and Broadway, surprised at her appetite. At two o'clock she went into the beauty salon. At four o'clock she changed her clothes at the 55th Street house, dressing with care until she was satisfied with how she looked, then she rode up Park Avenue in a taxi. Half-way there she began to pound heavily on the seat of the cab. "Hey, lady," the driver said, "watch that seat. I'm an independent."

She pushed the doorbell and heard it ring clearly inside the flat. No one answered. She took the key out of her purse and opened the door. She did not try to walk softly. She moved toward the guttural gasping sounds that were leaking from the room directly ahead of her. Then a shrill woman's voice cried out, "Oh, my God! Oh, my God!" Irene opened the door. Edward's naked body was lax above a mass of arms and legs and hair. Irene pulled a chair beside the bed and sat as she had at the Sante Croce Hospital, her eyes almost on a level with the closed eyes of a gasping slack-jawed girl. The girl's eyes opened. "Jesus Christ!" the girl said. Irene fell to her knees beside the bed—her eyes level with the girl's eyes, level with Edward's eyes as his head turned—and weeping silently, began to recite the act of contrition aloud, her hands clasped in front of her. Edward spun his body like a log, rolling away from her off the bed, half falling on the floor. Somehow he scooped up his underwear, shirt, trousers and one shoe and bolted out of the room.

"What the hell is this?" said the shocked girl. "How the hell did you get in here, fahcrissake?" Irene's fingers disengaged themselves from each other and took an iron grip on the girl's wrist, pinning her down while she continued the prayer and then concluded with "Hail, Mary, full of grace—." The confused, naked girl lay there and struggled to get free, her breasts moving violently from side to side like one-eyed spectators at a very fast tennis game. Then she gave up the struggle. She closed her eyes tightly and gritted her teeth against the humiliation. Then she spoke urgently. "Baby, listen. I got to douche. I mean I'll be in trouble if I don't." Irene stopped praying and stared. "No kidding," the girl said. "This is serious. I'm a very fertile chick."

Irene let go of the girl's arm. She stood up. The girl scuttled off the bed and ran out of the room. Irene followed her slowly. She passed the girl, who was knocking persistently on a door. "Eddie, open up. It's me. Eddie! Open up! I got to douche!" Irene ran out of the apartment.

CHAPTER SIXTEEN

Eddie was on the phone to Tobin. The girl said "Gee, I'm sorry, Eddie."

"It's not your fault, Alouette," he said grimly. Into the phone he said, "Willie? Be at the Palm Court at the Plaza in thirty minutes." He hung up. "I'm going to send you a little check by messenger, Alouette. It will be here by noon. Can you be packed and out of here by five tomorrow?"

"But, honey, what's the difference? She knows. I mean, why should we quit?"

"Read the check I'm going to send, then get out of here by five. Okay?"

"Where'll I go?"

"Try Hollywood. You'll do great in Hollywood."

"Honey, I don't know anybody in Hollywood."

"I'll send you train tickets and a letter of introduction with the check. Okay?"

She shrugged. "Okay. Listen, who knows? I might make a great little actress."

Willie was waiting when he got to the Plaza. He had ordered a bottle of ginger ale and two glasses. He told Edward that Carmela Palermitano had called him to say that Irene had been to see her in the hospital. Edward sent Willie to get to West Wagstaff as quickly as he could and told him to get a police escort to make sure. "Irene likes you. She trusts you. If you can get her talking, you might just save her from making a terrible mistake." Edward's back-chamber Gelbart accent had gotten thicker with the emotional strain.

Irene got to West Wagstaff after Willie arrived there. She
had been talking with a priest, who had said that she must
continue to live with Edward because marriage was forever. She wanted to talk to the cardinal. She said it didn't
seem possible that any intelligent, humane religion would
force her to allow herself to crumble into ashes to be scattered over the ice of their feelings so that Edward wouldn't
slip. "But what can I do, Willie? I have this sense of duty
and this contract to respond positively. Is all that merely
a substitute for what passes for thinking with atheists?"

Tobin was helpful just by listening. She was able to push
out some of the shock and shame and the crippling pain of
betrayal that had come to her as quickly as a train wheel
comes to the leg that it severs on the track. At the end she
said she would agree to meet with Edward if there was only
the two of them and if Edward was prepared to listen to her
ultimatum.

They met at the seal pool in Central Park at eleven o'clock
in the morning two days later. Willie was able to watch them
from above as they greeted each other stiffly, as they walked
slowly and awkwardly around and around the circular pond.

". . . I have even talked to the cardinal, who says exactly
what Father Corkery says. But I cannot. Perhaps a year
from now. Do you know what those letters called you, Edward? And they were accurate. A pervert. You paid a
woman to beat her, and you almost killed her by beating her
for your sexual—sick, insane emotional—pleasure. I might
have been able to adjust to infidelity. But that isn't any form
of love."

He was ready. "Would I beat a woman? You know me.
Would I beat a woman for such reasons? Have you inquired
what she had done to me, Irene? Have I ever as much as
raised my voice to you? She inflicted the most incredible
and unexpected pain on my—on me, and I struck out reflexively. She fell. She hurt me, but almost entirely she hurt
herself."

"No."

"How else could it be?"

"I have been to see her three times at the hospital. She

is mentally retarded. She can respond only to money. I paid her. We talked."

"You paid her and she told you what she thought you wanted to hear. That is her work!"

"No. She explained that there were quite a few girls who wanted to turn lump tricks, as they are called in your milieu, because you were known to pay so very well. She sees nothing wrong in it. She said that was the way you liked to make love. She was being very considerate of you, she thought."

"You'll have to believe her or me. A whore or the man you've lived with for fifteen years."

"I believe her."

"Then why are we here? Why are we talking?"

"Because we have a son. And because we are Catholics. I tell myself that if you were an alcoholic or a paralytic I would stay with you and love you and that, in those terms this—this *disease* you have—" She had to turn away from him and pretend to watch the seals for a while.

He said, "I will put myself in the hands of a psychiatrist."

"Will you?"

"Immediately."

"Are you ready to tell a man all the secrets of your life, all the terrible things you have done somewhere that have brought you to the need to maim women with your fists?"

"What do you mean?"

"Edward, do you have any conception of what psychiatric treatment is? A doctor has to know everything so that he can help you."

"I have nothing to hide."

"Oh, Edward, Edward," she sobbed.

"Has anyone—I mean beyond those letters—has anyone even suggested that I could have anything to hide?"

"I think it is I who must go to a psychiatrist. I have the habit, but I will not continue the habit with a priest. I *told* him what you had done and he insisted that my place was with you."

"The Lord moves in mysterious ways, Irene." He tried to take her hand, but she pulled it away with a gasp of fright, as if it were the touch of a leper. "We've got to give all this a chance to heal, Irene," he pleaded.

But he had been warned. He would not go near any psychiatrist. They had designed all of this to box him in, to force him to walk toward the converging lines of the triangle, where they would have their psychiatrist waiting to pump him of every shred of information, preserving all of it in his own voice on recordings so that they could expose him on the national networks and, by pulling him down, bring communism to America.

"Why don't you beat *me*?" she said in a broken voice that was loud enough and so hopelessly entreating that it startled people at the railing ten feet away, who turned to stare with shock. Edward reversed their course, holding her elbow, walking them away from the seal pond. She let herself be led. "The difference between you and me is that if I had known that you had to beat a woman, I would have urged you to beat me. You would have accepted that as a fair, a safer offer. But if I had needed to beat someone almost to death, it would not occur to you to ask me to beat you. But that was four days ago. I understand you now. I can see that you want to be beaten and I shall beat you. Not with my hands, not with a club—I'm not strong enough to please you—"

"Irene, don't talk like this! You'll make yourself ill."

"You had better listen to me, Edward, because I am going to hurt you more than you have hurt all those poor little whores in the darkness of your life." They stopped walking. There was no one near them for many yards around. "I remember somebody you told me was the lowest slime alive. Do you remember that?"

"Now, please, Irene—"

"I am going to find him. And I am going to be with him everywhere that people gather to hate each other in this rotten city." She was entirely unpracticed in hitting people, so she did it badly, even gracelessly. She pulled her right hand far back and looped it in a long arc and crashed her palm into his face.

It excited Willie Tobin more than he had ever been excited as he watched them through binoculars from his Fifth Avenue window.

CHAPTER SEVENTEEN

Food made her ill. She forced herself to get out of the house. She walked four miles every day. She had an electric bicycle sent from Abercrombie's. She volunteered for work at the Great Neck Hospital, and she stopped going to church because prayer had the effect of driving her back into herself. The exercise helped her appetite. The hospital got her mind engaged. After five weeks she noticed that the detectives Edward had assigned to watch her movements had gone away. He must have decided that she would remain in seclusion at West Wagstaff and had put aside her threat to humiliate him.

Edward telephoned many times, but she hung up when she heard his voice. He came to the house several times, but she would not see him and had the locks changed on the doors. Danny was at summer camp because he had said all the other boys would be there and he just couldn't afford to be left out. As the end of the camp season came around she decided she would call for him there and they would drive up to Canada for a few weeks. Then he could go directly to school and wouldn't have to come home to that empty house until she had become more used to it herself. He probably wouldn't even mention his father, because normally they met only about two times each year, and the boy wouldn't be likely to miss him.

The house gave her solace. It helped her to remember what "transitory" meant. The house would go on and on for centuries after she and Edward had escaped each other in death.

But the long Canadian visit with Danny changed everything. Totally. All the strength of her terrible resolve left her. He made her see her selfishness. This trundling from camp to school to camp couldn't go on. Let attendance at the Gelbart Academy be Edward's illusion, and let him have the chance to see his son and live with him. Thanksgiving Day would be there soon. Danny would be home. She would have to try explaining the inexplicable. She had to practice now seeing Edward as a *guest* in the house—her house—not as a stranger but as a person removed from her feelings and entitled to her best courtesy. She must work at this until a habit formed and until a hard shell grew over the habit. Everything had changed. She had to make her peace with the fact that life never had been meant to be what it had been before. Change was the only consistency. Change was a masquerade. Some change seemed cruel, some even brutal. Some changes were sweet and most changes invisible, but there was only change from nothing into the human form— from nothing to life, then to death, then from death the change underwent its own change.

Edward had changed. If he had died she would not have sat beside his corpse for years, but in this change he had died for her and yet she would not leave his corpse.

She called Bill Tobin and asked him to drive out for dinner. She talked it all over with him. He was more helpful and understanding than the priests had ever been. He saw clearly why she must accept the essence of change and open the doors of her house to Edward again, forgetting conceits and the tyranny of regulating his life if he were to be allowed to stay. Either he had been sick and was now cured by their joint experience—just as she had been cured of her innocence—or he was still sick. If he was sick she and his son had to help him. She would take Danny out of that damned school and send him to the school down the road where they could see Edward together every day.

She would have called Edward the day she decided all that, but it was a Thursday. Monday would be the first day of a new month. The letter arrived on Saturday morning, typed on the same defective typewriter. She opened it casually, because she knew that nothing like this could touch her any more. He had done the worst and it was over, no matter what this note would say.

The letter said that Edward owned eight of the principal brothels in New York, three of the largest gambling houses, that his long tenure as a leader of the prohibition movement had been criminally insincere, because he had been active in that movement only in order to profit from the criminal organizations he controlled throughout the United States. Had she read about Owney Madden, Legs Diamond, the Purple Gang, Al Capone, Little Augie Orgen, Egan's Rats? They worked for her husband. "All these are startling allegations," the letter said, "and most certainly require substantiation. Therefore, if you will show this letter to William Tobin, executive vice-president of Horizons A.G., with offices in the West National Bank Building, your husband's employee in charge of illegal liquor procurement, and to Arnold Goff, Park Central Hotel, Seventh Avenue at 58th Street, New York, your husband's employee in charge of all underworld financing, you will learn that this letter is accurate and true. Sincerely, A Friend."

She remembered the Silver Slipper and Goff, and Edward's frightened reaction to Goff, and Bill's telephone call to Goff to book the table. Irene solved the newest rats' maze by getting pneumonia.

Time became a blur. Edward and Danny and priests were there. She thought she had spent time with Clarice and wept when she came out of the fever and remembered she would never see Clarice again. One afternoon Bill was beside the bed. She had been asleep. She opened her eyes and he was there with such pathetic sadness in his face that it seemed as splintered as a broken mirror.

"Bill?"

"Irene!"

"What does Horizons do?"

"We are a Swiss company."

"What kind of a company?"

"A holding company."

"Do you control gangsters?"

"Irene!"

"Do you?"

"I don't understand the question. You've been very ill. You've been delirious. Do you know how long you've been here?"

"No."

"Five weeks. You almost died."

"I tried to die."

"Irene. Please, no." His face had fallen into shards again. She realized then what had happened to him. He was in love with her. She compressed time so that she could feel the past. Yes. He had always been in love with her. She must not torture him any more. She went to sleep.

She returned from Arizona in April. She was very thin and very brown. She looked very, very fit but quite dead. The outside was flawless and there was no inside. She let the house at West Wagstaff run into her emptiness for two days, then she called Arnold Goff.

"Mr. Goff, this is Irene West. Do you remember me? Edward West's wife?"

"I most certainly do." He had been weighing heroin on a jeweler's scale with three wholesalers with whom he was about to close. He could not turn his back on the three men, not with nine kilos of heroin on the table, yet he could not have them see his shock, so he relied on moulinage, the process whereby the raw silk becomes processed silk and reels itself around the bobbin.

"I called to ask if you would give me a card to your friend, that darling Mr. Levin. I would adore to get some of his clothes at the true wholesale prices."

Goff was almost unmanned until he realized what had come over her. She was bored with her husband and had gone gangster-happy. She was in that wicked, romantic-pirate stage of fifty other women whom he had allowed to take him into their beds, and he was possessed concomitantly with the keenest pleasure at the thought of surrendering to E. C. West's wife. He thought of Bella. He thought of five million dollars worth of Liberty bonds. He thought of Joe Masseria and Frankie Yale and Frankie Marlowe.

"Mrs. West, *nothing* would give me more pleasure. Shall we meet at one at Moriarity's tomorrow?"

"That would be simply *wonderful*, Mr. Goff."

"Please call me Arnold."

"If you'll call me Irene."

Jane Winikus told Edward that she had seen Irene lunching with Arnold Goff at Moriarity's. He told her she must be mistaken. She replied that she had thought she must be mistaken herself, so she had stopped by the table and had spoken with them. She had called Edward because someone else who hadn't talked to Irene might have called him, and she wanted to be sure that he knew that the lunch was entirely innocent. Mr. Goff was going to take Irene to Levin's Covered Buttons & Sequins Dresses Inc. to buy clothes wholesale, and every woman enjoyed buying clothes at wholesale once in a while.

West put watchers on Irene for the second time, but it would take a sandstorm to hide a tail out in the country.

Propinquity is a reliable aphrodisiac. Goff became so absorbed in getting Mrs. Edward Courance West into bed in order to have it on her husband that he convinced himself she was the most desirable woman he had ever seen. But the more he pressed forward to climb her thighs the further she retreated. Irene became intensely aware of her extraordinary desirability, and it thrilled her so fulfillingly that she began to feel dizziness about this man who could find her so desirable. She could taste lust at the back of her throat. She could feel talons digging into the floor of her stomach. But if she got into bed with him before she found out what she had to know, she was afraid he would fall slackly out the other side, a free man. She had to keep a lock on him, but, in a manner that she had never felt before in her life, she had to have a man soon—any man, anywhere.

After three weeks in which Irene and Goff had been seeing each other five and six times a week at race tracks, in nightclubs until dawn with gunmen and con men, West sent for Goff even though in four more days they would have been having their regular quarterly business meeting.

"What are you trying to do?"

"With your wife, you mean?"

"Answer me!"

"I am trying to screw her."

West started involuntarily out of his chair, but he caught himself. He settled back, trembling. "Have you forgotten Joe Masseria?"

"You did that once, West. You can't make it stick now. All I care about is screwing your wife. And the crazy thing is I am so crazy about her that I can sense a lot of things about her and one of them is that you can't even understand what it is I feel about her because you never felt it yourself."

West looked like death, death that was dying and death that brings death. At last he spoke. "I love her. Can you say that?"

"I think I probably loved Bella the way you think you love your wife. But if that's all it is, then nobody would have had any kids from the beginning. I mean I don't want to live without your wife, and if she doesn't want me, then go ahead and have me killed and do me a big favor. You go right ahead and tell how you love her. That's how I feel about her."

"I may do you that favor."

"That's fine. Good. That's the best way. No horseshit. Whoever wants her the most gets to keep her." He stared at West contemptuously. "You're just another hoodlum to me, E.C. I've seen a thousand of 'em. And hear me, pal. You aren't the only one who can hire a gun. And let me tell you something else before you remind me how you made my fortune. I have enough on you in my files at the hotel to blow up this whole nice, big bank you have here. And I happen to have figured out exactly how to use it."

A spear went through West with enormous force, pinning him to his smothering fear. Goff was the Communist plant! Here was the enemy out in the open! With a controlled effort West pulled the invisible garments of the Mafia over himself. He became the restrained, quiet-spoken man of respect.

"There is nothing else to say, Arnold. Get out."

Goff got up. He walked across the room toward the door, then turned. "Actually there is something else to say. I don't want you to think I am altogether a heel."

"What is it?"

Goff began to laugh. Whatever he was going to say was giving him such enormous pleasure that he might not even be able to say it. "I don't want you to think——" He had to hold his side with one pressing hand while he laughed uncontrollably. "I don't want you to think I'd tell Bella Radin what we talked about today." He opened the door and tottered out of the room. The door closed behind him, but West could hear his laughter ringing and receding as he walked away.

West talked to Tobin on the direct line and told him to come right down.

"Arnold Goff is your Commie rat, Willie. He's been keeping a thirteen-year-old file on me at his hotel."

"He said that?"

"Get him out of the hotel tonight for as long as possible. Call Rei and have him find you a locks-and-safes man. Comb those files tonight. I want everything out of there. Take them to Fifty-fifth Street, and we'll burn them in the fireplace."

Tobin had Rhonda Healey write a letter to Goff on a sheet of Irene's West Wagstaff notepaper and had her sign "Irene." He took the letter to the Park Central Hotel and gave it to the bell captain with a dollar bill to be taken up to Goff's apartment. Tobin sat in the lobby facing the elevator bank, screened by moving people. It was twenty minutes to seven.

When Goff came out of the elevator he wasn't looking for anything in the lobby. He moved jerkily toward the Seventh Avenue exit. Tobin followed him, and through the window of the florist's shop he watched him get into his car. Then Tobin went to a telephone booth and called the house on 55th Street. West answered at once. "Goff just left for West Wagstaff," Tobin said into the telephone.

"West Wagstaff?" West was shocked.

"He was very excited, Ed."

"What time did he leave?"

"Just now. Maybe at a quarter to seven."

"Have you seen his files yet?"

"Not yet. I'll go up as soon as the expert gets here."

"Don't miss anything, Willie." West was working to stay calm—Tobin could almost hear him screaming at himself inside his head to stay calm. The telephone crashed into its cradle.

Tobin left the telephone booth and returned to the chair in the lobby. The specialist, Doc Yankel, arrived at seven-fifteen. He was a small, alert man of fifty who carried a doctor's satchel. He went to the bell captain, who directed him to Willie.

They walked sedately down the corridor on Goff's floor. "This is it," Willie said. The door had three locks. Doc Yankel peered at each lock, then selected keys from his

overcoat pocket and opened each in turn. They went in and
Willie bolted the door. Tobin looked in every room and
every closet and he pounded walls for hollow places but he
could find files only in ordinary filing cabinets in a walk-in
closet. Doc Yankel drank a celery tonic with his gloves on.
Willie asked him to open the files. Yankel tried five keys before he got the right one. "It takes a little longer," he said,
"but I think it's better than forcing." There were twelve file
drawers in all. Willie began by taking *A* to *F* out to the
table and started reading at seven-forty. He finished at ten
after ten. He filled his small suitcase with the papers that
mentioned West, Rei, Horizons or himself, but the papers
he left behind were hot enough to burn big holes in some
very big hoods and civilians in the country.

Doc Yankel locked the files and they left the flat, locking
the three locks securely behind them. Yankel left through
the 58th Street exit. Tobin went out to Seventh Avenue.

Irene almost ran into the living room, unable to believe
the servant had gotten the caller's name right. It was he. She
stood swaying at the raised entrance to the room, staring at
him with excitement. He was very pale. He was breathing
unevenly as though he had run to her. They walked toward
each other without speaking. Her arms went around his
neck. His hands slid over her. They kissed and her legs gave
way as though they had been turned to water. She crumpled
to the floor, pulling him down upon her as Edward smashed
a stone bench through the window far across the room.

They sat up like electrified puppets, eyes unblinking,
totally alarmed by tribal guilt. West climbed through the
window as the butler and the downstairs maid appeared
in the doorway. West spoke to the servants first. "I want
everyone out of this house and on the way to New York
within the half hour. Telephone the bank for instructions
tomorrow morning. If you are out of here and in the station
bus in a half hour you will receive a handsome bonus. If you
are not, you will have to sue me for back wages. Get out."

The two servants fled.

Edward rushed to Goff and pulled him to his feet to
knock him down again. He was wearing brass knuckles that
tore away a large piece of flesh from Goff's cheek. Irene
screamed and pulled at Edward, but he flung her away.

Goff kicked out from the floor, catching Edward in the chest, but he was badly dazed from being hit and he was ineffective. West pulled Goff up and began to beat him rhythmically, blood spattering everywhere. Irene lay on the floor. Her head had hit the corner of a fireplace and she was unconscious. When Goff was a mass of blood—face, hair and clothes—Edward dragged him up the three small steps to the main hall, across the hall, leaving solid tracks of blood on the white carpet, out the front door and across the graveled yard to Goff's car. He got into the car and backed it up, then drove it so that its cowl touched the building wall, pointing directly into the ruined living room through the smashed window. He sat the groggy Goff behind the wheel and made sure he was awake, then he went into the room through the open window to where Irene was whimpering and stirring. As Goff looked on hazily, Edward pulled Irene into a sitting position, then grabbed her bodice with his right hand and ripped the dress away from the front of her. He kept ripping and tearing until the front of her was naked. He dropped on top of her. When he had finished he stared down into her shocked, wild eyes. He spat into her face.

Goff and his car had gone. Irene pulled herself to her feet and put on Goff's topcoat. She ran out of the room, sobbing. Edward left the house unsteadily and walked slowly along the path to the garages. People were getting into the long airport buses that West Wagstaff used to transport the servants. Kershaw, the butler, came forward to steady him. "Everyone is out, sir," he said.

Edward nodded. "Send them into the city and have them put up at any hotel. You get one of the big cars out and roll it to the front of the house, then go into the hall and shout up the stairs to Mrs. West that it is you and that you have the car ready to drive her to New York."

"Very good, sir."

Edward called Willie at 55th Street from the estate office in the garage. "Did you get the files?"

"Yes. Everything."

"I want you to do two things."

"Yes, sir."

"I want Goff hit tonight. Call Rei. Goff will be back at his hotel within the hour. Then I want you to find a cement contractor and send him to West Wagstaff with triple crews."

"Eddie! Is Irene all right?"

"She's all right. I'm sending her into New York."

When Willie hung up he called West Wagstaff, Irene's private number, immediately. The phone rang for some time, but she answered. "Irene? Bill. Thank God I got you. Are you all right?" She began to sob softly. He said, "Has there been trouble?"

"Terrible. Terrible."

"Kershaw is going to drive you into New York. You must go to my place. Do you understand?"

"Yes." She hung up.

Rei was in New York at the Waldorf. Tobin reached him there just as he was going to bed and gave him Edward's message.

"That's a very important contract," Rei said in his reflective way. "You're absolutely sure there's no mistake?"

"I'm sure."

"I'll have to handle this myself. There's going to be one helluva big mess over this one."

Edward manhandled the four drums of gasoline onto the hand truck with the large buckets. He pushed the truck across the areaway from the garage to the main house laboriously. At the back door to the house he began to fill the buckets with gasoline. He could handle only two buckets at a time. He lined the floor of the small elevator with filled buckets, leaving just enough room for himself to stand, and rode with them to the third floor. He took them out, two at a time, and walked with them to the farthest of the servants' rooms. He sloshed the gasoline all over. He took the buckets from room to room and emptied them wildly until the top floor was saturated.

He rode down with empty buckets, filled the lift again, then saturated the second floor of the beautiful house, returning once more with a second car full of the oil so that he could be sure that the room where they had lived was sodden. Then he worked methodically to saturate the main floor of the irreplaceable flawlessness, and at the end he dragged the quarter-filled drums into the living room and overturned them on the floor where he had raped Irene. The gasoline glistened across the surface of the room in the moonlight.

He raced up the stairs and opened all the windows on both floors. He ran down to the main floor in an insensate frenzy and smashed windows open by throwing Sheraton chairs through them. He was filthy with his work. He could not get the mocking image of his mother out of his mind, and he wanted to get at her somehow, to tear her to pieces. "She should be burning in here," he screamed. "She should be nailed to this floor." He sprinted out of the building to the garage. He soaked brooms under the gasoline from the pump, then he lighted them, all eight of them, and began to run in a circle around the house flinging the torches into the beautiful work of art, hearing the dull boom as the fire touched the oil and spread, until he had to fall back, then farther and farther back from the heat, and a hundred yards away he could still feel it. He stood under the trees and watched it go, and after a while he heard the fire engines coming. He fell down on the grass and went to sleep so that he could get the rest he would need to manage the work of cementing over the foundation of the house into one seamless slab that would entomb all of the shame all women had made him feel throughout his life.

Rei called Goff but there was no answer, so he got dressed slowly, then, sitting on the edge of the bed, he screwed a silencer to the end of a .38-caliber revolver and put it into an attaché case. He had to telephone twice again at fifteen-minute intervals before he got Goff.

"Arnold? Ben Rei."

"What can I do for you, Ben?"

"I'm at the Waldorf. I have a large can of the finest. I'll bring it over."

"Not tonight. I don't feel good. I'm going to bed."

"I'm sorry you don't feel good. But it has to be tonight because I leave in two hours for Chicago."

"Can't you leave it in the hotel safe?"

"Arnold, you know I can't do that. This is a big jar of the purest. I wouldn't hand it over to anybody but you. What is this? It'll take two minutes!"

"Okay."

"Fifteen minutes."

"Ben?"

"Yes, Arnold?"

"Knock three times. Slow. I don't want to see anybody else tonight."

Rei knocked three times, slowly. Goff opened the door. He had put a dressing on the side of his face. Above the dressing his face was badly bruised and swollen. "Hey," Rei said, "you took a real fall there." Goff did not answer.

"Where's the stuff?"

"Right in here." Rei sat down, resting the attaché case on his lap, his hat and light topcoat still on. He was wearing gloves. "I got a little indigestion, Arnold," he said. "Can you let me have a little shot of cognac?"

"Sure." Goff turned away to go to the bar at the far wall. Rei moved silently. He drew the revolver out of the case, released the safety, then fired once at Goff's back—the kind way, the Mafia way for friends of the friends, so that the victim would not know he had been killed. Goff fell forward on the carpet. Rei stood over him and fired a *coup de grâce* into the back of his head. He turned the body on its side with his right foot, then fired the silenced gun once more to blow the larynx away so that if, through some miracle, the man stayed alive, he would not be able to talk.

Rei replaced the gun in the attaché case, then removed from it a party tray of cards and chips and a paper bag. He dealt out six poker hands on the round, green baize-covered table on the side of the room away from the body and distributed the chips unevenly. He put four ash trays on the table and filled them from the paper bag with a used burned cigar and cigarette butts. He tossed some match boxes and books on the table, then stepped over the body to fetch three glasses, which he half-filled with rye and water and placed near the cards and chips on the table. He moved six chairs up to the table, approximately near the cards, to look as if they had suddenly been abandoned, then he picked up the attaché case again, saw that it was closed carefully, and let himself out of the apartment.

The body was discovered by a chambermaid, Mrs. Mary Gonnerty, at 11:35 P.M. that evening. The extraordinary prestige of the murdered man and the remaining contents of his filing cabinets caused such consternation and so many dangerous published newspaper conjectures that New York City Mayor James J. Walker found it necessary to request the resignation of his police commissioner, Joseph A. War-

ren and to appoint Grover A. Whalen to investigate the case.
Carrying the investigation forward vigorously, Whalen also
changed the automobile traffic pattern of the city, instituting
one-way streets for the first time. Traffic became so snarled
that the public attention paid to the Goff murder was merci-
fully lessened.

Congressman Rei waited for instructions at the Waldorf
until ten o'clock the next evening, when Edward West telephoned to him to call John Torrio out of retirement to take
over Goff's duties as a short-term commercial banker for
Horizons A.G. enterprises. Business was able to continue
as usual within the week without inconvenience or financial
loss.

CHAPTER EIGHTEEN

After the fire companies had left, Edward made an inspection. The foundation was still smoking. He fished out a brass sextant that had belonged to Walter Wagstaff, of whom he had been fond. The garage was intact. Before he went to bed in the staff quarters over the garage he called Willie to ask about the cement contractors. Willie said the crews would be there at eight-thirty the next morning. It was one forty-five. He asked Willie to ring him at eight o'clock, then he took a hot bath because he knew he could expect to be stiff when he awoke after manhandling so many gasoline drums. He washed his shirt, underwear and socks, brushed his suit, then went to bed.

He awoke refreshed when the telephone rang.

"Where is Irene?" he asked Willie.

"She's here."

"Good."

"She's seen the morning papers."

"The papers?"

"She knows about the fire."

"Good."

"And about Goff."

"Goff?"

"Goff was killed in his hotel apartment last night by a person or persons unknown."

There was a silence.

At last Edward spoke briskly. "Call Congressman Rei. Tell him I want John Torrio called out of retirement to

take over Goff's work and invite him to dinner at Fifty-fifth
Street at seven."

"Irene leaves for Palm Beach this afternoon and she——"

"Please acknowledge the instructions concerning Congressman Rei."

"Rei instructions acknowledged. Irene is going to take
Dan to Florida with her."

"Anything else?"

"The contractor's name is Nonie-Wintour. They'll send
a triple crew and four rolling mixers."

"Thank you, Willie."

The cement people were twenty-five minutes late. Edward
made himself a pot of coffee. He let them wait in the burned
area, calling his name, until he had finished his coffee,
then he went out. Some of the crew saw him and passed the
word. They found the boss, who came up to him saying,
"We been looking all over for you."

"Not all over."

"Where's the job?"

"You're twenty-five minutes late."

"We got lost."

"I want that building foundation cleared to whatever
point you decide it has to be cleared before it can be entirely
sealed over with cement. I want the job finished by five
o'clock this afternoon."

"All sealed in? Smoothed over? You want it like a
parking lot?"

"And please have a man bring me a chair out of the
garage and place it wherever you think I'll have the best
view of the work."

"You gonna stay here till we finish?"

The job was completed at four o'clock. It was a wonderful day to sit outdoors, one of those rare Long Island days,
soft and nearly hot in the April sun. He sent to the village
for a straw hat at eleven o'clock when the contractor had a
car going into town to get food. He and Mr. Wintour ate
submarine sandwiches, as Edward called them, or Guinea
Heroes, as Mr. Wintour called them—loaves of long French
bread cut in half, then packed with salami, ham, zucchini,
beans, sausage, olive oil, parsley, garlic and Swiss cheese.
His sandwich was so good that Edward accepted a tumbler

of homemade Chianti wine. "You Italian?" he asked the contractor.

"Yeah."

"What kind of a name is Wintour?"

"Izza company name. My fadder-in-law. My name is Angie Gennaro. Whatta you makin' here?"

"It's a grave," Edward said cheerfully. "I am entombing a house and everything that was in it."

"I told the boys to grade it good. You might wanna make a tennis court some day."

"Thanks, Angie."

Willie had a car standing by at noon. Edward left at four-ten and was in town at six. He bathed, changed, made eight telephone calls in response to business messages and was ready to receive his guests when they arrived at seven.

As Congressman Rei had prospered he had filled out. He was as stocky as a bucket of sand, and his lumberyard cheekbones made his head seem even bulkier than it was. He was a well-disposed man who enjoyed work or play, and the dinner jacket he was wearing, like shellac over an Iron Maiden, had required twenty-three fittings. "Good work," was the only comment Eddie made about the Goff business, then it was necessary to tell Willie, before he forgot, that he talked to London and that a syndicate of Scottish distillers would be arriving on the *Mauretania* and he wanted them to be royally entertained and sounded out as to whether they would consider selling all or part of their distilleries. The value estimates would be on Willie's desk in the morning. "Prohibition will be fading fast," Edward said. "We face a major overhauling."

The guests had two cocktails each before dinner. Edward drank the excellent Spanish Solares water. They dined well on ptarmigan (which Willie said he detested), spaghettini alla Siracusa, which was a miracle of oregano, capers, eggplant, black olives, garlic, anchovies, green peppers, tomatoes and olive oil combined with the pasta of Torre Annunziata. They rounded off with abbachio alla cacciatora, a Rei favorite, with some braised escarole and an eggplant pie. They drank Falerno wine from Naples, bottled by Giulio Coppola. When they had finished they smoked cigars and Edward said, "Did you reach Mr. Torrio, Ben?"

"I had the call out all day. He got back to me half an hour before I left for here. The proposition is okay with him. He'll be on the first boat, and he'll have everything all tidy in three weeks."

"I want him to have a year if he needs it."

"A year? You know John!"

"Goff worked for me because we started that way in 1911. But Mr. Torrio doesn't know who I am or if I'm on earth, and we'll keep it that way. Mr. Torrio will work for you."

"Fine."

"At the end of a year you and he will have to be ready to lay it on the line, to have all the affiliates working together. The way they work now is all right for prohibition, but in four or five years prohibition will be gone."

"You really think so, Zu Eduardo?"

"Yes. I'll even help it along a little."

"Why?"

"There is too much waste this way. As long as liquor is against the law the affiliates will go on making the messes they are making now. The Detroit people are impossible. The Chicago people are ridiculous. Capone has to go. No, no!" Edward added hastily seeing the consternation on Congressman Rei's face. "Not now. And there won't be any gang wars when he does go. What we are doing right now is setting out what we are going to do. The first thing is the basis of the plan for the affiliates so that they can understand the coming prohibition tapering off without panic. You and Mr. Torrio have to build this plan in detail so the affiliates will see the advantages of working in combinations, sharing enforcement problems, getting the maximum out of labor-union opportunities and reinvestment possibilities, coming under a common umbrella of political protection and many, many other advantages. Why, with narcotics alone—"

"You think this can work?"

"How, work?"

"The pool idea, group advantages—the cartel idea?"

"Of course it will work. You're as trained a businessman as I am. You just haven't thought about it. True, you'll have the job of making a rather strange conglomerate of mentalities and responses understand what you'll be talking about."

"They're not so dumb, Zu Eduardo. We can make them see it. Anyway, this is what I'd like to say. Legal liquor aside —forgetting that prohibition can disappear—this is an imperative thing you have conceived, because it is the only chance for continuity. I mean, in theory anyway, they could kill each other off unless there is some centralization. What I am saying is that I see in what you are telling us that if there isn't a common stake in the whole country and a sense of national cohesion, as the old men die or are knocked off— What do the young men know? They know muscle and guns. But if there can be continuity, the families will not have to react so opportunistically. They can have their young men educated as business leaders so we have to get stronger. You put your finger on what has been worrying me for a long time. What happens when you go—when I go? Is all this work going down the drain or have we started something here such as my people started in Sicily three hundred years ago? That was small—I mean, nothing compared to what we have here and can have here in fifty years, a hundred years. But what we have now is like ninety-four separate little General Motors companies instead of one big cohesive unit —a major force, a part of the American culture, if you will—an elastic, flexible organization with the advantages of centralization where that applies and decentralization where *that* applies. What you offer us is the only possible way we can go if we are to become the factor in American life that I know we can be."

"Well!" Edward preened. "Thank you very much Ben."

"And may *I* say," Willie put in, "it's the only way you'll ever control the offensive publicity that indiscriminate killing generates. A Goff is one thing. There have to be Goff eliminations of course. But killing civilians or just killing people in another neighborhood gang because of some old-time feud only leads to difficulties that make trouble and a great deal of unnecessary expense to put things on ice."

"Enforcement has to be centralized of course," Edward said, "and how that is done will be reflected in the reorganization as a first order of business. But the major consideration here, as I see it, is that soon we most certainly will be facing an altogether different economic climate, and will have to be fit functionally to ride that out. This market is insanely overpriced. The money mania that grips all the people is grotesque—as though they *believed* the credo of an equal chance for all! The economy is going to collapse."

"Well, I'm not so sure about that," Congressman Rei said. "I talk to a lot of people in my neck of the woods and everybody thinks——"

"Let me put it this way, Ben, because it will save time. Will you sell when I tell you to sell?"

"Yes."

"Then you'll be all right, and that 'lot of people in your neck of the woods' will be in the gutters. When the easy money goes down the drain and the people get frightened again on a permanent basis, that's when we have to be prepared to buy cheaply, to exploit a helpless labor movement that will need a strong point of view and other things, all on the one hand. But on the other hand, when the easy money stops, the same people aren't going to be thrilled and amused and entertained by a lot of hoodlums swaggering around shooting and scrounging. We have to prepare for both those very real problems. Add to those problems that beer and liquor will be legal, so that the payoffs to politicians are necessarily reduced to a fraction of what they had to be when these were illegal, and you'll find a lot of vicious, hungry and discontented politicians and police on your hands. So bear those things in mind. The big racket is about to depart. We have to develop and have ready substantial, national, profitable new rackets—or I should say expanded old rackets—to take its place or this marvelous political weapon so carefully developed will become just a disorganized mass of shake-down artists all over again instead of a controlled division of corporate personnel."

"Zu Eduardo," Rei said, "you really think with your head."

"We have one job, as I see it. We've got to protect our one-sixth of the gross of every affiliate's turnover from all sources, and we've got to keep them dependent upon our available short-term commercial credit," Edward said flatly.

"Very sound, Eddie," Willie said.

Edward was overwhelmed with work throughout 1928, mainly in supervising the pumping of a Horizons A.G. "special" fund into the American, French, and British stock exchanges from bases in Europe and six American cities. He moved on the pooled information of Horizons partners, driving the fantastic listed stock prices still higher and higher with the fund.

Throughout the intense work his mind had never really been away from the thoughts of Irene, some wonderful thoughts of the past, some of regret, but many, many thoughts of the future. He couldn't accelerate the arrival of that future because of the pressure of the work and also because he had calculated that a certain amount of time would be needed to heal their breach. He missed her at all hours of the day.

It was not until January 13, 1929, that Edward learned that Irene was in the Harkness Pavilion and about to have a baby. At first his mind went back as he convinced himself that this must be Goff's child, but he could not be sure of that, and Irene was in New York and he could not concentrate on his work any longer. The news came in the late afternoon. It was vague. Willie had been told by Rhonda Healey who knew a girl whose sister was a nurse at the hospital, and she had said that Mrs. Edward Courance West was expecting a baby there. Willie had checked the hospital immediately but they told him they had no record of any patient of that name. Edward pressed him to call Dan in Palm Beach. Will got Dan, who said his mother had gone to New York to have the baby and that Mr. Tobin could reach her at the Harkness Pavilion but he didn't know what room, so Rhonda had to pass bribes through the chain until the room number came back. It was the morning of January 14 when Edward went to see Irene. She had died in childbirth by the time he reached the hospital.

Edward collapsed. His breakdown could have been induced by the fear of losing her, the shock of her loss and his grief at now really having to live without her, but part of it was overwork and undernourishment. He was admitted to the hospital and he stayed there for thirty-two hours of amber and purple twilight while Willie handled the funeral arrangements.

Edward was aware of Willie sitting beside the bed with red eyes. Edward said, "It was Goff's child."

Willie shook his head. "No, Eddie. I saw it. He's your child."

Edward closed his eyes again and realized that all through

the passing year while he thought he was punishing Irene he must have been punishing himself, and he could not understand it. It was as though he had been staring himself down in terrible judgment (of *what?* what terrible thing had he done beyond protecting his name and his hearth?). He would stay away from her for one year because that was right, she deserved that punishment. It would also give her time to savor the marriage she had almost thrown away. They could forgive and forget and he would take her back again in spite of everything she had done to him. But he saw his guilt in a flash. He had hurt her grievously, and he was using the full and formal year to help her, bit by bit, get over the loss of the house she had loved and perhaps slowly come to understand why he had to burn it down. Bit by bit he had been giving her time to forget those poisoned letters, to have the chance to come to yearn, as he had yearned, that they could go together again, so that everything could be the way it always was meant to be.

"Willie?"

"Yes, Eddie?"

"I want the best private detectives."

"Why, Ed?"

"I want to know who sent Irene those letters."

"Okay, Ed."

"Now. Do it now. Get it started."

"After the funeral."

"Whose funeral?"

"Irene's."

Edward began to weep.

Only Edward, Dan, Willie, Charles Pick, Jr., and old Marxie Heller attended the funeral. Edward and Dan rode together in the limousine behind the hearse. They had invited Willie to ride with them as a member of the family, but he had declined.

"What would you want to do now, Dan?"

"Stay with you."

"But you have to go to school."

"I can't go back to Florida."

"Well—Gelbart."

Dan nodded.

"We'll have the summers and all the holidays together. Just the way my father and I used to have, and we'll go anywhere you say. Would you like to meet a champion or have lunch with the cadets at West Point? Do you like the races or baseball games? Would you like to go to Europe? Whatever is the most fun, that's what we'll do."

Edward threw himself into the work of reorganizing Horizons' affiliate concepts. He worked with Congressman Rei, who in turn worked with John Torrio. Rei called the meeting at the President Hotel on the boardwalk in Atlantic City for late April. It lasted three days and four nights. It was entirely successful. On the first day of the meeting Capone was told he was through, and he seemed relieved. He grinned at the news. "Game fish and fast ponies," he said. "Florida for me." He played it with class, like a board chairman stepping down for a younger man, but that night he went to Rei's suite and he was so frightened he was trembling. He could not believe that they had meant what they said, that he had not been marked for death. He was convinced that Congressman Rei was the *pezzinovanta* who had ordered his execution. In Rei's presence he pleaded with John Torrio to intercede for him, to convince Rei that he must be saved. He clung to Torrio's arm and begged for help.

To prove Al was mistaken, Rei said they would make any arrangement he wanted. Capone began to calm down. Torrio suggested that if he felt this way right now perhaps he would feel safer in Europe. Capone shook his head. "They're a bunch of foreigners to me, John. It was different for you. You like opera and you have your mother over there."

"Look, Al," Congressman Rei said. "We wish you well, like I keep saying. But I can see it might be good for you to cool yourself off, because, who knows, when the word gets out and some junky thinks you took a fall, he could take a shot at you in the first couple of months."

"Jesus. I didn't think of that yet."

"Look, Al. Pick a city. Any city in the country except, of course, Chicago. I'll arrange for you to take a pinch there and you can cool off in a big, comfortable cell, in a big, safe building where money counts for something."

"Yeah?" He looked at John Torrio for confirmation.

"When you, personally, are satisfied, Al," Torrio said, "when you can guarantee yourself that everything is copasetic, then you can go to Florida or do whatever you want."

An important point that was decided at Atlantic City gave much of the impetus to the "Americanization" of the mobs that began immediately thereafter, truly coming out of the inspiration, with which everyone heartily agreed, that a slush fund should be established for the proper education of promising young people to give them a chance to learn business administration the scientific way, the way Congressman Rei had learned it at the Wharton School of Business of the University of Pennsylvania, so that they could assume their proper roles as executives in the new interlocking organization, to cope with the already complex and sophisticated industrial problems that had arisen.

It was agreed that in the meantime a lot of impossible old-timers, the real inflexible Mustache Petes, would have to be eliminated, because every day they were proving that they just didn't have the elasticity to keep up with the modern operation. Joe the Boss was knocked off. Frankie Marlowe, Frankie Yale, the whole Diamond gang, Fats Walsh, Monkey Schubert, Johnny Guistra, Carmelo Liconti, Gerardo Scarpato were all killed, Sam Pollaccio disappeared forever, and Salvatore Maranzano, leader of the most reactionary of the Mustache Petes, was murdered in his office on the twelfth floor of 230 Park Avenue by Bo Weinberg, actually Dutch Schultz's chief gunman, as a favor to Charley Lucky. They were the headliners. Across the United States on September 11, 1931, fifty-six Mustache Petes were executed, and the new administrative team to co-align all national interests of Horizons A.G. was selected by Congressman Rei, headed by Charley Lucky and Vito Genovese. Edward West was enormously pleased with the changes that Rei (and the original Atlantic City conference) had effected. He was now confident that the enterprise would prosper and expand to an even greater degree than ever before realized despite the fact that prohibition itself was doomed.

Since February Edward had been using women as an anodyne. He didn't drink. He had a revulsion for drugs. His nerves had been laid bare and he was haunted by wonderful memories of Irene and pursued by the need to find out who had sent those letters. He pressed on Willie hard and Willie in turn pressed on the agencies working on the investigation, but they were getting nowhere.

Rhonda Healey had set up a beautiful girl named Baby Tolliver in a flat on Park Avenue, staked her out with a colored maid, some furs and nice furniture, and kept her in spending money. Willie handled the bills. Edward saw other women at random too, but Baby Tolliver was programed in as a staple, two or three nights a week, dipping in out of nowhere, always after one in the morning, sometimes at five in the morning. As the summer went on he saw less of the girl because the market was at last showing signs of real weakness. He moved into the apartment in the bank building next to his office and ran out his guerilla lines for buying, selling, raiding and wrecking from there to eleven action stations on either side of the Atlantic, all aimed right back at New York and finally causing the ruinous sure trend that capsized the market. Meanwhile he manipulated to get the two billion four hundred million dollars of the swollen Horizons "special" fund out of the market on May 4, 1929, moving into the short position on September 5. However, on October 25, after the profit had been taken on every dollar he had taken out, something very bad happened that required him to leave the country. He had discovered that Baby Tolliver had been operating a house of prostitution in the luxurious home he had made for her, and he had gone berserk with resentment and frustration, and it was possible that he had hurt her badly. Also, although he had not known it had happened at the time, he had beaten up the colored maid. But that was adjustable and Willie adjusted it. But a beating wasn't enough for the girl after what he had done for her. Willie handled the police and the DA's office through and with John Kullers, and they nailed her on maintaining and operating and on charges of compulsory prostitution and attempted bribery. However, it was decided that it would be a better thing if Edward got out of town or out of the country, so he sailed for Europe with Willie on October 27, 1929, and told the horde of ship news reporters who had crowded into his stateroom that he was "seriously concerned with the immediate financial future of the country."

Just before Christmas, Willie got full confirmation that the poison-pen letters which had been sent to Irene, almost shattering the West marriage, had been sent by agents of the

Soviet government. The revelation was shocking, staggering, mind-tilting news to Edward: for its starkness alone, as well as for its gargantuan implications.

He could not believe the documentation that Willie laid out so nervously before him. The story was there however, and in fact undeniable. Willie explained with a shaking voice that after the detective agencies had found only dead ends, he had, on a hunch, veered to friends in the American labor movement—Louis "Lepke" Buchalter, for example. In time, and through Lepke's connections, he had come upon certain implications that he had not liked at all.

"What implications?" Edward had demanded sharply.

"We discovered that more and more left-wing elements —I mean *far* left Commie elements—had it in for you."

"I should goddam well think they would. I've taken their goddam unions away from them."

"Not that sort of thing at all, Eddie," Willie said. He seemed to have gained confidence after Edward's reaction to the initial announcement. "This is all a matter of the feel for this thing that I've developed. At my own expense, so that you couldn't possibly be connected with it, I put operatives on this in Europe—and when I say Europe, I mean Moscow."

Actually, Edward had suspected what was coming at him for a long, long time—since his first deep, confidential talks with Mitchell Palmer. Then had come the overthrow of the Russian government by the Bolsheviks, and he had devoured miles of newsprint and ticker tape and State Department reports on how those bandits had torn apart the wealth and culture of centuries in a mad scream of "revenge," as their leaders called it. The Wobblies had been an even more threatening experience within the United States, and he had been appalled to look into the minds and hearts of fellow human beings and see hatred and envy of himself in there. When the big strikes had been attempted, strikes at industries as vital to the heartbeat of America as big steel and other great industries, in which he and many of the invisible Horizons partners were particularly committed, the entire pattern of the Soviet's blueprint for world power had become clear to him.

The USSR had launched her plan to annex the United States. Then, combining that with her own land mass, and resources such as minerals and cheap labor, and adding to it the power and prestige of the United States plus the wealth that would be stripped from Edward Courance West and his friends, Soviet Russia intended to take over the world as a possession of a handful of men in the Kremlin. Edward Courance West had stopped them. It was he, working with Horizons gang affiliates that provided the manpower from big cities, who had been able to organize the tough, mercenary civilian soldiers, the army of capitalism that had smeared the Commies across metal gates and speared them on pike fences, breaking backs and legs as they broke the concept of Moscow-inspired strikes for a fourteen-year period, which had been long enough to take them up to the war and to turn back, then paralyze Soviet Russian plans.

Here was the evidence in connected report upon written report that the Soviets not only knew who had stopped them but that they were now out to stop him. Here was immutable proof that Soviet agents had sent those poisonous letters to Irene, based upon material and information that Arnold Goff had given them. Goff was a Jew and undoubtedly a Communist, and he would do anything for power or money. The Kremlin had destroyed Irene. The Kremlin had tried to wreck his life. The Kremlin could have as many as *five hundred* counterespionage people investigating every (visible) cranny of his life, and if they could find out what they thought they could find out, they were going to try to crucify him on the tallest cross in history.

"What are they after?" he asked Willie shrilly. "What do they think they can find out?"

"Ed, take a good, hard look at yourself. You are one of the greatest Americans of your time—perhaps of any time. Forty years old—*forty years old,* but a banker among bankers, an industrialist, a visionary, a patriot—above all, a towering leader."

"But what——"

"Listen to me, Eddie. What do you think it would do to the capitalist system if such a man were exposed as having plotted prohibition for America—"

"I didn't plot prohibition. The people wanted it. The churches wanted it. The press wanted it!"

"No, Ed! I'm with you. What I am trying to do is to bring the picture to you from *their* point of view. So I will ask again—trying to put it in their words—What do you think it would do to the capitalist system if such a man as you were exposed as having plotted to bring prohibition to the United States for reasons of self-profit, thereby causing more graft and corruption, more crime and lawlessness and loss of respect for all law and authority than any other event in the history of the world? What do you suppose would be the effect on the capitalist system if Soviet Russia could produce facts proving that this same leader had conducted the American labor movement as an industry for private gain and private profit? What would be the effect on the capitalist system if they could show that this man had crashed the Western economic system down upon the heads of the world, causing untold and uncountable hardship and misery? *That is how they are trying to paint you, Eddie.* Not with truth, but with slime, claiming that you have sold out mankind for power and money. My God, Eddie, that's the case they are trying to build and that's why they've got to be stopped."

Edward got up and began to pace, asking piercing questions, giving orders to begin to set up the information network that would reach into every country on earth and would earn him many tens of millions of dollars as well as becoming the shield that would protect him from the enemy. He stood before Willie and vowed upon his beloved mother's name and spirit that he would fight Russia to his last breath and that before he was done he would bring her crashing down to her knees broken and dying. He vowed on the Constitution of the United States, which he had always preferred for oath-taking over the Bible, to sacrifice himself, his reputation and his entire meaning to the world in pursuit of that cause.

He took three powerful sleeping pills from Willie, for the first time voluntarily, and sat, drugged and upright, in a high-backed chair until midday the next day. Most of that time Willie sat across from him, adoring him.

In 1932, working it all out with the West public relations people so that the conferences could take place on the same day, Yale and Harvard simultaneously offered Edward honorary degrees—Yale, Doctor of Humanities; Harvard, Doctor of Laws. Total press silence was imposed after the arrangements had been settled, but Willie had driven to

Gelbart to visit Dan over a weekend and had confided the news to him, and within three days the ancient, collapsible Professor Gelbart himself was removed from some entombed glass case by the trustees of the school and somehow transported from New England to the West National Bank in New York. He was wheeled into Edward's office by his great-grandson, one of forty-six. Professor Gelbart was said to be one hundred and three years old, but he could still speak quite clearly. He congratulated Edward on winning his *G* in life and was wholeheartedly happy about the dual degrees that were about to be conferred upon him. Then he asked, simply and irresistibly, if Edward would come back to Gelbart on the day before he would receive his degrees from Yale and Harvard to accept Gelbart honors first, at the side of his own graduating son. Yale and Harvard withdrew their plans for Edward for that year.

The Gelbart degree became *the* commencement news. By the act of accepting Dr. Gelbart's invitation Edward raised $1,319,812 for the building fund of the school, to which he added two hundred and fifty thousand dollars.

Commencement Day was organized among the press, newsreels, radio, wire services and trade journals of those industries in which Edward Courance West was a leader, and for the student body and alumni, for June 17, 1932.

In April 1931, for the second time in his life, Edward had almost fallen in love. He thought of it as "almost" because he had pledged in his heart that there could never be a love that might even seem to equal the love he had felt for Irene. The girl's name was Mary Lou Mayberry. She was a showgirl in the Cotton Club revue, which was a great big joke on the management of the club because she was *not* a nigger. She had proved that to him the first night they had been together. For one thing, she did not have purple fingernails or gums. His own mother had had purple fingernails and she was as white as the Virgin Mary (in a racial sense). His mother had been quite dark, Sicilian dark. Mary Lou had exactly the same coloring as his mother, the same long ectomorphic body with the same swelling, full chest. Mary Lou, just as his mother had, dreamed of becoming a dancer someday. Mary Lou, it was revealed under probing, was a Sicilian herself. She had been reluctant to say that at first, she had told him, because she was sure he wouldn't like Sicilians. She couldn't speak the dialect because she was second-generation and had grown up in California. Her parents were dead. Around the Cotton Club (he was there only twice) she spoke in the patois of Harlem as protective coloration so that her bosses wouldn't find out she was not a nigger, which would make her lose her job. She was a terribly exciting girl and like some insane gamefish in bed. He thought she was deeply in love with him until June 16, 1932.

He had established her in an apartment on Madison Avenue, at the corner of 70th Street, that he had had decorated by José Maria Sert, which Willie Tobin had leased under the fictitious name of Professor Julian Smith. Edward visited the flat—an elegant graystone private building having two other luxury flats, no doorman and a self-service elevator—only after Mary Lou finished work uptown, so that no one made him Mary Lou's great and good friend. As had been the policy since Baby Tolliver had run a private little cat-house right under his nose, Mary Lou had been assigned a chauffeur (male) and a secretary (female), who took her to work and back and who stood guard over her in one way or another throughout each twenty-four-hour day. Mary Lou loved it. At the Cotton Club she was much more important than the star of the show.

Mary Lou's bodyguards had been engaged by Willie. The only possible flaw in the plan to shield Edward's identity would be if Mary Lou told the secretary or the chauffeur or anyone else who her lover was, but that certainly didn't seem likely. The girl was head over heels in love with him, and he had explained clearly and well why it was necessary for his name to remain secret, and what difference did that make anyhow?

As time went on and Edward remained raptly interested in the girl, Willie became more and more restive.

On June 16, at a quarter to one in the morning, as Edward was changing from dinner clothes into street clothes after a pleasant dinner and evening with Clare Padgett, first Horizons investor and now president of the investment bank for whom he had made such a historic connection, Willie arrived at the 55th Street house greatly agitated. "I have some very bad news, Ed," he said and had difficulty in getting even those words out.

"What is it?" Edward's voice was querulous. He was due uptown in forty minutes. And he considered himself beyond other people's conceptions of what was bad news. Except for Dan. "It isn't Dan?" he asked.

"No."

"What is it, goddammit?"

"It's Mary Lou."

"What? What happened?" He was suddenly enormously interested.

"I have just come from one of my regular, routine conversations with the driver. As you know, we pay each of the two of them a little extra on the side, as it were, as though it weren't a part of their salary, to keep an eye on the other one. It's just good security, if you know what I mean."

"What is the bad news?" Edward had grown pale and seemed all at once very tense.

"He offered to prove to me tonight that Mary Lou has been having this lesbian relationship with Miss Williams, the secretary we've had on the job."

Edward swayed as though stricken by a rush of fever. His face became mottled, more lack of any color than its accent. He breathed with difficulty and his eyes became filmed with fixed horror. He moved diagonally and sideways like a drunk crab toward the bathroom, but he couldn't get there in time. He vomited on the floor, then sat on the carpet beside the pool he had made, falling heavily, then leaning back against the wall. "I have to be alone, Willie," he said in a ghastly voice. Willie left the room and the house. He watched the house from across the street.

Edward contemplated this information called by Willie "bad news" when he knew well that his money and his power had placed him far behind common annoyances like that, and he saw it as the worst blow of his life. The second worst blow, then. Worse than the loss of Irene. Worse than what Goff had said to him that last day at the bank. Second only to the nightmare of his mother fleeing from him with her arms around that woman—and all of this had come back to him as the blade of a guillotine falls upon the neck. As he sat on the floor, dazed and unclean with vomit, he imagined he could see his mother's note, gigantic as a billboard, floating upon a shimmering ocean: THIS IS GOOD-

BYE. I AM LEAVING YOU FOR A WOMAN. I LOVE
THIS WOMAN. I AM A WOMAN LOVER AND I HATE
YOU. GOODBYE. His father had cradled his own head in
his thick arms on the kitchen table and Eddie had read the
note. He had read it again and again and he had snatched his
father's arms out from under his head and had screamed at
him to tell him what the note meant.

He had never believed that the note had been written to
his father. It had been written to him. She would never have
bothered to say goodbye to his father. She felt nothing for
him. Hate was too intense a recognition for his father from
his mother. She had written to *him*. All that time she had
hated *him*. She had run away from *him,* leaving him power-
less and without meaning—without any power to help himself, without any meaning to anyone else in the world.

Edward screamed beside the pool of vomit and pulled
himself with desperate need to his feet. He changed clothes.
He looked at the clock. It was two-seventeen. Where had
Willie gone? He left the house and walked from 55th to 70th
Street—Willie following a block behind. Edward was talking
to himself and to his mother, telling her this was the end,
that she should never again frustrate him into heartbreak,
that he had tried to withstand from her more than any
creature of God's was meant to withstand. He entered the
elegant graystone building, took the elevator up to Mary
Lou's apartment, let himself into the flat with a key and
murdered her brutally.

Willie followed Edward back to the 55th Street house, and
when he was sure he was safely within, took a cab to his
own apartment and called Congressman Rei in Chicago. He
gave the names and addresses of the chauffeur and secretary
and explained that he felt it was something of a rush job.
That done, he had but one thing on his mind. Edward had to
get to the commencement exercises at the Gelbart Academy,
because an extraordinary concentration of the national press
would be there.

He went to the 55th Street house at a quarter to eight
in the morning, bringing the early editions of the newspapers. He went directly to Edward's room. The room had
been aired and the messes cleaned up by the valet. Edward
was asleep, in his pajamas. When Willie touched him on the
shoulder he came awake at once and said, "Oh, my God!

Oh, God, what a terrible dream. I couldn't get out of it. I couldn't get out."

With sad, sympathetic eyes Willie handed him the newspaper. "That dream happened, Eddie. It's real." Edward took the paper and stared at it. His hands were shaking violently. "What am I going to do?" he asked.

"There's only one thing you must do. The Gelbart commencement exercises are today and you have got to be there."

Edward began to weep. Willie went quickly to bolt the doors. Eddie stopped weeping. He stared at Willie through his pale blue eyes. "They'll trace the apartment to you," he said. "They'll try to put the blame for this on you."

Willie shivered. He said, "There is nothing to trace, and I have called Congressman Rei about the chauffeur and secretary, just to be sure."

"Oh, *God,* Willie!"

"It's my fault, Eddie. If you can ever forgive me. It's not your fault, not any of this. It's all my fault."

"What are you saying?"

"I got a written operative report yesterday afternoon late. I didn't open it or read it. I don't know why. I suppose I was busy with something."

"What do you mean?"

"I opened it this morning. It was all there in black and white. The chauffeur and the secretary were both Communist agents. The woman seduced Mary Lou to try to drag information out of her."

"But she didn't know anything!" Edward screamed. Willie went to the bathroom and returned with a glass of water. He gave it to Edward, then shook two large red pills out of a vial he had in his vest pocket.

The sun was bright and hot upon the open platform facing Gardner's Green at the Gelbart Academy. The flashbulbs of the massed news cameras seemed more blinding and insistent than the sun. The microphone had been lowered to the level of Dr. Gelbart's blank, serene face as he read from the parchment scroll sitting in a wheelchair.

"Here, then," he read, "is the meaning of America, hallowed upon an altar within the spirit of Edward Courance West. He has lived out before the very eyes of our world the multiple meanings of the humanities. Here, then, beside us, in our midst, always welcoming our touch, is America itself in the meaning of Edward Courance West, this Atlas whose shoulders lift up and support the significance of our modern society, arching our glorious future above him, keeping it for us, lifting toward a heavenly tomorrow for all because of his deeds. A titan of democracy, the quintessence of all that truly *is* America—Edward Courance West!"

The applause was deafening. The color commentator had taken over from Dr. Gelbart on his switched-over microphone to combined networks and eighteen Canadian stations. Dan stood beside his father, proud and tall at eighteen years of age, his eyes shining. Edward had stood up with slow majesty made the more majestic by more of Willie's red pills. He felt superhumanly tall. Professor Gelbart's quavering voice, electronically amplified, rang like the Liberty Bell in his ears. He stepped forward and bent over, genuflecting humbly on one knee so that Professor Gelbart might slip the silken sash over his doctoral robes, then he stood and faced the microphone to deliver his address (now anthologized), "Hope Is a Promise That Is Always Fulfilled, Hope Is Our Mighty Land," that had been written for fifteen hundred dollars by a striving poet, so poetic and so American that he had once been named as Librarian of Congress.

Edward fell apart in the tiny bedroom of the suite Willie had arranged for them to use at a village tavern some miles away from Gelbart toward New York. Before they left the commencement festivities he had had the chance to tell Dan that his father was very ill and that this must be kept secret. Willie asked Dan if he would take the train to New York alone, then meet them aboard the *Aquitania,* which would be sailing at eleven o'clock that night for Southampton and Cherbourg.

"Where are we going?"

"Your father wanted you to have a grand tour of Europe."

"Oh, boy!"

"I'll see you aboard, then? Just ask the purser where we'll be."

"You bet!"

Edward moaned in his coma and sweated profusely.

Willie didn't call a doctor. Edward had morphine poisoning and Willie had begun to administer the antidotes himself. The private ambulance would be there at seven and they would drive straight to the pier and have Edward aboard before anyone else arrived for the sailing.

Willie pulled his chair up to the edge of the bed and looked tenderly down at Edward's ravaged face. None of this would have happened if Eddie had listened to him and had given up that girl before the whole affair became so complicated that it might even have led to something permanent and embarrassing. But what else could he have done? Eddie might have married that girl. A nigger. He had had to frame her. What else could he have done? He was genuinely sorry it had turned out the way it had. He loved Eddie West. He had been put on earth to serve him and to save him and it didn't matter that Eddie would never know how he felt and how forlorn and helpless it left him. He thanked God for his gift of paranoia to Eddie because it made him manipulable, rendered him content to be manipulated, and thereby saved him from his own genius. It was an inescapable fact that communism had to be fought. Eddie saw that need so much more clearly than the rest of the world and had contained that need within his paranoia. Only Willie really loved him. Only Willie really served him. Only Willie really could save him. He belonged to Willie now.

Willie hated Dan for the rest of his life for monopolizing his father that summer. While Willie and Dan toured southern England looking for druids, smugglers and admirals of the fleet, Edward recuperated at the Bürgenstock. When they arrived at the Grand Hotel two weeks later he seemed to be his old, stalwart self again and was doing prodigies of business by transatlantic telephone.

Edward and Dan had the first time together in their lives. It was a wonderful summer. Dan left them in September to return to enter Yale. The Bürgenstock's season was over at the end of September, but Edward was able to persuade Herr Frey-Furst to lease the hotel to him for the winter. When spring came again and it was time to reopen the hotels in May, Edward seemed to have no intention of ever leaving. Willie had made three round trips to New York during the year. Business demands were extremely active, because the

price of every possible investment in America seemed to
have fallen to its permanent low, and the Horizons partners
were impatient to have Edward return to the scene to begin
to buy the country for them.

But Edward was at the Bürgenstock, living with the
innocence and cleanliness and love of Irene again. At her
side at the Bürgenstock he was safe from the consequences
of any evil he might have done—and this he felt with a certain bewilderment, because Mary Lou Mayberry's murder
was the only evil he had ever been aware that he had done.
But Willie told him he was worried and even frightened to
have Edward live in Europe even within the protection of
Swiss neutrality. It would be too easy for the Kremlin to
kidnap him from there and to fill him with various truth
serums they had developed and possibly get what they would
consider a "confession" from his lips. Business needs were
actually becoming oppressive. The Horizons partners were
desperate to have him home. Edward could ignore Horizons
but he could not overlook the patent truth that Willie had
stated: Soviet Russia would have direct access to him, and it
was possible that he might not be proof against their drugs.
But although he became more wild-eyed and reclusive, he
could not make the decision to leave Irene.

Then Willie helped him to decide. He revealed his elaborate and detailed plan to recreate the Bürgenstock in America and to take Irene back there with them.

Edward threw himself into this miraculous opportunity.
Swiss architects went to work to reduce every square foot of
buildings and terrain to quarter-inch specifications. Land
scouts were sent out along the eastern seaboard of the United
States, in the Great Smokies, in the Ozarks, the Rockies, and
the Sierras of western America to find the site that would
be most likely to match the setting of the other Bürgenstock.

Edward became totally normal again. Or at least he returned to what passes for normal on every street of every
town and city and country lane of his nation.

BOOK TWO

THESEUS AND WIFE

CHAPTER ONE

The country of the Ashanti people formed an irregular oblong upon Africa with a triangular projection southward into the lands of the Adansi. The Ashanti were a more poetic and learned people than any in the East African coastal zones. It was their teachers who wrote, "If you are a child do not deride a short man" and "Nobody coughs secretly" and "Nobody measures the depth of the water with both legs." It was their talking drums that called out to Asase, the Spirit of the Earth, thus:

"Earth, condolences/ Earth, condolences/ Earth and dust/ The Dependable One/ I lean upon you/ Earth, when I am about to die/ I lean upon you/ Earth, while I am alive/ I depend on you/ Earth, while I am alive/ I depend on you/ Earth that receives dead bodies/ The Creator's drummer says/ From wherever he went/ He has roused himself/ He has roused himself." It was the Ashanti singers, standing before the assembled instruments who sang, almost as Horace had sung his beautiful dialogue ode "Donec gratus eram tibi," thus: *First Woman Singer:* "My husband likes me too much/ He is good to me/ But I cannot like him/ So I must listen to my lover." *First Man Singer:* "My wife does not please me/ I tire of her now/ So I will please myself with another/ Who is very handsome." *Second Woman Singer:* "My lover tempts me with sweet words/ But my husband always does me good/ So I must like him well/ And I must be true to him." *Second Man Singer:* "Girl, you surpass my wife in handsomeness/ But I cannot call you wife/

A wife pleases her husband only/But when I leave you you go to others."

Most of the Ashanti country was covered with primeval forest. Bombax trees grew to heights of over two hundred feet, ferns were abundant and throughout the forest spread the lianas, called "monkey ropes" by the Europeans, hanging in endless festoons from tree to tree, giving a weird aspect to the forest whose tall tangle was seldom relieved by flowers—except mimosas sixty feet high—or by birds or animals.

But the land surrounding the towns was highly cultivated. The fields yielded grain abundantly and also yams, other vegetables and fruit. In the northeast the Ashanti country was like a beautiful park—plains covered with high, coarse grass, dotted with beobabs and with wild-plum, shea-butter and dwarf date trees. There were many animals—some elephant, leopard, many antelope, many kinds of monkeys and many venomous snakes. Large and small hippopotamuses and crocodiles were in the rivers, and the gorgeous parrots were everywhere.

The rivers in the north were the Black Volta and the Volta, running north and crossing the eastern part of the country. At the center were the Ofin and the Prah. In the west were the Tano and Bia rivers, which emptied their waters into the Assini Lagoon. Apart from the Volta, these rivers were navigable only by canoes.

The Ashanti came to their country in the sixteenth century, just before Queen Elizabeth I came to the English throne. They were driven south from the countries on the Niger and the Sénégal by Moslem tribes. When they obtained possession of their region of impenetrable forest they defended themselves with a valor that became part of their national character and raised them to the rank of a powerful and conquering nation. They were of the purest Negro type. Originally they had been of the same race as the Fanti, who lived nearer the coast and spoke the same language. The Fanti lived on *fan,* a potatolike plant. The Ashanti ate *san,* which was maize.

Their government was a mixture of monarchy and military aristocracy. There were chiefs of clans and subchiefs with hereditary rights and they formed the King's Council. The land was held in common by the tribes, which were attached to the office of the head chief. Polygamy was practiced by all who could afford it. The crown descended to the king's brother or to the sister's son, never to the king's offspring, because he might have hundreds of wives, many of them in menial positions. The people were spirit worshippers who showed repugnance to the doctrines of Islam.

The Ashanti were the noblest warriors, and in their late history they fought the British Army five times, defeating them four, but they also wove fiber cotton, and their pottery and jewels were famous across the land. The Ashanti goldsmiths made masks and headdresses of beaten gold that hung in the king's palace at Kumasi, from which the ancient caravan routes went to the trading centers far inland.

Osai Tutu was the great founder of Ashanti power. He built Kumasi. He subdued Denkera and the Moslem countries of Jaman and Banna. He extended his empire to the east and to the west by conquests. He was slain in 1731. His successor was Osai Apoko, followed by Osai Tutu Quamina, who desired to make communication with the white nations. When the Fanti refused to deliver fugitives on the coast, Osai Tutu invaded their country and drove them to the sea, where there was the British fort, Anamabo, the principal slave-trading station of the Gold Coast. The fort stood on a hard rock shelf five hundred yards from the foothills. Its walls were built of crimson brick, lightly whitewashed. It had a spiral staircase and cool arcades. Kwaka Adai, the king's messenger, though he lived to be very old, never forgot it. There was also a thriving industry around the fort devoted to the manufacture of manacles, fetters, chains and padlocks as well as branding irons.

On his first visit with his warriors Osai Tutu destroyed the town and slaughtered eight thousand of its inhabitants. The king refused to treat for a truce except with the governor of the Cape Coast, Colonel Torrane, who came to Anamabo, where he was received with great pomp. In 1819 the British government sent a consul to Kumasi, Mr. Joseph Dupuis, who conferred with the king. A second treaty was drawn by which the British government acknowledged the sovereignty of the Ashanti over the territory of the Fanti—truly the territory controlled by the great slavers.

The British repudiated the treaty. The Ashanti attacked again, putting ten thousand men into the field, killing the

British commander, Sir Charles M'Carthy, whose skull was thereafter used as a drinking cup at Kumasi. On the day of Sir Charles's defeat, January 21, 1824, Osai Tutu Quamina died of natural causes. His successor, Kwaka Dua I, sent his son to the commander at Anamabo to convey the news of the succession so that a council could be assembled at once at Kumasi. The son's name was Kwaka Adai; he was called Kwaka after his father and Adai because he had been born on the first day of Great Adai, when prisoners of war and condemned criminals were sacrificed to the spirits as a sentiment of piety toward parents and other connections.

Kwaka Adai was captured by a party of white slavers as he came out of the forested foothills. He was chained in the slave compound to be shipped aboard the *Corsican Hero,* Captain Hiram Shawcull owner and master.

The going rate for young, healthy male slaves was thirty-five pounds sterling on the Gold Coast, but Kwaka Adai brought fifty pounds, not alone because he stood six feet, four inches and was of great strength and beauty but because he was an Ashanti royal messenger. Ashantis were prized and feared above all other African slaves by the owners of the American plantations, to whom they were sold in chains. Christopher Codrington, governor of the Leeward Islands, had written to the British Board of Trade: "The Ashantis are not only the best and most faithful of our slaves but are really all born heros. There has never been a rascal or coward of that nation; intrepid to the last degree, send us more like them." Robert Burbank DuBose, the Carolinian planter, observed that "No man deserved an Ashanti that would not treat him like a friend rather than a slave," but he warned that they had a gift for organizing slave revolts. Colonel James Nolan, owner of the enormous Solebury Plantations of Georgia (the man who wooed and won the formidable Dame Maria Van Slyke with epistolarian fervors), wrote of buying a parcel of Ibo and Ashanti boys and stated that during the breast-branding that followed, the Iboes screamed dreadfully, but the two Ashantis were only amused by the Iboan antics and came forward laughing and of their own accord, received the two searing irons on their chests without flinching, then snapped their fingers under the noses of the branders. Nolan at once informed his distant lady love that "African and European nervous systems are different. These people don't even feel pain."

Kwaka Adai had never seen the ocean before. He could not understand what had happened to him. He was the king's messenger but he had been beaten and chained. Until he was off-loaded on the other side of the Atlantic he thought it was a direct plot against his father. He was only one of twenty-six million men, women and children who had been taken into slavery in Africa for distribution in North and South America, but one of only fifteen million who survived the crossings.

Below decks the heat was so excessive that ship's surgeons fainted. The air was so thin that candles would not burn. Slaves were chained in rows, lying on their backs two and two together, with five feet of headroom ledge upon ledge, packed with enormous skill to yield the most cargo. Women gave birth while they were chained to corpses, and the white crews worked on the half deck with camphor bags gripped in their teeth because the stench struck at them like the beaks of vultures. While Kwaka Adai crossed, lying in his own excrement, sloshed with pails of vinegar, sixty bodies were lost to smallpox, and the survivors were dosed with rum so that they might help to put the corpses over the side. Then all forty-two survivors were dragged on deck and made to dance and sing under whips to give them exercise and to fill their lungs.

Kwaka Adai, age sixteen, was sold for eighty pounds sterling in the wholesale market at Bridgetown, Barbados, on May 15, 1824, then transshipped in July, to be resold at Charleston, South Carolina, for one thousand six hundred dollars, a top price. The auctioneer proclaimed to the crowd of buyers, "This man is Ashanti. Ship's master gave special papers on him. A king's son, this boy, and you all know the value of an Ashanti boy—none better in any market." Kwaka Adai was bought by the planter Peter Carvell and baptized with the name of Moses Ashant. He was put in a building with eleven males, coast blacks from as far north as Sénégal and south to the Guinea bight. He was set to work in the field until he learned to speak with the other slaves and his masters, then Miss Dorothy said she wanted him for her coaches.

Moses Ashant lived to be eighty-six years old and died

in Charleston in 1894, a well-to-do man in the chandler trade. His daughter Matty was born a slave. Her daughter Smitty emigrated to New York in 1918, large with her only child, Bertha. Bertha, Mayra Ashant's mother, had never known a man in the family, and her mother had never known a man in the family, and the only man Matty Ashant ever knew in her house was old Moses Ashant, a king's son, who cursed in wonderfully clear English at all the men who managed to get into his women without ever waiting to get into his family.

All the Ashant girls could cook, sew, sing, read, write and understand numbers and money. They had been taught that knowledge was the way out, because what it took to move up and out, Moses had taught them all, was confidence in self, dignity for self, pride in self, until all the rest of everything had to follow. They all knew everything about Moses Ashant and where he came from and why he was strong and wise, and each daughter told her daughter. But they were all further armed for the strenuous life. They were taught to be proud and grateful that they were Ashanti, and (like the French, English, Japanese, Spanish, Filipinos and Mexicans who had immigrated long after they had) they wholly believed it.

Walt said he wasn't so sure she'd been very shrewd marrying into the West family, because if they had any children, people could call them Ashanti Irish.

Her mother had explained that being black meant you had to teach yourself that you had to trust your enemies but not your friends. Whitey not only wasn't giving anything away but he was going to yell like hell if the blacks started taking any. But if you don't ask, you don't get. And you got to get for yourself, because the people who got ain't about to give. Just don't put your trust in the friendly liberals, something they call themselves. When you're being killed you don't want somebody clucking over you like a hen and saying they meant to clip the coupon and send in the five dollar contribution that could have prevented all this. Liberals, Mama said, were the people high up in the stand where blood couldn't get on them who were the first to turn their eyes away when the mean folks let the lions in among the Christians to entertain the liberals. The liberals are even against Muslims, Mama said, but the Muslims were the only ones who could prove Jesus was black.

Mayra knew how lucky she was to have Mama. Everybody lived with relatives or in hospitals or they had like boarders walking around and grabbing you by the cooze. Mama was a worker because she was proud, and the most Mayra had to do that she didn't like to do was to stay in the city nursery until she was old enough to go to school, and her Mama worked to get that money to keep her in there so she wasn't out walking around throwing rocks at rats and playing show-me-what-you-got under the stairs. Mama was somebody to look up to, and they all did just that, because she could throw like Jackie Robinson, hit like Joe Louis and talk two times faster than A. C. Powell. She bore down hard on studying. That's what she wanted from Mayra. She said the word "Slav" came from the word "slave," and look where the Jews had got because they studied. They knew. They never stopped, day school and night school, and they were getting someplace, while the black man stayed down resting on the bottom of the barrel because he wouldn't learn the secret. "We got to be sharper than sharp. We got to be superready, honey, and when that door opens just a crack we got to know how to zip on through, then to stay there when we get there."

They did all right in the fall, winter, and spring, but they were a little light in summertime, because that's when Mama mostly got laid off after she quit working for the big case-ace broads. She was a laundress now, because after Miss Mary Lou was murdered she said she'd seen just too much. But being a laundress with steady families downtown meant she had nothing to wash when they all went away for the summer.

Mama and Mayra always counted Emancipation Day from June 1947, no matter what the Republicans claimed. Mayra was fourteen when their manumission came through. It was a little before the end of the school year, and to start to get ready for the August days when The Credit would get on the tight side at Relleh's, where the food came from, they had moved into a basement flat between Manhattan Avenue and Eighth, which Mama said was a big rat resort for only the snobbiest rats and cockroaches. Rat traps loaded with jack cheese sat in wait and got cleared out every morning. They had a high bed and a good stove.

It was late afternoon. Mayra was doing homework. Mama was ironing and delivering her regular sermon on hustlers as a lesson for Mayra never to be tempted to go into that line of work. She never discoursed on icy-assed spade chicks standing under some lamppost on a winter night. Mama had known the big time up real close. The *big* big time. When the top white broad she would be working for as maid and pacifier took a pinch and went downtown, or broke her heart on junk or booze, Mama would go back to being a laundress in buildings between Lexington and Fifth in the Sixties until she spotted the wicker basket she'd been looking for, the one that seemed to hold only towels, then she'd find out whose laundry that was and go on upstairs and present herself with her credentials. She had the hard-money credentials because she had worked for Miss Baby, the most ambitious, money-stacking hustler since the Dutch bought New York.

Mama was thirty-four years old in June 1947, and she'd been in the profession for sixteen years before she backed out of it, sliding down her own screams. She knew what she knew and she didn't hold anything back, because Mayra was growing up to be a beautiful girl. She wanted to prove forevermore that there was absolutely no percentage in turning tricks. She would tell how, at first, when she started with Miss Baby, she had picked up a few case twenties herself when the men would drop in with a big hangover in the afternoons and Miss Baby and her roommate, Jewel, would be sleeping or doing their thing. Miss Baby was an Italian girl like who was so big-time that she had managed a Southern senator into saying, in print, that she was his niece, and right off the bat the going rate to lay that little debutante was like triple. Miss Baby didn't care if Mama obliged an afternoon customer and turned a trick in the off-hours. Like it kept men from wandering off to somebody else's pad. But Miss Baby made Mama tell her every time and how much they paid, because if they paid less than twenty she'd have the doorman downstairs bar them from the building. The tips were good. The pay was just fair, but the tips doubled it, sometimes better, so except for the summer months when the big broads in the business moved out to the Hamptons and to Saratoga, they never had to wrestle for credit at Relleh's—only in the summertime.

Mama got clothes from Miss Baby that were like new and cold-cream samples from a wholesale druggist customer that kept coming in her name for two years after nobody saw the wholesale druggist anymore. Miss Baby ran a tight ship, but she was always fair. Only she was a real nut about everybody wearing clean underwear. She gave Mama four sets of underwear so it would be clean every day whether anybody was going to see it or not. Miss Baby was in love with this one roommate, Jewel, but when Jewel came out for a party in dirty underwear Miss Baby threw her right out on her ass and she stayed out. Dirty underwear turned Miss Baby off, and she figured it must turn the customers off.

Miss Baby was Mama's first really big hustler, and the job lasted for almost three years. Then they hit her behind the neck. "I mean money wrecked her, she was so greedy. She found this john she told me was so rich he could like buy her a hook-and-ladder fire engine every day if she wanted some, and he was crazy about her. He got her to close up her business and move to a new pad at Eighty-second and Park. He gave her like a guarantee of more money than she was making free-lance just to be his chick. Now, she must have moonlighted on him. She had to be sneaking other johns in when I wasn't there, because he come in one night—I was washing underwear—and he beat the living shit outta her. Honey, I mean she was *wrecked,* with like eleven fractures. And he stayed so crazy mad that he come in and spread me out on the bathroom floor and give it to me, then he beat the living shit out of me, but not so bad, because he was tiring, thank God. Then he went out, and instead of like a couple of ambulances a lot of cops came in, and they booked Miss Baby for running a house of prostitution and trafficking in drugs and fencing stolen goods. I mean, I'm telling you, you never heard of some of the things they dropped on her and I know I'm in real trouble, but a little man comes in and all of a sudden they unbook me and a doctor is handling me right and the man gives me five hundred dollars and says forget it. When they got done with Miss Baby she done nine years and was dead in jail with tuberculosis. I went to see her plenty of times when she was still in Woman's Detention, and like all her looks was

gone. I kept asking her what she did to him to make him so
mean and she kept shaking her head. I asked her straight
out if she moonlighted on him and she says she never did it.
I said maybe that little chick she kept around made him hot.
Nobody ever knew, but let me tell you, that's the worst kind
of man—but what I'm saying to you is, she got herself into
the worst kind of work. Sure she was taking it in as a free-
lance hooker before he got there, but she was paying out
to the precinct and the building people that run the house
and presents for the roommates and a very expensive horse
habit and all that underwear, and when they hit her she had
nothing. I want to tell you that in the end, downtown, she
looked like one of those chicks who'd do it for an apple.
I tell you, Mayra, hustlers have nothing but trouble. The
customers turn them off. They're all dykes, or something's
always going wrong with pimps or cops or clap or junk or
booze. The sporting life is full of only bad surprises. There
isn't any way to win."

Mama said that if she could have stayed thirty years old
for like about twenty years she could have made lifetime
credit at Relleh's. She got out for good and stayed with
washing clothes for good when Mary Lou Mayberry got
herself murdered.

Miss Mary Lou was a show girl who used the shows as
an advertising medium to advertise her ass, which made the
real money for her. Mama never wanted to talk about coming in and finding what some john had left of Mary Lou
Mayberry.

"Losers loaf, winners work," that was the motto that
Mama emblazoned on Mayra, who was going to keep on
going to school as long as the credit lasted at Relleh's, and
she was going to learn to type and run an office. And she
was going to get into civil service, where the federal laws said
they had to treat you right, where nobody could jim-crow
you, where no smart-ass could fire you if you did your work
according to the clock, and where there was a pension. If
Mayra found she didn't take to working in an office, she'd
work in a library or a hospital, and Mama had a list of all
the civil service jobs there were from Delehanty's.

The body hit the courtyard outside their room, which was
flush with the areaway, and Mama watched it plummet down

for the last twenty feet or so. It didn't make a sound as it came down. But when it hit, the sound was like a giant melon exploding on the concrete. Mama put the iron down, pushed the ironing board out of the way and rushed to the window, throwing it open. Mayra leaped up and ran after her. The body was about seven feet away and it was leaking blood from the length of its back. Money had shot out of its pockets on the impact; big cartoon rolls and flat packs of bills had whooshed out and were settling on the blood like green boats and barges. Mama climbed out of the window like she was fourteen years old and the house was on fire. "Come on!" she yelled over her shoulder to Mayra. "Pick it up! Get it!" and Mayra dove out the window.

They heard shouts from above. They looked up. Two honkies with gray hats were staring down and yelling from the roof, six stories up. They were yelling that Mama and Mayra should get the hell outta there and keep their hands off that stuff, and it made Mama laugh, but she was busy. She was harvesting on the far side of the body while Mayra worked the near side. They picked up the money like an animated cartoon. Mama kept talking. "I told you, Mayra. I told you. Something always turns up. Here we got Iron Charley Jackson, the Policy King. Wasn't so iron after all. Straight down from heaven, and they threw him right at us, but they forgot to roll him first. Poor Iron, lucky us." She piled her crop on top of Mayra's and said, "Go run and put it in that suitcase."

Mayra ran to the window, dropped the money over the sill and dove through, Mama bent over Iron Charley while the men still yelled at her from above. She stripped off his watch and rings and lifted a gorgeous cat's-eye stickpin off his necktie, then streaked back through the open window. They hadn't been outside more than fifty seconds. Mama put her scrapbook in Mayra's schoolbag and dropped that on top of the money in the suitcase, slammed the case shut, grabbed Mayra's arm and they both sprinted out of the door. They went up the back stairs to the street floor, and as they went out the front door they could hear the hoodies pounding down the stairs from above, banging into garbage cans, tripping on roller skates, cursing and shouting about two floors above them, maybe three, making noises like parrots in a pet-shop fire.

Mama and Mayra sailed onto the pavement from the front stoop, ran about eleven yards toward Eighth Avenue, then a cab came along and Mama flagged it down. She threw Mayra and the suitcase into it and jumped in beside them, slamming the door. "The Bronx!" she yelled.

"Where in the Bronx?" the driver quibbled.

"Who cares where in the Bronx?" Mama yelled. "Get outta here! Move it, man!" She threw a five-dollar bill in the driver's lap and the cab zoomed away. It turned the corner fast at Manhattan Avenue, heading north. Two breathless honkies wearing gray hats whammed out of the front door of the building, looked up and down the street, then grabbed a man who had been sitting on an orange box at the foot of the stoop. "Did two women just come runnin' outta here?" the smaller man yelled.

"Nobody outta here in more'n a haffa hour."

"They got to be downstairs still," the little man said. They ran back into the building, and the street watcher walked rapidly toward Eighth Avenue.

The cab went two blocks uptown, when Mama suddenly told the cab driver to go around the block. The cab turned right to Eighth, went down a block, then turned west on the street just north of and parallel to the street where the men were searching for them, then doubled back up Manhattan Avenue, where Mama had the cab stop in front of Relleh's. She took off her apron, which had blood on it from where she had wiped her hands, and said, "Always pay off for The Credit." She went into the store while Mayra waited in the cab. Two men in gray hats went speeding past the cab, heading north on Manhattan Avenue at fifty miles an hour, but Mayra wouldn't have known them if she had seen them. "I give Relleh an extra five," Mama said as she came out and got into the cab. "I told him it was on account, but if we don't get back by winter then to lay out five dollars worth on somebody who needs it." She told the driver to turn the cab around and take them west to the 103rd Street subway station, up the hill on Broadway.

As the cab made the turn Mama said, "That's a new specialty they have now, throwing their man off the roof. It started with Abe Reles and they found out it scares hell outta people, so they revive it like now and then for the advertising. A shooter walked right up behind a man on Gunhill

Road on a contract for Lepke and he put the gun right up to
the man's head till it touched and shot it. Bullet went in the
back and kept on till it come out between the man's nose and
eye, and the man lived. I mean like he was back at work in a
couple of weeks. I got that straight from a police captain who
was a freebie on top of Miss Eloise. When they throw off the
roof he don't make a sound coming down because they sap
him before they toss him and he's sitting straight up like he
was in a dentist's chair. I knew what it was before he hit,
when I saw him coming down."

They got out of the cab at 103rd Street and Mama only
took three dollars change back out of the five. They walked
along the side streets, primly, carrying their proper suitcase
for room hunting. Once Mama didn't want what they had
and once the landlady didn't want Mama. Then they saw the
"Rooms" sign in the window of the brownstone on 95th between Columbus and Amsterdam. It was two nice light
rooms—no rats, no bugs, no leaks—with a nice little
kitchenette and a bath with an inside toilet. Mama paid
the lady for three weeks in advance, then she locked the
door.

"Wowee-wow," she said. "It's come our turn to lead the
band. Two more weeks and school is over till Labor Day
and we got the whole summer to look for a nice place on
the Island or maybe New Rochelle or Mount Vernon."
She sat down and lifted the suitcase up to her lap. "Pull
down the shades, honey. Then write down the numbers as
I call them out." She handed Mayra the schoolbag when
the shades were down. She put the watch, the rings and the
cat's-eye stickpin on the tabletop, then she began to wipe
off and flatten out the paper money and sort it into de-
nominational piles. When that was done she counted it
slowly and carefully and had Mayra write down the amount
after each ten bills. When she finished, Mayra added it up,
Mama checked it out, and they found they had come into
twenty-one thousand six hundred and eighteen dollars. They
were stunned. They were quiet for some time, then Mama
said, "Now figure this out. We're going to live right. Sixty a
week. How long will the money last at sixty a week, not
counting Iron's jewelry?" Mayra's pencil worked over the
pad. Her eyes got bigger and bigger. "Just about seven
years," she told her mother.

"Then we got it made," Mama said. "Seven years and you'll be in the civil service and safe for life. I go back to work after Labor Day at a dollar and a quarter an hour plus carfare and lunch. That's ten bucks a day, five days a week. Every week fifty, for forty weeks a year—just like in show business—so we only need to drag down ten from this kitty to make it sixty, then sixty out for the twelve summer weeks. How much time do we buy that way?"

Mayra calculated. "Close to forty years," she said.

"That's too much. Makes me nervous. We got to adjust. Well, there's Christmas and doctors. There's birthdays and extra shoes and you'll soon be needing some sharp extra dresses, so let's cut the extra free time down to twenty-five years. I'll be fifty-nine when we run out. You'll be thirty-nine and close to getting your pension and have a husband with a good job, so how can we miss?"

"Thirty-nine?" Mayra said blankly, unable to conceive of such an age.

CHAPTER TWO

At the end of her last year in high school Mayra Ashant was
a tall girl who gleamed at the world with skin that was between mulberry and acorn in translucent layers of warm
color, soft and luminescent. Her mouth was pink cushions
and white tombstone teeth; her eyes melted tar on oyster
shells. The nose was too delicately proportioned for the
chin and cheekbones—the nose of a Harari woman of
Abyssinia, of the incredible beauties bred by crossing Galla,
Somali and Arab—but the rest of her face insisted that the
nose should have been formed like the noses of the Congo
west of the Stanley Pool.

About three months before Iron Charley Jackson had
been thrown off the roof Mayra had been having tactical
trouble with her art teacher at high school. Mama's counsel
had always been, "Smile when they start to press you. Make
them know you admire them for being men and how it
could have been a fairy tale of a lay if it wasn't that you had
had your cooze cemented over." The advice had always
worked with the men she had to cope with just by walking
along the street, until the middle of the third year of the
high school art course, when a scholarship to the Shannon-
Phillips Institute of Art somehow got itself involved with
Mr. Seligson's feelings. Mayra wanted the scholarship.
Mama wanted Mayra to get the scholarship. Mr. Seligson
was in a position to see that she couldn't get it, and it was
one of those things where if a fuss was made over the rea-

sons why Mr. Seligson might stop her from getting it, then everything could get worse than ever.

Just before Christmas, at the end of the year, before graduation time in June, Mr. Seligson asked Mayra to stay after school. He was a light-framed, wiry man who wore glasses and who could speak rapid French with a strong Washington Heights accent. Mr. Seligson had lived and painted in Paris in his student days.

Mayra went to the art classroom at three-ten. Mr. Seligson closed the door carefully and pulled down the shade over its top glass panel. He stared at her and Mayra thought he got very pale. His breathing wasn't good either, and she knew all the signs. "You wanted to see me, Mr. Seligson?" she asked tentatively, smiling the awful smile she and Mama had worked out. He took both of her hands in his. "I think you have tremendous talent," he said. "I want to be allowed to build on that talent." (That night Mama said he meant he wanted to erect on that talent.) "I have a dream for you, Mayra Ashant," he murmured. ("A wet dream," Mama commented later.) Mr. Seligson slipped his long, slender arm lightly across Mayra's shoulders. "Hold your breath, Mayra, and listen." He gripped her fiercely. "What would you say if I could get you a scholarship at Shannon-Phillips?"

"What's Shannon-Phillips?"

"Shannon-*Phillips?*" He was having such difficulty breathing that he left her side and walked to the window, gripping the metal handles tightly with each hand. "The best art school in the entire world, that's what Shannon-Phillips is."

"Oh."

"Well?" He turned to face her.

"What would I say to what?"

"What do you mean?"

"You just asked me, what would I say if you could get me a scholarship."

"Well! I meant would you like that? Would you be free to take it? Is your family financially secure enough to let you have two years of real art study?"

"I thought the scholarships paid for that."

"They do! But I mean your family might want you to be out earning money or something."

"Or something?"

"To bring in income. To help support!"

"My family wants me to try for civil service. I mean, well, like if there was anybody who gave out scholarships to the Delehanty Institute, that would be more what my family thinks."

"That would be a tragedy! That would be real, stark tragedy!" Mr. Seligson said. He started toward her very slowly. "Mayra, sweetheart, listen to me. Call me Mort if you want to. Right now there are maybe a thousand young painters in Paris. Some of them very talented, *and let me tell you this*"—he reached out for a front grab at her shoulders, but she began the awful smile and backed away—"there isn't one of those talented young painters who wouldn't give five years of his or her life to get a scholarship to Shannon-Phillips." He inhaled and exhaled slowly. "You're not just another schoolgirl to me, Mayra." He shuddered. "You are a *woman*. Of great sensibilities. You can be a great painter. In my humble opinion." He had her with her back to the blackboard. He got the fleshy parts of each upper arm and began to knead them absent-mindedly, and a dry smell, like steam, came away from him. She turned the whole force of the awful smile on him. His hands dropped away. He dug the back of his hand into his forehead. He turned away to the desk and picked up a large manila envelope. "Show this to your family. It has everything about Shannon-Phillips and an application. The holidays start tomorrow. We'll be apart for nine days. You'll have a chance to think about everything. *Everything.* And if you feel you need me—if you want to talk it all over much more thoroughly—my home address and phone number are in that envelope." He stared at her solemnly, wheeled away, walked to the window and gripped the window handles again as he stared out at the cement tennis courts. Mayra left very quietly with the envelope.

She was doing her French homework when Mama got home from work at seven-thirty, bubbling. Every customer had come through with Christmas loot and they had all paid up any back money that was due. She had a hundred and thirty-six dollars in cash and therefore a solid line of credit with Relleh's. "And that ain't all," she said triumphantly. "Looka here." She lifted a sky-blue nightgown with a lacy top out of the deep shopping bag. "Just happens to be your size."

"It's beautiful!"

"Now, this here is some kind of Filipino perfume that somebody give to Mrs. Gibson, but she never heard of it so she give it away. Unopened. She didn't even smell it! It says 'Made in Manila, P.I.' so she didn't want it. I bet you it costs ten bucks." Mayra was holding the nightgown up to herself in front of a mirror. "Looks real good," Mama said. "And we got an electric juicer. This lady's husband— the new people from Dover, New Jersey?—he won't let nothing German in their house. I got a ten-pound turkey, and I say to hell with waiting two days till Christmas, let's cook it now."

"My art teacher's got big eyes and hands for me," Mayra said.

Mama began to unwrap the turkey. "What'd he do?"

"He told me to come back after school. I think he locked the door—anyway, he pulled down the shade—then he said what would I say if he said he might be able to get me a scholarship to the best art school in the whole world, and I said what would I say about what?"

"That was good." Mama looked up at the wall at the painting of two somber Puerto Rican children crossing a field of golden wheat under a brilliant blue sky. She did a rough arm's-length fitting of the large turkey and the tiny oven. "Never get that bird in there. I got to take it to the baker's and get them to slide it in the oven."

"I'll go. You read this." Mayra gave her mother the manila envelope. "It's all about the scholarship. He gave it to me complete with his home telephone number."

They had a wonderful Christmas weekend. They kept eating turkey, went to two movies, watched TV and went to the Apollo. They were living in a top-floor apartment on Manhattan Avenue near the Monongahela Democratic Club, where Mama was a registered building captain, facing the cathedral, which Mayra could stare out at and sketch, not far from the highest point of the Ninth Avenue El, which was a very popular suicide leap. Mama worked hard for the Monongahela Democratic Club because she said that the leader, Jimmy Hines, by cooperating with Dutch Schultz, had brought prosperity to Harlem, because he was doing so great himself and he always paid off for loyalty. On Christmas Day at about four o'clock Mama turned off the TV and said that the time had come to talk about the scholarship. "Now, I got to tell you straight out. I hate a cockteaser, because that always makes trouble. But this here teacher has got to be handled without any problems, because you're sixteen going on seventeen, you're getting out of high school, and you're too young for civil service. We got to play this art teacher by ear, baby. We got to get that scholarship, but we got to block him good."

Mr. Seligson seemed much less tense when school started after the holidays and she turned over to him her application to Shannon-Phillips. He was pleasant but impersonal. They got through January and most of February that way. At the end of February she asked him if there had been any news about the scholarship and he said he'd be happy to look into it for her. In the first week of March he said he had some news but that it wouldn't be fair to discuss it on the class's time, so they could meet after school to discuss it. Mayra needed advice from her coach first, so she said she had to go to the dentist's that afternoon and they made it for the next day.

She and Mama examined the options. First, he might be a harmlessly genuine admirer of her painting, but they skipped that possibility without discussion. Second, it didn't seem likely that he would make his big move in the classroom, no matter how late he could persuade Mayra to stay, on whatever pretext. If he did make the move, then Mayra would have to work her smile or keep moving out of reach or deliver a kick in the seeds, but the kick could mean the end of the scholarship, although not necessarily. If he worked it all out with care and boxed her into a place where she had to leave the school with him to go somewhere, she should flatly refuse unless the excuse was built around art—which was what it was most likely to be, because they had nothing else in common—then she had to say her mother was an art bug and that her mother would have to go along too. "After all, you're sixteen going on seventeen," Mama said, "and you can get away with stuff like that." They decided on two constants: She was not to be alone with him anywhere outside the classroom and she was never to laugh at him no matter how silly he might become. "Laugh and we lose him," Mama told her. "Keep a straight face and we got a chance to wear him down, but the main thing is to keep pressing on him about the news on the scholarship, and we can work from there."

It was a bleak, dirty day. The tarnished winter city lay stiffly outside the windows of the classroom. Mr. Seligson kept his back to the wall on which had been tacked the work of Van Gogh, a sure anaphrodisiac. Directly over Mr. Seligson's shoulder Vincent's mean little red-stubbed face glared at her. "Ah, Mayra," Mr. Seligson said, as though she had surprised him in a reverie on art. "Good afternoon. Come in. I have the application papers all prepared. Would you like to see them?"

"Where are they?"

"Right here on my desk."

"Oh. Yes. Then I would like to see them." But she didn't move forward. She remained in her *querencia,* shuffling her feet, and Mr. Seligson sidled across her terrain as cautiously as though he were concealing a hole in the seat of his trousers. He moved to her left, while she sidled just as carefully, moving to her right, always facing him, and keeping her arms as stiff as horns so that she could hold him off if he should lunge. They made it to the desk at approximately the same time. "Here they are," the art teacher said hoarsely. He reached out to lift the form, but his hands were trembling, so he withdrew slightly and nodded at the desk top instead. Mayra watched him peripherally. Curiosity gripped her and she leaned over the desk to read the forms and as she did she felt Mr. Seligson enclose her, pretending to lean over the desk to look with her in case the Board of Education should bust into the room, but his offside hand cupped her breast and she could feel the bulge of his trousers at her buttock. She stepped backward, felt her high heel touch his instep, then she shifted her weight to bear down fully. He stifled an outcry. She apologized, and as he fell back, picked up the application form and moved out of reach to stand in front of the window.

Mr. Seligson fell into an approximation of Cheyne-Stokes breathing. His eyes jerked wildly, toward then away from each other in a deeply disturbed labyrinth. Each cycle became more intense and was followed by what seemed to Mayra to be total cessation for fifteen or twenty seconds until the rales would begin again, and through the labored

gasping he tried to speak to maintain the illusion of normal
composure. "As—you—can see—my dear. All—is—in—
order. All. Complete. I shall pop it in—it shall be popped—
into the mailbox—this—very—afternoon." He groped to
his right to find the chair, then sank into it slowly. Mayra
said, "I'll mail it, Mr. Seligson." She jammed it into her
purse. "I just can't thank you enough." She crossed the
room, walking backward, and opened the door to the corridor behind her. He waved at her weakly as a captain from
his bridge might salute the last departing lifeboat. The door
closed. He put his arms across the desk and rested his head
on them silently.

Mama read the application very carefully, then she had
Mayra make a copy of it. She studied Mr. Seligson's signature and said that the open loops and high letters indicated
a very artistic nature. They went out together that evening
and mailed the letter at the post office slot, not just in a mailbox. Eight days later, on a Friday afternoon, Mr. Seligson
invited Mayra to tea at his apartment on the following day.
She asked if it was to show her his paintings. He said he had
many of his paintings there and she was welcome to see
them but that there had been some developments about
Shannon-Phillips and they needed to have a long talk. She
said she thought she'd better bring her mother if it was
about Shannon-Phillips. "You are not to bring your mother,"
Mr. Seligson said primly, "and that is final."

Mama said there was nothing to do but to follow through.
They could do nothing on a Friday afternoon, tomorrow
would be Saturday, Shannon-Phillips would be closed, so
they couldn't find out whether she was accepted or not—so
she'd have to take her chances. If Seligson actually was legit,
okay. If not, the first time he tried to put his hand down her
dress or up her dress she was to kick him in the ankle if they
were standing up or drive her elbow into his stomach if they
were sitting down. Then while he recovered she was to run
all over the apartment, leaving her fingerprints on every
surface she could think of, all the unlikely places—such as
the ceiling of the refrigerator—and remember where she
left them.

"You know, baby, there are all kinds of indirect ways of
getting things done, but the kind way is the best way. You
remember Miss Pupchen, the little blonde chick on Forty-

eighth between Fifth and Madison? Well, this very, very,
very rich john stashed her there. We won't talk about him.
I mean if we can work it out that way we won't even talk
about him. He had a lock on her with a chauffeur who was
really like a stoolie and a bodyguard—she couldn't do nothing. And a Chinese secretary who could watch her in the
places where the chauffeur couldn't go. The john dropped
by whenever he felt like. All crazy hours or maybe not at
all for like two weeks. Miss Pupchen was flipping her wig,
except it was good money and lots of good sharp clothes,
but she had this thing about herself that she was oversexed and she needed more than anybody else, but she
couldn't even score the chauffeur or the secretary because
those two was being paid to cancel each other out. Like
they didn't even talk to each other. I was referee. The john
knew me from when I was with Miss Baby, way back. I remember I had no connection at the moment and I was doing
laundry at Four seventy-one Park and this very smooth,
skinny guy came around and he offers me solid money to
be maid for Miss Pupchen. She was no hustler, you understand. She just always had a rich john keeping her, so there
was no tips in it for me, and besides being the maid and
all like that my job is to keep an eye on the chauffeur and
the Chinee chick and to call a certain number if either one
of them chopped at Miss Pupchen.

"Well, it's a living. And that Miss Pupchen was a little
doll. She used to cry so hard. She says she's so oversexed that
it hurts her when she don't get it and that I have to help her
get a little relief for which she is willing to pay well. I see
what she's after, and it makes me sad to say it but I tell her
I only know how to pitch righty but thanks anyway, and why
don't we just play gin to get her mind off it? Well, we played
gin. I'd win a couple hundred, then she'd win a couple hundred—mostly we broke even. But she keeps talking about
her troubles, and I tell her it would be nice if she was to
call up her mama and just breeze. Just talk. Because, I mean,
I know that's a good thing for anybody. So she did. She says
why didn't she think of that? We were on East Forty-eighth
in New York and her mother lived in Vienna, Austria,
that's in Europe, and Miss Pupchen kept an open line going
right around the clock. And Miss Pupchen had her mother
hire the neighborhood drunk or somebody like that, because

it was all in German, and that man sat there Sats, Suns and
Hols to call the mother to the phone, and she kept that open
call going for five and a half months. She'd come bare-ass
out of her shower in her itty-bitty mules with the big pom-
poms and she'd pass the phone laying there and yell
'Loodvig!' into it and he'd answer. If it wasn't late at night
there the mother would get on and they'd breeze about the
weather or whatever, and the idea that she was oversexed
went right out of her head because she was not only always
talking to her mother but she figured she was getting even
with this rich john.

Well, we waited. Five weeks went by and the phone bill
had to be sent to The Man. Nothing. Nobody says anything.
We waited four months, but nothing. Finally, one night
when the john is laying on top of her she starts to yell at him
right in the middle of it. She tells him he's a big chump and
how she's been taking him for his roll with the telephone
and how she kept that open line going all those weeks, and
you know what he said?"

"What'd he say?"

"He said he was proud of her that she thought that much
of her mother and that it was one of the nicest things he
ever heard. I mean, that's what he said."

"What'd she do?"

"She had a nervous breakdown right after that. I don't
suppose she sent her mama even a post card ever again. And
that's the whole point, baby. Hustling johns is a loser's
racket. You can't win in it. But what I mean is, it was a *nice*
way to handle her differences with that john, and you got to
figure out the same approach with this horny art teacher."

Mr. Seligson's apartment was on Washington Heights
between Broadway and Audubon Avenue. He was so nervous waiting for her all day that he couldn't stay in the
apartment and went to a Jack Holt double feature in a
revival house, and what with the pressures on him he broke
out in pimples all over the backs of his hands, so he bought
a pair of white cotton gloves to give the rash a chance to go
away by five o'clock. He wished he had gone to a Turkish
bath instead of the movie. He worried about making love
to Mayra with gloves on. It could give her a fixation and
he'd be responsible. And worse, he ought to be thinking
about what he'd be missing with gloves on. Never had there

been such skin. His legs turned to water when he thought about it.

Mayra was precisely on time. He led her to a chair, then went to the kitchen for the tea and the cookies that he had bought in the Hungarian bakery where they also sold bean soup to take out. Mayra started talking the moment she arrived. She kept talking when he left the room, she merely spoke more loudly. "Surely Giorgione represents the finest High Renaissance painting of the Venetian school, don't you think, Mr. Seligson? He outgrew Bellini, no matter what anybody says about the 'Virgin of Castelfranco,' and no one could spiritualize a landscape the way Giorgione could do it."

"You're absolutely right," he yelled from the kitchen. He took down the English cookbook to check that he was making the tea the right way. He could hardly concentrate on the printing the way she was demanding attention.

"And as for those rebellious Pre-Raphaelites," she yelled as though being drawn into his English polarization, "it seems quite clear now, doesn't it, that they simply were not the rejected outcasts they pretended to be. When have painters ever been such darlings of the speculators? I mean, aside from right now, can you think of a more marketable period for art, plain supermarket art?"

"No. No, I can't," he shouted back at her. He peeked under his white glove while he waited for the tea to finish steeping. The hands had definitely improved! It was going to be all right! He stripped the gloves off. He wished he had the talcum power in the kitchen. No matter. He'd use flour.

"And let's face it," Mayra was bellowing. "The Louvre has its drawbacks. It's dark whenever the sun isn't shining, and their own painter, David, recorded his scorn in 1795 when he said the gallery produces false illumination almost always unfavorable to the paintings." Mr. Seligson rushed in with the tray of tea and cups and cookies. He lowered the tray to the table in front of the sofa where Mayra was not sitting but where she was supposed to be sitting, where she was when he left the room. "I won this samovar with Green Stamps," he said.

"It's beautiful."

He filled her cup, then his. He put hers on the table in front of the sofa, his beside it. He sat down and motioned

to her to come over saying, "I have some rather good news
for you, Mayra dear. Please. Sit down." He motioned again.

"I'm fine. This is a wonderful chair." She darted across
the space and got the cup. She returned to the chair, gripping the cup with both hands. She was wearing an old black
dress of her mother's and no lipstick. It had been her idea,
but Mama had said she didn't understand—nothing could
make her look less than sensational. "Are those some of your
paintings, Mr. Seligson?" she asked.

"Call me Casey." He had always liked the name. His name
was Mort, but he had always liked Casey. He had never before suggested that anyone call him that, but he had never
before been about to take himself a gorgeous Negro mistress
either. Age sixteen, maybe seventeen, tops.

"Casey?"

He knew he would have to wait until "after" before she'd
call him Casey. "It looks very much as though I have been
able to get you that scholarship at Shannon-Phillips."

Mayra clasped her hands under her chin, her face as expressionless as a face can become.

"I sent along a portfolio of your work, of course," he
continued, "but I very much suspect that it was my endorsement and my twenty-three-hundred-word analysis of
your work that clinched everything."

"I am grateful," Mayra said. "I am very grateful."

His eyes suddenly filled with tears. "It was a privilege.
An honor. I lay myself down as a bridge over which you
may carry your talent into the world." He slid to the end of
the couch, directly beside her. "You must go forward into a
greater appreciation of the gifts God has seen fit to accord
you." He slid his left hand swiftly along the channel made
by her tightly closed legs and moved straight toward the
treasure. Her torso leaned forward as though to receive the
hand, but the movement was to free her right hand, which
slammed like a steel building wrecker's ball into the side of
his jaw. She sprang to her feet and ran to the kitchen. She
opened the refrigerator door and impressed her finger and
palm prints upon its enameled ceiling.

She fingered all the eggs in the egg compartment. She
fingerprinted the bottom of a roasting pan she found in the
oven, the steam pipe and the side of the stove. She returned
to the living room and sat down in a straight-backed chair,

her purse and her white gloves neatly in her lap, her feet together.

"That did it, Mayra. Just forget it. Forget the scholarship. Forget even passing your art course—and see what that does to your graduation."

She listened politely. The side of his face was red. He did not open his eyes as he spoke to her. "Monday morning I go to Shannon-Phillips and tell them with regret that you have been caught stealing art supplies from my class and that severe doubts have been cast upon your morals because you were seen having sexual relations with three men in Van Cortlandt Park. You'll be sorry for the rest of your life that you turned down my friendship."

"Mr. Seligson?"

"Too late! Never mind. There's nothing you can say. Let actions speak now. Maybe, and it's a big maybe, if you get those clothes off and get over here—"

"Mr. Seligson, I have been leaving my fingerprints in different places all over your apartment, and my mother is waiting for me right across the street. The police station is right over on Audubon Avenue, and a business friend of my mother's is a reporter on the *Daily Mirror.*"

"Are you blackmailing me?"

"I thought you were blackmailing me."

"Listen here, Miss Smartass—" His lower lip began to tremble. "Just how far do you think your word is going to carry against mine? Hah? You think they'll take the word of a little—a little colored girl—over the word of a respected educator, eleven years a teacher with the Board of Education, City of New York?"

"I'm a minor, Mr. Seligson."

"Go! Out!" His face pressed itself into grimaces of humiliation, then she gave it to him to save him. She gave him the smile that showed him how much she truly admired him and how very much she would have wanted to lay him if only her parts had not been cemented over at infancy. "Goodbye, Casey," she said. "No hard feelings. I'll do you proud with that scholarship." She let herself out of the apartment. Casey poured himself a cup of tea and began to peck at the pile of Hungarian cookies.

CHAPTER THREE

The scholarship to the Shannon-Phillips Institute of Art was the cloud upon which the Virgin Mayra ascended to womanhood. The Institute confirmed that she could paint and that there was indeed a world existent south of 110th Street that was not (necessarily) exclusively for whigros, the word Mama used for whites or, when she got real mad at them, whiggers. Indirectly through the Institute she was caused to yield her maidenhood without any of the dismaying diversions, such as the need to convince herself that she had fallen in love, and she got high pleasure and much spiritual excitement in return. Even Mama approved of the cherry-taker and in more ways than several.

His name was Caspar P. Lear, Jr. He was a black art teacher, a painter, a spiritual follower of Mao, a graduate of City College and a *possible* contender, he told Mayra, for the light-heavyweight championship, although he didn't exactly say of what. He held a degree as a chemical engineer, had been offered good jobs as a chemical engineer. He was also about the handsomest man she had ever looked at. But all that was not what had decided her to topple over in his bed.

They had their art and health and color in common, but he had never set a straight course on seducing her, nor she him. He preferred to discourse on the many forks ahead in his road, which he thought he might take and what he'd do when he got where he figured to be going. He was never dull, but she wasn't altogether pleased with his perfection either.

Everything about him was just maybe a little too much to think about living with forever, but he gave her more than the one thing she had not yet encountered—the possibility of revolt, the open door to rebellion. No hat-in-hand waiting around for whitey to run you for alderman or drag you screaming into the membership of his country club. Caspar P. Lear, Jr., believed in the expanding promise of black revolution.

After she had looked dreamily into his eyes, showing the high glaze of lust as they lay side by side on the big daybed in his apartment on 95th off Central Park West, and she had murmured "Let's fuck," she wanted to move in with Caspar because he did everything as well as he did everything else, but Mama talked her out of it. She said living with the first man you made it with was too habit-forming, and sometimes people never got out of the habit. She agreed that he sounded like a good man, but that didn't mean Mayra had to go and live with him. Mayra capitulated when Mama suggested that she just try it out on Friday and Saturday nights. The Ashants were living on Long Island, and that was the right way to arrange it. It was a wildly exciting love affair once it got started, and once it did get started they didn't talk about black revolution much any more. It lasted four months, then Caspar decided to accept a job in the petro-chemical division of the Morania Oil Company in Philadelphia. There wasn't much romantic sadness. They both knew how they felt by then, and she said she understood why he wanted to try the square side of the tracks for a little while. He told her not to be too sure, to keep reading the sports page, and anyway Philadelphia was only ninety miles away. "And, hey," he decided to tell her, "one thing. You might like to hear that the Institute thinks you're the most talented student painter they've had in almost fifteen years."

Her eyes got misty.

"Whassamatta?"

"I don't see how they can think that." She turned away. "And I'm not fishing."

"Why can't they?"

"My stuff comes out okay, but I don't *feel* anything about it. I don't hear any bands playing in my head. I can't smell much life coming off the canvas."

He grinned, "They said 'student painter,' didn't they?"

Her face brightened. "Yeah, I forgot that."

He touched her cheek. "Technique first, always technique. When you got a lock on that, time enough to pour yourself all over it."

After he left, Mayra was in the rhythm of staying in town Friday and Saturday nights, and she'd meet Mama and they'd have dinner, then go to a movie, then check into a mid-town hotel and do some shopping Saturday morning. Mayra got to brooding about technique, and one Saturday morning when Mama had agreed to go uptown to a laundry customer's to sit with two of her kids while the woman took the littlest to an eye doctor, Mayra went to the 42nd Street Library and began to look at books in the art room. The first book she picked up was a book about *trompe-l'oeil* painting by a Martin Battersby, and as she read it and studied the illustrations she lost her sense of time and she kept looking at *trompe-l'oeil* books until an hour before closing, about twenty minutes before she was supposed to meet Mama at Penn Station. She was so quiet all the way home that Mama wondered what was going on. "Just trying to figure something out about painting," Mayra said. She kept figuring all day Sunday, then she cut classes on Monday and went back to the art room and read it all over again. On Tuesday she began to ask questions at the Institute. She was told: "After all, no one takes *trompe-l'oeil* especially seriously, do they, Mayra?" and "Offhand I wouldn't have the faintest idea who you could go to to teach you *trompe-l'oeil*" and "But it's all so technically difficult, and to what avail, my dear girl?" At home she went over the whole thing with Mama, who said finally, "If you want pot you don't go to United Cigars, baby. Go ask the man who wrote the book to tell you how to paint that way."

So Mayra went back to the library and was shocked to discover that Martin Battersby lived in England. England was farther away than the moon. England took money, and no Institute scholarship went that far. So she wrote to Caspar P. Lear, Jr., in Philadelphia and explained how her life had been changed in the art room of the 42nd Street Library, and what could she do about it? He sent her a telegram. He told her to apply for a Fulbright or a Guggenheim, or if she wanted to go first class all the way with the most, she could ask John Moodie at Shannon-Phillips how she could get a

fellowship from the E. C. West Foundation, and that he
wanted to be her number-one witness on the application
forms, but that it might be a good idea to write to Martin
Battersby first just to find out if he would agree to teach
trompe-l'oeil painting.

May 14, 1954

Dear Mr. Battersby:

I am an art student at the Shannon-Phillips Institute
of Art in New York who will soon complete its two-
year curriculum. The faculty has said that if you will
consider accepting me as a pupil they will supply high
endorsements of my seriousness and ability. If you accept me as a pupil I shall apply for an E. C. West
Foundation fellowship. I am Negro, almost twenty
years old.

Very truly yours,
Mayra Ashant

Battersby sent his letter of acceptance in six days. His
fee would be one-half of the amount of the fellowship after
return travel had been subtracted and if the remainder was
sufficient to cover her living expenses. She must guarantee
to give not less than one year, hopefully two years, to her
studies, but if she were late for class or if he found her abilities were not up to his standards she would be discharged.
He looked forward to seeing her references from the faculty
of Shannon-Phillips. Second to being laid by Caspar P. Lear,
Jr., it was the most exciting moment of her life. She applied
for the fellowship and Mama's signature gave parental con-
sent.

"I got news," Mama said.

"What?"

"You know who ended Miss Baby's career?"

"Who?"

"And you know who was Miss Pupchen's sponsor when
she kept the open line to her mama in Vienna?"

"Who?"

"Edward Courance West, that's who."

"Mama!"

"I think I can get through to him. He'll remember me,
baby."

"But, I—"

"Won't mean nothing to him. It's all tax deducts, I read. And anyway, he never gave a damn about that open line to Vienna for five months. He'll just tell somebody to set it up, and off you go to get what you're after."

"No, Mama. I can't. This is something else, and I have to do it with my work. I mean I'm not saying it isn't great the way you're always there to get anything for me, but with this they got to take me because I'm a painter they'll be proud they got started."

"Now you talking, hon."

The Institute's austere director, John Moodie, arranged everything, and the Foundation demanded (beyond the Institute's recommendation and photographs of three of the most representative pieces of her work) that she provide an affidavit stating that she was not then and had never been a member of the Communist party or a sympathizer with its aims. Caspar P. Lear, Jr., had instructed Mayra that Communists were almost as crazy to burn down the world as Republicans, so Mayra had no trouble signing that. Her application for scholarship was accepted and the scholarship/fellowship granted on July 3, 1954. Casp came up from Philadelphia and joined Mama and Mayra for dinner at Longchamp's on lower Fifth Avenue. They didn't talk politics. Mayra told him she was sailing on the *Elizabeth* on July 17, and, as though he were joking, Casp asked Mama what she would do with herself when Mayra had gone off to England and had left her all alone. "Mostly sit around waiting on you to call, Caspar," Mama said because she knew he wasn't making any jokes, and as she told Mayra later, the whole thing gave her more confidence in her mirror. Casp was nine years older than Mayra, who was up to being twenty, and Mama was only nine older than Caspar, and besides she had a lot of flair.

CHAPTER FOUR

Walt's anxiety was fastened to tracks that ran from his first consciousness to the ever-retreating terminal, the present. His anxiety was a swiftly scanning eye that transmitted all minutiae, never ending in its search for clues that might lead to the discovery of why he had been painted with such wet and sticky guilt. The frantically roving eye had never been able to find any explanation in all the almost thirty years of its shuttling desperation. It had raced over switches and across endless tracks of experience reporting back its bafflement—but it could not be stopped.

When Walter West had been five days old, in 1929, his father had assigned his rearing to the Wall Street firm of Pick, Heller & O'Connell. When he was ten years old he had asked Mr. Pick whether many of the firm's clients had consigned their children to Mr. Pick. The lawyer had stated, "In effect, yes. Death occurs to clients (and others) at all ages. We have had young, deceased clients who left children and substantial estates, and although we had not been instructed specifically to administer the child as well as the estate, we did have the executor's responsibility in that the children had become the primary clients."

On the morning of the first meeting with Edward Courance West regarding his son Walter, five days following the death of Irene Wagstaff West, Mr. Pick appeared at the Harkness Pavilion discreetly dressed as befitted a serious samurai. West laid out the retainer slowly but clearly and charged Pick, Heller & O'Connell with final responsibility for the rearing of his son, whom, he explained he did not intend to see ever again. He suggested that Switzerland would be a good place to settle the infant. He wished Mr. Pick to draw a trust agreement into which Mr. West would pay seven hundred and fifty thousand dollars on January 2, 1930. Until that date, just less than a year away, he told Mr. Pick that he would invest the amount for the infant Walter and assign any profits to the infant's trust. He gave Mr. Pick a power of attorney to act for Walter until it was decided whether Mr. Pick should be appointed by the court as Walter's legal guardian.

When Irene West's estate was probated, the Walter Wagstaff West trust fund was enormously appreciated in that Walter and his older brother Daniel were the equal and sole legatees of her estate. Irene West had been the sole heiress to the estate of her father, Walter Wagstaff, leading American railroad manipulator and operator. The morning after Mr. Pick had advised Edward West of this accrual of funds they held a meeting in Mr. West's Pierce-Arrow, on the Harlem River Drive, motoring up and back twice past the Polo Grounds under High bridge to Dyckman Street. Mr. West told Mr. Pick that, in his wife's memory, he wished to take over Walter's inheritance, as he had already done with Dan's, that he would combine Walter's legacy with the seven hundred and fifty thousand dollars already in hand, and that he would, of course, sign all necessary papers and place in escrow all necessary collateral to guarantee the amount of Walter's inheritance against loss. Mr. Pick reminded him of the approximate amount in millions of dollars that would be involved in the escrow agreement and Mr. West nodded absent-mindedly.

Walter West's fortune began to multiply five days after his birth on January 14, 1929, a date forty-one days after President Coolidge in his final State of the Union message to the Congress had said, "No Congress of the United States ever assembled, on surveying the state of the Union, has met with a more pleasing prospect than that which appears at the present time." The statement was a certainty on December 4, 1928, the day of the President's message, the day the Goldman-Sachs Trading Corporation was formed. By the time Walter West was eight months old and settled in Switzerland it was less true.

Carrying the capital of his two sons as casual baggage, Edward West had provided the bulk of the financing in England, through the unidentifying and unidentifiable resources of his own bank, for the illegal Clarence Hatry operations, a vast industrial and financial empire that was built around vending machines and that had expanded into investment trusts, then to higher finance, then to the issuance of unauthorized stock, and even to the forging of stock certificates. When Edward West suddenly withdrew his entire investment, without warning and without risk to his own reputation, he left Hatry behind in England in a maze of peculiarly financed investment trusts, to collapse in September 1929, shaking world confidence in the highly speculative American stock market. Then, operating from his New York base at the West National Bank and buying from seven other offices in the United States and Europe, Edward West helped to drive up the value of the shares in Boston Edison to prices so far beyond their true values that the Massachusetts Department of Public Utilities refused to allow the stock to be split four for one and consternated the stock market on October 11, 1929, with the words, "Due to the action of speculators no one . . . on the basis of earnings . . . should buy it."

Mr. West took the short position in the market on September 5, 1929, and played it like world championship billiards through the next six weeks, taking his son's legacies along with him. He worked well hidden behind the screen of the West National Bank, as always before he had worked behind the scenes in all of the extraordinary enterprises that had originally provided his extraordinary capital. He liquidated everything, from two high-leverage investment trusts to several companies he had built from two-thousand-dollar investments into stock issues worth thirty-seven million dollars, dumping shares onto the New York Stock Exchange, the Curb Exchange and onto markets in Boston and Cincinnati. On the afternoon of October 27 he gave Mr. Pick twenty-three checks made out to Walter's trust fund, and he sailed for England that evening, telling ship news reporters that he was "seriously concerned with the immediate financial future of the country." Hundreds of thousands of investors in all parts of the world were selling wildly behind him, hoping desperately to save something, but there was nothing left to save.

In following the demands of his acquisitive, not to say rapacious, nature and in acknowledging his respect for his dead wife's last will and testament, he met his responsibility as Walter's father for the first and last time. Walter at eight months of age had become the sole owner of one of the toweringly great American fortunes at a time when all investments at every level of the American financial structure had become "bargains." However, Mr. West instructed Pick, Heller & O'Connell not to reinvest Walter's funds until he issued instructions. Twenty-three months after the collapse of the stock market he told them to begin to reinvest. They did, and the trust held outstanding interests in stocks, real estate and bonds, as indicated by Edward West, all through the thirties, all through the war economy.

When Walter reached his majority in February 1950 (while he was in Korea as an infantryman) his estate had multiplied to proportions nearly immeasurable, because it insisted on growing even while battalions of accountants and bankers tried to count it. In a desperate caricature of the allegedly traditional system of opportunity offered in his native country, Walter West not only had enough to feed, clothe and house entire cities of crippling slums but he had not earned a penny of his fortune nor was he able to comprehend either what he owned or how he had acquired it. He personified the motto of the United States, *E pluribus unum*—one out of many.

In March 1929, through Natural le Coultre of Geneva, Switzerland, Pick, Heller & O'Connell purchased a comfortable seven-acre property for Walter—Les Haubans—on Lake Genève, between Hermance and Anières. It was a large, sturdy house with a sizable barn that was renovated and extended into a gymnasium, and a tennis court, squash court and indoor swimming pool. The law firm then caused the infant Walter Wagstaff West to emigrate from New York in the charge of Dr. Abraham Weiler, a young pediatrician, and a baby nurse, Evelyn Gonkums.

At the age of three Walter's training was taken over by an English nanny of formidable reputation, Miss Rosie Currie, firm but fair, who trained his straight hair into a natural wave. She returned to England after a four-year

tour with Walter, the last two years of which had been conducted in German and Italian; English was spoken only at
meals and on Sundays. Walter learned French and Spanish
from the housekeeping stewards of Les Haubans, Henri
and Louise Emmet, who, after he had reached ten, taught
him the grave distinctions among cheeses and wines; after
he was fourteen Mr. Emmet taught him the embellishing
distinctions of dress. Because of Mr. Emmet, Walter was
never to travel in later years without packing two dinner
jackets, in the event that sauce mousseline or any other
staining agent was spilled on one of them.

Mr. Pick brought Gordon Elphinstone and Mr. Takamura to Walter on the boy's sixth birthday. Gordon Elphinstone was an associate professor of education at Columbia
University and held a doctorate in American history. During
the two years he spent at the Institute for Advanced Study
at Princeton he wrote his brilliant analysis of the Ballinger-
Pinchot controversy that won the Keifetz Prize. Professor
Elphinstone (calculating Mr. Pick's options) signed a ten-
year contract to educate Walter that provided grants and
research assistance, as well as salary deposited in New
York, which would enable him to publish every two years.
He was to teach Walter all formal subjects except languages
and physical culture. For his own enlightenment he began
his tenure with the preparation of a history of the flaws in
the American credit and currency structure that had brought
about the panic of 1907 and had been directly responsible
for the passage of the Aldrich-Vreeland Act—which is to
say, to specialists of American history if not entirely to all
others, he was a stimulating man. He was short, thirty-six
years old, a bachelor and intensely aggressive. He was white
and Presbyterian—perhaps superfluous information.

Y. Takamura took charge of Walter's physical training
and renewed his Italian and German. For twelve years,
until Walter was eighteen, Mr. Takamura taught him calis-
thenics, baseball strategy, tennis, skiing, bowling, *pétanque*
and curling, mountain climbing, figure skating, billiards,
ballet, swimming, boxing, trampoline, small-boat handling,
karate, ballroom dancing, automobile operation and maintenance, flower arranging, photography, gliding, fencing,
controlled concentration, and how to watch bull fights and
court tennis.

Pick, Heller & O'Connell had assembled a small surrogate family for their client. Elphinstone interpreted the passage of time, past into future; the uses of pen, speech and mind; mysteries and humanities. Takamura brought control and uses of the body. The Emmets introduced the essentials of sensuality, perpetual and life-lasting. Pick, Heller & O'Connell leased to him a conscience and judgment. Together all of them built a steady and reliable, if dull, young man.

Walter Wagstaff West cannoned out of adolescence to become an architect and was determined to show his father that he, too, was an achiever. He was a gifted architect who applied himself through late hours. When he had decided how he wanted to practice his profession he asked Pick, Heller & O'Connell to locate Derek Adler, a friend from the United States Army in Korea who had studied architecture with Miës van der Rohe at the Illinois Institute of Technology.

It took the law firm's London detective agency two days to locate Derek Adler. When found he was trying to decide whether to accept a job in U. S. Army Ordnance as an architectural consultant/maintenance engineer or to become a playwright, which his British wife favored. As Adler had become more and more British his wife had become more and more American, until by the second year of marriage his only concession to American mores was to use peppermint-flavored toothpicks at $3.50 per thousand to dislodge his wife's cooking, which consisted almost entirely of things like Two-Alarm Texas Chili and frozen hush-puppies. The Adlers had met through the *Marriage Herald,* a monthly magazine published in Chalcot Road, N.W. 1, that stated its sixty-two-year-old institutional purpose was "to arrange marriages between ladies and gentlemen of suitable character, tastes, attainments and intellectual standards," maintaining at all times an awareness of "undesirable characters and adventurers who would bring the agency into disrepute."

Derek Adler confirmed his disciplines for architectural design by believing in the logic of brokered marriages. His parents and grandparents had met and married by such means. One could be far more certain of making a successful marriage, because both partners would have demonstrated the degree of their interest in marriage by advertising for it;

therefore both were more likely to be ready for marriage than partners acquired at random. Adler did not believe in the single life. Single, he felt like a magnificent recipe that had been torn in half before it had been savored, and he sought to find the completion of the recipe when he advertised in the *Marriage Herald* in 1955:

> American architect, bachelor, age 27, height 6 ft. 1 in., dark-to-olive coloring, athletic build when dieting, Jewish parents, comfortable income, wishes to correspond with/meet attractive, healthy, non-kinky, Jewish, Gentile, Mohammedan, Zoroastrian, or agnostic girl who does not smoke, is well-groomed writer, painter, architect, musician or even sculptor, income unimportant, must be willing travel anywhere; object, matrimony.

He got four responses. One criticized him for wanting to mix religions; one was looking for a mate who would be willing to become one-half of a ballroom dancing team; one got lost or stolen en route to a meeting that they had scheduled; and the fourth was the woman he would have designed for himself if architects had been given the power to breathe life into quarter-inch specifications.

Jane was a writer perpetually at work on an exhaustive biography of Cardinal Newman, author of *Lead, Kindly Light* and more than any other individual credited with the expansion of Roman Catholicism in Britain and the United States—which, in her view, was an invidious record indeed. She was a fine cook, he a splendid eater. She was a writer, he was a reader. Jack Sprat and his wife never had it so good in so many ways as did the Adlers. In fact, the only way their union could have been more perfect would have been if she were a transvestite and could have worn his hats, of which he had an extraordinarily representative collection.

Between her immersions in the biography of Cardinal Newman, Jane Adler was a free-lance journalist who happened to be entranced with *trompe-l'oeil* painting. She met Mayra Ashant at Battersby's studio in Brighton. Mayra was about to try to break out as a professional painter in London and Jane invited her delightedly to stay with them while she looked for a permanent place to live. It was Jane's theory that the more art surrounded her husband the more he would be likely to turn down the job in Army Ordnance and become a playwright. Six weeks later, at tea time, while she and Mayra were hammering at him to make him agree to write a play on the experiences of the lewd rector of Stiffkey who had passed on in 1936 as a result of having been partly eaten by a vaudeville lion, Walter West rang the Adler doorbell. When the door opened Mayra was standing there. At lunch the next day he and Adler worked out the details of their partnership. To be licensed in a foreign country would be next to impossible, but they could operate as consultants to a licensed firm.

CHAPTER FIVE

Pick, Heller & O'Connell opted to secure a large bank loan for the operations of the new firm called West & Adler, Consultants to Perkins & Flicker, and yet another business manager was installed by them to operate West to West Ltd., a realty firm simultaneously established.

"I think I should meet the client," Adler said.

"Why?"

"If I don't meet the client, then I'm the inside partner, and the inside partner is always the heavy."

"What's wrong with that if you never meet the client?"

"Also, I'd like to try to get a feel of what the client will instinctively try to botch up."

"We're the client," Walt said abruptly.

"Did your father—uh—?"

"No."

"Who?"

"Questions can make a lot of trouble, Derek."

"Answers make the trouble. And I'm your partner. I got a right, right? What I mean is, suppose you're hit by a car, God forbid, and I have to run everything. Does Charley the business manager know who the client is?"

"Not really. It's sort of a chain. We hook onto him and he hooks onto another business manager at a realty company who hooks onto an English law firm who hooks onto a New York law firm who hooks onto a bank who hooks onto the client." Walt rumpled his hair, pinched his nose, stared out the window and made a face. "But you're right. You have to know. I'm the client."

"You're the *client?*"

"Derek, now hear this. What I've told you is very confidential information. First, it won't do the firm much good if people know we're our own clients. Next, I don't want people to think of me as anything but an architect, and that includes being known as Edward Courance West's son. I don't want to be known as that either. You've got to respect that and you've got to keep all of it as a confidence."

"Sure, Walt. Certainly."

"It's just a piece of land and a lot of lawyers. We have to create something of value on the land—design it and see it built. That's all that matters. Do you see that, Derek?"

"Sure, Walt. Absolutely."

Walt felt the way he thought his father must have felt when he had put his first great big deal together, and this exhilaration was even more heightened when he found a message at his flat that Dan was waiting for his call at the Savoy Hotel. He called before he took his hat off, to be ready to rush right out again. Dan sounded tired. He said he was in town for about two days and that he'd been tied up at the embassy all day. He asked if Walt could get free to join him for dinner in his hotel suite. Walt said he was on his way.

Dan looked tired. He drank three fairly dark-brown highballs before dinner and most of a bottle of Haut-Brion with dinner while Walt ate everything in sight and talked excitedly and with a considerable amount of triumph about West & Adler, Consultants to Perkins & Flicker and West to West Ltd. He said, "I think even Father would agree that this is sure-fire stuff. And I hope you'll pass the word along."

Dan had been staring blankly over Walt's shoulder across the river at the lights of the Royal Festival Hall. "I don't have to tell him anything any more, Walt," he said. "He knows everything that happens to you and to me every hour of the day and night."

Walt was startled and not a little thrilled. "How do you mean?"

"He's built the largest private intelligence organization anywhere in the world and he has to keep it working. His new men probably practice on you and me."

"Why does he have that?"

"To protect himself from the Communists—what else?"

"But what does he need to do that for?"

"Because he's become insane—if he wasn't always insane."

"Now, just a minute, Dan—"

"He's the whole wind behind Joe McCarthy. I won't even speak to McCarthy, and McCarthy thinks that's very, very funny, because most of his money comes from my father, who is the sure-thing backer of any and every crackpot anti-Communist scheme they can dream up. He's scared out of his mind about Communists in Washington and Communists in Moscow, and someday someone is going to whisper to him that it could be that the Vatican is packed with Communists, and he'll race into the breach with another five million bucks."

"Oh, well," Walt said, "that's just national fermentation. It's the usual historic process that made the nation great."

"What the hell do you know about it?" Dan's voice was tight and his eyes were hard. "I live with it in the Senate. I live with it under his hate. You should get a good close look at how great America has become—in the same room with Joe McCarthy drunk and clowning and the old man so certifiably insane that he should have been committed five years ago except that he's too rich to be committed and you and I don't have the nerve to sign the papers anyway."

"Dan, don't talk like this. He's our father. We should be defending him."

Dan shook his head and stared at the floor. "Maybe you'll find out someday," he said bitterly. "I'm chained to him. I can't get away and I'd give anything to get away. You're as free as a bird and you want to be chained to him." He stood up and trailed off unsteadily toward the bedroom. "Good night, kid. I'm sorry I talked so much. I'm sorry about a lot of things."

Mayra and Walt began by seeing each other for dinner once a week. Then he'd call her and ask if she could have lunch because he had an idea for interior patios high up (and once a plan for a waterfall that was to fall from the roof of a sixty-story office building into a gorge and would create all the electricity used by the building). Then they saw each other for lunch on Tuesdays and Saturdays and dinner Mondays and Thursdays, and by that time they had found out that they were in love so they began sleeping with each other, and in the third month Walt moved into her basement flat permanently. He brought one suitcase.

"You sure travel light," she said.

"Oh, I keep a few things at the office."

Mayra cooked. They ate in restaurants on the same two evenings each week and lunched in restaurants on the same two days, but she cooked and kept the flat in shape and made the beds and handled the laundry, and they were happier than either of them had ever been in their lives. It wasn't a very big flat. It had a large living room-studio that had good light in the afternoon, a small bedroom, a good-sized kitchen and a hallway. Walt asked her if maybe she'd like to have him find her a studio with a north skylight, but she said she worked better at home where the heavy work was, so he brought her a set of elaborate architectural blue-white Dalites.

Jane Adler was a very good journalist. This required excessive curiosity and physical pain if the curiosity wasn't satisfied. From the day Derek took her to see the enormous piece of property on which West & Adler, Consultants to Perkins & Flicker, were to build a multiple dwelling for five hundred families, she had to know how they had suddenly happened to land a commission like that.

"I courageously stopped a runaway horse carrying the only daughter of the richest man in Europe." Adler shrugged. "Naturally, he demanded to be allowed to discharge the obligation by rewarding me somehow and——"

"Oh, bosh!"

"Watch it. You're sounding more British than American."

"How did you *get* the commission, Derek?" She asked him in bed, while dancing, during friendly quarrels and once while they were making love. She pushed, pressed and cajoled. She got tough. She got hysterical. Her purpose was so much stronger than his that, at last, as she had known he would, he got bored with the inquisition and told her (swearing her to eternal secrecy on the pain of their loss of everything held dear) who Walt was, who his father was, how

Walt operated as his own client and how they might just keep on expanding forever.

The only thing that impressed her was that Walter, her friend Walter, her guest, her companion, the man she had introduced to her friend, was the son of Edward Courance West.

"Do you have any *idea* who Edward Courance West is?"

"Sure. I read the *American Weekly*."

"Bosh! No matter what you read—by God, I think he owns our newspaper!—no matter what you've heard, you couldn't remember it and put it all together and see it in one piece."

"What am I, an obit writer?"

"To begin with, he's the richest man in the world."

"Big deal. And I mean that from the bottom of my heart."

"Walt is his son? I mean, you *know* how I love Walter West, but—"

"I didn't say he was Walt's father."

"You did too."

"I said Walt said the man was Walt's father. Walt may be a secret masochist."

"Bosh!"

"You've got to quit these obscenities, Jane. No kidding. Besides, Walt's father is a complete nut."

"Oh, come off it."

"He and McCarthy and about a dozen other hustlers are practicing right now to put everybody in jail. By me that's a nut. And I am beginning to have the horrible feeling that I must be some kind of a nut myself for telling you that that nut is Walt's father."

So Jane told Mayra and Mayra took it big. Mainly because she hadn't known, and she was hurt and angry because Walt hadn't told her. And because Walt hadn't told her (because he didn't feel he should recognize his father if his father hadn't recognized him) Mayra decided that Walt must certainly have thought that she would lunge at his money if she knew, and she got into a sick rage, lost her head and bolted. A firm in Beauchamp Place came into the flat and in two hours had emptied it of everything except Walt's packed suitcase. She left London on the three-o'clock flight to Rome, where she stayed for two nights in a hotel off the Via Condotti. Then, through a restaurant cashier, she found an apartment off St. Agnes in Agony Street, behind the Piazza Navona, and grimly set to work to see if she could paint herself out of any memory of ever having known the son of a bitch.

She left complete demoralization behind in London. Walt strolled from the bus in Sloane Street to Hans Place, whistling merrily off-key, carrying two bottles of pink (Swiss) champagne because it was the luniversary of the day they had met, trooped lightly down the outside staircase, let himself into the flat—and she was gone, the place was stripped and his suitcase had been packed untidily. He called Derek Adler.

"Mayra's gone."

"Gone where?"

"She moved every stick out of the apartment except my packed suitcase."

"Why?"

"I don't know. When I left this morning she was—she was—"

"Hysterical? Angry?"

"No! She was very happy. She was ecstatic."

"Maybe she got a cable from home. Somebody could be dying. Maybe she had to fly out."

"And take all the furniture and twenty-three paintings, fahcrissake?"

"Take it easy. Let me think."

"I don't want opinions. If you don't know where she is, that's all I want to know."

He slammed the telephone down. He called C. L. Pick in New York. Mr. Pick was in Washington but Mr. Heller was there. Would Mr. West speak to Mr. Heller? He asked Heller for a detective agency in London. Heller said he'd have someone call him from London. Walt said please rather have them send their best man or men to him at 19, Hans Place instantly, basement apartment. Heller asked if the matter were serious enough to require legal assistance. Walt said no.

Derek sat Jane down and pulled a chair across from her so that she would have to face him. "Everything busted wide open," he said.

"Where?"

"Mayra's gone. She cleaned out the flat. Everything's gone."

"Why?"

"You tell me."

She began to cry, and she didn't cry easily.

"Did you tell her about him?"

She nodded, sobbing.

"When? I mean, Jesus, when did you have a chance? I didn't tell you until one o'clock this morning."

"Ten o'clock—no, a quarter to ten—this morning." She looked at him, frightened and appealing. "I thought she'd be proud! I never thought she'd leave him just because——"

"Some mess. I don't even know what to do. Anyway, it's not your fault. He told me not to tell anybody and I did. It's my fault, honey."

"Now you quit that, Derek."

"We'll just have some coffee and wait here. No booze. We'll need clear heads." He poured them each a short glass of whiskey. "He'll come here and we'll tell him what happened."

"Oh, Derek!"

"It's okay. I can always write a musical about the rector of Stiffkey."

"It's pronounced Stew-key."

"For that matter, Walt can always shoot himself."

When Jane had telephoned to tell her who Walt was, Mayra had felt cold hostility cover her like hair spray and hold her in ѡ rigid net. He was the son of the West Foundation. They'd been together for three months and she had thought they'd been everything it was possible to be to each other, but he had been afraid she would find out who he was, because she was black and he was ashamed of her. So many things he did habitually began to convince her more and more that he had just been using her until he got tired of using her. Like the way he was so cheap, pretending to like Swiss champagne more than French, or always taking buses, or having two suits of clothes to his back, all so she wouldn't think he was that rich man's son and try to take him the way he figured that's what she'd do the minute she found out. And the way he babbled about astrology, and theosophy and faith cures and nature healing, just like he was some goddam idiot who never got out of grade school and who had to cover up and show off like a little boy how smart he was, all so she wouldn't know he was that rich man's son with a mess of colleges behind him. And how he never knew anything about the West Foundation. And the way he'd look at her Foundation check when it came on the first of every month and keep turning it over in his hands and looking at both sides of it and saying he'd get it cashed for her. Then when she packed his goddam bag she found all three Foundation checks tucked right in there, never used, like he thought his rich goddam honkie father could trace them to a nigger girl if he cashed them.

The agency men found her in thirty-two hours. Walt chartered an Executive Jet and went to Rome. Mayra had been in her new flat in the Via Parione for fifty-three minutes and was already painting hard, thinking hard, not a stitch unpacked, when he knocked at the door. She knew someone was making a mistake, knocking at the wrong door, so she answered it.

"What the hell happened?" Walt said. Her jaw dropped. She stood and stared. "What made you run out of London like that?" He entered the apartment and she offered no resistance. He shut the door. "Christ, Mayra, you scared hell out of me," he kept on. "You should have left a note or something." Mayra began to cry softly. He put his arms around her and she let her forehead rest on his lapel and she bawled. They got it all straightened out in about ten minutes. She found out what his father felt about him and she forgot all about all the things she had dreamed up against him, felt sorry for him on the one hand and very proud of him on the other, but most of all, gloriously most of all, she knew who he was, not by name, not by baptismal label, but who he was.

There was also an indirect consequence of their reconciliation. West & Adler, Consulenti à Di Georgio e Bonetti was formed by a Roman lawyer retained by Pick, Heller & O'Connell together with estate agents who found a large very desirable piece of property on the far side of the Villa Borghese. Derek and Jane Adler flew in from London to set up offices and crews that would duplicate the construction of the building being designed in London, insofar, that is, as Roman building laws would permit the design without modification.

CHAPTER SIX

After her first show, after she could speak pretty good Italian, after the new architectural offices were established and Derek was commuting from London, after everything was simply marvelous and simply couldn't possibly get any better, Walt spoiled everything by demanding that she marry him. The more he pleaded and bullied and wheedled, the more certain she became that she would not marry him. She spent seven months fighting off his maniacal resolution, and once when they were in a desperate argument in the street she pointed up at the street sign proclaiming St. Agnes' agony and yelled at him with muscular Italian therapy that it wasn't only Agnes who was feeling pain. But he wouldn't stop and she couldn't stand it any longer, so one day while he was at the office she hired two men with a truck and broad shoulders and they packed everything in the flat in the Via Parione, including her new paintings, for shipment to Paris to an address she was to cable them. She left only Walt's packed suitcase.

She flew to Geneva, then took the train to Paris, where she found an apartment on the first day in the Avenue de Neuilly, which she rented in the name of a *notaire* so that Walt's detectives couldn't find her. She remained in the flat for four months, leaving only to shop for food in the neighborhood, and then heavily veiled. At the end of that time she felt she had almost forgotten him. She had accumulated twenty-seven new paintings in all, and the afternoon she met with the dealer she thought most capable of handling her show, she was tagged by Walt's people, who followed her home. Walt rang the doorbell at nine-twenty the next morning and his appearance almost broke her. He was thin and sick-looking, almost dead-looking—just large eyes and sunken white cheeks and thick, hanging ketchup-colored hair.

"Walt! My God!"

"I'd like a cup of Bovril."

"Bovril?"

"Don't you have any?"

"How did you find me?"

"I just had people covering the *trompe-l'oeil* dealers in Europe."

"In *Europe?*"

"We got a line on your being in Paris from your letters to your mother, but they had no return address on the envelope and I was quite strict with the people about not daring to open them. But we knew you were in Paris from the postmark, and we knew you were in Neuilly, but we couldn't seem to pick you up until you showed at the gallery. May I come in?"

She stood aside for him and he entered the flat wearily. She closed the door and she knew that she had not forgotten him at all. She threw her arms around him and kissed him tenderly, then hungrily, and she cried.

After five weeks he had responded to her cooking. He moved his single suitcase in with her, turned rosy again, was extremely careful about not mentioning marriage, and everything was wonderful again. Derek came up from Rome and they established West & Adler, Consultant à Elaine Hewlett et Grellou, and bought a marvelous, large piece of property on the Boulevard Jourdan through the land agents for West to West Ltd. Mayra had refused to marry him, but she aided his career vastly. Three offices, three rather huge building development complexes that would alter the housing standards of thousands, and a total of seven realty-architectural-administrative companies had been formed because of her. She told Walt that maybe if they lived long enough in the goddam apartment it could mean advanced housing for all of Europe.

But she couldn't paint and cook and defend herself all at the same time. They were married on September 27, 1958, at the Chelsea Registry Office in London, with the Adlers as witnesses. They went to a restaurant in Basil Street, where they drank champagne but ordered no food, and Walt played the piano and sang to them until Derek was inspired to make a Bauernschmaus. So they bought two magnums of champagne and climbed into what Adler called his Rentley, a hired Humber, and swanned into Soho to buy sauerkraut, pork, paprika, sausages, onions and carrots, while Derek assured everyone that Bauernschmaus was merely a light Szekely Gulyas. It took an hour and a half to cook and two hours to eat, then the bride and groom were returned to the basement flat in Hans Place, which Walt had generously leased from Mayra during the almost two years they had been away from England.

The cablegram arrived on December 15, addressed to Mr. and Mrs. Walter Wagstaff West.

Walt tore open the envelope and flattened out the message sheet. He looked, grew pale and dropped the cable. She picked it up. "It's from my father," he said shakily. "Read it to me."

"Hawk Bay, New York. Nine twenty-two——"

"No, no. The message."

" 'Cordially invite you and your bride to spend Christmas Day with your brother and myself at Bürgenstock West and to remain here to see in the great promise of the new year. Mr. Tobin will telephone you to make all arrangements. Your father, Edward Courance West.' "

Walt walked unsteadily to a large chair and sat down. "Now, what did he do that for?"

"It's natural. Christmas, and you have a new black bride." She sounded easy, but she was frightened, and she didn't know why this was.

"We won't go."

"I wish you would. I'd like you to meet Mama."

"Let's fly Mama over here."

"You know she won't fly."

"But what can I say to him?"

"Hell, honey, you'll think of something."

"I'm going to call Dan." He picked up the phone and put the call through to Washington. "After all these years of being go-between Dan ought to know that I've finally been

called in to meet my father about a month before my thir-
tieth birthday."

"Well, sure."

"I hope it's not too late."

"Baby, why should it be too late?"

"I don't need it now the way I used to need it when I was
a kid."

"But you're curious. You've got to be curious."

"That's what it is. That's what it's reduced itself to—just
curiosity. When your own father is one of the most important men in the world, how can you help being curious about
just meeting him? Right?"

"That's right." The telephone rang and Walt picked it up
instantly.

"Dan? Walt. Hey, what do you think happened to me?
I just got a cable. Father sent me a cable inviting Mayra and
me to spend Christmas and New Year's with him at Bürgenstock West."

"He did? But—how come?"

"I thought you might know."

"No. In fact I can't think of anything that would be a
bigger surprise. He must want to ask your wife if she's a
Communist."

Walt laughed. "Do you think I ought to go?"

"Of course not."

"You don't?"

"Listen, Walt. You're in love, you have an exciting career
going for you, everything is coming up roses, so what the
hell do you all of a sudden need an insane man on your side
for? Forget it. You're safe where you are. Stay safe."

"But just the same, Dan, I——"

"So you're going anyway?"

"Well, I——"

"Okay. I know. I mean, really, it's okay. You were raised
to answer that way. Nothing you can do about it."

"It's not that, Dan——"

"When do you leave?"

"Well, I suppose we'll have to leave tomorrow to get there
by Christmas Eve, because we want to spend some time with
Mayra's mother in New York."

"I can't get there Christmas Eve, but I'll get there on
Christmas Day. I have to see for myself what it all looks like.

You can't be there all alone with that son of a bitch, because he's sick and he wishes no one well and if he makes any effort at all, on anything, in any direction, it's only for one reason—to feed his sadistic insanity."

"That's pretty strong stuff, Dan."

"I know. I wish—ah, what the hell. I'll look forward to seeing you and meeting your bride on Christmas Day."

Walt hung up.

"What was pretty strong stuff?" Mayra asked.

"Oh, Dan and Father had some family fight. It's nothing that won't be all fixed up by Christmas."

CHAPTER SEVEN

When the big West plane stopped and Mayra looked out the window she saw Mama waiting. And Mayra wasn't ready for that. Mama thought she had married a fair-to-struggling young architect, and now a big Learstar slides in from across the ocean and only two people get off, one of them li'l Mayra. Mama stood straight and looked just great, but there was gray in her hair. She looked just beautiful, but she wasn't the young Mama that Mayra always thought she was. She had a stack of Christmas parcels in her arms and she was smiling wide, getting ready to be happy, carrying it all off as though she was always getting driven out to meet her daughter stepping down out of a private, transatlantic plane. She had on a mink stole and she wore it over a gorgeous red dress, her long, slim legs rising above red shoes. There stood Mama. Mayra grabbed Walt and said, "There she is, that beautiful black lady!" She shrieked with happiness and buried her head in Walt's chest.

The engines stopped. The steward opened the door. Mayra flew down the ramp, across the cement and into her mother's arms. Mama gave Walt a big kiss straight off and he blushed five shades of red and pink. "He may not be black," Mayra said, "but you got to admit he's colored. How's the credit, Mama?"

"Perpetual at last. I got a food store that sells everything. Big, fat German fella from Dover, New Jersey. His wife says he eats cold spaghetti. I swear. I started him off with a cash deposit of a hundred, then second time I give him one-fifty, then third time round he says why bother to pay it in front, my credit is good with him, and I tell you he sure could give lessons to that Relleh on Manhattan Avenue."

When they got to Mama's house she made them tea but she backed it with gin, Scotch, beer, ice and setups. They sat around the dining room table grinning at each other, Walt shy and Mayra manic, Mama calm and happy. They talked about the housing Walt's firm was working on and Mayra's hat and dress and Mama's hat and dress and mink stole. "How about that stole," Mama said. "Did that almost knock you down? You know where that came from? Remember Miss Lily the—the lady on Madison Avenue and Sixty-fourth a long time ago?"

"The blonde one?" Mayra asked. "The one on cocaine?"

"That's the one. Well, she died about five months ago and she remembered me in her will. I cried like a baby. She left me that beautiful fur thing."

After a short while Mayra lied. "Walt, I know you have to see Mr. Tobin and don't you worry about Mama and me —we have plenty to talk over after all these years—and maybe if you go now you'll be able to be back in time for dinner."

Walt knew that Mayra knew that Willie Tobin wasn't waiting for him anywhere, but he got the drift. Anyway, it was a chance to have a good uninterrupted look at the Seagram Building, so he said, "I can get back here by six. Will six be all right?"

"Then is the hour," Mama answered.

"Looks like you got a good man," Mama said.

"Maybe better than that."

"What about that plane? What about that Rolls?"

"Belong to his daddy."

"Who his daddy?"

"That's the crazy part. Our name is West because his daddy is Edward Courance West."

Mayra expected her mother to be startled, agape with awe, wholly astonished and maybe even speechless for a little minute. But she hadn't ever expected to see the shock and then the fear that came over her mother's face. "Mama! What's wrong?" Mayra asked quickly. The older woman shook her head slowly but did not speak. Mayra could hear clocks ticking. Mama reached out and poured some gin into a glass. "I know that man, honey. He's a bad man. Baddest there ever was for women. I know him. He even screwed me once on the floor of Miss Baby's john—and that's a long time ago, when he was the most famous man in America, and he's bigger than that now. He put her in that pad and she moonlighted on him. He maybe figured she'd sew or like that between the times he felt like stopping in. He didn't put bodyguards and secretaries on his meat in those days and he had chicks all over. A little guy name of Willie Tobin used to come around and pay off. Miss Baby was careful not to ball him and I didn't wear no uniform when we knew he was coming. I played like I was the cook and cleaner. Miss Baby was greedy, that's all. She got that pad and clothes and a lot of roommates to stay on with her because, like she told Mr. West, she got lonesome—plus he gave her a thousand bucks a month, and that's in the Depression. Well, Mr. West found out and, man, he *wrecked* her, and he knocked me around plenty too. Then he calls up the *cops*. He rates, I mean. The place was full of police inspectors and assistant DAs, and they work out of me a statement that Miss Baby had been running a house of prostitution and trafficking in drugs and compulsory prostitution and fencing stolen goods —and those last ones were just dreams. He dropped everything on her. Then they took her down town and they made it all stick in court, and she died in jail with tuberculosis after she done six years. And why? Because she cheated on Mr. West, that's why."

Mama began to cry. She hunched over in her chair sobbing and mopping her face with a napkin. "Then he almost killed Miss Pupchen. For nothing. She didn't do anything. He just came in with crazy eyes and he broke her into pieces, and when it's all over he's clear-eyes. Yeah, Mr. Clear-Eyes. He give me five hundred bucks, because he said he lost his temper when he come on me and screwed me the time before at Miss Baby's, then beat the shit outta me. But this time he didn't do me nothing. He give me a check for a thousand and he say, 'Take care of the kid,' and he start out. I run after him. I say I can't, I don't know how, and she's hurt bad. She's all wrecked. He says for me to call Willie Tobin, and he strolls out, all clear-eyes."

"Walt's not like that. Walt's not anything like that. And he's never seen his father in his whole life."

"His father killed Mary Lou Mayberry. Murder, I'm talking about. He killed her, and I know that, and he's so bad I wouldn't be alive right now if he knew I knew that. I found her. I come in at ten in the morning and I found what was left. She hired me one day before, and for once he didn't know I was going to be on that job. She told me who was paying all those bills, and I come in and I saw that mess of brains and blood and I run outta there before they could put my name in the papers and he could know I knew. His girls got darker and darker. Mary Lou Mayberry was a beautiful black girl. A beautiful black girl just like you."

CHAPTER EIGHT

Edward Courance West finished dining alone in the main *salle* of the Grand Hotel at Bürgenstock West. It was an L-shaped room holding sixty-one tables to seat one hundred and seventy diners. All the tables were set with gay flowers, silver, elaborate service plates, linen and glassware—but there were no other diners. The maître d' hôtel stood near and behind Mr. West. Six *chefs de rang* and eight *commis* were at their stations. The very tall, very thin sommelier waited with his two apprentices to respond instantly on signal. A carver wearing a tall, white starched hat stood at a silver serving cart. Nine large crystal chandeliers hung from the ceiling, tall plants stood in each corner, and ancient Chinese porcelain bowls looked out from niches in all the walls. Eleven heroic oil paintings of princes and battle lords looked down hungrily at the central serving buffet, nine feet by nine feet, which was laden with hors d'oeuvres, salads, cold meats and fowl, cheeses, fruits and desserts. Flanking the outer edge of the L were high glass doors leading to gardens and high terraces.

Mr. West lifted his napkin to his mouth, then placed it beside his plate. The maître d'hôtel withdrew the chair gently from under him as he rose. He walked unhurriedly across the forty-foot diagonal to the door leading to the main hall, held open by a *chef de rang,* who said, "Good night, Mr. West."

He continued slowly along the corridor. Ahead of him the main hall, ninety feet long and forty-two feet wide, was a sea of vast Persian rugs on which floated sixty-one Louis XV and XVI chairs, eleven settees and sofas and twenty-five tables—but it was empty of people. The room was brilliantly lighted by five chandeliers. The chairs had been set to draw a long scarlet line down its center, flanked on the four walls by fifteen majestic oil paintings. The high ceiling was touched by a white colonnade of six arches that made a graceful aisle along one side.

At the end of the corridor, the beginning of the main hall, Mr. West turned left into the compact reception hall of the hotel. The uniformed concierge hastened out from behind his desk bringing with him a goose-down-lined greatcoat and a hunter's hat with earmuffs. As he dressed the upper part of Mr. West a porter put his feet into high, warm, insulated boots. "It is getting colder, Mr. West," the concierge said.

Mr. West left the lobby through the revolving door and stood looking out at the floodlights that were fixed on high poles placed thirty feet apart, seventy yards away from the entrance, seeming to curve on both sides of the long line of poles as though encircling the whole property. It was raining, and the tall lights transformed the falling drops into ropes of tinsel. Beyond the light there was blackness, as though Edward Courance West and his building were all that were left in the world; as though this were a way station on the sunless road that led downward and downward into the tenebrous, rock-locked regions of the underworld. It was as cold as Nifleheim, that ancient German concept of hell; by morning or sooner, the rain would change to snow. It was snowing only twenty-one miles to the north, and heavy snow could slow down the car he was waiting for.

The Rolls-Royce glided to a halt in front of him. William Tobin opened the door from the inside. Mr. West got in. The concierge tucked a beaver robe well around them, then closed the door. The car started up the long, gentle, sloping road.

"The first checkpoint telephoned," Tobin said. "They are right on time."

"Good."

The car drove two hundred yards to a wide plaza and turned on the circle so that it was pointed back toward the Grand Hotel. There was no one in the plaza. Mr. West had come there to stand at the edge of the cliff fifteen hundred

feet above the lake and search the formless horizon, hoping
to see the lights of the car appear as it climbed the mountainside or to see the lights of the helicopter above the car to tell
him that they were coming closer and just how close they
were. He knew that as intently as he would look he would
see nothing, but he could not have waited for them all that
time, sitting in the hotel. When he had stared at the night
and had seen nothing he would go back to the library and
wait for them to appear on the closed-circuit television
screen, watching while his chief guard at the second checkpoint did what he had been told to do with his hand-held
dummy camera. He wanted to see them unadorned, in a
clutch, as it were, unaware that they were being studied.

Mr. West got out of the car at the center of the seven
thousand two hundred and twelve acres of forest he had
leased from the State of New York. Tobin got out on the
other side. Mr. West walked toward the cliff. He felt Irene's
presence all around him. He felt forcefully her approval of
the arrangement that it would be only the family gathered
for this Christmas dinner. Everyone would be there except
Irene's physical manifestation. But she was there.

He watched a guard who wore shining black rubber and
held two police dogs on leash, straining to see something
beyond the night, something that had departed from him
decades before, something he willed to return.

He took the watch with the two faces out of his jacket
pocket to check elapsed time. It was the only watch of its
kind in the world, built for him for sixteen thousand dollars
by Patek-Philippe in Geneva in 1913 when he had taken
Irene on their honeymoon to the Bürgenstock. It had taken
two years to design the watch, seventeen months to build it.
It could deliver fifty-three separate calculations of time and
tide simultaneously, making it as unique as its owner, Irene
had said.

It would be forty-one minutes more before they could
reach the lower funicular landing. As he returned to the
plaza Tobin fell into step beside him. They began to talk
about the impending installation of a desalination plant on
the western coast of Morocco.

They got into the car and glided along the two hundred
yards to the Grand Hotel. The concierge opened the front
door just as Mr. West stepped down from the car, his green

and black uniform colors giving Mr. West inner satisfaction. He and a porter helped Mr. West to take his coat and boots off and Mr. West walked into the main hall, turning right to go to the library as Tobin turned left to telephone the police detail about restricting the dogs and to get the kitchen started thinking about the Christmas menu.

The library walls held books with green and black bindings. It was almost a square room, about thirty by thirty-two feet, with a mural-sized Rubens painting, "Diana, the Huntress," all pink bosoms and flying teats that sped across the canvas like wind, and two large oils by Frans Snyders, the meat-and-produce painter of the Rubens assembly line, "In the Larder" and "The Game Merchant." It was an exact reproduction of the room where he had sat with Irene at the Bürgenstock forty-six years before.

He pushed against the center panel of a book shelf, reversing it, showing several hundred other books on the shelves within. He chose a book carefully, closed the panel and sat down to enjoy what he thought of as "lust of the eye." As he turned the pages slowly, savoring the extraordinary illustrations, he could feel the carnality stir in him, but he could not concentrate on that lesser pleasure. His mind was on the car that was moving up the mountain on the far side of the lake. He looked at his watch, then clicked on the television receiver of the closed-circuit channel.

The car stopped in a brightly lighted area where the road had widened to three lanes, directly across from the guardhouse of the second checkpoint. Two men wearing shining, black rubber coats and hats, holding machine rifles, appeared at either side a dozen feet ahead of the car, their breathing creating clouds of vapor.

A third man came out of the guardhouse, his rubber coat hitched up at the side so that the bone handle of a big revolver showed. He walked with tiny steps, placing one riding boot directly in front of the other, girlish and comical. His shoulders were so squared he could have been wearing a clavicular cross-splint. He rapped sharply on the window at Walt's side. Walt pressed the switch that rolled the window down. The guard's scarred face stared in at them, then withdrew to examine the driver.

He minced back to the guardhouse, laying his pointed

toes down like a high-wire walker. He dialed a wall telephone, talked to somebody, then lifted up a black box they
could see clearly. The box was attached to a heavy cable. He
carried it across the road nearly to the open window of the
car, then he lifted it and pointed it at Walt and Mayra. He
touched a switch. An intensely bright light hit them with the
force of a punch. Mayra cried out. Walt yelled at the guard
and shielded Mayra from the light until the guard lowered
the box and leaned into the car. "Y'all 'spectin' tuh go on
up tuh the main house?" he asked nastily. Walt glared at
him, going into a rolling boil.

"Ahm gunna trah again," the guard said. "An' this tahm
don' you go blockin' the broad's face."

"Broad?" Walt was incredulous. "The—the *broad?*" He
threw open the door with all the force of his body and it
staggered the man backward and knocked the camera to the
ground. Walt jumped out of the car, grabbed the man's tie
with one hand and began to punch his face splinteringly with
the other. The guard fell backward with such force that
Walt had to release the tie, but he stood over him and kicked
him steadily in the ribs and head, wholly lost inside his fury,
as though the two of them were the casts of all the television
shows ever produced.

The driver came tumbling out of the car yelling at the two
riflemen who had started their sprint toward Walt, holding
their guns as clubs. The driver was yelling, "Easy, boys!
Watch it! This is Walter West! This is the boss's son and Tex
musta been outta his mind." He talked them into a slow
pace, then into a full stop, their eyes dumb with confusion.
The driver and Mayra pulled Walt back into the car, then
the driver jumped behind the wheel and the car moved away
up the dark mountain road.

"You were wonderful. Oh, you were wonderful," Mayra
said, holding his face and kissing it again and again. "Where
you been keeping that terrible temper, man? You like a
double tiger. Oh, baby, that's who you are, my double tiger."

Mayra stared at the pillar of light far across the lake, perhaps seven miles away, which seemed taller than any city
skyscraper. It glowed as it towered as though it had been
stuffed with ancient angels or with all of Mr. West's gold. It
was a shining shaft as long as the sword of the Avenging

Angel. Walt stood behind her and stared with her. "That is Hammetschwand West," Walt said. "It's a glass elevator shaft to the top of the Tritten Alp West. It is nine and a quarter miles away."

They left the launch and boarded the funicular on the other side of the lake. The car moved them backward on its stunningly steep ascent, drifted them upward away from the lights of the launch and pier, backing into the darkness of the mountain.

They were afraid. They were afraid for different reasons, but Mayra had never felt such fear.

The funicular car stopped. They were at the top of the mountain. They walked into the floodlighted plaza. Across the plaza the tall, gaunt, old man left the huge automobile and began to walk toward them. He shouted something at them but the wind took the words away.

BOOK THREE

THE LABYRINTH

CHAPTER ONE

What had seemed an evil amusement park lighting up the top of a mountain changed into something more unreal and sinister. The contrasts were overpowering. As they had begun the ascent in the cable car, to give Walt strength in the presence of this legend they were about to greet—a skyscraper filled with newsreel clips, picture magazine covers, radio decibels, newspaper front pages; a fountain of honorary degrees, medals, international foundations, foreign decorations, authorized and unauthorized biographies, libraries, gigantic possessions, exalted national art galleries; of pomp beyond the captains and the presidents; *the* Defender of the Republic against the Communist beast, the richest man in the world and also, remotely, her husband's father, then, more remotely, a religiously devout sadist and a murderer, the punisher of black women—she had given Walt the news that was more than two months overdue, the news that he was going to be a father soon—if she escaped from this place on the mountain top.

The lights that blared as intensely as the sound of cities struck upon the snow and banished shadow. It was black-enclosed night light, as perpetual and shadowless as the glow through which Proserpina had walked into Hades. The snow fell through the light as though the air were *Geldwasser*, just as though Mr. West had ordered it for this jolly Christmas season from Abercrombie & Fitch, an old-fashioned Yule-tide-confirming machine fixed to pour out longed-for white

Christmases from just above the lights where the blackness enclosed everything.

Across the plaza, through the pointillising snow, they could make out the diffused outline of a large automobile. A tall, thin man was walking away from the car, moving slowly through the thick light. They could see him wave and shout, but the wind took the words away. Walt ran toward his father crying, "My wife just told me we're going to have a baby!" Mayra could see Mr. West's gaunt face grimace in sharp revulsion as he envisioned a mottled black baby, but the face recovered its cold aloofness almost at once. It was a long face with a large, sharp, pitted nose framed by thick white eyebrows, and a straight, thin blue-toned mouth, like a carving designed to conceal human expression, a face that had been carved out of America's fantastic economic originality until, in countless ways, its owner had become the Lenin of capitalists, the Nijinsky of banking and the Rudolf Valentino of money. He was old and very thin, old and very tall, old and very cold.

Walt moved like a supplicant, stopping ten feet short of his father. Mr. West, Mayra noticed for the first time, had with him a large dog, the largest dog she had ever seen. The dog neither followed nor preceded his master. He was with and beside him, silent and frightening, as Mr. West glided forward just as silently for a mooring with his son—the first time they would ever have touched each other. He lifted a yellowed hand, pulled out of a goose-down-packed glove, a claw of bones and veins, a quest of long fingers and enlarged knuckles that were sculpted unnaturally under the incredible lights. They shook hands. Mayra moved in to join them, commanding dignity from her body as she heard the huge beast growl. Mr. West did nothing to still the dog. Walt put his arm around her. "This is Mayra, Father," he said proudly.

She made herself think of the Ashanti. She was a gift to this house from Kwaka Adai and from the kings before him. This man was the head of his house, so it was for him to smile and welcome her, then she would be free to smile. She could feel his revulsion for her as clearly as she could hear the revulsion of his dog, as though she were being impaled upon it. He stared at her zinc-orange skin, looking across

what Mama had called chocolate-to-the-bone like a taxi-
dermist at work. He said, "My mother was very dark."

"So is mine," Mayra answered.

The man seated inside the car opened its door and called
to them. "I'm Willie Tobin," he said in a musical voice that
had no gender. They turned. They walked to the car. Walt
introduced Mayra to Willie, then himself. The great Irish
wolfhound waited until Mr. West climbed into the car, then
he leaped aboard and sat erect between the jumpseats. Mayra
had to slide across the jumpseats, moving under the dog's
long, ferocious muzzle. Walt seated himself as Willie fixed
the beaver robe snugly around Mr. West's legs. As the car
glided forward all of them sat primly, hands folded on laps.
The large car made the small circle around the central flower
bed, then moved at five miles an hour down the slope
through the brightly lighted snow toward the Grand Hotel.

Walt broke the silence nervously. "Do you have many
miles of road on this side of the lake?" Mr. West did not
acknowledge the question, but Willie came in smoothly
under the tiny pause and said, "We have about four hundred yards of road, actually."

"Not much for a big car like this, is it?" Walt asked. "How
many miles do you have on the car?"

Willie spoke to the driver through a tube. "How many
miles on this car, Hayward?"

"Fifty-seven, sir."

"That's extraordinary," Walt persisted. "How old is the
car?"

"How old is the car, Hayward?"

"Four years, sir."

The car stopped at the hotel entrance. The driver helped
Mayra out, then Willie. Willie took Mayra's arm and moved
her into the hotel's revolving door. They were greeted by
Herr Zendt, managing director of the Grand Hotel, who
wore a frock coat and striped trousers. He welcomed them
with a Swiss-German accent. The concierge helped Mr. West
remove his outer clothing while his assistant struggled with
Mr. West's galoshes. Behind Herr Zendt two stuffed chamois
and a mountain goat, festooned with edelweiss and posited
upon a papier-mâché boulder, faced the reception desk and
the ceiling-high key rack.

"But this is just like a hotel!" Mayra exclaimed.

"My dear lady," Herr Zendt replied, "it is a hotel."

"Haven't you ever been to the Swiss Bürgenstock?" Mr. West asked Mayra.

"No."

He turned to Walt. "Have you?"

"Yes, sir."

"Then I think you should have explained all of this to your wife." He walked past them and disappeared into the main hall as Willie said smoothly, "Shall we meet in the bar in just one hour? We're far out in the country, but we adore dressing for dinner."

They moved through the crowded hugeness of the main hall, filled with hundreds of pieces of furniture, enormous paintings, Lobmayr chandeliers, with everything arranged to accommodate transient ghosts who had come to the mountain from a past that was so far away only Edward West could remember it. Herr Zendt showed them into the lift and Willie waved goodbye. "It is a very great honor and pleasure to have you here," Herr Zendt said as the door closed. "Your brother we have known for many years, Mr. West."

"Is my brother here now?"

"Not yet, sir."

"Is he expected tonight?"

"Not any more tonight. Tomorrow he comes in with the helicopter in the morning. But the dogs will be loosed soon. No more landings tonight."

"The dogs?" Mayra asked blankly.

"Oh, yes. Magnificent. We have nine killer shepherds. They make security like nothing else."

Herr Zendt showed them through the rooms, explained that their baggage had been unpacked, showed them the three balconies that looked out over the lake fifteen hundred feet below, then bowed himself out, walking backward. As soon as he had closed the door Walt grabbed her and whirled her. "How could you keep such a wonderful secret?" he asked. "When will the baby arrive?"

"I don't know myself," Mayra said. "Maybe only six more months."

"You know what? You're blushing."

"How can you tell?"

"What a day, what a day! I went and collided with two

generations at the same split second. Isn't Father magnificent? What presence! What authority!"

"And what a dog," Mayra said. She patted his cheek with one hand and opened the balcony window with the other. They stepped out upon the balcony and into the horrendous brightness. "Man, now we know how night ballplayers feel," Mayra said. Sixty yards away a man wearing a shining black raincoat came out of the woods followed by two large dogs. "Probably the fire patrol," Walt said.

"I'll bet." She was thinking that maybe Mama shouldn't have told her what she had told her about Edward West, because that had been a long time ago, but it sure had changed the way she looked at things.

When they went into the bar at the end of the main hall Mr. West had been transformed into charm itself by Willie's magic pills. The bar was seventy feet long and thirty-five feet wide, with a dance floor in the sunken crook of the L shape around which two dozen tables were placed. The room was paneled in polished dark wood. The back bar was long and high, lined with a large mirror and fronted with terraces of bottles. Mr. West and Willie stood at the far end of the bar. The gigantic Irish wolfhound, which no one ever seemed to acknowledge to be there, sat beside Mr. West, facing the door, and as they entered the room, he rose to his feet and growled. Willie had a Manhattan cocktail in front of him and was gazing up at West's white cropped head with indulgent hero worship, giggling at some joke that Mr. West could not possibly have made. In the far corner behind them stood a tall, overdecorated Christmas tree.

Mr. West flushed deeply as he stared at Mayra moving toward him in a dress of white St. Gall lace with amethyst ribbons and an amethyst sash, glorifying the glorious color of her skin. She seemed as dark as he remembered his mother, and she moved like a dancer. She was very beautiful.

The barman poured champagne for the guests and filled Mr. West's glass with Henniez water. They lifted their glasses and clinked them together. Walt wished them all a merry Christmas.

Mayra walked with Willie along the main hall to the dining room, following Walt and his father at about twenty paces. She watched them. They seemed to be having a disagreement. Walt shrugged and Mr. West seemed to flare, then the double doors of the dining room were opened ahead of them by the maître d'hôtel. As they came up to the door he began to move backward rapidly, guiding them to their table. He was the famous Smadja, imported from La Chasse Rouge in Paris. This was his great specialty. He had memorized the placement of the tables and could almost sprint backward among them, beckoning Mr. West onward as ego had beckoned St. Paul, never colliding with an obstacle on the course.

There were two huge rooms in L-shape having sixty-one tables for one hundred and seventy-five diners who would never arrive, each table set with crystal glasses, jade service plates, silver and many flowers.

The family group was seated at a round table placed off-center in the room, toward a corner that was flanked with high French windows. The sommelier poured champagne. His assistant filled Mr. West's glass with Swiss Henniez water. The wolfhound sat at Mr. West's left hand.

"I had first visited the original Bürgenstock in 1913, you see," Mr. West said, plunging without pause into one of his most cherished stories. Over the years his Gelbart Academy accent had become stronger, almost identical with the undershot pronunciation of the mandarin, Professor Gelbart himself. "It was quite different from what you see here, you may be sure. Not a painting in sight and the main hall packed with wicker furniture that was painted blue and red. Horrible. And no plumbing. Then, in 1929, just before and just after Walter was born, I spent considerable time there, and it had been beautified in an extraordinary manner. When the season ended I persuaded Herr Frey to allow me to lease the Grand Hotel with staff and I stayed on there alone—except for visits from Willie, 'iere—and found I liked it very much.

"I saw at once, of course, that the Bürgenstock is simply the most beautiful place in the world. I had many business friends who had recreated the usual European castles here in America. Deering's Vizcaya, Vanderbilt's Biltmore—very perfect, by the way—San Simeon. I confess I was drawn to the concept, but I also admired Rockefeller's Kykuit and Edsel Ford's charming Cotswolds visitation, though I thought it small. But above all I wanted a functioning unit that would exist to serve me. It had to pull its own weight, so to speak. I love the Bürgenstock. I think of it as a place my mother would have loved. My wife loved it. Just as you will fall in love with it tomorrow when you see it fifteen hundred feet above the lake on this cliff, with that long ridge descending from the mountaintop, with the sweet, green Swiss valley falling away into the other side."

"It took Mr. West four and a half years to dig that valley," Willie said.

"The site wasn't too hard to find," West explained. "There was the mountain, the ridge, the cliff and most of the lake, but no valley."

"It cost Mr. West two million dollars to make that valley," Willie said.

"We enlarged the lake," West said in a slightly louder voice, glaring at Tobin, "and we had to put blue industrial dyes into it to match the Lake of Lucerne. We used fill from the valley to build the golf course, where, I am proud to say, some of our great professionals have been delighted to play. We have fifty-two buildings on the estate, and I keep my automobile collection in the Palace Hotel."

"Sixteen hundred and eighty-one cars as of last Friday," Willie added.

"But do note the valley tomorrow. Wait until you see the sweet little dummy farmhouses and hear the dear sounds of cowbells morning and night when the herds would be ascending or descending to and from their mountain pastures. This isn't dairy country, of course. Too wooded. But I've gotten the wonderful cowbell effect without the cows— electronically, through carefully placed amplifiers." The maître d'hôtel was hovering. Mr. West nodded to him. The maître d'hôtel snapped his fingers and waiters converged on the table bearing paté of beaver.

"I've had two Presidents of the United States here," Mr. West continued, "and three Vice-Presidents. The Secret Service people have told us that we have dream security. It isn't possible for a stranger to get on or off the property within a thirty-one-mile radius." Mr. West directed his explanation to Mayra. "That is, without being electrocuted or shot or blown up or torn to pieces by the dogs." He shifted his gaze away from Mayra. "We are a superbly functioning Swiss unit here. I have my two hundred and thirty-nine Swiss hotel artists, just as the Pope has his Swiss Guards. But all that to one side. Bürgenstock West exists for the most important reason of freezing the years between 1913 and 1929. To keep my wife alive beside me as happy as she was at the Bürgenstock of long ago, to have her here with me as she was before Walter killed her by being born."

Walt and Mayra were in bed at 9:42 P.M., having declined to attend a Victor Mature movie which was being shown at the Palace Hotel.

"Were you having a little trouble on the way to the dining room?"

"It was pretty disgusting stuff, actually," Walt said.

"What did he say, honey?"

"He said it was a terrible disappointment to have me in his house at Christmas and to find me unfit to say Mass."

"Jesus."

"I told him I'd say Mass if it would amuse him, and I said that if he'd invited me to his house when I'd been a priest I would have said Mass right around the clock for him."

CHAPTER TWO

The news that Edward Courance West's younger son had been ordained in the priesthood after service in the Korean war had made a large forty-eight-hour splash in the papers. Walter even cooperated to keep the comment strident because he hoped it would flush his father out, but West remained silent and invisible. Then, to get out of the spotlight, he called on Dan to use his influence, and Walt was whisked out of sight to become pastor of a tiny parish in the back country of New Mexico, to work with a congregation of Mescalero Indians. He and his flock got along fine. Walt was a good priest and because he was rich, he provided, as a good shepherd should—a new hospital, community tools, a roof for the school. He was happier than he had ever been. People were calling upon him for love and service. He expanded and fulfilled himself.

Then without warning, five months after he had been installed, his father began to write long letters to him; intimate, fervent, embarrassing letters that repeated over and over how much it meant that his son had taken holy orders, then had expanded that mission of his life into beatitudes of meaning for Edward West's mother and Edward West's wife, who were then in heaven glorying in the presence of God, rejoicing with Edward West in the knowledge that Walt was allowing all of them to serve him through a devout son. Walt was elated all through the first three letters, but even they were fairly morbid stuff. Had Walt and his father lived normally together through even a part of their lives,

Walt might have considered discussing the letters with the family doctor, but as it was, this great legend of America had finally and formally acknowledged that he was Walt's father, and the young man was inundated, almost drowned by his gratitude for this. By the time the fourth letter arrived he was receiving a series of direct orders about which there could be no question but of obedience. Mr. West ordered Walt to pray for his immortal soul. Very soon the letters specified the combinations of litanies that were required. The litanies became so complicated that Walt was sure that his father had called upon the hundreds of obligations among bishops, mothers superior, cardinals, the entire curia (including the Pope), for obscure, long, wearying and obfuscating forms of prayers. Finally Walt found that he had become a walking prayer wheel within a numbing wall of confusing words and entreaties and supplications for the salvation of the soul of his earthly father. By his seventh month in the little church beyond Fort Stanton he was devoting three hours to praying each morning and four hours each night, in addition to saying extra daily Masses for his father's salvation. The church was no longer a church for the Mescaleros. It belonged to a congregation of one, whom he had never seen.

As the brutalizing demands for more and more complicated prayers poured upon Walt, his father would compromise him further by donations for the reservation through the Department of Indian Affairs, then by bestowing scholarships upon the young people (which were made so easily available that the number of Walt's flock was halved and the labor force of the community seriously threatened as the young people went off to find the world, temporarily subsidized). But the greatest bribe of encumbered money was required to be spent for baroque stations of the cross, shipped from Italy, and fantastically huge, painted statues of the Virgin with bright blue glass eyes, shipped from Cuba. Throughout the constant redecoration of the tiny, remote, country church—gold leaf on the ceilings, marbleization of the pews and the floors, gold-plating of the altar rails—the Indian congregation conveyed to Walt their clear impression that no continued hard work would be necessary by them, that their priest's historically exalted father was prepared to endow them with everything from the cradle to the grave;

and Walt's purpose as pastor was effectively destroyed. In the fourteenth month after he had arrived in the parish Walt suffered a complete nervous collapse and had to be hospitalized in an institution above Denver for more than three months. He never returned to the parish or to the priesthood or to any religious service of any church.

Later, in Paris, he told Mayra, "My father has developed the tremendous power of controlling people from a great distance. He can't be accused of cruelty because he is too far away to be really aware of what he is doing. But what he did to me, and must do to others, was the ultimate in refined cruelty. He pressed upon my need for him to take me to him as his beloved son until I had prayed myself out of whatever faith I had ever had. But as I prayed I gradually saw something that enabled me to understand him. I saw that if he really did believe that my mother and his mother had this direct access to God in heaven, then he could not have believed so desperately that he needed my prayers for his salvation. If he had loved his wife, if he had loved his mother, and if they had loved him, then he should have had the faith that they would intercede for him. And as I prayed I remembered popes and princes of the church and bishops and monsignori who had clustered around his money. I remembered the cities of religious buildings he had caused to be built. I remembered that he was such a great benefactor of the church and of individual arms of the church that armies of priests and nuns and lay brothers throughout the world must have been instructed to send up millions upon millions of prayerful pleas, supervised prayers and Masses for the salvation of his soul. And yet, despite all of that tugging at the sleeves of the robes of God, he demanded seven hours of hopelessly complicated prayers from me each day—from me, the son he despised. So I saw that he must have done something unalterably evil and that he must have a scalding reason for fearing damnation throughout eternity. He must have sinned beyond all sinners and he must dread the everlasting fires of his most Catholic hell."

CHAPTER THREE

Edward West's habit of collecting intelligence (which began for the most intelligent supervision of American gangsters and the American government for Horizons A.G.) grew to international proportions when the menace of world communism revealed itself to him, then doubled and redoubled within industries and governments of countries throughout the world in personnel, equipment and expenditure as his responsibility grew for reinvesting his gigantic sums of capital and credit in the business and industry of the planet. His facilities for gathering intelligence anywhere were so prodigious, his paranoiac need to confirm/allay suspicion so deep, that he used this suborganization for all manner of things, things beyond politics and industrial espionage. Among these investigative interests was Walter Wagstaff West, then in her turn, Mayra Ashant.

When he received a report that his son had dated a nigger seven times in three weeks, Mr. West was indignant and not a little hurt. At Mr. West's own instructions to Charles Pick, Jr., the boy had been raised and trained to understand that the slightest nuance of change in his public posture could be misinterpreted by the press and the heroic West reputation made to suffer. The idea of his own son being attracted to a nigger was both degrading and viciously exciting to Mr. West, and he resented the boy's power over him in both respects.

Then photographs of the girl arrived, together with a detailed statement of her background, career and interests;

and staring at that dark face (and actually believing for a second that he was seeing his own mother again), then reading that she was a gifted painter—an artist as his mother had been an artist—thrilled him and revolted him more distinctly. He had Willie assign a photographer to her for fullest hidden coverage. She was photographed on the streets, in restaurants, in her bathtub, in Walt's arms, painting, dressing, undressing, dressed and naked—for three years, from the time she met Walt until they left for Bürgenstock West—in London, in Paris, in Rome and in many lovely country towns and grubby cities in between. The photographer, Bryson Johns, had become so accustomed to espionage photography that it is to be doubted whether he could still take a successful straightforward portrait in the sunlight. He used infrared, masked cameras screwed permanently within fixtures inside her flats, which he serviced daily, removing film and reloading, while Mayra did household shopping. Consequently, of the two thousand-odd photographs of her in Mr. West's files there were none showing her with grocers or butchers.

Mr. West would sit in the library at Bürgenstock West and go over Mayra's lovely body inch by inch with an enormous magnifying glass, spending a half hour studying her haunch, staring for twelve or fifteen minutes as she sat on the toilet seemingly staring directly at the camera. He had details of her anatomy greatly enlarged: her long hands, her mons Veneris, her ear, her eyebrow, her bottom, her mouth. His passion was renewed all over again when he was told that she was studying Italian, and Bryson Johns was then assigned to make tapes of her speech, which was capable of exciting Mr. West strangely as he had never been stirred before. His years seemed to melt away. He became capable of erection, and once again—but surely the last time in this short final period of his life if he could bring this black woman to him upon the Bürgenstock—he had Willie fly whores in from New York, and he survived two orgies in which he poured champagne into the girls, every part of them, then drank it out of them.

A leading Italian architect was hired through the West Information Services in Rome to become acquainted with Walter, then to invite him and the black girl to dinner at the architect's villa, where Bryson Johns had rigged up a secure sound motion picture recording unit and was able to expose one and a half hours of uncut movies of Mayra complete with sound track. Mr. West screened it again and again. He had it scored with wailing Sicilian music, unmusical music but moving nonetheless. He had the right to these things. Nothing in his life meant anything if, with the fruits of his prodigious labors, he could not bring his mother back to him in the form of youth, moving with such frightening grace, speaking hoarsely in the speech of her people, which, if not quite Sicilian speech, was close enough, Italian enough. This was his right. This was what each man should give his life to—his own past, his own youth, the few precious moments of utter, total untarnished happiness with his mother before she left him. But she had left him. She had gone *forever*. F o r e v e r. F O R E V E R. She had to be punished. She had to be found and fondled. All the joys that she was so capable of giving needed to be abstracted from her, then she had to be punished because of the word "f o r e v e r," embedded so inextricably in his soul. But he must not hasten the time. Savor everything slowly.

Gradually Bryson Johns worked out techniques whereby sound motion picture installations were possible and effective in her bedroom, in her workroom and in her bathroom. The man was a wizard, and Mr. West saw to it that he was bountifully rewarded. As the film was shipped into Bürgenstock West, expert editors would shape it into many separate forms, into features and featurettes, as it were, so that if it were Mr. West's mood to enjoy her walking across Paris, in parks, entering and leaving shops, he could do so; with this went a narration by Mayra herself, a narration taken from the recordings of her accounts of the day to Walt. If it was Mr. West's whim to hear them rage together in quarrels over why she would not marry him or to listen to her heartbreak when she discovered that he had once been a priest, this was on film with words and music and really excellent photography. He luxuriated with her in her bath, he agonized with her at her easel. He would run close-up after close-up of her gasping twisted face during orgasm after orgasm. The cost-accounting sheets allocated one million three hundred nineteen thousand eight hundred and fifty-four dollars and nineteen cents to the project. The films of her asleep were the most serenely rewarding because sleep, in its external essence, is so much like death, and he would dig the nails of his fingers into his thighs in the screening room and often cry out to the screen in his need to punish her and bring death to her, because she was an artist, because she was his mother, because she spoke in that ancient evil tongue and because, most of all, because she was a nigger.

He would lead her to the mountaintop, drugged into a twilight sleep. He would remove her clothes slowly and he would enter her. Again and again. Over and over, as long as his power was there. Then he would beat her. He would smash her face and break the bones of her arms and her chest and her legs as he had been forced to do so many times before when they needed punishment. But she was his mother and a nigger, and he would drag her to the edge of the mountaintop, then cast her down, down into the pit, down into the ultimate punishment. Then he would be renewed and he would start again, wholly cleansed, his mother ripped out of his sensibilities forever. When he finished her nigger punishment he would start again and cause white America to rise up and tear and break and smash down the sickening threat of the nigger living everywhere within the America he owned and loved, threatening white America like an invidious disease.

He did not tell Willie his plans. He was not as sure of Willie's loyalty or judgment any more. He would wait. When the punishment was over, his mind would be clearer. Some sign would be given to him to know what he was to do and whom he should choose to help him in his crusade.

As his archives expanded with her image and her voice, her grace in movement and her beauty, she came to be everywhere he turned. The black woman was there. And the black man was behind the black woman—all Communists, all animals. She was everywhere he turned, and the nigger was more and more everywhere across America, possessing what was not his, threatening the home, the farm, the blood strain. His mother must be kissed and loved, but the artist she had reached out so feebly to become must be denied, because the soul is not free, the soul is bounded and baled by the strong cables of religion, which long, long before had mapped the way of the soul's journey through all life. The soul was not free. Art is a lie. The mother must be cherished, art denied, and the alien-animal nigger punished. Punished wonderfully and terribly. More than terribly. Worse than terribly.

CHAPTER FOUR

Willie looked elegant and as outdoorsy as a cigarette commercial in a green and white hounds tooth-check jacket over a trendy Norwegian sweater with a long, trailing green woolen scarf that he called his Cratchit. He wore a Tyrolean hat at a jaunty angle and extra-long, narrow hiker's knickerbockers and high-laced moccasin boots. They walked up the sloping road toward the funicular plaza and Willie identified buildings as they went. They strolled past the Park Hotel to the Palace, and he turned them into the building to show her part of the West automobile collection. "I started it in 1923," Willie said, "then he saw it and made me sell it to him. He gave me his watch collection—as though that could make it all up. However, it is an unusual watch collection—watches of only people who have appeared on the covers of *Time*."

The main hall of the Palace was seventy by forty feet. Nine twenty-two-feet-high pink marble pillars supported the ceiling, six large paintings were hung over deep-bellied Louis XVI commodes under massive Lobmayr chandeliers. Three automobiles relaxed like lazy cats on Persian rugs. A white Dusenberg stretched out in the foreground. Beyond that was a highly polished, robins-egg-blue Dobles steamer, and beyond that a rich Lincoln-green 1907 Compound. "Except for the mechanics and polishers, every guest on every floor of this hotel, and on nine floors sunk into the ground, is a vintage automobile."

They walked along the path to a reproduction of a dark

brown, wooden eighteenth-century tavern, where Willie put them both aboard a Vespa that he rode along an ascending left-hand fork in the path, past a small, exquisitely beautiful church, then upward into the forest. "We'll take the Hammetschwand lift to the top of the mountain," he said over his shoulder. "It's the finest view in the central Adirondacks, just as the real thing is one of the finest views in Switzerland."

The shaft of the lift was enclosed in glass. It was illuminated at night, Willie explained, and looked like a pillar of golden fire when seen from the pier on the opposite side of the lake, six miles away. "The Hammetschwand lift at the real Bürgenstock is the fastest elevator in Europe. This is a precise duplicate of the one Herr Frey built when he was outraged to hear that Adolf Hitler's elevator at Garmisch was said to be the fastest anywhere." They got off the Vespa and into the elevator car. "It's straight up now for six hundred and thirty feet to the mountaintop, which puts us at about twenty-one hundred feet above the lake. And the fall on this side of the mountain is as straight down as the sides of two and a half Empire State buildings, one on top of the other."

The view was breath-taking. Below them, along the mountain ridge that was the high, narrow spine of land between the emptiness above the lake itself and the soft, green valley mantled with snow on the other side, balanced the buildings of the Bürgenstock. They sipped icy cold Dezaley wine at a tiny replica of the souvenir stand and café that rested on the Swiss Tritten Alp, and Willie showed Mayra the footpaths by which one could descend to the ridge without taking the towering lift. Willie looked at his watch and said they must go down soon to join the others at the entrance to the church for Christmas services, which, as Mr. West performed them, meant instant slumber for all.

The concierge of the Grand Hotel leaned across and wrapped Mr. West warmly in the beaver robe. He closed the door, and the heavy Rolls glided silently for two hundred yards down the hill, where, at the end of the road, the driver turned the car around. Walt could look downward at the helicopter's landing pad at the foot of a long escalator stairway. Walt and his father had not spoken to each other beyond their greeting in the hall of the hotel. When the car stopped they could hear the sound of the chopper and their eyes followed it down. Walt stood on the brow of the hill in the clear sunshine, deep in snow, and watched Dan get out of the plane.

Dan was wearing a black homburg, a white silk scarf and a black overcoat with satin-faced lapels over a dinner jacket and black tie. His face was a high color. He glided up the escalator, talking as he came. "Where's your wife?"

"Willie took her out on a special morning tour."

"How is you-know-who behaving?"

"Fine. He's right here."

"You look great, kid."

"You look pretty fit yourself."

"Don't believe it. I flew in straight from an all-night party at Rockrimmon. I'm not exactly dressed for a Christmas day lunch." They embraced, then Dan leaned into the car and shook hands with his father. "It's a long climb," he said, grinning. "Can't we get a high-speed escalator?" Mr. West took up a dictaphone from inside the arm rest and spoke into it. "Investigate high-speed escalators," he ordered into it. The driver packed them in under the beaver robe. Dan smelled of the very best bourbon. Mr. West said, "What does State have to say about Roncalli?"

"He'll make a good Pope, Father."

"My people say he's some kind of a liberal."

The driver got behind the wheel. The car moved sedately up the hill. "De Gaulle was elected with a seventy-eight-point-five percent edge over Communists. Maybe sanity has come back to France." To Walt their conversation seemed coded, as if they were speaking in some private shorthand. But the timbre of his father's voice had changed. He no longer sounded like a querulous old man. "There are nine hundred and eighteen computers in use in this country. My companies operate one hundred and seventy of them. There are a hundred and fifty-four computers working in Europe and my people operate sixty-three of those. All those computers and my own sure sense tell me that we're going to make a real killing in France in the next five or six years, and I don't want your State Department rocking the boat." The car stopped at the Grand Hotel. "No, no," Mr. West said. "We're going on to the church."

"Not me, Father," Walt said, opening the car door. "I'll look for you at lunchtime, Dan. In the bar?" He shut the door, and the car moved forward as Walt went into the hotel.

"I have my doubts about your brother," Mr. West said. "An unfrocked priest who marries a nigger and refuses to go to church sounds like a Commie to me."

"Please," Dan answered wearily. "No communism. It's Christmas. Why did you invite them here?"

"He's my son. I am entitled to curiosity about my son."

"After thirty years? After my appealing to that curiosity three dozen times in the past fifteen years? Why did you invite them here?"

"Did you invite yourself all the way here just to ask me that?"

"Yes."

Mr. West shut his eyes. "I am old, Dan," he said. "I'll be dead soon. I wanted to make my peace. Maybe I made a terrible mistake with what I did to that boy. I don't know. I have to find out. I wanted to see him here and in a little while to be able to talk to him. Maybe he has big dreams. He's young. Why not? Maybe I can help him. That's what fathers are supposed to be for. That's why I invited him here at Christmas time. That's why I'm so confused for one of the few times in my life."

"I hope that is why you invited him here."

Mr. West turned the full power of his eyes upon his oldest son. "And if it isn't? Are you threatening me? Do I hear that in your voice?"

"Yes, Father," Dan said, regarding him steadily. "You do. If anything wrong is done to that boy or his wife, you and I will break apart and I will fight you from their side."

"You are a silly man to volunteer a thing like that, Dan," his father answered and closed his eyes.

Mayra and Willie and Dan filed into the church with the small congregation of hotel employees. It was a strikingly beautiful church interior, an exact replica of the church at the original Bürgenstock. It was simple beyond simplicity. Hand-carved, painted statues stood in elevated niches. The altar was a multicolored triptych illuminated by the sun. All around was immaculate white plaster upon which the sunlight fell from stained-glass windows on either side and high behind the altar. The congregation seated itself, then folded up its collective mind and tucked it away. Dan went to sleep immediately. Willie sighed and settled himself for shock waves of boredom as Mr. West appeared wearing a long, black robe and moved to a place behind a lectern.

He gazed out fiercely into the blanked faces of his audience and intoned. "On this supreme of all birthdays, let us pray." He led them in the Lord's Prayer, then opened the large Bible in front of him. His eyes shone. He spoke only to Mayra, but the other three dozen people had been so turned off by previous sermons that no one was aware of the intensity of the attention he paid to her. What he said was written in the Bible, but he seemed to know the words as though they were his own: "Let her kiss me with the kisses of her mouth, for thy love is better than wine. Draw me, we will run after thee, the king hath brought you into his chambers and we will be glad and rejoice in thee, we will remember thy love more than wine: the upright love thee. Set me as a coal upon thine arm: for love is as strong as death; jealousy as cruel as the grave: the coals thereof are coals of fire, which hath a most vehement flame."

She felt fear. She heard her mother tell once more about Mary Lou Mayberry, a coffee-bean girl. His eyes glowed above the Bible, and only Willie, excepting Mayra, had come to life with what was happening, following the beam of his master's eyes to Mayra and connecting it, all of it, backward in time, with Mary Lou Mayberry, with Baby Tolliver and with all of what Rhonda Healey had called "Eddie's black dagoes." Mayra could not break her own gaze fixed to West's. He no longer stood before them as a peculiar old man, but as a bull god. "Many waters cannot quench love, neither can floods drown it: Make haste, my beloved, and be thou like a roe to a young hart upon mountains of spice."

Mayra knew she was more alone in the white, white world than she had ever been before.

CHAPTER FIVE

She asked the concierge to tell Walt that she had had a sudden headache and would he please lunch with Dan and she'd see them both later? She lay staring at the ceiling, and her bewilderment increased. Three days before, she had been a safe painter married to a safe architect who was doing well. They had a dinky apartment behind Harrods in London, an even smaller one in Rome, and a bigger one in Paris. They had good friends. All of it was more than she and Mama had mapped out together, because it was a helluva lot better than civil service. The way it had worked out up to three days ago had added up so right that she wanted this baby as a magnet to fling at the moon at the end of a rope of hope that everything would stay exactly as it was. Then had come the private transatlantic airplane and after that Mama's news. Now they were on top of the mountain and Walt was sitting as wary as a leopard and they were walled in until the afternoon of New Year's Day. She rubbed her belly longingly and said aloud, "Come on, little baby, grow up and come outta there."

Willie stared at West, who was listening to sounds in the room upstairs through large, padded earphones, which he took off with impatience and tossed on the table in front of the monitoring equipment. "What is your impression of the young people?" Willie asked blandly, but West knew him too well. This sly man was up to something, he had some axe to grind.

"You've been with her all of the morning, what is your impression?" West answered, just as blandly.

"I am very favorably impressed," Willie answered with deliberate emphasis.

"What impressed you?"

"They are both first-class young people. She is about to be a mother, and that in itself is a wonderful thing."

"Do you think so?"

"By George, I wish they were my young people. What a thrill it is to watch something really constructive and worthwhile when it gets started on its way."

"How can you tell? What have you ever observed that was constructive or worthwhile?"

"I have my instincts, of course. And I read a lot."

"What is all this blather leading to, Willie?"

"Idle curiosity. I wondered what you had planned for them."

"What would you have me do?"

"I'd have you give them your blessing and send them back home to get on with their lives—after a merry Christmas and a happy new year here, of course."

"What is so extraordinary about that?"

"I haven't suggested it was extraordinary."

"You have engineered an entire conversation about the obvious."

"Yes. So I have. Forgive me, Ed."

"What did you think I planned to do with them?"

"Well, I knew you had been spending a great deal of time with your collection of photos and films of Walt's wife that the Intelligence Department had gotten together and—"

"Do you begrudge me that little indulgence, Willie? Since my pride has not allowed me to bring myself to talk to my son, do you begrudge me this pathetic attempt to observe his life from afar, at second hand?"

"No, no. I do not. I think you have shown a father's interest and hope in a most discreet and characteristic way. But she is dark, isn't she?"

"What do you mean?"

"I meant to say that we are much alone up here. It is my belief, as your dearest friend, that those photos and films of Walt's wife excite you and—"

"Excite me? That is disgusting!"

"You qualified it, not I, Ed. In fact, I am certain that those films and photos excite you, because it has been several years—several years before these photos of Walt's wife began to arrive—since you asked me to assemble girls here for your pleasure. You seem to have had your manhood renewed by something, Eddie. And it is my belief that the cause of that renewal was the photos and films of Walt's wife."

"What if I proved to you that I have cause to believe Walt's wife is a Communist? That I had to make sure? That everything in my life forced me to make sure whether she was or she was not?"

"Years ago and until this moment, Ed, you put me in charge of that active part of our operations, and I can assure you again, as I have assured you before, that during the months before she and Walt were married I devoted almost all of my time to convincing myself, and you, by every test and inquiry, that she was not a Communist."

"Willie, exactly—I mean precisely—what is it you have on your mind?"

"I am worried, that's all."

"Worried about what?"

"About you."

"Me? You have been talking about Walt and his wife."

"I remember very bad trouble we almost had. Mary Lou, for one. I know how excited you get, how charged up you can force yourself to be—"

"Now, just a moment here, Willie—"

"My only concern is you, Ed. Only and always you. You are all that counts in this world, and I cannot stand by to allow even you to harm yourself." Willie got up. He took a small brown bottle from his side pocket and poured a glass of water from a carafe. "And you know I'm right, Ed. You know in your heart that I am right." He extended the small pill to West, who put it on his tongue. He gave West the glass of water and West drank it down.

Sergio, the bartender, was telling Dan and Walt about the Arab party that Dan had arranged through the State Department to visit Bürgenstock West for family business reasons.

"You should have seen what they did to the second floor,

Senator West," he said. "The prince brought four wives this time, so the bodyguard was bigger, and there were all those kids. The prince always ate downstairs with Mr. West, but all the others cooked on the floors of their rooms. They just made fires on the rugs and they burned through the wood to the concrete. And they did everything else on the floor. Every night your father would bring the prince down here to drink champagne, a religious slip, and they would sit here and work on the oil leases all night. When they left, after ten days, he gave everyone on the staff a Patek-Philippe watch that had his portrait on the face in four colors. Two hundred and forty Patek watches, but it took the crews eight days to clean up and restore."

Christmas dinner was very quiet. Mr. West did not appear throughout the day or evening after the church services, and Dan left for Washington the next day without seeing him. On the night following Christmas night, at a quarter to twelve, after Walt and Mayra had retired to bed, Walt was summoned to his father's apartment by a telephone call from Willie Tobin. He dressed, grumbling. Mayra said the main thing to remember was that there were only about five more days to go. When Walt finally found his father, having been passed from his father's apartment to Willie's quarters on the other side of the hotel, to the library off the main hall, Mr. West was serene and even Olympian, nearly jovial. They sat as strangers in the large square room among copies of Rubens and Frans Snyders, and Mr. West began by explaining what really fine copies all the paintings at Bürgenstock West were and how, when the copies were made, he had had them follow scrupulously the system of separate painters doing parts of each painting, just as in the Rubens atelier, where Rubens had done the figures, De Voz the animals, Snyders the food and produce, and Wildens the landscapes. Then he asked Walt if he was or had ever been a Communist. Walt said his mind didn't run that way. "I am only a liberal in politics," he explained, "which Mayra says means that I wish well for all sides providing there is no inconvenience to me."

"Mayra says? Did you find yourself a Negro to do your thinking? Are you an ant?"

"In many ways. I am industrious and patient. I have a keen attention span. Are you an ant?"

"No forced humor, please."

"As for being a Communist—if I were one I'd have to give all my money away. Don't you think?"

"Is your wife a Communist?"

"No. She has over four thousand dollars in the bank. And she's a painter and she examines the world piece by piece."

"Can you arrange your affairs so that you could practice architecture in the United States?"

"Theoretically, yes."

"I have acquired three large tracts of land. One is between Washington and Baltimore. The second is in the Midwest. The third will serve Los Angeles, San Francisco and Nevada. I want new cities to be built on the land and a first-class feeder plane or monorail system devised that will keep them safely decentralized." He watched Walt closely. Walt was wide-eyed with fascination. West said, "I've averaged out at about one hundred and eighty dollars an acre, and if the labor force can move in at the moment the housing and the factories are ready, we'll get forty thousand an acre for the industrial sites and a relative markup for the homesites plus the banking and construction business. Do you want the job?"

Walt and Mayra went walking along the high path to the Hammetschwand lift and he told her about the offer. There wasn't much either of them could think to say against it because it was precisely the work Walt had been pointing toward since he and Derek had gone into business. There would be a lot of traveling among the three sites, but Derek could handle that until the baby was born, and while they waited for that, while they got an American office together they could find a house on Long Island somewhere near Mama. In fact, the more they talked about it the better it sounded. They decided Walt should seize the chance. He said he would have to leave for a few days to look over the land sites with his father's partner, the former Congressman Rei, who was a Midwest banker, but he'd be back by Saturday, and they would leave for good by Monday noon to return to New York. He said she probably wouldn't see much of his father, who, Willie said, spent much of his time in his rooms, but Willie looked forward to entertaining her, and there were movies every night, bowling, indoor tennis and squash and swimming and a lot of heroic visions to be painted. Mayra said that sounded fine.

Congressman Rei had done such a great deal to advance the cause of international aviation that Walt looked forward eagerly to meeting him. In the twenties and thirties, to an almost legendary degree, the congressman and his widely publicized personal pilot, Captain Guill Rael, had flown great and greatly reported distances in the Rei Ford Trimotor, almost always with a passenger list of the most delicious sort of celebrities. And these feats of glamour had kept aviation in the forefront of the news. The plane would show up in Havana, Mexico, Canada, throughout the Caribbean, and Rei had a press agent waiting at every stop. What was not as widely known as his keen interest in aviation was his even keener interest in the importation of narcotics. Every plane the congressman ever had could carry up to sixty kilos of heroin or cocaine in concealed compartments, and the consignments always whooshed past the customs in a blur of celebrity dust.

On the morning of Walt's departure to join Congressman Rei for a tour of the new city sites, he and Mayra were greatly surprised, when they entered the car that was to take them to the pad, to find Edward West seated there, dressed for travel. "I have business in Chicago and Washington," Mr. West said. "I do not want State to upset General de Gaulle in any way." Mayra saw them off, waving at the helicopter as it rose into the sky, then set off toward the West airport at Hawk Bay.

At lunch time she called Willie, but the room did not answer, and Gubitz, the concierge, told her he thought Mr. Tobin was busy with the mechanics at the car collection in the Palace Hotel. He asked if she would like him to locate Mr. Tobin, but Mayra said not to bother him. She decided not to have lunch in her apartment because she wanted to feel what it would be like to have an entire dining room brigade available to serve her alone, so she went to the dining room, where she chose lightly from the enormous menu. At three o'clock, six vague and formless hours after Walt and his father had flown away, she slung her portable painting kit over her shoulder and set out along the mountain trail to the Hammetschwand lift and the magnificent view.

For the first time in her three visits, there was no one in

the Berghaus. The colored post cards were in the racks. The bar stood gleaming inside the plate glass window and the tables were set for the snack lunches that were so rarely served, but there was no staff. The sun had begun to hint at departure within the hour but its low angle and her high place gave her magnificent color and light and shadow in the forest and snow below her. She felt alone on top of the world, and because it was a temporary feeling, it gave her a sense of exultation, as though she had survived alone the hydrogen bomb, the viscous pollutions of water and air, and the voraciousness of politicians. It made her sad for Mama and Walt, because it was an exalting game to play. Then she set up the easel, propped up the canvas and began to think about what she would paint.

She watched the colors shift and heard the low wind and began to sketch the complex of Bürgenstock buildings far below. She worked quickly and surely. Very soon it was clear what she had set out to do. Then she heard the voice behind her. It said, "Why did you marry my son?" She turned in fright because the voice was very frightening, not only in its unexpected suddenness. Mr. West was standing on the shallow porch of the Berghaus, ten or twelve yards away. He wore a coachman's hat and a half-cape overcoat that had a collar he had pulled around his face, whose lower part was already muffled in a heavy black wool scarf. His face was beyond paleness. It was dead white. His mustache was white on white. She stared at him. He spoke again. "Why did an Italian-speaking nigger marry my son?"

"That only matters to Walt and me," she said. Her voice shook. Her eyes were widely opened. She gripped the paint brush with both hands as though it were a railing upon a very high, swaying place.

"You deserve to be punished for what you've done," the cold-eyed old man said. He stood stiffly, with his head and torso thrust slightly forward, his ungloved hands clenched tightly, his arms rigid at his sides, and each time he paused he chewed on his lower lip. "My family is the most honored American family in this country's history, which means it is the most honored in the world. You are a nigger. You have shamed my family's name." His voice carried harshly across the hastening darkness. They did not move toward or away from each other. "You are a nigger Communist. Niggers are sex-crazy. My son had a life that was meant to be devoted to God, and you dragged him into your bed, and you must be punished for that. Punished in this life." She could watch the thin line of spittle march out of the left side of his mouth. "I had photographs taken of what you do with him. I have over a hundred photographs of every bed you've dragged him into and I know. I know niggers are sex-crazy, and I have the proof of what you did with my son, whose life was meant to be spent in the service of God."

She thought of wide spaces of blue sky and deep sunlit depths of crystal water to clear her mind of panic. She concentrated on remembering that Willie Tobin had said that there were cowpaths going down from the mountaintop into the valley behind her. She tried to resolve that she would not run from him. He was an old man. She was Ashanti.

"You should be beaten until your bones are broken and you bleed from every orifice of your body. Until you scream with pain and want to die. Then you should die. You must be cast down from the heavens. From this mountaintop. That is my right and my duty, to cast you down from the highest place into the pit, where you will enter hell to receive eternal punishment for thinking only of satisfying your body, for using your body again and again and again for pleasure under a white man of God. Because you degraded my son and degraded my name and because you live for your body and its insatiable appetites."

He began to move toward her slowly. His eyes were glassy, shiny but not shining. His eyes seemed to be looking inward as he moved toward her, and the spittle was freely running out of the side of his mouth. She tried not to cry out, but she did. She tried not to run away from him, but she was spun by the force of her fear and sent running away from him with her hands clasped over her ears. The winter dusk was closing in, but she came upon the clearly defined path immediately. She did not look back. Two miles down toward the valley the long, high ridge on which Bürgenstock West was settled stretched out, and as she began to run, its lights came on like a beacon. Fifty yards down the path she halted to look upward and back, but no one was behind her. He was no longer on the mountaintop, but she didn't know how the other paths on the mountain ran or if he had ways to head her off, so she ran. She fell over bushes and ran into trees as she descended. She was more apart than together when she reached the level of the ridge. She couldn't remember when the dogs were set loose to roam the estate, so she kept running, gasping for breath, but she didn't weep, and twenty yards before she reached the entrance to the Grand Hotel she stopped and did her best to put her hair in place and catch her breath. She walked slowly and with dignity to the revolving door, entered the hotel and asked Gubitz to find Mr. Tobin and ask him to join her, if he could, in her apartment.

When she got upstairs Gubitz telephoned. He said that he had located Mr. Tobin in the Palace garages and that Mr. Tobin would be happy to join her in a half hour.

Willie was in the blandest good spirits when he arrived, apologetic that he had been tied up in the garage all day and hadn't been able to lunch with her, but looking forward to a gala dinner. He explained that two really fascinating cars had joined the collection that morning and that he just had not been aware that so much time had sped away.

"I went up to the Berghaus this afternoon to paint a little bit, and a sad and frightening thing happened."

"What happened?"

"Mr. West followed me up. He must have come up just about ten minutes after me on the big elevator, and he said a lot of sick things. Like he said he was going to punish me. What's the matter?"

Willie was looking at her with dismay that was mixed with anxiety and even consternation. "Mayra, dear," he said "when did this happen?"

"About an hour and a half ago."

"But it couldn't have happened an hour and a half ago."

"Why not?"

"Mr. West is in Chicago with your husband."

"He is like hell."

"Yes. He is." Willie wet his lips. He rubbed his hands together. "Now, there is nothing to be concerned about here. You're pregnant. You've been traveling a great deal unexpectedly and you've had all kinds of contrasts. The fact is this sort of thing happens with many pregnancies."

"Not this sort of thing. But, okay, never mind. We'll let it go. Where can I call Walt?"

"They're all at the Drake Hotel in Chicago."

"Will you put the call in for me?"

"Certainly." Willie glided across the room to the telephone and gave the instructions to Gubitz. They waited somewhat uneasily for ten minutes, then Gubitz reported that Mr. Edward West and Mr. Walter West were out of the hotel. "They're probably out looking over the housing site," Willie said. "In fact, I'm sure that's where they are," he said, holding his hand over the mouthpiece.

"Please ask when they'll get back."

Willie asked. "They'll be back for dinner," Willie said after Gubitz had fed the question to the hotel in Chicago.

"May I speak to the hotel, please?"

"Certainly." Willie extended the phone.

Mayra spoke to the desk clerk and asked him to be certain to leave word that Mr. Walter West was to call his wife as soon as possible.

Mayra said, if Willie didn't mind, she thought she'd rest for a little bit while she waited for Walt's call. Willie started to reassure her again that it most certainly must have been a trick of light and the wind, and she listened so patiently and nodded so compliantly that he lost heart and began to leave, asking her to call him, please, after she had talked to Walt and saying that he hoped they could have dinner together.

Walt called at eight o'clock, which was seven o'clock Chicago time, three and a half hours after she had come down from the mountain, four and a half hours after she had been threatened by Mr. West.

"Walt?"

"Yes, honey?"

"How's everything?"

"Just fine."

"Your daddy with you?"

"He's in the hotel, not with me, but down the hall somewhere."

Mayra shut her eyes tightly. Then she spoke again after a long pause. "Were you out to look at the site?"

"Just got back. Marvelous piece of land."

"Walt?"

"Yes, love."

"Did your daddy go out to the site with you?"

"No. We had an early lunch, then he decided to take a nap and make some calls. He's too old to go tramping around the countryside."

Her eyes popped open. "What time you finish lunch?" she asked.

"About twelve-thirty. Why?"

"You just get back?"

"Yeah. Just now."

"Been in to see your daddy since lunch?"

"No. Say, what kind of a crazy conversation is this?"

"Don't pay me no mind. I just wanted to talk. The words don't matter, do they? So long as we just can talk. I guess I'm lonesome."

"Well, not for long, you won't be. This is Wednesday. I'll be back Saturday. We'll be having dinner with your mama on Monday night in New York."

"Call me right after dinner?"

"Sure will."

"I'll be waiting right here now. Love you, baby."

"I love you, sweetheart."

She called Willie and apologized. She said he had been quite right. Mr. West was in Chicago, and she felt very bad about what she'd said. Willie implored her not to think about it, please not to think about it, it was their secret and everybody knew these things happened all the time, and she simply was not to give it another single thought. Mayra promised not to, but she said the whole experience, even though imaginary, had tired her out and she thought that maybe the best thing was to turn in early and have a real good rest.

Walt called from Chicago at ten-twenty. Everything was fine. His father was in the best spirits and was really very, very enthusiastic about the project. Walt and Congressman Rei would be flying out to California early in the morning. His father would be going on to Washington and he hoped to get back to Bürgenstock before they had to leave.

"Walt?"

"Yes, baby."

"You have more money than most countries, so why do

you need this deal with your daddy? You can buy land. I mean, why do we need him even a little bit?"

"It's not just the land, hon. I could have done that years ago, but you know this new city stuff is my whole dream. If it was just buying land, hell, I could have done that with Derek instead of building the same apartment complex all over Europe. But it's very tricky stuff. Mostly connections. Connections to swing tremendous financing. For instance, nobody but my father or some insurance company could have lined up three of these enormous projects simultaneously. It takes connections more than financing to bring the residents who are the labor force into the houses at exactly the time when the factories are ready—sometimes chemists, sometimes lens grinders, sometimes just ten or twelve thousand wig makers—who knows? Everything has to balance, and it takes connections and special merchandisers, everything very special and solid but very organized. They have to match and be at the same place at the same time. It takes political connections. All kinds of specialists have to be recruited and right there, not only ready to work but ready to be paid, like teachers and butchers and movie projectionists and golf pros. I'm just an architect. I have the money for the openers, but I wouldn't know where to go to line up the dovetails. So that's why I need my father if this kind of work is the work for me. That's how it is."

"It's going to be a damned interesting winter," Mayra said. "How long between when you left your daddy after lunch and you met him for dinner?"

"I don't know, maybe about seven hours. Didn't you ask that before?"

"That's how the whaling captains' wives passed the time. Imponderables. You sure we're going to do all this out of New York?"

"Well, I'm not sure. Maybe better out of Chicago."

"Oh. Sure. Chicago. Hurry on back here, Walt."

"At the very latest, Sunday morning."

Mayra sat up, staring at the lovely wood fire that had been made in her sitting room. She didn't believe they would be allowed to work in New York or Chicago. She didn't believe Edward West intended for them ever to work anywhere else, except maybe Walt for a short time, and then mostly traveling, for all the most convincing reasons in the world. So she had to convince Walt. Nothing easy about that. Maybe Mama could just fall out of a barber chair and win that kind of an argument, and if she could do an hour or two of figuring the scam out with Mama she knew she could beat it—but forget it. If she called Mama she'd be talking through a bug, and as soon as she began to lay out the problem she'd get cut off, then with the kind of loot this cat had, in twenty minutes some high-priced mimic who sounded exactly like Mama would call back, and nobody wanted Mama's advice that secondhand. She'd just have to study up on how to think like Mama or she'd be dead and this little thing who wasn't even formed into a baby yet would be dead. If anybody could ever learn to think like Mama it should be her. Never mind this Ashanti shit. That kind of highchin swanning could get her right to the bottom of the cliff under the Hammetschwand. She had to sleep on it. Man, she had to think on it and dream on it and maybe send out for a Ouija board to cone in on Mama. Mama would hear. Mama would transmit. It was just a matter of locating the tuner.

The answer didn't come until the next afternoon, and then—even though what they began to do to her was, for them, so hopelessly debasing and demoralizing because of the rotten misery it brought and the murderous hypocrisy that attended it—the extra-special Mama-wave came through and she was able to begin to form a clue about what she was going to have to do. At least a tiny part of what she would have to do.

CHAPTER SIX

After breakfast the next morning Mayra became about as miserably ill as if she had the worst kind of seasickness. She retched continuously and couldn't find any position that gave her any comfort. By two o'clock she decided that the only way to pass the intelligence test would be to see if the place had a doctor, so she called Gubitz, and in ten minutes a steady, reassuring-looking man named Dr. Garrison arrived with Willie Tobin. The doctor asked Willie to wait until he had completed an examination, then he talked to Mayra in a calm, confident way, explaining that he was Mr. West's staff physician and mentioning the various glorious hospitals at which he had been chief of staff, then he asked her questions, discovered she was pregnant, took medicine from his satchel, made her swallow it, and in no time at all she felt safe for the first time in almost six hours.

Willie was deeply concerned, and conveyed that he felt himself to be responsible for Mayra while Mr. West and Mayra's husband were away, in that order, and seemed to be listening to Dr. Garrison's prognosis, while his hands clenched and his feet were drawn tightly together. Mayra couldn't piece it out why they hadn't let Willie in on the plan. Dr. Garrison said, "What Mrs. West has been suffering is a rather pronounced form of morning sickness. Usually these things happen somewhat earlier on—she's never had the slightest symptom of morning sickness before, she tells me—and usually the mother-to-be is well over this sort of discomfort by the end of the third month—which Mrs. West tells me is about two weeks away—but this morning's attack was so acute that we'll just have to wait to see if it recurs or whether, possibly, she has been afflicted with some form of food poisoning—although she tells me she had cinnamon toast and tea for lunch yesterday, and nothing for dinner last night but tea, so that doesn't seem likely. We'll just watch and wait for these subsequent mornings to see what happens."

Mayra thought she knew what was happening, and when, the next morning, she was even more violently ill, and Dr. Garrison said that the best treatment would be for her to remain right in bed until the usual time for that condition was passed, she thought she ought to ask him if there was any guarantee that it would be all over by the end of the third month of pregnancy. He said, not necessarily. He said that frequently—in fact, it was amazing how frequently—expectant mothers remained in bed throughout their pregnancies and never did get over being violently ill until the day of birth. He said they'd just have to see that she had the best obtainable care and that he knew that, if required, Mr. West would fly in the best obstetrical team in the United States for the duration, and that she was not to worry.

So that afternoon she called Mama.

"Mama? Mayra."

"Hey!"

"How's everything?"

"We're winning. How're you?"

"You know. A little baby-wonky. In the morning."

"Miserable, but standard."

"But they got a fine doctor here, and he says if I rest it out in bed I'll beat it."

"Oh, you'll beat it."

"But I will be in bed for a while and"—Mayra took a deep breath—"I thought maybe you'd send me up in the mail the old family scrapbook and I could pass the time leafing through it and maybe filling in a couple few pages of snaps of Walt and me that I been lugging around."

Mama dug. Mayra could tell by the change. Not a big take. Not a power hose of questions. Just "The *scrapbook*?" softly, no emphasis in particular, but just like she wanted to be sure they were talking about the same thing.

"Yes. The family snapshots and your diploma, and all like that."

"Oh. Sure."

"Think maybe you could get it in the mail today? Special delivery, registered, would be the quickest, and mark like *Scrapbook* right on the front of the package. The best way."

"Uh-huh. How's Walt?"

"He's just fine. He had to go off on a business trip, but he'll be back tomorrow."

"You meet his father?"

"Yes, indeed."

"Is he like they say?"

"Oh, yes. Just like you thought. But he's away right now too."

"That's nice. Well, I'll get right on out to the post office. Think you could phone me every day at about this time?"

"That would be just fine, Mama."

"Okay then."

"If you don't hear from me, maybe you could call Walt here, because if I'm feeling poorly he'll take the message and pass it on. It's Hawk Bay number one, Herkimer County, and Information has it."

"What if I can't get you or Walt?"

"Then maybe I could ask you to call Walt's brother? The senator? In Washington?"

"How do I get him?"

"Just call Information and tell her you want the number of the Senate Office Building, I guess."

"You all right so far?" There was alarm in Mama's voice for the first time. It was naked and off guard.

"Just that little bit of morning sickness. 'Bye now, Mama." Mayra hung up before Mama could say anything else, because she was sure the room was bugged. She knew what to look for and where to look because Mama had once gone out with a police captain, and the captain was an electronics man who talked about nothing else. He'd told them two dozen times that most of the rooms of the world were bugged, and he would lead them all around and show where and how and keep describing the different ways. Come to think of it, Mama had been friends with two different police captains in her time.

Mayra went over the room carefully, inch by inch, but she

didn't find anything until she started unscrewing the mouth-pieces of the four telephones in the two rooms and the one in the john. Every one of them had a cadmium-nickle miniaturized transmitter packed in under the mouthpiece, and it was the kind of a gimmick that picked up whether the telephone was on or off the hook. She let them be. When Walt got home and she had figured the whole damn mess out and was ready to talk, she could handle all of them with a few pillows.

She got back in bed and turned on the radio. She noted that the sick feeling left almost the moment she took the medicine. She also noted that they were working to pin a bad pregnancy on her—like it had made her blow her wig because the first thing Willie had said to explain why she had thought she had seen and heard Mr. West, who everybody in their right mind knew was in Chicago, was that everybody also knew that those kind of hallucinations were just an everyday part of being pregnant. Now they were laying on a little mild breakfast poison. Well, she had to play. Then she heard what the radio was saying.

". . . reports that the private aircraft of Edward Courance West, which was carrying Mr. West's younger son, Walter, age thirty, and former Congressman Benito Rei, the promi-nent Chicago banker and great friend of American civil aviation, together with pilots A. Ehrlich and C. Anderson and Chinese steward Mat Sun, was reported missing today in a flight between San Francisco, California, and Washing-ton, D.C."

She stared at the radio. The doorbell began to ring hur-riedly, then the door opened and Willie came into the living room, pale with fright. She watched him cross the room toward her before she was able to nail down into her con-sciousness what the radio had said.

"Mayra," Willie gasped, "I have bad news. I just talked with Mr. West in Washington. Walt—"

"I know. I just heard it on the radio."

"No, we must not panic. Mr. West was very clear about that. The fact that the plane is missing does not mean that there has been an accident. It is entirely possible that it was just forced down by some mechanical demands, and Mr. West has a country-wide search of the flight pattern being made right now by the air force and civil authorities."

"How could it be forced down? I mean, where could it land that there wasn't a telephone?"

"But that's just it. Mr. West even anticipated that question by saying what reason would they have to telephone when they wouldn't even have known anything had happened to them? The pilots would naturally figure they could radio the changed ETA when they were airborne again."

"Oh, my God."

"Please rest. Please let Dr. Garrison help you to rest." He sat on the edge of the bed and held her hand. "Please try not to think about it."

"I'll think about it. I can't not think about it." She watched Dr. Garrison through the open door as he proceeded with stately pace across the living room carrying his black satchel. "But I won't believe it."

"That's good. That's fine." Willie said.

"I won't believe it because I know it hasn't happened. It's just another stunt. It's just one more sadistic trick." She watched Dr. Garrison slide the needle of the hypodermic syringe into the ampoule. Willie wasn't just holding her hand to pat it, she noticed. He was holding her arm. So it was okay. Walt was safe and sound, and it was all done just to move her around a little bit more, to set her up so that nobody, not even her own precious, wonderful Walt, could believe that she was all right in the head. Going crazy is just a part of being pregnant, Mrs. West, she told herself as Dr. Garrison slid the needle into her vein.

CHAPTER SEVEN

"They found her unconscious on the floor of the Hammet-schwand lift at 6:38 the next morning. The helicopter spotted her on its first morning patrol because the elevator car had stalled somehow, halfway up the transparent, illuminated shaft, and the pilot had alerted the police command post to investigate. Four men went up the mountain trail in two motorcycle trucks, bringing a maintenance technician who activated the lift machinery and brought the car to the base of the shaft. Mayra was sprawled across the floor of the car. The police sent for a stretcher and Dr. Garrison, and she was carried down the mountain, still unconscious." Willie spoke slowly and with great seriousness. Mr. West listened intently. Walt simply wasn't able to comprehend what Willie was saying.

"But why? What does it mean?" he asked.

Dr. Garrison spoke next. "I have taken the liberty of calling psychiatric colleagues at Johns Hopkins in your absence, Mr. West," he said, speaking directly to Edward West, "and I hope, under the circumstances, that meets with your approval. They are flying from Baltimore now."

"Indeed, it does meet with my approval, Dr. Garrison. And we thank you."

"Dr. Garrison," Walt began, "will you *please*——"

"I have asked these distinguished men to come to confirm my own diagnosis because this has evolved into a serious matter."

"*Evolved?* Evolved from where? You had never set eyes on my wife when I left here three days ago."

"I think Mr. Tobin might begin with the first symptoms of the evolution of the patient's illness," Dr. Garrison said stiffly.

Willie cleared his throat delicately. "Uh—you see, Walt —on Wednesday afternoon—the day you left with your father for Chicago—Mayra took her paint box and gear to the top of the Tritten Alp. I was engaged in meetings with Mr. Zachary, our chief mechanic. At about six o'clock, maybe a little before that, Mayra sent word through the desk that she wanted to see me. When I arrived at her apartment she seemed to be in tip-top form, entirely healthy in every way, then she told me that your father had assaulted her verbally on the mountain top and to escape him she had had to flee down the valley trail."

"But how could she—"

"Yes. Precisely. I told her that what she had experienced was illusory, because Mr. West was, of course, in Chicago. She refused to discuss that condition of fact but instead said she would telephone you in Chicago, which, I assume, she did."

"She did. Yes. But she was entirely normal. She said nothing to me about any delusion, I mean about Father being in Bürgenstock when he was in Chicago."

"She didn't mention it at all?" Dr. Garrison asked.

"No. She asked if Father was in Chicago. Yes. She did cross examine me in a fairly pointed way about when I had seen Father last and when I expected to see him again that day. But that was all."

"Didn't you think it was odd or strange that she asked so many detailed questions about your father?"

"I did for a moment, yes. I commented on it to her. But she said she was just making conversation to keep talking to me because she was lonesome. But the hell with this. I knew this. I want to know why you have sent for Johns Hopkins psychiatrists to see my wife."

"Take it easy, boy," Mr. West said.

"The next morning, that would be Thursday morning, Mayra was violently ill—sick to her stomach and so forth. And when she saw it wasn't going to stop she called Gubitz and asked him to send a doctor," Willie explained, "and

Gubitz immediately told me. I arrived at the apartment with Dr. Garrison."

"As you know," Dr. Garrison continued, "it was my first examination of Mrs. West, I found her to be suffering a perfectly normal manifestation for an expectant mother—it's called morning sickness—and I prescribed for it even though there was a possibility that it could have been food poisoning, although she had eaten nothing more than tea and cinnamon toast the day before. Mr. Tobin then asked me—or rather he told me about Mrs. West's delusion of the previous day—*then* he asked me if I felt that the delusion could all be a part of a reaction from the pregnancy. I said that this was possible."

"She was very ill the next day, Walt. Worse than the first day, the poor dear," Willie said. "Then in the afternoon, after she had agreed to stay in bed and follow Dr. Garrison's orders, she turned on the radio at just about the same moment that I hung up on your father, both of us hearing the news about the same time that your plane was missing."

"I want to have an investigation and find out who the son of a bitch was who gave out that ridiculous goddam story," Walt said.

"Then, after that news, at some time during the night, after she'd heard the news, she wandered out of this hotel and up the mountain trail to the Hammetschwand."

"But why didn't you tell her that the story was false? Surely someone told you the story was false."

"Your father told me the moment he knew," Willie said. "But Dr. Garrison had sedated Mayra rather heavily, and it would have been the wrong thing, I felt, to try to awaken her to tell her. I was eager to tell her that everything was all right the first thing this morning."

"All right, All that happened. But why did that mean you had to fly in psychiatrists, for Christ's sake? Gynecologists, yes. Obstetricians, certainly. Why psychiatrists?"

"Because of my fears, which in my opinion were confirmed last night and early this morning when your wife was found," Dr. Garrison said.

"Fears of what?"

"Fears that in her present condition your wife might be intent upon harming herself—or even destroying herself."

Walt shook his head slowly and compulsively in a caricature of patience. "That just isn't possible, doctor," he said. "You just don't know Mayra. It's simply impossible."

"Well," Dr. Garrison replied, "very shortly you will be able to have the prognosis of two of the best psychiatric men in this country."

"When can *I* see my wife?"

"She's in a sedated sleep right now. She should awaken in about two hours, when the doctors should be here. Their examination may take an hour or an hour and a half, but you will certainly be able to see her as soon as they have talked to her, and then you'll be able to see her when you've been armed with their very special response to her condition."

CHAPTER EIGHT

"Your wife's condition is wholly classical," Dr. Palmer said, evenly and sympathetically. "It is called Doctorow's Syndrome in our work. It is potentially very dangerous because of two things. First of these, of course, is the destruction the patient wishes to turn upon herself. Second is the patient's total unawareness that she is ill, her denial of any delusions of self-destructive ambitions. If she can be watched at all times, the prognosis is simple. Watch her, wait until the baby is born, then know that all danger has passed. If the patient cannot be watched—and we believe these patients must be watched, not by members of the family, whom such patients can convince that they are rational, but by strong, impersonal psychiatric nurses—then we would urge that the foetus be aborted to save the patient from harm."

The three doctors faced Walt seated in an arc. They were grave, mature, obviously intelligent men of considerable experience. Flanking Walt were his father on his right hand and Willie on his left. It was a terribly effective, terribly convincing scene. Walt began to weep. He put his face in his hands and he sobbed as though he were alone. Willie patted him softly on the back. "I've got to see my wife," Walt said. He stood up, averted his face and walked out of the library to the elevator in the main hall. He ascended to the top floor. He let himself into the apartment with his key. Mayra was fully dressed and was arranging flowers in a crystal vase. She turned and grinned as he came into the room, dropped the flowers and flew across the room into his arms. She kissed him again and again and tasted his tears.

"Please, baby. Don't get yourself sick with this. I see they convinced you. Well, that had to be. That's the way it was set up for you. What the hell. But pay it no mind, because not only is this whole thing a fantasy, but I am going to prove it is a fantasy."

Pillows were piled upon the two telephones in the room. The door to the bedroom was shut.

Mr. West was seated at the monitoring equipment, fiddling with the gain dial. "Something has gone wrong with the transmitters in that room," he said to Willie. "I'm not getting anything. I can't hear one word they're saying." He took off the earphones and wheeled in the swivel chair to face Willie. "What the hell is the matter with you?" he asked.

"I'm sick of this," Willie said. "I think this has gone far enough."

"What has gone far enough?"

"Ed. Please."

"I ask you again, what has gone far enough?"

"What you are doing to this girl."

"What I am doing? Are you mad? Do you mean flying doctors in here to help her or putting up with a half-crazed woman pregnant with a half-caste baby?"

"Those men aren't doctors."

"Dr. Garrison isn't a doctor? Is that what you're saying? You hired Dr. Garrison out of a half-dozen alleged doctors two years ago, and all this time you led me to believe he was a doctor."

"Garrison is a doctor. He's a crook or you have something on him, but he's a doctor."

"He's a crook?"

"I mean those two actors who were supposed to have come here from Johns Hopkins. I can't prove anything else, Ed, but I can prove they aren't doctors."

"How?"

"Do what I did. Call Johns Hopkins. They don't have doctors named Palmer or Youngstein in *any* department, and in the psychiatric department no one has ever heard of Doctorow's Syndrome."

"I don't understand this. Garrison arranged to bring them here. He handled everything."

"The way he handled putting the stuff in her food to make her sick was more efficient, Ed. Or knocking her out so you could have the security men ride her up the mountain and dump her in that lift."

"Willie, there's been something wrong with you for a long time now. I haven't trusted your judgment for a long time now, and this is proof that I was right. You've gone rotten on me, Willie. Your mind isn't the same. You're older than I am and I think you're senile."

"Okay. But nothing is going to be done to that girl any more, and you're going to tell those two young people that you are too tired to stay on through the winter up here on this mountain and that you're going to leave in the morning for Palm Springs and you'll send them back to New York."

"I am, am I?"

Willie stared at him, not answering.

"Willie, did you know that I've had you stacked to take the fall for Goff—just in case something like this came up? I have the gun. I have your prints on the gun. Doc Yankel is still alive. He runs a chicken farm in southern Illinois with his grandson, and he's there to tell how you broke into the apartment, holding a gun on him to make him get you in, and that you then shot and killed Goff because of a woman. Jesus, what a scandal that would make."

Willie couldn't speak. He sat down weakly.

"For the past few years you've had the idea that because you've got me isolated up here you are the real boss, because you think you control the boss. Isn't that so? Well, that hasn't bothered me. You worked hard and you're entitled to kid yourself if you want to. What the hell. But you never tried telling me what I was to do. You bossed flunkies and felt real good, but you never made mistakes like this before —over this nigger girl who doesn't mean a damn to you, except you like the taste of being boss, and you thought I'd gone soft and old, and you thought you'd make a test run to see if you could move me as you wanted to. Well, I haven't gone soft, and I'd break your back just as quick as I broke Goff's back or Capone's back or Warren Harding's." He stared at Willie with distant contempt, colder than hatred, as though he were unable to justify how Willie had ever somehow gotten into his life. Willie's eyes filled with tears. He turned away from West as he sat in the chair and hid his face in his left hand. West said, "You've always been worth about what a full spittoon is worth, Willie, and we both of us know it."

"I'm trying to kill myself, right?"

"That's what the three doctors said."

"Okay. Now I'll lay it out straight. And I'll even have exhibits like they do in court. Like you'll have to eat my breakfast in the morning just to sort of bear out what I'm going to tell you. Then—but we mustn't talk while we're doing it—I'm going to show you how your daddy has this place bugged and how he's either been listening in or recording everything we've said since we've been in this room. I got a lock on it now, so we can say what we want—but I can see you're looking all wary like what I'm saying is proving that I'm crazy. I better start at the beginning."

"Honey, let's just get out of here. Let's just pack up and go home."

"I don't think we can."

"You don't think we can?"

"No."

"My father is holding us as sort of prisoners?"

"Yes." She looked at him levelly. "Did your father say we could leave Monday?"

"No. As a matter of fact he—well, because of what's happened to you—anyway, he said he'd prefer it if I set up an architectural office here, in the tennis house, and bring draftsmen and Derek and so on up here so he could be in the closest touch with the job from the very beginning."

"I see."

"I said okay, but now I've changed my mind."

"Baby, listen. Please. Let me talk. You're the one who has to stay loose, because as long as you're convinced I'm sick, you can move in and out of here. He was on that mountain at about twenty to five Wednesday afternoon. You saw him last at twelve-thirty or so in Chicago, and there was plenty of time for his Learstar to take him back here and back to Chicago. But I'll let that one go by. It can all be proved from the outside, and maybe that's why you've got to stay loose. Tell him we're leaving, and he's got to put a lock on you. Tomorrow morning I'm going to ask you to eat my breakfast because—"

"It takes two and a half hours to fly to Chicago. I didn't see him for six and a half hours," Walt said dazedly.

"Oh, sure. No doubt about it."

"But what did he *say* to you?"

"He said I was a sex-crazy nigger and that I had to be punished for marrying you. I had to be beaten until I bled from every orifice, then thrown off the mountain down the cliff beside the elevator shaft—'cast down,' he called it—so I could be punished through eternity."

"But why would he say such things, Mayra?"

"You ever see me have morning sickness?"

"No."

"I don't think anybody in my family ever had it. That's for true. But tomorrow you're going to have it."

"Me?"

"You're going to have it right after you eat my breakfast, then I'll give you the antidote and you won't have it any more unless you eat my breakfast the day after that. You know about the dogs here?"

"Yes." He felt sad. He could never be found by his father now. His eyes had turned inward upon his grief, but his grief was being suffocated by his rage. Mayra was pulling at his lapels. "They got nine killer shepherds. All bigger than wolves. All trained to tear anything that moves into dead, bloody pieces. They're loose all night. But I walked from this hotel to that Hammetschwand elevator and nothing bit me. And there was deep snow, but my slippers weren't wet and my feet weren't cold. How come?"

"How?"

"Because they doped me to make it look like I'm in psychiatric shock because your plane was missing and me being in a very delicate condition as any doctor will shortly prove, then they rode me up the trail and put me in that elevator car and stopped the car halfway up the shaft."

"Why? Why?"

"I told you why. Because he's crazy. And because he wants you to think I'm crazy so when they find me dead at the bottom of the mountain everybody can say poor girl, too bad." She closed her eyes and began to sway. He held her tightly by the shoulders. "But why should all these people conspire with him to kill you?"

"Not all these people. Just Willie Tobin. Willie fixes up

my morning breakfast before it comes in here. Willie brain-washes that dimwitted Dr. Garrison. Willie took me up the mountain to make sure I'd know the way if I wanted to paint up there. He's done it all before. Your father has murdered Italian-speaking niggers before."

"Mayra!"

"Mama's scrapbook will be in the mail Monday morning. When I can show you that I'll tell you all about it."

"What's in the scrapbook?"

"I can't say until you see it under your own eyes. Nobody could believe what I have to tell you unless they can look right at this scrapbook."

"What are we going to do?"

"First, you have to believe him or me. One of us is crazy."

"I believe you. I believe in us."

"Then everything ha/to be okay. He can't kill me if you believe he's trying to kill me. Next, you've got to believe that he can keep us here as long as he wants us here. He controls all the transportation. All the cops. And he controls the telephones, so we just aren't about to call out to your brother Dan to send in an air force and some troops."

Walt looked ill. "But I can get out," he said. "If you can stand to take the chance to stay up here alone with him, then I can get out and get all this finished."

"How?"

"Business. I'll tell him I've got to meet Derek in New York to line up a drafting crew. I won't even tell him. I'll keep it casual and just ask Willie to arrange to have the plane take me into the city."

"Then what will you do in New York? What can you do? I mean, if you bring Dan back here with you, then he'll just be one more prisoner."

"Dan and I can have him committed. Maybe I couldn't do it all alone without a big fight and without its taking a long time. But if Dan and I both sign the papers, we're the only sons. And Dan is a United States senator. I can convince Dan—I know I can—because over the years he's as much as said that Father isn't right in the head. We can get it all done in twenty-four hours—the court order committing him, the psychiatrists, and we can come back here with all of it, and his whole force of security police won't dare go against the law."

"That's it. That's how we could do it."

"But—but, I can't. I can't leave you here. I can't do it, Mayra."

She was trembling violently, so she sat down suddenly. She sat on her hands, and that held her arms rigidly at her sides, so that he could not see that she was shaking with fright. "It's the only way," she said, as easily as she could. "If we don't do that, honey, we are cooked. We dead." Her face seemed gaunt from all the morning retching as she stared up at him, and her eyes were desperate, but the steadiness of her intelligence and her courage overwhelmed all that. "Fix it up to get out of here Monday morning," she said lightly, "and we'll have all day tomorrow to figure out how he can't get near me."

CHAPTER NINE

After Walt told Willie he had to go to New York, Mr. West called Walt to say that two psychiatric nurses would be standing by to return with him, but until they got there, how did Walt think his wife could best be protected from herself? Walt said Mayra was quite calm, that she reacted marvelously to sedation, and that he thought the best plan would be to post a security officer in the hall outside her door.

Walt and Mayra spent Sunday inside their apartment. They ate only unpeeled fruit. They talked about fashioning weapons, but Mayra said she wouldn't know how to use them and that she would rely on her own agility to defend herself.

"That's not enough. We have to hide you."

"Where?"

"This is an enormous hotel. I'll get a set of skeleton keys from the desk late tonight and sometime before dawn we'll plant you in one of the smaller hotel rooms and you'll stay right in there until I get back."

"I can't hide until the mail comes tomorrow. I've got to have Mama's scrapbook because it's a tremendous weapon. The best defense is an offense. Man, that scrapbook is really an offense."

"How is it a weapon?"

"No use trying to tell you unless you see it. But it's what he did to women a long time ago. Mama knows. She worked for the women. He thinks it's all blown over. He thinks nobody ever connected him with what happened. If he can get the idea that somebody knows he killed a woman—yes, he did, baby, yes, he did"—Mayra held her hand over Walt's mouth as he started to press for more information. "I say, if he knows somebody knows he murdered that woman, then his head is gonna be so full of the fear of that that he isn't gonna come for me—man, not the first night anyhow, he'll be so shook up—and you'll be back here before the second night, and then it will be over."

"But how are you going to tell him? How can you tell him you know and expect to get away from him, to hide from him?"

"I'm going to tape pages from that scrapbook up on his door, then I'm going to be out of there before anyone knows I've ever been there."

"But *why?* How can that help anything?"

"Baby, how can I make it clearer? Suppose you were the safest man in the world, then all of a sudden everywhere you looked there was a big poster that told everybody you had killed a woman. Suppose you knew, all of a sudden, that somebody near you knew you were a killer. What would you do? I'll tell you. You'd start thinking only about yourself and stop playing games with black girls until you could get this first bad thing all straightened out. Dig?"

The scrapbook came from Mama as promised, and because Willie had cleared it days before, after West had played back the tapes of Mayra's call to Mama, it was handed right over to Gubitz, unopened. Walt called Willie's room. He was told Willie was in the lobby waiting for him.

"Why do we want Willie?" Mayra asked. Walt said he had been told that Willie would be riding with him to New York and that Smadja and Herr Zendt would be riding with Willie. "The explanation is," Walt said in a thin, shaking voice, "that we're coming to the time in the staff contracts when one-third of them are revolved back to Switzerland, and they are going into New York to line up replacements. But that's better than it's bad. I'll get you a key to Willie's room so that you'll have a second place to hide if he flushes you out of the first."

They couldn't use the elevator because of the sound it made. They ran together along the carpeted corridor to the red light over the exit staircase at the end of the hall on the top floor. Mr. West's apartment was directly below theirs.

He took her to a single room at the end of the long hall on the floor below his father's. "You know where Willie's place is?" Walt asked her at the door to the small room. "The floor below this? Placed the same as our apartment and my father's, directly facing the stairs?" She nodded. He kissed her desperately. She locked herself in the room, then Walt sprinted two floors up, then along the corridor to his apartment. He telephoned his father to say he was leaving and that he'd like to be sure a security guard would be posted outside Mayra's suite before he left. "How does she seem this morning?" his father asked.

"She's fast asleep. She promised to take the same medicine when she wakes up."

"Good."

Walt waited until the security man knocked at the door, then he left the apartment and locked the door behind him. The man carried his suitcase to the lift, and Walt told him that Mrs. West was resting easily and that undoubtedly she would be as quiet as a mouse all day.

Willie, Smadja and Herr Zendt were waiting in the lobby. They were all driven to the helicopter pad. As he said good-bye to his father in the hotel lobby Walt had difficulty in controlling his trembling. He looked as though he were going to be sick.

"What's the matter with you?" his father asked. "You look terrible."

"My breakfast must have disagreed with me," Walt said. "How do you feel, Father?"

"Never better." Mr. West looked remarkably fit and quite sane. Walt stared into his father's face, examining every part of it, peering into his father's clear, rational eyes. He was overcome with the conviction that what he was doing was all wrong, that Mayra could be just as ill as the three doctors had said and for the reasons the doctors had said. Her stories were calm and cool but what they said were wild. That scrapbook. His father appearing on the mountaintop when he knew himself—had seen with his own eyes—that his father was with him in Chicago. This was all as crazy as both of them were working so hard to prove it was. One of them had to be right. If Mayra was mad, perhaps it was she who had decided, in this terrible insanity, that it was her duty to kill his father, just as she had proved to him so craftily that his father had decided to murder her—working step by step as she developed her case against his father while he developed his case against her, as though they had become the synthesis of all white Americans opposing through riot and fire unto death all black Americans. Just as all blacks had been driven mad in their desperate need to defend themselves and their meaning and, by the force of a collective, murderous syndrome, had set out simultaneously to destroy.

Insanity was irrational. White against black was irrational. Could both his father and his wife have gone mad? But he stared into his father's face and knew it could not be so. And he saw the great roll of honor that was his father's history and America's history and he knew it could not be so. But he could remember Mayra too. He could see her face and hear the strong, sure rhythms of her voice and knew, too, that she could not be mad. He could remember too much, too many moments of her ever to be able to believe that she was mad. What was the right thing to do? Where should he stay?

"Helicopter's waiting, Walt," his father said.

"I've been thinking hard all day yesterday, Father. I think I'll let Derek wait in New York and I'll take Mayra out to a New York hospital today."

"That is out of the question."

"I don't think so. And as her husband, I'll decide these things if you don't mind."

"No."

"You can continue to say no, but it is my decision."

"It was the decision of three distinguished, experienced doctors. They decided that it could be fatally dangerous for her to travel, and she is not going to travel. You have your job to do. Go and do it."

"Yes, Father," Walt said grimly. "I have my job to do." He turned away without farewell and began to descend on the helicopter.

CHAPTER TEN

At ten o'clock that night, standing behind a heavy plum-colored drape, Mayra looked up the sloping road that led to the funicular plaza and the Park Hotel, where the staff lived, and watched people in civilian clothes move out of the hotel to the funicular station by multiple dozens. The Bürgenstock was being evacuated. Soon a skeleton crew and the security police would be the only people scattered at different stations around the grounds. By now, except for security police, perhaps, she and Mr. West were the only two people in the Grand Hotel.

She waited for night to come. She pulled a small bed lamp down to the floor. She put it under the bed before she lighted it so that none of its glow could be seen through the window outside the hotel, then she began carefully to take apart the scrapbook. The words of the past seemed as eerie and terrible as the scenes themselves must have seemed to Mama. Pictures of dark, shapely, somehow Italianate women were displayed prominently on the pages. Miss Baby looked like a slut. Miss Pupchen looked like a child. Miss Mary Lou Mayberry—well, it was fairly possible that Miss Mary Lou Mayberry did look a little like her. But the eerie and uncanny thing, with her perceptions now so frightened and heightened, was that all of them, somehow, looked in some way like each other, so they must have looked like someone else who was buried deep, deep, deep within Edward West's tenebrous mind.

She had transparent acetate tape. She took up two pages

of brutality, viciousness and murder, put out the light under the bed and moved toward the doorway that led into the corridor. She unlocked the door. It clicked heavily. She began to tremble, leaning against the wall. She could not make herself open the door. She talked to herself. She told herself that she had to go out into the corridors and do her work. She was so soaked with sweat that her hand slipped as she tried to turn the doorknob. But she opened the door.

The corridor was softly lighted. She was at a far end on the first floor. The other end was approximately eighty yards away. The door into Mr. West's apartment was on the second floor, positioned at the center of the corridor, facing the staircase and the entrance to the elevator. The building was as silent as a mortuary. She stayed close to the wall and glided silently along the heavy carpet to the staircase. She hugged the wall of the staircase as she moved herself, against her will and against her fright, down the stairs—impossibly slowly. She made herself think of what she had to do and how she must study well, in advance, how it must be done, so that she could flee to her hiding place again. This time to Willie's room. She reached the second floor. She was facing the door to Mr. West's apartment. She started to move toward it when she heard a sudden sound just above her and she almost cried out. She felt physical pain from the tension of the muscles of her neck and face. She clung to the wall, waiting for light to fall on her. Moments passed. She remembered the security guard Walt had said he was going to post outside her door. He had kicked his chair or had leaned it against the wall.

She made herself move again. She chose the full newspaper page, mounted on black cardboard. A screaming headline said: SHOWGIRL BRUTALLY MURDERED. POLICE VOW CAPTURE OF KILLER. There was a three-column portrait of Mary Lou Mayberry.

She tore off a strip of tape and fixed the page to Mr. West's door. She anchored it there with two more pieces of tape. She backed away to the elevator door and taped Miss Baby's newspaper page on it. She held her hand tightly across her mouth and lower jaw and gripped hard, so that she could not cry out, and moved like an undersea diver across the corridor again. She came up to Mr. West's door as though she were in a trance. She pressed the door bell heavily. The dog barked frantically inside the apartment. She turned and ran. She went down the staircase and disappeared. She was on the second floor landing and was moving swiftly and silently downward when she heard Mr. West open his door. She reached the first floor before she heard his scream of horror. She ran desperately along the first-floor corridor to Willie's apartment. Fumbling with the skeleton key, she let herself in, then locked the door behind her, gasping for breath. She moved into the living room. Willie was sitting there; smiling up at her.

CHAPTER ELEVEN

Mr. West opened his door. The wolfhound padded out into the corridor, searching in both directions. West moved into the hall to look to his right and left, and as he turned to enter his apartment, he saw the yellowing newspaper page hanging on his door. He flicked on the light switch in the entrance hall and looked at the page closely. He screamed. He slammed the door into the wall violently, pushing it away from himself with both arms. The security guard who had been posted outside Mayra's door came bounding down the staircase.

"There is someone in the building," West said hoarsely. "Find him. Bring him to me." He took the page down and entered his apartment, slamming the door. The security man ran down the stairs.

West sat on a low hassock in front of a coffee table, the dog sitting alertly beside him. He stared downward at the large portrait of Mary Lou Mayberry as a show girl, beautiful and nearly nude. The doorbell rang. He shouted to come in and turned the page down on the coffee table. Arno Ehrlich, the security chief, glided into the room, alarmed. Two subordinates remained in the background as Ehrlich held out a mounted newspaper page to Mr. West. "What's that?" West asked shrilly.

"It was taped to the door of the elevator, sir."

"Why are you here? Get out of here," he screamed at Ehrlich. "Find the man who was able to break through the most perfect security of all time and who is waiting out there to murder me." Ehrlich left at once, on the double, the two men right behind him.

He wanted them out of the building. He didn't need them. He knew who had done this reckless and capricious thing. Willie had decided to blackmail him to get the nigger girl. Willie had done this. Only Willie could have saved these crumbling records for all these years, because from the beginning he had meant to use them for blackmail. Blackmailers must be dealt with. Blackmailers must be put down and broken, never to rise again. He left the apartment, the gigantic dog at his side, and moved to the lift. When he entered the lift with the dog he pressed the button for the first floor. He left the lift and crossed the hall to Willie's room, to Willie who had so carefully said he had to go to New York with Smadja and Herr Zendt to recruit the new hotel staff people. West took the master key from his pocket.

CHAPTER TWELVE

Mayra's legs gave way as she stared at Willie. She had no adrenaline left to hold her on her feet, and she slid on her spine down the lintel of the door to Willie's living room and collapsed into a sitting position on the floor. He darted across the room to her. He rubbed her wrists and murmured to her soothingly. He ran across the room to an elaborate bar and poured cognac into a large glass and brought it back to her. He made her drink it.

"You went to New York," she gasped. "You were sent out of here with everyone else—why are you back?"

"It's all right," he said. "Everything is going to be all right and nothing nor anyone will harm you. Walt will be back tomorrow. Dan will be with him. I know. That is why I went to New York with them, so I could call Dan to tell him that the time had come to commit his father to institutional restraint—as I had promised him I would when that became necessary. Then I ordered the plane to take me back here, so that I could stand between you and him until this night was over. You have nothing to worry about. I can handle him. I have spent my life handling him."

They heard the key in the lock. Willie pulled her to her feet and jammed her behind a heavy drapery at the nearest window, then moved out into the center of the large area to face his visitor.

"Willie, we've come to the end of the road," West said. "You've done what you thought you had to do and I am sick and tired of you."

"What was it I thought I had to do, Ed?" The two old men were about eleven feet apart. Neither moved closer to the other. The huge dog sat at West's side and watched both of them.

"You're too big, Willie."

"I'm sorry. I don't understand what you're trying to say."

"You are trying to blackmail me. You are trying to get that nigger girl for yourself. You are trying to bring me down. After all these years. After I made you a multimillionaire and a friend of some of the most important people in this country. What would your father have said? He would have touched his cap to you. And if he knew you had accepted everything I brought to you and then plotted to bring me down—he would have died of a broken heart."

"Ed, you've got to take a pill. The veins on each side of your head and across your forehead have become throbbing pieces of rope."

"Never mind that. You're finished, Willie."

"Finished, Ed?"

"Your life. It's finished."

"At least sit down while we chat. Sit down and rest."

"I'm going to kill you."

"Why? Please—sit down and tell me why?"

"Don't talk to me as if I were an old woman who had to be humored. Beg. Beg me. Do you want to die? Plead with me to let you live. Tell me what you have done for me. Soften my heart. Confess your lifelong devotion, you two-faced messenger boy." Mr. West was breathing irregularly and shallowly. He seemed to totter for a moment. Willie backed up toward the side of the room, away from Mayra's feet where they seemed to be hung from the draperies at the windows. West appreciated Willie opening a greater distance between them. He came farther into the room and sat down heavily on the nearest chair.

"You'll have a stroke if you don't watch out," Willie said. "Dr. Tumulty warned you. He said that if you agitate yourself, as sure as nightfall you'll have a stroke."

"A stroke could save your life," West gasped. "Pray that I have a stroke."

"If I thought you *should* have a stroke, there are things I could tell you, Ed," Willie said. "If I thought you had set yourself to beat and break that girl, I'd give you a stroke—

for all you've meant to me and mean to me." The two men were talking in the accents of the New York streets of their boyhood with overtones of Paddy's brogue and Jiggs' Galway speech. Gelbart Academy had not been forever.

"When you're dead I'll go for her," West said. "She's all of them. She's Mary Lou come back and my mother too. She tore my son away from the church, and she has to be punished. She's a nigger Communist and she lives for her body, so she has to be punished."

"Then you must have your stroke," Willie said. "Do you know how I used you all these years and led you around by the nose?"

"What are you talking about?"

"Well—the Communist reports from our operatives all over the world. I wrote them all. I copied them out of newspapers. I fed silly Joe McCarthy's vomit back into you with a spoon."

"You're a liar."

"I did it to get you up here. Safe up here. To get you out of the world before you began to kill all the women you met and had to be put into a crazy house. Because you're starkers, Ed. You belong behind bars, not for what you've done—you couldn't help that. For what you are—sick and insane."

West shouted out at him, his face blue, his eyes popping out of his head, but his strength had left him. He clawed at his tie and got it pulled away from his throat, then he ripped open his collar and breathed in heavy, broken gasps.

"Did you ever wonder who sent Irene those letters, Ed?"

"Who? Who did?" West made himself ask thickly but with renewed life, as though the hope of finding the answer to that secret would lead him to the greatest vengeance of his life.

"I sent them. And every time it seemed as though Irene would give in to her compassion and forgive you, I sent another and another. Too bad for Goff. Too bad for Irene. But not too bad for you. I saved you. I had to get you away. I had to tear you out of that insanity that was overwhelming you and separate you from the world, to get you to this mountaintop so that I could save you."

West pulled himself to his feet. "You killed Irene?" he mumbled hoarsely. "You did that to—*Irene?*" He shambled toward Willie, his face jerking, his face lined with the need to bring death. Willie took a pistol out of his jacket pocket. "Stay right there, Ed," he warned. "Don't move one step closer to me. I'll kill you if I have to, Ed. I'll kill you. You know it."

The Irish wolfhound fastened his upper and lower jaws on Willie's hand and crunched them together. The pistol dropped out of Willie's hand as he cried out in pain.

"Bring him," West said to the dog and turned away, walking to the door. Willie cried out to wait, to wait until they could talk all this over so he could show the reasons why he had to do what he had done. The dog pulled him along. They followed West out into the corridor. West walked unsteadily ahead. Willie's hand bled heavily on the rug along the way. "Ed, for God's sake," he shouted after West, "please call this dog away from me. He is taking my hand off. The pain is terrible." West neither answered nor turned. "Where are we going? What are you going to do?" Willie screamed at West as he was dragged forward down the main staircase to the main hall. The dog dragged him to the lake side of the hotel, where a locked glass door led out to the terrace upon the bluff, fifteen hundred feet above the lake. The burning, brilliant lights on their high poles made the whole area pitilessly shadowless. West unlocked the glass door.

"Eddie!" Tobin screamed. "No! Jesus Christ, no, Ed! The dogs!"

West took him by both lapels and threw him backward to sprawl upon his back out on the floodlighted terrace, then shut the door and locked it. Willie scrambled to his feet with frenetic, desperate fright and began to beat on the double glass doors, pleading with West to let him in. His face was distorted with terror and the blood gushing out of his right hand stained the glass as it smudged and streaked downward.

Two dogs came loping in from the left. One came sprinting from the right. They all leaped for his throat, knocking him to the ground. The lone dog got to his throat first and ripped it out. The other two tore at his face and arms.

Mr. West placed the mounted newspaper page showing Baby Tolliver beside the beautiful page showing Mary Lou. He sat down slowly beside the low coffee table, staring with enormous pleasure at Baby's sluttish face. He could remember their contrasts sharply, as though he had just been with each of them.

All of the faces he had ever beaten came funneling into his mind, and he saw for the first time that, in this little way or in that large way, each of them had been somehow like his mother. The faces began to stack themselves neatly on top of each other, the long, full-breasted bodies registering their outlines upon each other. His sight darkened. His left arm hurt terribly. He could hear himself making lowing, guttural sounds deep in his throat, but he saw his mother's face, then her body, come to rest on top of the towering sculptured stack, and his only meaningful past with this horde of dark women fused into one face and one body, and he saw that this new woman whom his son had brought to him was his mother, returned to trick him again. She was hiding from him. She had to be punished before she ran away from him again. He wheeled upon the hassock, then stood up, his strength renewed. He ran out of the apartment with the great dog beside him, straight up the staircase before him. He stood swaying and gasping for air at Mayra's door. He fumbled for the master key. He entered her apartment. The lights from the high poles poured upon everything, but she was not there. He crashed open the door to her bedroom, smashing it into the wall and shouting out obscenities to begin her fright. She was not there. He ran from bathroom to dressing room. There was nothing. He ripped one of her dresses from the closet and held it under the dog's muzzle. The dog darted out of the room ahead of him. He took up an iron poker from the fireplace as he went through to the main door, then followed the dog as he went down the staircase, breath coming to him in shattered sobs. He watched the dog circle around and around outside of the West apartment, then go to the elevator door, as West clung to the balustrade, then the dog began to descend the stairs again, turning right along the corridor on the first floor and padding parallel to the long line of blood that Willie's hand had dropped upon the carpet. West staggered behind him, striking at the doors of the rooms with the iron poker and yelling as he splintered the doors that her punishment was at hand and that she would be flung into the pit.

The dog turned at the end of the hall and doubled back.

West had pulled himself into fanatic energy. The dog halted outside Willie Tobin's apartment and began to bark.

Mayra heard the key slide into the lock. She stood erect in the center of the room. There was no place to go. She waited for him. The door crashed open. He careened into the room, his face greenish-white. He lifted the poker over his head and ran at her. Then he fell. The poker rolled out of his hand. She ran to him and rolled him on his back to help him breathe. He stared at her. His eye could move. He was alive. He could see her.

She leaned closer to him. "Blink once for yes, and twice for no," she said. "Can you move?"

The eyes blinked twice.

"Can you talk?"

The eyes blinked once, feebly. There was a rustling sound from his throat as he tried to speak. She came still closer and put her ear just above his lips. *"Volevo essere un ballerino,"* he said to her.

*Biggest dictionary value
ever offered in paperback!*

The Dell paperback edition of

THE AMERICAN HERITAGE
DICTIONARY
OF THE ENGLISH LANGUAGE

- Largest number of entries—55,000
- 832 pages—nearly 300 illustrations
- The only paperback dictionary with photographs

**These special features make this new, modern dictionary
clearly superior to any comparable paperback dictionary:**

- More entries and more illustrations than any other
  paperback dictionary
- The first paperback dictionary with photographs
- Words defined in modern-day language that is clear
  and precise
- Over one hundred notes on usage with more factual
  information than any comparable paperback
  dictionary
- Unique appendix of Indo-European roots
- Authoritative definitions of new words from science
  and technology
- More than one hundred illustrative quotations from
  Shakespeare to Salinger, Spenser to Sontag
- Hundreds of geographic and biographical entries
- Pictures of all the Presidents of the United States
- Locator maps for all the countries of the world

A DELL BOOK 75c

If you cannot obtain copies of this title from your local bookseller, just
send the price (plus 15c per copy for handling and postage) to Dell Books,
Post Office Box 1000, Pinebrook, N. J. 07058. No postage or handling charge
is required on any order of five or more books.

75¢

Dell
0207

DELL
75¢
REF

Based on the new best-selling
AMERICAN HERITAGE DICTIONARY—
the freshest, most innovative, most useful dictionary
to be published in this century

THE
AMERICAN HERITAGE
DICTIONARY
OF THE ENGLISH LANGUAGE

• Largest number of entries—55,000

• 832 pages—nearly 300 illustrations

• The only paperback dictionary with photographs

440-00207-075

DELL

30 weeks on *The New York Times* Best-Seller List

THE ANDROMEDA STRAIN

by Michael Crichton

This is the breathtaking story of "Project Wildfire"—the crash mobilization of the nation's highest scientific and medical resources—when an unmanned research satellite returns to earth lethally contaminated.

Four American scientists, chosen in advance for their experimental achievements, are summoned under conditions of total news blackout to Wildfire's secret laboratory five stories beneath the Nevada desert. There they work against the threat of a worldwide epidemic to find an antidote to the unknown microorganism that has wiped out all but two inhabitants of a small Arizona town. "Terrifying . . . one of the most important novels of the year."—*Library Journal*

A DELL BOOK $1.25

If you cannot obtain copies of this title from your local bookseller, just send the price (plus 15c per copy for handling and postage) to Dell Books, Post Office Box 1000, Pinebrook, N. J. 07058. No postage or handling charge is required on any order of five or more books.